HEATHER McCORKLE

BARED &
BETRAYED

CHILDREN OF FENRIR BOOK THREE

CITY OWL
PRESS

BARED & BETRAYED
Children of Fenrir, Book 3

CITY OWL PRESS
www.cityowlpress.com

Cover Design by Tina Moss. All stock photos licensed appropriately.

Edited by Yelena Casale.

For information on subsidiary rights, please contact the publisher at info@cityowlpress.com.

Print Edition ISBN: 978-1-64898-078-7

Digital Edition ISBN: 978-1-64898-077-0

Printed in the United States of America

For those who have felt their destiny was out of their hands.

PRAISE FOR HEATHER McCORKLE

"Kickass women, Icelandic warriors, and plenty of action!"
— *Kait Ballinger, Bestselling Author of The Execution Underground Series*

"The characters have lots of depth to them and are strong, sexy and fun. A fabulous story line full of magic and danger that I was pulled into from the first page. I can't wait to read more of this series. I loved it."
— *Petula Winmill, Book Reviewer*

"Holy werewolves, Batman! What did I just read!! A winning combination of romance and heat, action, and drama, not to mention plenty of Norse lore and mythology to make a paranormal lover combust! This story was unique and quite different from the shifter stories we've come to know and love. Ms. McCorkle did a marvelous job with weaving her story and I am so looking forward to what's coming next."
— *Katrina Berry, Book Reviewer*

"Excellent book!! Not your average shifter book. I really like the Norse bent to the storyline. Couldn't put it down and anxiously awaiting book 2 of the series."
— *Susan Hall, Book Reviewer*

"What a great story this is! One of the best things about it is that I can't think of a book to compare it too. The reason why I love that, is because the story is just so unique. Which is why I kept turning the page! Loved it!"
— *Ali Cross, USA Today Bestselling Author of Young Adult Fantasy*

"There's trouble in the Dragon Empire, the kind that could start a war between dragons and the races of people...For those who love fantasy, dragons and a sweet love story, this book is definitely a must read for you!"
— *Geeky Book Gal*

"Channeler's Choice is definitely my choice for a fantastic story. Heather McCorkle turns the heat up in her second novel of the Channeler series... McCorkle is an outstanding storyteller, and she totally blew me away again."
– I Heart YA Books

CHILDREN OF FENRIR

RECOMMENDED READING ORDER

Clawed & Cornered (novella)

Bitten & Beholden

Tempered & Turned

Bared & Betrayed

CHAPTER ONE

RAUL

The acrid stench of recent gunfire made my fangs extend. My lips drew back out of a self-preservation instinct. Nose scrunched up in distaste, I crept through the thick pine trees. My atoms quivered with the urge to shift to wolf form and go into track-and-attack. I resisted. I needed to keep my head in the game for this.

Through the tree line ahead I spotted sunlight gleaming off the red hood of a truck. The breeze carried something else to my nose—blood, death, and the musk of wolves. Not werewolves, but the kind natural to this world. The knowledge of their deaths still pissed me off. As I moved, I drew my duty weapon, keeping it in a low-ready position. The grips of the Glock .40 felt slick and light in my hands. A man walked around from the other side of the truck. A brown, furry shape hung over his shoulder. He flung it onto the open tailgate. It landed softly, on top of other carcasses from the sound of it.

Anger-spiked adrenalin focused my already sharp gaze. Fit but middle-aged, the man posed little threat to my life, especially considering the outline of his rifle on the rack in the window of his truck. The only weapon on him appeared to be a knife belted at his waist. I checked the air but didn't smell any other people.

The snap of a twig sounded beneath the heel of my Danners. The man made no indication he heard the sound. I slid through the underbrush and out into the small clearing.

As I leveled the gun on him, I commanded, "Hands above your head, right now!"

The man flinched and moved like he was going to dart around the other side of the truck.

"Don't give me a reason!" I warned.

He froze, which proved him to be smarter than most criminals. The threat in my voice must have revealed how ready and eager I was to shoot his ass. I gave him a series of commands that he followed to the letter. Once he was prone, face-first in the dirt with his hands out to his sides, I holstered my gun and moved in.

"Don't move!" I commanded as I put a knee on his shoulder.

In a matter of seconds, I had him cuffed and was hauling him to his feet. I patted him down in a search for weapons. Considering I'd be able to smell whatever he was packing, it was more of a routine precautionary thing than anything else. But muscle memory habits acquired at the academy died hard. Before turning him around, I found my cool and made my canine fangs retract.

"What the hell, man? Since when do the forestry po-po arrest guys at gunpoint for hunting?" the man complained.

"Poaching," I corrected.

He spat a hunk of chew onto the ground. "Like hell. I was protecting my employer's cattle. Damn wolves have been taking out the calves lately."

"Bullshit," I called him out. He scoffed at me but didn't respond. "You are on private land set aside as a wolf preserve. Let's cut the shit and stop wasting each other's time."

The man stared at my mouth. A hint of fear widened his eyes. Shit.

"What the fuck man? You got two sets of incisors? That's some weird crap. And what the hell, do you sharpen those things?"

I turned him around and started marching him toward my forestry department Cherokee. Down the overgrown road, a dark Ford Explorer with a light bar on top bounced in my direction—Hemlock Hollow PD.

When the poacher stumbled, I dragged him, one of my hands beneath his arm, the other on one of his wrists. His complaints of pain were music to my ears, especially when we passed the tailgate of the truck and I saw how many wolf carcasses were piled in it. Half a dozen. He'd slaughtered the entire South Fork pack. And because they were normal wolves and not shifters, all I could do was arrest him.

He must have picked up on how pissed off I was because he started to try to justify himself. "Come on man, you've heard about all the wolf attacks. People are being killed. People!"

I had no comeback for that. I couldn't tell him normal wolves weren't doing it.

"You can't arrest me for protecting American citizens. It ain't right," he went on.

"I'm not."

He relaxed and stood up a bit taller, walking on his own now. We reached the back of my Cherokee. The Hemlock Hollow Police truck rolled to a stop not far from us. The tall, broad, blond cop who got out nodded to me, then opened the back door. He stood there waiting, face stoic, pale eyes staring straight ahead, prepared like the good ex-fullback he was.

The poacher started to protest as I walked him toward the truck. "What, no, but you said you weren't arresting me for protecting American citizens. You said!"

"I'm not. I'm arresting you for poaching and for trespassing on private property."

The man's murky eyes widened as they took in the name on the side of the police Explorer. The police officer grinned at him. "You're lucky one of the owners of this private property didn't shoot your hick ass," he said in a voice so mirthful, it was downright disturbing. It made me smile in return.

"I didn't know I was that close to Hemlock Hollow, I swear! I must have got turned around. I'm so sorry. I'm so sorry!" he said, voice rising with each word.

I shoved him into the Cherokee and slammed the door. He pressed his wide-eyed face to the glass and continued to scream out apologies. Ignoring him, I turned to the officer.

"Thanks, Jörgensson. Another minute and I wouldn't have been able to resist tearing him apart," I said.

"Welcome, Captain." His nose sniffed the air and his blond brows pulled together. "That the South Fork pack?"

I nodded.

"Dammit. Thanks for catching him." One wouldn't think a person could pack so much sincerity into so few words, but Jörgensson was like that. "You gonna drop by to fill out the paperwork, or you want me to?"

I patted his shoulder. "No reason for you to stay late. You have a new baby at home. I'll be by. But I am going to go for a run first, see if he left any survivors behind, make sure he was the only one out here."

Jörgensson gave me his tight-lipped version of a smile. "In that case, I'll take the long, bumpy way back to town."

I laughed and he joined in. "Kiss that baby for me," I called as he walked around and got into the driver's seat of his rig.

He nodded. "Will do, Captain."

The old nickname drove away a bit of the chill of death that clung to this place, but only for a second. I put my duty weapon and radio in my rig, locked it, then walked back into the forest. Once I got deep enough into the thick, fragrant pines, I stripped down. I placed my folded clothing on top of my boots beneath a low-growing pine bough. A late summer breeze flitted across my bare skin. It felt better than good, stimulating almost. The damn, unnatural polyester blend of the uniform itched. But that's what I got for working for the forestry instead of Hemlock Hollow PD. Like most of the world, the majority of the forestry department was oblivious to the existence of my kind.

I exhaled and let my human form go. My paws brushed the pine-needle-covered ground a second later. I shook out my brown and white fur, starting at my nose and ending at my tail. The movement left me feeling charged, ready to go. Thoughts focused down to the comforting state of need and instinct. The scents of the forest stretched before me into dozens of different trails. But only one interested me today.

I picked up the hunter's scent immediately. It tainted everything around it with the stench of gun oil and spent powder. Nose to it, I settled into a fast trot, eating up the ground at a speed that would make a human dizzy. About two miles later, the scent trail led me to a small cave in a rocky hillside. The darkness yawning from within it was thick with bad vibes. The place reeked of death, recently spilled blood, and the musk of wolves—normal wolves who had been slaughtered because one of my kind had murdered people and made it look like an animal attack.

Mind stuck in a haze of anger instead of being in the game where it should have been, I almost missed the soft sound of a whine. The high-pitched sound wasn't one an adult could make. So much sorrow filled the pitiful little voice, it pinched at me. Not wanting to scare it, I crept slowly inside. The whine turned to the low growl of one still figuring out how to make the sound. The fact it even tried impressed me. My werewolf eyes adjusted quickly to the dim light of the cave. In the back, a ball of brown and white fluff growled at me through tiny, bared fangs. A male from the scent. It was barely bigger than my front paws put together. To its right lay the still body of an adult wolf. The scent of congealing blood surrounded the carcass.

As I approached, the pup took a step toward me. He gnashed his teeth. I made a chuffing sort of bark at him. The sound wasn't unfriendly, exactly, more disciplinary. His head perked up, then cocked to the side. I lowered my snout to his level and half-closed my eyes. Little claws clicked on stone as he trotted up to me without hesitation. He rubbed his face along the side of mine, let out one whine, and then trotted over to the carcass. When I didn't follow, he let out a bark.

Sympathy overrode impatience. I walked over to him. For good measure—and mostly to appease him—I nudged the dead wolf with my nose. A gunshot wound had made a mess of her stomach, and yet she had managed to drag herself all the way back here. This had to be her pup. I let out a short whine, took a step back, and turned from the carcass. The pup let out a series of pitiful cries that sounded eerily like human weeping. He ran over and rubbed against my leg. Careful as I could, I picked him up in my jaws by the scruff of his neck. His whimpering faded away and he relaxed in my grip.

Leaving him here wasn't an option. He'd just die. I trotted back toward my truck. Lucky for this one, we had a new mom in town, kind of a rare thing for us. He remained still and quiet the entire way back. A mixture of bravery and sorrow wafted from him—part scent, part a feeling I picked up on.

I stopped at my clothes and sat him down. He sniffed at the two piles of material, then backed away until he bumped into my leg. A startled yip popped from him. The sound turned into a growl as he stared my clothes down like they were some kind of threat. I licked the top of his head and he fell silent. A quiet chuff got his attention fully on me. I hated to put him through this, but there was no other way. To minimize alarming him, I sat down on my haunches before I shifted to human form. Eyes popping wide open, the pup growled and scampered backwards until he had climbed halfway up onto my shirt. I chuffed at him again. He froze, head cocking to the side. Staring me down, little growl still rumbling through him, he hiked his leg and peed on my shirt.

Moving too quick for him to react, I snatched him up and moved him away from my stuff. He growled and snapped at me, squirming in an attempt to get some part of me in his jaws. I held him up and gently blew into his face. He immediately stilled. Another breath and he had my scent. His fan-like tail swept to the side once, then twice. This time, when I sat him down, he stayed put.

I grabbed my clothes—the dry ones, at least. "I don't like it much either, but you didn't have to pee on it."

Lips curling up from his teeth, he watched me with suspicion. The growl-bark noise I emitted made him plop down on his butt. I put my pants and boots on and picked him up by the scruff of the neck. He didn't struggle, but I put an arm beneath him anyway. This close, he would notice the scent of my skin wasn't much different than the scent of my fur. He relaxed against me, nuzzling his head into my abs. Cradling him in one arm, I picked up my offending shirt, holding it well away from us both.

As I walked from the trees, I repositioned him so he could bury his nose in the crook of my arm. No sense in him seeing the poacher's truck and the grisly remains of his pack in the bed. He had suffered enough for a lifetime, let alone for today.

CHAPTER TWO

ELEXIS

S uspicion made me sniff twice at the dark concoction in the black ceramic coffee cup with the Hemlock Hollow PD shield on the side. My nose detected no sugar or cream, just like I'd asked for. I stared the chief down over the rim as I took a small sip. It was good, which deepened my suspicion. What kind of a police department made good coffee?

Chief Balderson's full red lips quirked up into an amused expression that was almost a smile. "Good, isn't it?" he asked, his deep, baritone voice vibrating along my bones in a disturbing way.

The shine of his smooth, dark-skinned head made me wonder if his wolf form had fur. That thought disturbed me too. Hell, everything about this disturbed me.

"It is," I admitted, not bothering to hide the suspicion in my voice.

The chief chuckled. "Helga down in booking makes such a delicious pot of coffee, I'd keep her on for that alone. It's no surprise her daughter runs the Crescent Coffee shop. Apple didn't fall far from the tree there."

I took a longer drink. I'd have to visit this coffee shop. While I drank, the chief chatted about the hours, expectations, and benefits of my new position with the department. Half of my brain listened, but the other half tuned in to the chatter from the squad room on the other side of his office door. I'd always been good at picking up on faraway conversations, but this new werewolf hearing of mine took that to a whole different level. For one thing, I could hear through a door without even trying. That, and I could smell their agitation. Before turning, I hadn't known agitation had a smell. It wasn't pleasant, especially not so much of it.

The other officers talked among themselves. Some were curious about me, some excited to meet me, but even more were ticked I had been given a spot on the squad—as an investigator no less—when there were townsfolk who had been working hard at getting hired for years.

When the chief took a breath between talking about the sick leave policy, I jumped in.

"Thanks for the warm welcome, Chief, but you don't need to ease me into this. I can hear what they're saying out there. I know some are pissed, thinking I didn't earn this spot. And maybe they're right, but I didn't ask to be bitten in either." I took another drink of my coffee, not willing to waste it if I ended up storming out of here. "The PD doesn't owe me anything. Hell, Hemlock Hollow doesn't owe me anything. I can catch the son of a bitch who bit me on my own if need be."

His smile melted away, his expression slipping into that unreadable thing cops pulled off so well, myself included. "I am sorry we haven't caught James yet, but we have been trying, I assure you. And you'll have us at your disposal during your investigation into him."

After another drink, I sat the empty cup down on the corner of his desk. "Thank you. But look, I worked hard to earn my position as a detective with Jackson Hole PD, and even harder to earn the respect of the men on that force. I don't need to go through the same shit again." It wasn't easy to gain respect when one moved up fast through the ranks, and even harder as a woman. I gave him a deep, respectful nod and started to turn for the door. I'd been half-expecting this, which was why I hadn't bothered to book a hotel room. The other reason was, apparently, there weren't any hotels in Hemlock Hollow. Guess they didn't want humans staying in a town full of werewolves.

"What about what *we* need?" he asked, stopping me in my tracks.

I turned slowly back toward him. "Excuse me?"

"You think I hired you because you were a cop who was bitten in by one of our kind against her will and we needed to make it up to you. And that I brought you here so you could help find him to get some sort of closure. That about sum it up?" he asked, tone hard.

"About," I admitted.

"Then you have completely misread me, Detective Sandalius. You were one of scores of people who have been bitten in against their will lately. The crimes started thirty years ago and have grown worse in the last year." His eyes went distant, their amber deepening to a dark brown. "The man who bit you couldn't have been working alone because the crimes started before he was born."

I straightened to my full five-foot-six inches, five-nine if you counted my take-no-prisoners boots, which I certainly did. "You have my attention."

Despite the fact he now had to look up at me, the chief remained sitting. Twenty points to the chief. "The *uppskera*—the reaper—is after one man she thinks is behind the crimes. But I don't think he's the only one. Helheimr, I don't even think he's the main one behind it all."

While I was intrigued, I wasn't interested in having my ego stroked. "I'm sure you have some outstanding detectives, people who have been shifters their whole lives instead of a few months and have had all that time to hone their skills." People who stood on the other side of the door bad-mouthing me right now, calling me an agent of Loki, whatever the hell that meant.

He nodded. "Yes I do, some very fine men and women. But they all share the same problem, a problem you don't possess." The intensity of his tone told me it wasn't just a good hook and line, he meant it.

I took the bait. "What's that?"

"Enough distance from the situation, and all those involved, to remain objective." His eyes narrowed and he dropped his voice so low I had to lean in to hear the next part. "There are some rotten roots in our little town, and I don't know how deep they run. I need you to dig them up." His voice returned to normal volume. "Your chief in Jackson Hole spoke very highly of your detective skills. This force needs you. This town needs you. So I hope you'll give us a chance."

I resisted the urge to bite my bottom lip to stop a smile. I wasn't very good at retracting my fangs yet, and I didn't want to put a hole through my lip. "How long did you work on that speech?" I asked.

The grin that lit up his handsome, ebony-hued face might have got my hormones up if I hadn't already noticed the ring on his finger. Besides, who knew how old he was?

"All night." His quick, shameless admittance impressed me. The man seemed to be doing that at every turn. It was chipping away at my resistance.

I sighed. "In that case, I guess I have to at least give it a chance."

He unfolded his tall frame from his desk and clapped a hand on my shoulder. "Excellent! But, please keep in mind that the same goes for your *kennari*."

Did he mean the rotten roots or the part about needing me? My *kennari* was the person they were placing me with to help ease me into this lifestyle and town. I wasn't sure if I was comfortable with his meaning either way. I wasn't good with people needing me. "A *kennari* isn't necessary."

The chief held his hands up in mock surrender. "I know, I know, you've already made it through the *veröa* on your own—a very impressive feat, by the way. But the change isn't the only thing a *kennari* helps their *nemi* through. Becoming one of us has never been more dangerous than it is now. You must have someone to teach you about our ways, our town, and our packs."

"True enough," I admitted.

He opened the door and stepped aside to allow me to go through first. Apparently, gentlemen weren't all dead, they were just werewolves. Who knew?

Conversation ceased abruptly on the other side of the door. All twelve pairs of eyes in the squad room crawled across my skin. Some regarded me with curiosity, but even more with contempt, especially the two women. No surprise there. Women in a man's line of work always judged one another more harshly. I don't know why we did it, but we did. Part of me couldn't help but wonder if some of the contempt had to do with my tanned skin, where all of these people looked pale as the snowy land their ancestors had immigrated from, except for the chief. I hated to think so, but that was how it had been back in Jackson Hole. Then there were the blue highlights I had put in my shoulder-length black locks. I accepted blame for that one. But I had my reasons.

The chief's hard gaze swept across them, a tight smile on his face.

"Officers, you will join me in welcoming Detective Sandalius to the squad," he commanded.

I hid the cringe that worked through me. Why did those in charge never realize the repercussions of saying something like that? Half-hearted murmurs of welcome came from each officer. The chief beckoned to one near the back, a man whose blond hair was buzzed so close to his head it connected seamlessly with his cropped blond beard. His fit frame slipped through the others with a grace and ease that made me think he had been an athlete once. From the youthful look on his face, it couldn't have been too long ago.

"Gilmerson, track down Anderson and take our detective to him, would you?" the chief said, making the question a command with an easy smile and a hard tone. It made me wonder, for at least the tenth time, how this hierarchy worked since the officers belonged to different packs and the chief was only their alpha here at work. Such a thing had to divide loyalties. Which, I supposed, led to the very problem the chief needed my help with.

Gilmerson flashed a smile that didn't reach his eyes until his gaze fell on me. In a snap his smile turned from respectful to appreciative. His gaze took all of me in but landed on my breasts, despite the fact they were hidden beneath a bulletproof vest and a gray uniform shirt buttoned all the way up to the hollow of my throat. The moment I had stepped into the station wearing the vest I'd felt out of place. No one else wore them. It turned out werewolves weren't overly concerned about being shot like normal cops were. Now I was glad I'd worn it.

"Of course, Chief. He'll be in to fill out paperwork on the poacher in holding in a bit, though," Gilmerson said in a slight Montana drawl that made me think of cowboys instead of Vikings.

But then, his kind had come to this continent in something like 1400, so I guess it made sense for their accent to have changed. At least, that's what the woman said who had approached me back in Jackson Hole last month.

Chief Balderson shook his head. "You know Anderson, if he got sidetracked it could be all day before he makes it in. Our new detective needs to get settled into her new accommodations before worrying about getting settled into work." The chief turned to me. "I appreciate you showing up early to meet the squad and tour the department. We're happy to have you. I'll see you back on Monday."

I inclined my head to him. "Thank you, sir." I hadn't expected a four-day weekend, but I wasn't about to argue. Getting settled in sounded good, really good.

The chief nodded and smiled in return as I started to follow Gilmerson from the room. I met the gazes of those staring at me as I passed them, refusing to look away. A few of them looked down, up, or to the side, but most held my gaze until I passed. So that was how it was going to be. Fine with me. Nothing new there. Okay, a room full of werewolves trying to glare me into the ground wasn't the same as testosterone-charged cops getting their panties in a bunch because a woman had joined the force. But when you got down to it, the hostility and reasons behind it weren't all that different.

The pressure of all those eyes eased the second we stepped outside into the late July sun. I moved toward my circa 1970's Dodge Ram, but Gilmerson moved in the opposite direction.

"I'd like to take my truck so I don't have to come back for it," I called to his retreating backside.

"No can do. If you don't have a reason to come back, Raul might not come down and do his paperwork, which means I get stuck with it," he said.

My uncooperative side screamed at me to argue, but it was a problem I understood all too well. "All right," I conceded with enough reluctance in my tone to let him know I wasn't thrilled about it.

Without responding, he pulled a set of keys from his pocket and pushed a button. The "thunk" of locks disengaging drew my attention to one of the patrol cars parked along the curb. The sleek, black Charger sported the shield of Hemlock Hollow—a forest scene with the silhouette of a wolf in it—and the name of the PD. Another button clicked and the engine roared to life. The thing sounded as badass as it looked. Gilmerson walked to the driver's side. I climbed in and put my seatbelt on.

Inside, it looked like every other cop car I'd been in: shotgun mounted between the seats, computer built into the dash, radio mike hanging on a clip below the heater controls. But it smelled different. Mingled with the scents of guns and electronics was the musk of wolves. It was subtle, probably not even noticeable to humans, but I couldn't have missed it if I tried. The scent of any cop car put me at ease, but this one did so even more. As much as I might want to be disturbed, I wasn't.

Gilmerson folded himself into the vehicle, put his sunglasses on, and put the Charger in gear. He took a left onto Main Street, heading out of town. Instead of commenting on his lack of seat belt and the hypocrisy of breaking a law we had to enforce, I asked, "Is Anderson the type of cop who'd leave you with the paperwork?"

He waved a hand. "Not too often. The captain's a good guy. But he tends to get...distracted." He smiled and chuckled at the last word.

"Captain?" Hemlock Hollow didn't use that designation. They were far too small to have precincts with different captains.

"It's a football nickname from high school that followed him into college. He was the best damn captain and quarterback a team could wish for."

Great, my teacher was an ex-jock. The day just took a dive. Just because I loved football didn't mean I loved jocks anymore. "Oh yeah? What was your position?"

"MLB," he said, no doubt either testing or trying to outsmart me.

"Guess I should call you Mike then." I let silence fall between us, giving him time to absorb the fact I knew the nickname for a middle linebacker. Considered the quarterback of the defensive line, guys like him could be as cocky and full of themselves as the offensive quarterback. I'd dated my fair share of jocks throughout the years to know and be wary of his kind.

Gilmerson's brows drew down and he gave me a long look—too long considering we were now barreling down the road at over sixty-five miles per hour. "How much did they tell you about Raul?"

I shrugged. "Raul Anderson—forest ranger in the national forest surrounding Hemlock Hollow, of which he is a resident, member of the Reinhard pack," I recited.

"Well shit."

Back going rigid, I sat up a bit in my seat. "What?"

Gilmerson turned and became riveted by the road ahead.

"Tell me," I all but growled. The sound of my voice, so nearly out of control, irritated me even more. I hated that my control over my wolf side had slipped.

He grunted. "Guess they left it to me to tell you. I'll have to thank the chief."

When he didn't go on, I glared him down until a muscle in his cheek started to twitch.

"Raul's a good guy. He just got mixed up in some political crap. Remember that after I tell you the rest." The glance he shot my way was quick and hard.

"He's a good guy, I got it," I said, not bothering to hide my impatience. An old football buddy's opinion couldn't exactly be trusted. And the fact he'd opened with telling me Raul was a good guy made me fear the opposite.

"Too good. That's what got him into this mess. Loki targets those who are too good," he mumbled.

I don't think he meant for me to hear it, so I called him on it. "Loki? Hah! Assuming he does exist, you really think he's bored enough to screw with this Anderson guy?" When he didn't answer, I pressed harder. "What mess?"

"Being a *kennari*. He didn't choose it. It's his penance."

The quick way he answered made me change my mind. He had wanted me to hear, and he wanted me to ask about it. For the moment, I played his game. "What do you mean by 'his penance'?"

He sighed, the sound pulling from him as if he needed it to force himself to go on. "Raul bit in a woman without asking the council, and her, for permission. So now he has to be a *kennari* to do penance for it."

My vision went a little dark. "He what?" I think I yelled it.

Gilmerson held up a placating hand. "Now, now, he had his reasons. And he didn't attack her or force her or anything, he just hadn't had the chance to ask her."

"Hadn't had a chance?" Yep, I was definitely yelling. Blood roared in my ears, a constant rush accented by the pounding of my heart. Fangs sprang from my upper and lower jaws. I hated that I'd lost control, but dammit, this guy had done the same thing to some poor woman that had been done to me. Well, almost the same thing.

"It was a complicated situation, nothing like what happened to you. Raul isn't like that. He'd never attack a woman."

Several deep breaths helped me regain a touch of my composure. "That's a massive pile of frost giant shit!"

His brows rose as if my alluding to the Norse legend impressed him. It hadn't been my intention. I'd only meant to try and curb my foul mouth a bit.

I went on. "You don't think he's involved in whoever is biting in all these people against their will?"

"Hell no. He hates those guys. He helped catch two of them. One of them was the guy who bit you."

That didn't improve my plummeting opinion of this Raul Anderson by much more than a hair. The chief told me the story of how they'd caught the guy who bit me in, and then he'd escaped again—probably with help. And I disagreed wholeheartedly. If Anderson was willing to bite even one person in against their will, he could be part of the group behind this. I didn't believe in coincidences. "Then why did he do it?"

"Those are his reasons to tell, not mine. I'm sorry, I thought you knew. They should have told you." Though he played it up, this time his underlying tone was insincere.

No, what they should have done was assign me to someone else, anyone else. But I didn't say so out loud. Chances were they stuck me with this guy because I had already been through my first moon on my own and was comfortable shifting. They thought I'd be a good way for him to ease into this *kennari* thing. I fought the impulse to demand Gilmerson turn the car around. For six years I'd been a woman working in a man's profession. That time had brought a clear understanding of when a man was trying to get under my skin—and a stubborn resistance to allowing them.

What I couldn't figure out was, why did Gilmerson want to rile me up? It was like he wanted me to throw a fit and demand another *kennari*. Did he not want me around Raul? But why? What kind of a threat did I pose to him? Unless he did have something to do with the group biting others in after all.

"I know what you're thinking," Gilmerson said.

I remained silent.

"You're thinking you want another *kennari*, and it would be within your rights to ask for one. But Raul is a good guy. He cares more about this town and our packs than anyone I know."

Still, I kept my mouth shut. I know he expected some kind of response, which was part of why I didn't give him one. Mostly, though, I needed to work on reining in my anger and trying to get my damn fangs to retract. Both felt like a losing battle. Motives within motives lay in this guy and this town. While this news pissed me off, it also intrigued the investigator in me. And if this Anderson was involved with the group biting people in against their will, being close to him would help my investigation.

Pine trees stretching high into the sky whipped by outside the tinted windows. The forest became so thick on either side of the road, I couldn't see through it at all. Gilmerson remained silent as we turned off this windy road onto another just like it. After less than a mile, he turned up a paved drive. The address on the sign raised my suspicion a notch. A quaint cabin peeked through the trees, its two big windows like sleepy eyes gazing at me from beneath the steep A-frame roof. Simple, natural landscaping filled with plenty of native plants and flowers lined the road and occupied the center of the circular drive. A forestry truck was parked to the left side of the house on a cobbled area.

"This isn't Anderson's address," I said. I knew because the chief had told it to me since I'd be staying there.

"No. He texted me and told me he was stopping by here," Gilmerson said as he stopped the car halfway around the drive, right in front of the house.

A click sounded, and brief static came across the police radio a moment before a woman's voice. "Dispatch to Officer Gilmerson."

Gilmerson shot me an apologetic look and thrust his head in the direction of the cabin's front door. "Go ahead. I'll be just a minute."

It was all the invitation I needed. I was sick of sharing a confined space with someone I didn't know or trust. As I got out, I heard the click of the radio mic, followed by, "Gilmerson. Go ahead."

I closed the door on the rest of the conversation. Warm air, thick with the scent of pine, wrapped around me like an unwelcome blanket. But it was better than being in that car with Gilmerson and his hidden agenda. My already thin patience was getting downright anorexic. I marched up the steps as quietly as I could in my black Ariat boots with their moderate high heel. It wasn't out of a desire to be quiet so much as out of cop habit.

As I knocked on the door, I felt Gilmerson's eyes on my backside. It was possible he was just being a typical straight guy and watching my ass, but I didn't think so.

Rustling came from inside, claws clicked on wood, then the doorknob started to turn. I put on my cop face and prepared to ask for Raul Anderson. The naked blond woman who answered the door rendered me speechless. She held a towel against her otherwise bare breasts, the only stitch of fabric near her. The casual way she stood, not even trying to cover her crotch—the blond hair of which was trimmed so short I could see every fold of her sex—made me forget what I'd even been about to ask.

For a moment she looked confused, then her eyes widened and she smiled. "You must be Elexis. Welcome to Hemlock Hollow."

After a few tries searching for the right words, I simply said, "I am. Thank you." It came out harsh, but hell, I was lucky to even get that out.

"Raul, your *nemi* is here," the woman called over her shoulder.

I had no idea what *nemi* meant, and I wasn't sure I wanted to know. But the idea of me being this guy's *anything* made me grind my teeth.

From somewhere inside I heard the patter of bare feet approaching. A man came into view from what must have been a hallway. Biceps bulged as they scrubbed a towel atop a head of wet, brown-black hair just long enough to get in his golden-brown eyes. A bare chest pumped up with enough natural-looking muscle to make me salivate led down to a tantalizing V of muscle. From there my eyes followed a thin line of dark hair leading from an innie belly button into a pair of blue jeans fitting snug enough to outline a nice bulge.

My body reacted without my permission, sending blood straight to my nipples, making them press hard against my bullet-proof vest. Shit. Wolves could smell arousal, and I was well on my way there. I turned my attention back to the naked woman in front of me and allowed anger to replace desire. My fangs tried to lengthen and I fought them back.

"Sorry to interrupt," I said.

"Oh. No, no this—" the woman began, but I spun on my heel and marched back down the steps at werewolf speed. I'd had more than enough of this day and these people with their games and agendas.

Gilmerson was halfway between the car and the house, a bewildered look on his face. But his eyes sparked with something that made me think he knew exactly what was going on. He started to question me, playing the idiot, but I marched right past him, snagging the keys from his hand as I did so. He protested and reached for me. I bared my fangs and gave him a hard look of warning that stopped him cold. As I jumped in the Charger and started it up, I heard the woman say, "Not what it looks like," but I didn't care.

I was over this shit and over this day. The chief was going to have to assign me another *kennari* if he wanted to keep me. I slammed the cop car into drive and left rubber on the asphalt as I tore out of there.

CHAPTER THREE

RAUL

The old Dodge truck in front of the station wasn't a good sign. At least it was the only vehicle here. I breathed out a sigh of relief. No doubt the entire force had shown up for Elexis's briefing. I counted myself lucky they were all gone now. This would be bad enough as it was without half the heavy influencers of all three packs in attendance. I pulled around back, and still the two patrol cars Hemlock Hollow had on duty at all times were nowhere to be seen. No doubt the chief's doing, because I just wasn't that lucky. Ever.

I stepped out of the Cherokee and adjusted the too-tight crotch of my borrowed jeans. Not too tight because I had Elexis on the brain—though that would do it—but because Karman's husband, Leif, wore a size smaller than myself. The white print of the rune wheel on the borrowed Sólstafir rock band shirt I wore hugged the valleys of my pecs in a way that made the shirt look misshapen and strange. Tugging at the heavy-metal tee didn't do much more good than tugging on the jeans had. I gave up and strode to the back door of the station.

I forced my nervous hands to stop. What did I care? Elexis had already seen more than these clothes covered and gotten the exact wrong impression anyway. Still, for at least the hundredth time, I wished my uniform had made it out of the dryer on time.

By muscle memory alone, my fingers punched in the code on the keypad beside the thick metal door going into the back of the station. Inside, half a dozen desks filled the squad room. Tension flowed out of me on seeing them all empty. Only one computer screen was lit up as if it had been used recently. It had probably been Gilmerson, who had an ass-kicking coming as soon as I caught up with him. If bringing Elexis by Karman's had been his idea of a joke, he was about to find out just how funny I didn't think it was. Right now I had to deal with the fallout, though.

"That you, Anderson?" the chief's voice came from the next room.

I squared my shoulders and strode toward his office. "It is."

"Then by all means, get your tail in here."

The tiny hairs along the back of my neck stood and my fangs threatened to extend. I swallowed the anger down and put on a carefree grin. "Hey, Chief, what's—" The rest of the sentence died on my tongue as I stepped into his office and saw Elexis standing there.

I liked to think it wasn't because she took my breath away, but I'd be lying to myself. Hair so dark brown it might as well be black hung in loose waves down to her shoulders. In this light, I saw dark blue highlights throughout it, and while I wasn't into that kind of thing, it looked smoking hot on her, rebellious in a way cops usually weren't. She'd changed into civilian clothes—a black T-shirt with blue crosshairs on it, the V-neck just low enough to give me a good shot of her cleavage. C-cup, if I had to guess. Eventually, my gaze made it to her dark blue jeans and black cowboy boots —the utilitarian kind, not the fashionable ones. My tight jeans grew tighter.

When I finally got to looking at them, I found her blue eyes trying to burn holes right through me.

"Raul, it seems you have upset our new detective in record time. She's demanding a new *kennari*, which means you may have already failed at your first assignment," the chief said in a gruff voice.

Shit, I had forgotten he was in the room. My gaze shot from Elexis, to him, and back again.

"What? No. I didn't do a thing. Hell, we didn't even speak," I protested. The rock-hard cop look she gave me felt as chilly as the winds over the falls of Iceland in winter. My jeans grew even tighter. *No, dammit.* I would not be attracted to someone who knee-jerk judged me. I'd had enough of that shit.

"We didn't have to. I heard all about you, and meeting you confirmed what I suspected," she said in a voice a touch deep for a woman's, but only sexier because of it. She took a step toward me. "Not only are you an asshole who bit in a woman without asking her, you break protocol while on duty, and are more interested in wetting your dick than doing your job. I will not be saddled with an idiot like that," she went on.

I had to bite my lip to keep from grinning. Her words pissed me off, but the closer she got, the more I lost my mind a little. Her vanilla and gun oil scent drove me a bit crazy. "You're welcome to ride bareback." The words slipped out before I'd even realized I'd thought them. *Shit.*

She spun back around to the chief. "Point in case. Assign me a new *kennari* or I walk."

Double shit. I couldn't afford to fail with my first student before I'd even started. But I wasn't about to apologize. She'd made up her mind, and I was sick of being judged.

The chief held his hands up in a placating gesture. "Now, now. Don't be so hasty. Before you make your decision, hear me out."

She took a deep breath that made her breasts rise nicely, even beneath the redundant bulletproof vest, and motioned for the chief to go on. The almost imperialistic way she did it made my blood pump faster. Her claws extended a bit where they rested on her elbows. *Impressive.* Few could partially shift and not completely lose it. And here she was making demands of the chief of police, a powerful werewolf, and she didn't seem fazed by it. That thought drew my eyes back to her breasts, and I let them stay there. Because, why not? She'd already made her mind up about me.

A bit of the growl came from the chief, and my gaze shot to him. The warning on his face said he knew what I was thinking, or he wanted me to be quiet. Probably both.

"I assigned Raul to you for two reasons. The first is because I knew that, as a cop, you'd be best suited to be his first student. The second is because I know he is secretly investigating who is behind the bitings, and he believes they are rooted in Hemlock Hollow." The chief paused and gave me a long look. I gave it right back through wide, startled eyes.

I hadn't known he knew. Like most people in this town, I figured he believed the worst about me. The man was sharper than I'd given him credit for.

He went on. "He cares about this town and the packs in it—all of them—more than anyone I know. He is the ideal partner to help you investigate this matter."

Elexis lifted her chin. "I don't need a partner. I can investigate this on my own."

The chief nodded. "I've no doubt you can. But without Raul's knowledge and help, it will take you twice as long. And that is time we don't have."

Elexis uncrossed her arms, stood straighter, and turned to look at me. She stared for several long seconds, and I enjoyed the look all the more because it was hard, which made *me* hard. At least she didn't hide her distaste for me like so many in this town.

"And the longer the investigation takes, the more people get bitten in against their will. At least half of those bitten in die or don't make it through the *veróa*. Lives depend on you working together," the chief pressed.

She shot a narrowed look to the chief. "You didn't have to lay down the guilt trip. I was going to say yes based off his 'inside knowledge.' But If I'm going to work with him, I'll need a raise."

"Done."

My brows rose. I'd never heard the chief be so accommodating. He gave me a smile. "Anderson, if you want to get to that paperwork, Detective Sandalius and I will get to renegotiating her pay, and I'll have her back to you before you're done."

I nodded to them both as I backed out of the room. Paperwork had never sounded so good.

I pulled the Cherokee into the third bay of my garage and jumped out to go help Elexis. She stood beside her old truck, the handle of a roller bag in one hand and an army-green duffle thrown over the other shoulder. Her eyes were glued to my split-level house with its multitude of windows making it look literally like a glass house. I couldn't tell if that was disgust or awe on her face. I approached and reached for the bags.

"Let me get those for you."

"No." The amount of hostility in that one word raised my hackles. "Suit yourself. Right this way."

Her suitcase wheels clicked across the checker pattern of white and gray marble squares of my walkway separated by a gridwork of flowering moss. She cursed in frustration as she struggled with the terrain. Finally, the wheels stopped clicking when she picked the suitcase up. I opened the four-inch-thick glass front door for her and stood aside. Nose in the air, she refused to look my direction as she passed me. The top of her nearly black-and-blue-haired head came to my lips, an impressive height for a woman who wasn't of Norse descent. In fact, she looked kind of...

"So Sandalius, is that Spanish?" I asked.

"Don't know," she said in a distracted tone as she looked around.

I couldn't tell what the guarded look on her face meant. My style and décor weren't for everyone. Everything in my house was either red, white, or blue in honor of both the American and Icelandic flags. It was sparsely decorated, with modern art throughout depicting either wolves, travel, or digital art created by my sister featuring the nine worlds. Very few walls clogged the space, and every one of them that could have a window, did.

"Odd," I said.

She turned quickly to me with a wide-eyed look that made it seem like she'd forgotten I was there. "What?"

Her reaction made me smile. "That you don't know what nationality your last name comes from."

She sat her bags down and walked farther into the open foyer, eyes on the view across the room. Outside the wall of windows on the opposite side of the house stretched the hollow the town was named after. Across the hollow reached a steel footbridge with no guardrails of any kind. Seeing Elexis see it for the first time reminded me of why I had the house built to face it. But all I could look at was her.

"I've been in the foster system since I was three," she said as she walked into the living room, eyes glued to the bridge beyond the windows. She didn't sound bitter about it, just distracted. "What is that?"

"The town's version of a replica of the *Bifrost*."

Her nose wrinkled up in a cute-as-hell look. She didn't stop walking until she nearly pressed against the wall of windows. "That sounds familiar. What is it?"

"It's the bridge to Asgard, to Valhalla."

"Icelandic settlers." The wonder softening her voice stirred me, which tightened my jeans again. "You guys take that old-world stuff quite serious." She sounded impressed, but it still pissed me off.

"Oh yeah, like launching crusades to murder everyone who doesn't believe the way you do, turning an entire town into a religious center, and a country into a pilgrimage destination isn't," I countered.

Lush lashes pinching her eyes down to slits, she glared hard at me. "I never said I was of the Christian persuasion."

"Didn't have to," I snapped as I turned and started down a hallway.

Soft boots slapped the marbled tile right behind me. "You don't have to get so damn defensive. I didn't mean anything by it," she said.

"Right, no one ever does."

I turned a corner in the hallway and still she followed. "Well if I had known you were going to get your panties in a bunch, I wouldn't have said anything."

All the way down the long hall, she never slowed or backed off. Her power crawled along my back, enticing me to turn around. I resisted and kept walking.

"So what if I was of the Christian persuasion? You saying there's something wrong with that religion?" she demanded in a tone that itched for a fight.

I was just the guy to scratch it for her. "That's not what I said at all. But now that you mention it, there's something wrong with every religion. They're all about control, fear, and judgment."

"Someone like you would say that."

The comment got under my skin as surely as claws. Stopping at my open bedroom door, I spun around and faced her. "Someone like me?"

Instead of backing off like good sense should be telling her to, she took a step closer. "Yeah, someone like you, someone who would bite in people against their will."

Grinding my teeth as best I could with my fangs extending, I stepped right up into her personal space. "It was one person, *one*. And it wasn't against her will so much as without her knowing what I was doing," I said, forcing my voice to stay calm and controlled. It came out sounding all wrong, which only made me madder. And dammit, the words themselves sounded horrible, making me sound horrible.

"Right, if that helps you sleep at night." The flush in her cheeks made her look even hotter.

It didn't, nothing I did helped me sleep at night. The ferocity in her dark blue eyes sucked me in against my will and told me she saw my torment and wasn't moved by it one bit.

A growl of frustration tore from me as I spun away. If I didn't get out of these tight pants, I was going to bust the seams out of the crotch. Walking toward my bathroom, I pulled my shirt off and tossed it into the clothes hamper on my way. Elexis's boots clicked against the tile behind me. Ignoring her, I took the holstered gun from where it was clipped to the back of my waistband and lay it on the quartz countertop. I unzipped my pants.

"But don't you dare think for one minute that not giving a woman a chance to say no is consent. Guys who think like that belong six feet under," she said, voice slurred by what was probably her extended fangs.

Forcing my own fangs to retract, I stopped and turned back around to face her. She almost ran right into me. "I am *not* that type of guy. I would never raise a hand to a woman or do anything against her will." I knew she was right—by the gods, I agreed with her—but I wasn't about to reveal my deepest secrets to a stranger.

Inches apart, we stared each other down. The sunlight pouring in through the arched window over the tub made the blue highlights in her hair seem to glow. Dark locks framed her heart-shaped face with its perky little nose, making me want to brush them away so I could see her better. The hint of white fangs peaked out of her slightly open mouth. The flush in her cheeks made me want to rub my body along hers, cradle her against me, feel her heat. I had to get away from her.

I pulled my jeans down, then stepped out of them. She gasped but didn't move away. Her gaze went to my cock, which stood partially at attention.

"The guest room is down the hall to the right, unless you want to share my bed."

Fury flared to life in her eyes. That, and desire. She liked what she saw, and she couldn't hide it. Growling in frustration, she took a step back. To either side of the blue crosshairs printed on her shirt, her hard nipples pressed against the black material. A slow smile worked its way onto my lips.

"Like hell. I would rather sleep outside!" she snapped as she stormed from the room.

"There's a couch on the porch you can use," I teased.

Shoulder-length hair bounced as she retreated at a clipped pace. Her ass filled out the black BDUs she wore perfectly. I longed to have my hands on that ass, lifting it so she could straddle her legs around me. Dammit. I was going to need another shower, a cold one.

CHAPTER FOUR

RAUL

A loud boom woke me from a restless, dream-filled sleep. For several seconds, all I could see was the white landscape of the dream and the face of a foreign man so tall, he dwarfed my ancestors. The images lingered so strongly it felt like I stood both on that snowy mountain and lay on my couch. As always, it took several moments to shake off the dream and realize my couch was the real part. Another boom sounded—thunder. A storm must have moved in. It helped ground me in reality.

After another groggy second, I jumped from the couch. Elexis was still outside. A glance at the clock told me only an hour had passed since she'd retreated to the patio. Vivid as my dreams were, I still would have woken if she'd come in. Careful to keep my steps light, I walked to the back patio doors and peaked through the heavy beige curtains. Since I hadn't turned on any lights in the house, my *varúlfur* sight easily saw through the night's gloom. The dark shape of Elexis wrapped in a sleeping bag huddled on the blue cushions of my outdoor couch. Only her face poked over the top of the bag. The constitution of our kind meant it wasn't cold bothering her.

Beneath the couch I saw the corner of her carry-on luggage. A tablet sat on the edge of the side table next to her, the kind with keyboards too small for my fingers to type on. Beside it sat one of those travel-sized medleys of vegetables found in the produce section of supermarkets. All of her things were neat and tidy, nothing poking out of the carry-on, tablet closed, lid on the vegetables.

A howl echoed up through the hollow, making her jump. Her hands went white where they gripped the dark material of her sleeping bag. Another howl sounded, and she jumped again. The voices were too far away for me to tell who they were. It didn't matter. No one would come onto my property. But she didn't know that.

I moved back from the curtain before she could notice me. Even if the big bad wolf Fenrir himself came onto my patio, I didn't think she'd come inside. Before crashing on the couch earlier, I had tried to entice her in. Not even take-out from Mike's Malt Shop had swayed her. Though, for a second there she had wavered when she smelled the fries.

Three more successive howls sounded, followed by the barest whimper from Elexis. Stubborn, pig-headed, and quick to judge or not, I couldn't let her sit out there and stew in her fear. She didn't ask for—or consent to—this life. And I was her *kennari*, dammit.

Quiet as I could, I went to the kitchen and got a bottle of Syrah from the wine fridge. I uncorked it, filled two pearlescent blue, stemless glasses, and headed for the patio. She jumped when I slid the door open. Though she pretended to glare at me over the top of the sleeping bag, the relief in her eyes was clear. She sat up and crossed her arms beneath her breasts. Gods help me, she had no bra on.

"I'm not having sex with you. Alcohol won't work," she said.

I sat one wineglass on the side table next to her and turned to the fire pit in the center of the furniture. At the press of a button, flames licked up around the amber glass chunks, filling the stone and steel fire pit. I sat down in the big chair across the fire pit from the couch, resting my glass on the arm.

"That's not why I brought it. It's Thursday, and I unwind with a glass of wine on my patio every Friday. Just because you're here doesn't mean I should have to change that habit. But since I'm a good host, I brought you a glass too," I said.

She grunted at me as she emerged from the sleeping bag like a butterfly from a chrysalis. A smoking hot, blue and black butterfly in a skin-tight black tank top. She picked up her glass and brought it to her nose. I forced my eyes back to the flames and took a drink of my own wine. I wouldn't be able to handle seeing her lips touch the glass.

"Hmm, you struck me as a beer guy," she said.

Out of habit, I pulled a coin from my pocket and started to flip it through my fingers. It soothed me. "Apparently I struck you as a lot of things I'm not."

She grunted again, then took a drink of her wine. Her eyes widened as she looked from the glass to me. "And you have good taste in wine," she said in a shocked tone.

The mouthful of wine I had went down silky smooth, leaving behind a distinctive taste. "Naked Winery makes one of the best Syrahs I've ever tasted," I said.

Her gaze watched my fingers with interest, following the coin as it wove through each of them and back again. "You don't prefer Italian wines?"

My nose wrinkled up. "I'm not into the foreign earthy wines that leave an oak aftertaste."

"You're just full of surprises tonight, aren't you?" The tone of her voice made me think she was pleased, and irritated that she was pleased.

I laughed.

She looked harder at the coin in my hand. "What is that? It looks foreign."

I stopped flipping it around and held it out to her. "A one hundred kronur."

Eyes narrowing, she accepted it from me. "What kind of fish is this?"

"Lump fish."

"It's ugly."

I laughed. "Yeah, I guess it is."

Her fingers caressed it in a way that sent shivers over my skin. "And what are these, Odin and his flock?"

I laughed again. "No. It's the Icelandic coat of arms—a dragon, an eagle, a bull, and a giant."

"A giant? Like the frost giants of Jötunheimr?" she asked.

My brows shot up. "Could be. You certainly didn't read that in a comic book." I didn't want to be impressed, but I was.

"I read up on Norse mythology. Your Eddas are confusing as hell, but interesting."

Anger bristled through me. "The Eddas aren't mythology any more than the Bible or the Koran."

She handed the coin back and held her hands up. "Okay, okay, easy there. That's not how I meant it. So why do you carry around an Icelandic coin?"

Her lack of even an attempt at a smooth conversation transition melted some of my anger. Socially graceful this one was not. Oddly, that had a bit of charm to it. "It's the first 'dollar' I earned from my father. He gave it to me for mowing the lawn, told me I'd have to wait until we went to Iceland to spend it."

She laughed, an easy, carefree sound. "Did he ever take you to Iceland?"

I nodded. "Every spring, but it was summer, which meant I spent all summer and fall mowing lawns for Icelandic money I couldn't spend."

"But you still did it?"

"Of course."

Her eyes widened. Triumph rose in my chest. After a few long minutes of silence, during which I stared into the fire to avoid staring at her, she finally spoke again. "Listen, I don't need a teacher. I got through the becoming all by myself, and I'm doing fine. What I need is a partner for this investigation."

"And someone to help you get to know this town."

She tilted her head to the side. "Fine, that too. If you can be those things, this might work."

Staring into my wine so I didn't have to look at her lake-blue eyes, I nodded. I'd never seen blue eyes so dark. They were captivating, like a lure promising beautiful things, which then drove a hook through your mouth. "Fine, partners it is."

A grunt of part disgust, part irritation came from her. "So your kind—our kind—have gone centuries without anyone being bitten in against their will, without werewolves attacking humans to the point of drawing attention. What changed, Loki decide to start recruiting in your ranks?"

One of my brows rose. "Ha, ha. Very funny. No, I'm not a big believer in blaming the gods. Calder Valdísson started biting in random people thirty years ago. He discovered he was of the *uppskera*—the reaper—line.

He hoped to awaken the power in himself. At least, that's what most people believe," I said.

"But not you."

"No. I do believe that's what he wanted, and that's part of why he started doing it all those years ago. But only part. I think someone told him he was of the *uppskera* bloodline, and it got him started in the first place. I think they have a bigger agenda than awakening the first reaper and seeker in three hundred years."

She tapped her finger on her luscious lips as she thought. It was very distracting. "That's a pretty big agenda in itself. This seeker and reaper could be used as a means to another end. The chief said Calder wants werewolves to come out—so to speak," she said.

"Yeah, I think that's what Calder wants now, but I don't think it was his idea. I think there's someone behind it who planted the idea in his head."

Interest sparked in her eyes as she leaned forward. "What do you think they want?"

"I suspect they don't just want us to come out, but they want to take over." It sounded crazy out loud, which was why I'd never told anyone. Something about this woman just made it slip out, probably her cop vibe combined with how hot she was. It was a dangerous combination, one I'd always been drawn to.

Gaze casting out over my dark backyard, Elexis tugged at a blue lock of her wavy hair before curling it around her finger. "And who do you think that is?"

"More than one person, most likely. But I suspect the main one behind it is Bain Robertson."

"The alpha of the Draupnir pack?"

My brows rose. "Yes."

"Don't look so surprised. I did my homework." The cute half-smile she gave me followed the wine all the way down to my stomach—and kept going. I reminded myself of her lightning-quick judgment of me when she'd knocked on Karman's door. Because she had heard I'd bit Sonya in without asking her first, she immediately assumed I was the type of guy I hated most in the world. Nothing chafed me more.

"Why him?"

"He's a power-hungry, Loki-touched asshole. World domination is right up his alley."

She must have heard the resistance in my tone because she changed the subject. "Tell me about the seeker and reaper."

This could go south. "How much do you know about them?"

Her head cocked to the side and she listened to the distant howls for a second before answering. "Only that the power awakens in a person of a certain bloodline when the need arises, and there is always one of each, like yin and yang or something."

I nodded and filled in some of the blanks. "They find and save, or put down, the werewolves who lose their mind during the *verða*, the change, and others who develop a taste for killing. They keep us all safe by doing so."

Cradling her empty wineglass in both hands, she leaned forward. "So the seeker finds them—I'm guessing by her title—and the reaper kills them if the seeker can't save them."

I shook my head. "Not if *she* can't save them, if they won't save themselves. Neither the seeker or reaper decides a werewolf's fate. They decide for themselves, depending on their willpower and desire."

Her brows rose. "Wow."

"What?"

"I didn't expect you to be so deep."

I wanted to make a crass comment on exactly how deep I could go, but I refrained. When I didn't go on, she asked, "So there hasn't been a seeker and reaper for three hundred years from what they tell me. Why now? And why this Sonya and Ayra?"

Before answering, I took a long drink of wine and kicked my feet up onto the edge of the fire pit. "The seeker and reaper have always come from one of five different bloodlines. The seeker awakens first, usually at puberty if they are born with an active gene. If not, then they have to be bitten in and exposed to the reaper for their power to fully activate."

"So you bit the woman in because she was the seeker?"

"Yes," I answered without hesitation. I might as well foster the lie. It was better than risking telling her the truth.

"Why?"

The last drink of wine tasted far more bitter than it should have.

"That's enough sharing for the night." Glass in hand, I stood. "Come inside. At least sleep on the couch." I gestured to the outdoor throw pillow to her left, where I knew by the scents of metal and gun oil she had her Glock .40 stored. "If I do anything you don't like, you can shoot me."

Gaze going from the pillow to me, she almost smiled. "Promise?" Her playful tone almost made me smile too.

An engine purred softly and tires thumped over cobblestones. Both Elexis and I looked in the direction of the sound, though we couldn't see it since my patio was around the back of the house. The scents of both a werewolf and a normal wolf drifted to me before I even heard the car door open.

"Oh no," I muttered low enough the werewolf approaching from around the front of the house wouldn't hear it.

A querying whine sounded, then claws clicked out a fast rhythm on the cobblestones of my side walkway. Seconds later the South Fork pack pup trotted out of the dark, his little tail wagging like mad. He paused, gave Elexis a hard look as he sniffed the air, then ran right up to me. Yipping and barking, he circled my legs. Karman came around the corner a few seconds later. Blond hair all up in some kind of clip, shirt on backwards over a pair of sweatpants, she was the picture of frazzled. Guilt pinched at me.

She shot me a tired smile before looking to Elexis. "Elexis, welcome to Hemlock Hollow. I didn't get a chance to say that when I answered the door before." She gestured toward the pup. "Nursing and all, sorry about that." Her gaze turned hard as it landed back on me.

I beckoned to the other cushy chair on my patio. "Karman, have a seat. Can I get you anything?"

She looked longingly at the chair before waving her hand in dismissal. "No time, but thanks. What you can do is take this fella for the night. He won't sleep, and if he won't sleep, my baby won't sleep, and if she doesn't sleep, I'll go insane." She swung a pack off her shoulder and passed it to me.

"Is that milk I smell?" Elexis asked.

Karman nodded slowly, her heavy eyelids blinking so long I wasn't sure they were going to open back up for a second. "Yes, enough bottles to keep him happy until tomorrow. I'm sorry, Raul. You're welcome to bring him back then. I'll be at the coffee shop. Feel free to drop him by there."

I accepted the pack. "No need to be sorry. I'm the one who dropped off an unexpected second mouth to feed." I nodded toward the chair. "You sure you don't want to sit for a bit? I have leftover takeout from Mike's."

Smiling, she took a step back. "Thanks, but I'd better not. If I sit down, I won't get up, and Leif's at home with the baby, probably half out of his mind already."

"You need me to drive you?" I asked.

"Nope, got the Leaf. See you tomorrow. Nice to meet you Elexis," she called over her shoulder.

"You too," Elexis shot back.

A few seconds later, an electric engine hummed to life and tires thumped over cobblestones as she pulled away. Careful of the pup, I sat down. He stood on my foot and tried to jump to my lap, but slid back down my leg. After the second attempt, I picked him up. He walked a circle and lay down. Figured.

"Who did I just meet?" Elexis asked.

The bewildered look on her face made her look temptingly cute.

"Karman Paulsdöttir. She owns the Crescent Coffee shop on Main Street."

"And she brought milk for your puppy?"

A laugh slipped out before I could stop it. "He's not my puppy. He's a wolf pup I rescued today. Karman did me a favor by feeding him and watching him for a bit."

The brightness of her wide eyes banished the bewildered look. "She had a baby at home. By fed, you mean…"

"Nursed."

A multitude of emotions crossed her face—shock, distaste, wonder, and finally what might have been guilt. "So when I knocked on the door, you two hadn't just finished…" She gestured toward me.

I thought about torturing her by making her finish her sentence, but decided against it. "No, I like my balls right where they are, and Leif would do his best to make them into earrings if I ever touched her. Not that I would anyway. I respect Leif too much."

"Leif?"

"Yep. Leif Jörgensson, one of my best friends." Even after all the shit that went down, he had stayed by my side, not caring what anyone else thought. "She's his wife. He and I go way back."

"So she was nursing him and had shifted back into human form to answer the door. I get why she was naked now. But why were you coming out of the shower?"

I scratched the wolf pup's head. His eyes slipped closed. "He peed on my shirt. And I had to bring his pack's carcasses back to be processed for evidence. I couldn't get the two smells out of my nose, so she let me take a shower."

Elexis looked down at her lap. "Oh." Shoulders squaring, she looked back up at me. "I'm a bit of an ass then. Sorry I got the wrong impression. I thought maybe the little show had been Gilmerson's idea of hazing. You know how cops love to do that shit to the new recruit, especially when she's a girl." After a long pause, she sighed and went on. "The paperwork you had to do, it was on a poacher who killed his pack?"

"Yes," I said, trying to keep my tone neutral so she didn't realize how impressed I was by her owning up to being an ass.

For just a second before she hid it, I saw her eyes soften. "You saved him."

The crackle in her power settled like embers going out.

"We'll see. He's too young to be taken away from his mother, so he has a hard road ahead of him," I looked down at the sleeping pup while I smoothed the hair between his pointed ears.

"So the wolf preserve around Hemlock Hollow isn't just a cover."

"Nope. We share the land with two packs, the South Fork and the North Fork. Well, just one pack now, I guess." I had to take a breath to push my anger down. "We protect them, and they protect us by providing a cover story for wolf sightings. With all the wolf attacks all over the news, it's getting harder to protect them."

"The wolf attacks are actually newly bitten attacking people." Fear gave her scent a touch of a tangy smell, not like something bad exactly, more like limes or lemons. The wide-eyed expression on her face made me realize she was afraid of becoming like the ones attacking people.

"No, not newly bitten, condemned. There's a big difference. Newly bitten either haven't made it through the *verða* yet, or like you, they've made it through successfully. Condemned either went mad during the *verða* or were mad to begin with," I explained.

Her dark brows pinched together over eyes filled with bewilderment. "Someone bit in people who were already mad? Why would they do that?"

"Because they want to bring attention to our kind, to expose us."

"The chief's theory."

I nodded.

"But you don't believe that."

Though she was a pain, she was quick. At least that was something I liked about her, besides her scorching body and those eyes that looked right through me. "No, I think they want to distract from what they're really up to."

Her eyes sparked. "World domination. Sounds very Viking-like."

A half-smile pulled up one corner of my mouth. "It isn't as far-fetched as you might think. There are werewolves deep in the political system of all countries, many in influential positions."

One of her perfect black brows rose, giving her a quirky, cute-as-hell look. I fought the impulse to shake my head. Cute? What was wrong with me?

"Why doesn't that surprise me?" Her last word turned into a long yawn.

Between her and the pup, I was about to knock off again. Another howl in the distance made Elexis's eyes pop back open. Pretending not to notice, I kicked my feet up on the edge of the fire pit—well away from the flames—and repositioned the pup in my lap. "Hope you don't mind if we sleep out here for a bit. I don't think he'd like all the smells of civilization in my house," I said.

It was true enough that my tone didn't sound forced, but one of her brows rose again anyway. Blood rushed to my cock. Damn, if she was going to keep doing that, I was going to have a problem.

"Suit yourself." Relief lay hidden in her tone.

As she settled deeper into her sleeping bag and closed her eyes, I tried to tell myself I was staying out here for the pup. Trouble was, I couldn't bullshit myself. This woman was getting under my skin, and the itch wasn't entirely bad.

CHAPTER FIVE

ELEXIS

The last of the nearly scentless soap rinsed from my skin and disappeared down the drain. A turn of the brushed-steel knob shut off the water flow. I stepped from the gray tiled shower into a room so steamy, I couldn't even see the opposite wall. Guess I should have turned the exhaust fan on. But if I had and Raul decided to get all creepy and peek in, then he would have seen far more than I was comfortable with. That thought brought up the memory of his toned, bare chest.

Hell no. I was not going there. This guy was an ass, even if he did save puppies and sleep outside during a storm for them. I refused to soften on this or let my sex-deprived body get the better of me.

At least he had a good-sized home gym he let me use. I'd thought werewolves wouldn't bother with such things, being naturally stronger and faster than humans, and possessing a crazy quick metabolism. Something I was glad to be wrong about. All the supernatural abilities in the world couldn't keep me from working out. It wasn't a love of the burn or anything like that. Having been a cop for years, the need to be in optimal shape for survival was deeply ingrained into me. Not to mention, while I was now faster and stronger than most humans, I had werewolves to contend with.

I dried off and wrapped the crème-colored Egyptian cotton towel around my hair. The towel would no doubt end up with traces of my blue hair dye on it, but what the hell. If it stained, I'd buy him a new one. Even if the damn thing was a hundred-dollar towel like I suspected. I hit the button for the exhaust fan and slid open the pocket door leading into the powder room. This ridiculously opulent bathroom had a room for everything: the shower, the toilet, the sinks, and another door I still wasn't sure of. But I wasn't about to snoop. Yet.

Considering the monstrosity of a shower had three showerheads and could fit at least five people in it, I guess it warranted its own room. All the signs pointed to Raul living alone, so I could only imagine who he'd had in that shower. It had made me want to scour it with bleach before using it, but I hadn't smelled anything other than mild soap and cleaner in it. My heightened new senses wouldn't have missed the scent of bodily fluids associated with sex.

After a good scrub on my shoulder-length hair, I dropped the towel in the glass hamper near the door leading into the hall. The cool air of the fog-free room felt amazing against my skin, so I bypassed my clothing to brush my hair first. Raul was still zonked out on the patio furniture, meaning I had the house to myself, for a short while at least. Halfway through brushing my hair, I heard footsteps in the hallway. I dropped the brush and reached for the door.

Raul appeared in the doorway just as my hand closed around the knob. His golden-brown eyes darkened with desire as they opened wide and took in every naked inch of me, slowly and shamelessly. Dammit if that look didn't feel good, like a talented caress.

"Good to see you're already getting used to the werewolf comfort level of being naked around others," he said.

Mouth agape, hand on the doorknob, I just stood there. In only a pair of blue shorts, he looked hotter than an asshole like him had any right to be. He breezed past me into the bathroom. His scent wrapped around me as he passed—pine needles, clean water, and spice—or was it musk? It tugged at something deep in me, tried to get me to turn toward him. But I refused. I'd rather he get an eyeful of my bare ass instead of my hard nipples. Why my body reacted to a man I couldn't stand, I had no idea. I resisted the urge to search desperately for a towel, or anything, to cover myself. I didn't want him to realize he'd gotten under my skin.

"I didn't leave it open on purpose," I finally managed to say.

"Um hum, sure."

A little ball of brown and white fluff trotted into the room. The pup acknowledged me with no more than a flick of his ears before following Raul.

"Why does he look so fluffy?"

Raul opened the third door in the bathroom—the one I hadn't explored yet. A huge walk-in closet yawned beyond it. He and the wolf pup disappeared into it. "Lupine Naturals conditioner," he called back.

"What is that?"

While he was busy, I started to get dressed, fast. "It's conditioner from this great little shop in town, Lupine Naturals. They make all their own products, scent-free and earth friendly. I'll take you there next week. You'll love it," he said, voice echoing from the depth of the closet.

The thing had to be huge. What the hell kind of a closet could one's voice echo in? I was kind of afraid to find out. "You gave him a bath."

He poked his head around the closet door, a T-shirt halfway over it but unfortunately not covering his eyes. "Yeah, why not?"

Feeling more comfortable in my shorts and black bra (even if it was lacy and sexy), I put one hand on my hip. "What happened to him not liking the smells of the house?"

I caught one last flash of those hard abs before he pulled his shirt down. Damn, he must do a lot of crunches. Giving myself a good shake, I grabbed my own T-shirt and put it on before he could return to the bathroom. Just because he was being nice to me didn't mean I would allow myself to be attracted to him.

Sadness filled his golden-brown eyes. "He smelled like death. I couldn't have him meet the North Fork pack smelling like that. They'd reject him."

"You're taking him to the other pack? Already?"

"Yep. The longer he's around human things, the harder it will be for him to learn they're dangerous."

Why did he have to be good looking and sensitive toward animals? Animals and hot guys who loved them had always been weak spots of mine.

He walked by close enough to brush against my shoulder. Heat burned through me at the touch of those hard biceps. The pup jogged after him.

"When are you going?"

"Now."

I followed him into the hallway. "What about my training? What am I supposed to do?"

Shrugging, he kept walking. "Come with me. It will be a good...learning experience."

"What exactly am I going to learn about being a werewolf by hiking around in the wilderness?"

He stopped and turned to me with a bit of a bewildered smile. "Everything."

Aggravation forced my fangs to pop out before I could stop them. I'd opened myself up wide for that. His smile grew before he kept going. The realization he was probably right pissed me off, and I didn't like him being right. "And our investigation?"

"The forest will help clear our heads for it. A hike always helps me when I'm stuck."

We emerged from the hallway into the living room, with its vast ceiling and endless windows. All the evergreens beyond that glass called to me. The need to be outside, in the wild, struck me with a powerful desire. He was right again, and I hated it. I focused on the glass and steel elements of his house to try and calm myself. While the Wyoming girl in me longed for a more western traditional architecture, I was starting to see the draw of this modern-style home of Raul's. But it had its drawbacks too, like making me want to give in to my wolf side. That wasn't okay. Being a wolf felt too out of control for my taste.

"All right. I guess we can talk on the way."

Raul made a non-comital, almost amused noise. I ground my teeth. Man, he irritated me. He opened the front door and stepped aside to let me go first. It was an automatic reaction, muscle memory. I could see it in his face and stance. I didn't like that. It meant he was less of an asshole at his core than I had originally thought. Being wrong—repeatedly—wasn't something I was used to. I mumbled a weak "thank you" as I walked through the door.

The inside of Raul's white forestry department Cherokee was as immaculate as his house. This man had some serious OCD. The shared flaw made me feel a bit better. Just as I pulled my seatbelt on and rolled my window down, Raul climbed in and handed me a squirming ball of fluff. I held the pup up and away from me. His big brown eyes watched me with interest. Slowly, his tail started to wag.

"What am I supposed to do with this?" I asked in a voice two octaves higher than normal.

"It's a him, not an it. And hold him, preferably not like that."

"Is he going to pee on me?" I asked. His tail wagged faster.

"If you keep holding him like that, probably."

I sat him down on my lap so fast he grunted. Recovering quickly, he turned to face Raul, little tail going like a high-powered fan. One glance at the two of us and Raul let out a deep belly laugh.

"What?" I asked.

He started down the driveway. "You just look so uncomfortable." The surprise on his face offended me.

"Well, I've never had pets."

His eyes widened. "Really?"

"Why is that so hard to believe?"

After a shift of gears, he shrugged. "Single woman, cop, living alone, that kind of life usually comes with a pet. You do like animals, right? Because it would just be weird—"

"What the hell makes you think I fit that profile?"

A smile grew on his stupid, handsome face as he cast me a sideways glance. "You never check your phone. I'm not even sure you have one, which is odd enough in this day and age. No ring on your finger and no hint of the telltale tan line of one having been there. Your mannerisms ooze independence, capability, and stubbornness. I'm guessing your hookups are short, sweet, and infrequent, never forming attachments."

I didn't know whether to be offended or impressed with his deductive capabilities. I settled on both. He took a breath to go on, but I interrupted. "Okay, Mr. Profiler, why don't you do something useful with those skills and tell me why you think this Bain is our guy."

For several long minutes he concentrated on the road ahead. I hadn't expected to hit a nerve with the question. Finally, he spoke. "Bain lived under the shadow of his brother, Didrik, his whole life. Didrik was the alpha of the Draupnir pack since before Bain was born. Didrik followed the old ways, kept our traditions and culture. Bain is the opposite. He gained enough allies, grew strong enough, and rose high enough he was able to challenge Didrik."

When he paused, I asked, "Able to challenge? Can't anyone challenge the alpha?"

"Yes and no. If a wolf's standing isn't high enough, they have to fight their way through the alpha's *verndari*—kind of like their inner circle of lieutenants—to prove their worth first. But if the wolf is already a *verndari*, then they can challenge the alpha directly."

"Interesting system. *Verndari* means lieutenant in Icelandic, then?"

He shook his head. "No, it translates closer to protector. They are the protectors of the pack."

"Okay. So he challenged the alpha. Why's that make him our guy?"

His jaw clenched. "He challenged him in the old way, the way that doesn't allow the pack's *verndari* to challenge the new alpha if the current is defeated. When the alpha is defeated, all of their *verndari* are reduced to bottom members of the pack, if they're allowed to stay at all. It means they have to fight their way back up through a pack to gain the level high enough to challenge."

"That makes a kind of sense, I guess."

Raul's teeth pulled back from his lips, and I caught the flash of fangs. "It does, which is why Didrik embraced it. But Bain didn't just defeat Didrik, he killed him, and the way he challenged him means his *verndari* couldn't avenge him." The last words were barely more than a growl.

"And what of his female proxy alpha? Morene something-or-other-daughter?" I struggled with the last name, still not quite used to how the Icelandic American of Hemlock Hollow's surnames worked.

The chief had briefed me about all the alphas, and from that conversation I knew she had belonged to the Draupnir pack before the takeover and had stayed after, and that she wasn't Bain's mate.

"What about her?" Raul asked—or maybe snapped would have been a bit more appropriate term.

"If Bain is a main suspect, do you favor her as one too?" I asked what I thought was an obvious connection.

"No, I don't. She is a victim of his as well." The confidence and finality in his tone made it clear there was more to that story and he wasn't about to tell me now.

I let silence fill the Cherokee for a bit. We turned up an overgrown dirt road. The trees ticked by at a slower pace while we crawled along. Once Raul's breathing returned to normal, I asked, "Is it unusual to fight to the death?"

"Highly. And for a brother to kill a brother..."

This time I didn't press. I had no idea what it was like to have siblings, but I'd always wanted them. Now maybe I wasn't so sure. On top of the next hill a steel gate blocked the road. Raul brought the Cherokee to a stop and shut the engine off.

"We have to walk from here." He got out and held the door, looking to the wolf pup expectantly. Raul made a motion with his head, and the pup rose, licked my chin, and trotted across the seat. Without hesitation, he launched himself from the truck. Raul caught him mid-leap and sat him down on the grass. "Crazy pup," he said with a laugh.

The sound of his easy, deep laugh warmed me all the way to my toes. I tried to ignore how that warmth pooled in my groin. Raul shut the door.

"Stupid body," I mumbled to myself.

I climbed out of the lifted SUV.

"What's that?" Raul asked. Though his tone was innocent enough, I saw one corner of his mouth turn up.

"Nothing," I snapped. I walked around to the front of the vehicle to join him, trying to look anywhere but at him.

"Um hum."

My fangs pushed against my lips, forcing me to open my mouth or get pricked. Speaking of pricks... Ahead of me, Raul walked, all predator-like up on his toes, eyes scanning, but still at ease, as if the mannerisms were second nature to him. Hell, maybe first nature. The wolf pup ran alongside him, hopping over the tall grass, then disappearing into it. I struggled to get my mind back to the investigation, to what Raul had told me about Bain. Clearly the subject was a touchy one. But why? I couldn't help but wonder if it was because Raul had some connection to Bain and might be in on it.

I was about to push with more questions when he stopped next to a tree and took his shirt off. Nicely defined pecs and six-pack abs, combined with the pheromones he was kicking out, made me do a double take—and pissed me off.

"What are you doing?" I demanded.

He slid his shorts right off without missing a beat. My traitorous gaze went to his groin. Even limp and relaxed he was well hung. I squeezed my eyes shut, hard. Deep laughter rolled over me. "Maybe you're not as comfortable with nakedness as I thought."

"I'm perfectly comfortable with my own nakedness, thank you very much. It's yours I'm not comfortable with."

"Why does my nakedness make you uncomfortable?"

"Because I don't like you."

"So you need to like the people you see naked?"

I wanted to smack him. I opened my eyes so I could glare at him. My peripheral vision tried hard to distract me, but I refused to let it, even if the man did have a nice package. "Of course I do."

"That's going to be a problem."

"Why?"

"You're a werewolf now. We get naked a lot, to run, to howl together, to fight, and yes to fuck. But fucking is the least common reason we get naked."

Two spots of intense heat did their best to burn holes in my cheeks. Just hearing him say the word "fuck" made the muscles between my legs tighten. To prove something to myself, and to him, I began stripping, my movements fast and angry. My T-shirt dropped to the ground, then my shorts. The smug look on his face made me reach back for my bra clasp. His cheek twitched and his smile faltered as I slid the straps from my shoulders and let my bra fall away. I held his gaze as I removed my panties. His cheek twitched again, but he didn't look down. That scored him a few points, but it was still a blowout game he was going to lose.

I thrust out a hip and put my hand on it. "You wanna tell me why we're naked?"

"It's better to go the rest of the way as wolves. If the pack spots us in human form they'll never let us approach." He cocked his head as he looked at me. "I figured a Wyoming girl like you would know that."

The comment made me feel more naked than actually being naked did. I shrugged as if it were nothing. "While other kids were in FFA, I was in juvie, or bouncing around the foster care system." I hoped my casual tone didn't sound as hollow as it felt.

The barest hint of surprise widened his eyes. He obviously hadn't researched me as much as I had him and this town. That made me feel better. There were things about me I didn't want this guy to know. I'd said more than I'd meant to as it was.

"Sorry," Raul said in a soft tone that played along my skin like talented fingers.

Of course he would likely have talented fingers, ex-quarterback and all. I shook the thought away. Rather than answer, I drew a deep breath in through my nose, listened to the wind through the pine boughs, and tapped into my wolf. If I didn't hurry up and do it, I wouldn't, and I wasn't about to let him see it bothered me to shift.

Heat flooded me as my molecules started to vibrate. I crouched, and less than a second later my paws touched the ground. My vision sharpened, as if I'd put my eyes to binoculars, a million scents danced on the wind, and my hearing improved until I could hear the heartbeat of a squirrel in a tree twenty paces away. For a moment I just soaked it in. This was the part I loved, those first moments when everything sharpened and I felt more alive than I ever thought possible. But it was also the part I hated, because it felt so raw, so instinctual. It grew harder to focus, to think, to control instinct. Being out of control even a little made me edgy.

The wolf pup let out a querulous noise, cocked his head, and trotted over to me. This was more of the part I hated. The body language of wolves was foreign to me, and it was a language all its own. Not knowing what to do, I stood still while he sniffed me. A few seconds later, he licked my nose and trotted off. *Better than hiking his leg at me, I guess.*

Shimmering out of the corner of my eye cued me in to Raul shifting. I caught one more flash of his tightly stretched bare skin over well-developed muscles before he became a large brown wolf. His wolf form was just as filled out as his human one. And my wolfy instincts liked him, a lot.

It was all I could do to stop myself from turning my ass toward him. Damned instincts.

Struggling to think as a human, I went over his faults: arrogant, self-absorbed, snarky, rich-boy, and mass assault and conspirator suspect. Those last two were growing more questionable by the day, which was making it harder to hate him. Not impossible, but harder. The human thoughts helped drive back my traitorous instincts.

Was he smiling? Shit, I couldn't tell. I bared my fangs at him. At least I knew what *that* meant. He made a noise that might have been a laugh and jogged off toward the trees with the pup in tow. I shook my head—not caring if it was a very human thing to do—and followed.

We kept a slow pace for the pup's sake, but I was grateful for it as well. Jogging was something I'd never enjoyed as a human, and becoming a werewolf hadn't changed that. I preferred my cardio to be more of the full-contact variety. I'd yet to find a sports bra capable of keeping my D-cup girls from bouncing enough to be able to enjoy running. Then there was the fact I wasn't very coordinated as a wolf yet. If I overthought it—which I did all too often—I tripped over my huge paws.

Energy coiled within, growing stronger the deeper into the forest we went. It rolled off the trees and plant life almost like they were exhaling it. The energy didn't feed me so much as soothe and relax me. It felt good, familiar, like a favorite hangout, only better. And the company of the big brown wolf and his little sidekick wasn't entirely bad either. Raul guided the pup along with a patience that surprised me, not even getting mad when he ran off after a squirrel, twice. I couldn't be sure, but the sounds he made at him seemed encouraging, and his body language was relaxed. It even looked like Raul had to hold himself back from joining in.

I got that, more than I wanted to admit. The instinct to chase things, to hunt, was almost overpowering. The only thing keeping me from it was the potential embarrassment of Raul seeing me act like an animal. But the idea of him chasing a rabbit... That brought to mind a hilarious image of him as a kid chasing small forest animals. A sort of chuffing noise came from me. I think it might have been a laugh. Raul gave me a sideways glance. The corner of his mouth turned up, exposing a lot of teeth. Aggression or amusement? I couldn't tell. While I clearly needed to work on wolf language, Raul was the last person I wanted to ask.

He stopped suddenly, his nose going into the air. I took a long sniff, but between the trees, ferns, flowers, squirrels, rabbits, and more, I couldn't figure out what had alerted him.

Raul's movements became tense and slow. I concentrated on my hearing, sharpening it and allowing my other senses to dull and take a back seat. From some distance away came the sound of many paws landing softly against the ground—running in our direction. Wolves from the chuffs, growls, and occasional soft yip. At first the sounds came from the north, then they came from all around us. I moved closer to Raul. He gave me a long look, but I couldn't read what those golden-brown eyes tried to tell me.

The wolf pup let out a little whine as he looked from one of us to the other. His ears perked up, and his nose began to twitch as he sniffed the air. Raul moved between him and the largest group I heard approaching. I moved to the pup's other side. I didn't know if they'd be a potential threat to him, but Raul's movements made me think it was possible.

All around us, the forest came alive with the sound of approaching wolves. I had no idea how many there were, but it sounded like a lot. Why hadn't I thought to ask Raul earlier? A hunter would be able to tell, but I'd never been hunting. Unless criminals counted.

My heart thudded against my chest. The hair along my back started to rise. It tickled a bit, but not in a good way. Wolves began to step out of the trees. Two, three, five, eight. I lost count after that. The press of their energy told me there were at least ten. They revealed themselves but didn't approach. Several bared their fangs at us. Even more had their hackles raised. One wolf with white markings reminding me of a lion stepped out and approached. Stalked would be a more appropriate word. He walked all up on his toes, making his shoulders roll and moving the raised hair along them and his back. I didn't need to be able to speak wolf to know he was the alpha.

Not a single one was as big as I was, let alone as big as Raul. Tension coiled in me until I felt like a cocked pistol ready to go off. Raul looked long and pointedly at me again. I took a deep breath and forced myself to relax. His attention shifted to the alpha, almost casually, as if he saw no threat in him. But *I* saw threat in him, plenty of it. The two stared each other down. The pack's alpha let out a little growl. Raul remained quiet and relaxed. My instincts wouldn't let me relax. I was going to have one hell of a bad hair day when I shifted back.

After several long moments of a staring contest, both dipped their noses a bit. The North Fork alpha relaxed. Most of his hair smoothed down along his back. Raul moved one front leg to the side and back, not exposing the pup, but revealing him. I had to fight the urge to step between the alpha and the pup. Raul shot a very brief look at me. I didn't move. The alpha's stance relaxed a little more. He took a few steps closer, nose lowering as his nostrils worked. The pup lifted his own nose and sniffed in the alpha's direction. They couldn't touch each other because Raul stood in the way just enough to keep them apart.

Seeing the alpha so close to Raul made me realize how big werewolves really were, easily twice the size of normal wolves, maybe more. How anyone ever mistook us for wild wolves was beyond me.

The pup's tail started to wag. Something in the alpha's eyes softened. His shoulders relaxed. The pup's tail wagged faster. I relaxed as well but didn't move away. The alpha turned his head and let out a soft bark. The wolves in the trees to our right parted to let a female through. Gray head held high, she strode to us as if our size didn't intimidate her in the slightest. Her pack dipped their heads to her, tucked and wagged their tails, and made soft yipping noises.

She stopped before us, looking regal and proud. Her eyes met mine before flicking down to the pup. Not knowing what else to do, I inclined my head a little. She lowered her nose to him. I hovered right over him, hoping my posture made it clear he was under my protection. I'd never been the mothering type, so the instinct to protect him felt strange, foreign, like stepping into someone else's skin. Deep inside, the human part of me knew she'd never chance my wrath by trying to hurt him. But my wolf side disagreed. The pup took a step toward her. I tensed. They touched noses. She pulled back. He barked, spun in a circle, and stuck his nose back up to her. He licked her and began wagging his tail.

He took a step out from under my shadow, and she lowered her head to him. His little pink tongue flashed again and again as he licked her chin and face. The soft look in her eyes told me all I needed to know. She turned and walked back toward the trees. The pup bounded after her but stopped short of the tree line. He looked back at Raul for a long moment.

The female wolf made a sort of barking sound. The pup jumped and ran after her, tail wagging.

Raul and the alpha exchanged another long look. This time it didn't feel tense. The alpha dipped his head slightly, then turned and trotted into the trees after the pup and female. Slowly, the rest of the pack melted back into the forest. Soon the soft patter of retreating paws died away and we were left alone.

For a moment so long it almost grew uncomfortable, Raul stared at the spot in the trees the pup had disappeared into. The tension went out of him, leaving him looking drooped and sad. I thought he would have been thrilled to get rid of the responsibility of the pup. Seemed he was right about me being wrong about him again. Which really, really chapped me.

Before I could worry about him seeing my discomfort, he trotted back the way we'd come. I had to rush to catch up. We jogged the entire two-plus miles back to where we'd left our clothes, with me practically tripping over every twig on the way. At least he was ahead of me, so he didn't see. Deep down I knew if I just let my wolf side take over and gave into instinct, movement as a wolf would come naturally. But then I'd have to give up control, and I was *not* about to do that.

I turned my back to Raul as I dressed. Still adjusting my T-shirt, I turned around to find his back to me as well. The respect for my privacy caught me completely off guard. It didn't help that he looked hotter than a smoking gun, his bare back all taut muscle. He turned unexpectedly, shirt still in hand. My eyes flicked back up to his face, but it was too late. His damn, cocky smirk told me I'd been caught.

"Enjoying the view?"

That did it. "It isn't all about you all the time, you arrogant ass."

His grin only grew, making me want to punch him. "But it is this time."

I threw my hands up and stormed past him. "Ugh! Fine, yeah, it is, but not like you think. I was just marveling over the fact you cared about that pup. I didn't think you had it in you."

His lips tightened. "Don't believe everything you read or hear about me." His tone was teasing, but it had a hard underlying edge to it. The edge hid something—pain. But not just any pain. This felt like a pain so deep and old, it had scarred his very energy. All I caught was a brief feel, then it was gone, buried and hidden. I recognized it because I knew that bitterness, that kind of pain.

As a foster child who had gotten bounced from home to home for behavioral issues, I knew it all too well. The biting remark I had been about to say died halfway up my throat. Silence as thick as a Jackson Hole blizzard dropped over us as we climbed into the Cherokee. Neither of us broke it, and I was fine with that. What I wasn't fine with was Raul getting a little deeper under my skin in a way I totally hadn't expected.

CHAPTER SIX

RAUL

The front door let out a tiny creak as I opened it. I cringed and froze. I'd never had to sneak out of my own house before, so I'd never noticed the thing creaked. Five very long seconds passed without any sound coming from the inside house. I left the door open and crept across the stone paver walkway toward my Cherokee. No animals would enter my house. Despite how clean I kept it, the scent of werewolf remained. As for people, if there was anyone who would enter when I wasn't home, they wouldn't care if the door was open.

I sped up when I rounded the corner—and came to a jarring halt when the Cherokee came into view. Elexis leaned against the front fender, arms crossed beneath her breasts, pushing them up and increasing the already deep cleavage visible thanks to the low neck of her dark blue T-shirt. The color set off the blue highlights in her nearly black hair nicely. Not even a hint of the outline of a nipple showed, making me think she wore a bra. Bummer. Short shorts exposed plenty of her long legs.

"Where are you sneaking off to?" she demanded.

I stiffened and tried to hide it with a shrug. "Nowhere you'd be interested in. Unless, of course, you can't stand to be away from me. I would understand, since you've seen me naked now."

She threw her hands up and shook her head. "I'm not one of your conquests. That reverse psychology crap won't work on me."

My fangs ached to be released, but I held them back. The rage would be useful later. Digging the keys out of my pocket, I ignored her and walked to the driver's door. By the time I started it she was climbing into the passenger seat. I gripped the steering wheel hard enough to compress it a bit.

"Seriously, I have a personal matter to take care of," I said.

She blew air out of her pursed lips and put her seat belt on. "Your hot date can wait. I want to start questioning people of interest about the bitings."

"What makes you think I have a hot date?"

Her hand swiped at the air before me. "All that."

One corner of my lips lifted. "Detective Sandalius, are you saying I look good?"

More air blew through her closed lips. "That is not what I said. I have a list of people I think we should talk to about the bitings."

"It's our day off."

Eyes pinching together, she turned to nail me down with her hard glare. "So putting a stop to this and protecting our kind is just a job to you?"

The question shot into me like a harpoon. I returned her glare. "No, it isn't. Not that it's your business, but what I'm going to do is related."

"In that case, I'm going."

"No you're not." I leaned over her and opened her door. Gods it was hard to ignore how good she smelled—like vanilla and hemlock with a touch of gun oil.

Her breasts heaved as she took a deep breath and shut the door. Was that a blush in her cheeks? "Unless you're willing to throw me out of this vehicle—and you'd better think hard about it if you are—then I am going."

I shifted the Cherokee into first and took off, sending gravel flying. "Fine, but you aren't going to like it. Don't say I didn't warn you."

A huff came from her as she rolled the window down. "I haven't liked anything about Hemlock Hollow, or you. Why should that change now?"

I smelled a lie on her, but I couldn't tell about which part. I rolled my window down to let the July heat out of the vehicle. It also helped to blow her scent away from me, which I really needed right now. Focused on the road, I did my best to ignore the insufferable woman beside me. The way her dark hair whipped about her face, making her look wild and fierce, didn't help. It was going to be a long drive.

Three painfully silent miles later, I turned up a hemlock-lined cobblestone driveway. The huge wrought iron gates with wolfs' heads formed out of Norse knot work hung open as if waiting for our arrival. Elexis stared wide eyed at them as we drove through. The zesty scent of the eastern hemlock trees blew in the windows, bringing back a ton of memories. A gasp came from her as her attention shifted to the log home at the end of the drive. I couldn't blame her. It was a sight. The two-story main cabin had wings and outbuildings connected by sky bridges. It didn't so much sit on the property as sprawl across it. Longing stabbed at me from the depths in which I'd buried it.

"Where are we?" she asked in an awed tone.

"The den of the Reinhard pack."

"That is some den! Does the entire pack live here?"

I tried to sound like I wasn't grinding my teeth. "No."

She brightened as if she couldn't feel the tension rolling off me. As distracted as she was, it was possible she couldn't. "Right, this was your pack."

"*Is* my pack."

Her brows rose. "Really? They didn't kick you out when you bit Sonya in without her permission, or the council's?"

"No, they didn't," I answered in a cold tone I hoped would cut the conversation off.

She stiffened and looked back out the window. "Why'd you bring me here?"

"I didn't. You invited yourself."

She shot me a look that burned like the fires of Muspelheimr. "Fine. Why did you come here?"

"To fight."

"What?" she practically yelled.

I smiled. "Told you that you wouldn't like it."

A loud thump sounded before I'd even realized she'd moved to smack my dashboard. Damn, she was fast. Yet another thing about her that was too sexy for my own good.

"Ugh! What the fuck, Raul? Why would you drag me into something like this?" Her face was turning red. It was cute.

"It's not like that. I'm fighting to regain my standing in the pack."

"And you had to do that today?"

"I have to do it every day."

Her face scrunched up in confusion. That was cute too. "Why every day?"

"Because each fight I win gets me one more step up in the pack, and I have a long way to go."

I thought I saw her eyes soften before her cop mask covered her expression. "So you were pretty high up before you plummeted to the bottom?" So much for softness.

"I was one of the pack *verndari*." It came out cold and removed.

Her head pulled back and her eyes widened. My upper lip raised on one side, flashing a bit of fang at her. "What, you didn't discover that when you grilled the chief about me and the town?"

Red tinged her cheeks, and her brows scrunched up again. "Well, no. We didn't have time to get around to the specifics of the packs, just who their alphas were and how big the packs are. And he didn't tell me who my *kennari* was going to be. That surprise was left up to your buddy Gilmerson."

A growl escaped me. "Whose friendship is apparently questionable."

"He wanted me to see you at Karman's and get the wrong impression. Why?"

"That a great question, one I plan to ask him very soon."

She went quiet for several seconds. "The Reinhard pack has over five hundred members. That's a lot of fights."

I slowed to a crawl as I drove beneath the sky bridge to the left of the main cabin. "Not as many as it sounds. The bottoms decline and forfeit, so it drops over a hundred right off the bat."

"Still, that's a fight a day for over a year."

"Naw. Four fights a day for almost four months."

"That's insane!" She actually looked a bit worried about me.

I waved a hand. "Not really. The lower five hundred of the pack aren't at my level. The fights are quick and easy. Only the last fifty or so will even make me break a sweat."

An exasperated noise came from her. "Then why do they even bother to fight you?"

"So they don't lose their position in the pack."

"You're saying every werewolf has to be a fighter?" Irritation peppered her tone.

"Not at all. Just the higher-up members because they're the ones who protect the pack. As a cop, I thought you'd get this." The last part slipped out. I peeked at her out of the corner of my eye and saw her irritation ease.

"Depends. Do the higher members protect even those who don't fight?"

"Especially them, at least in the Hemlock Hollow packs. I can't speak for other werewolf packs."

A sort of humming noise came from her, and she nodded.

"What?" I asked.

"I get why you have to work your way back up. You're meant to protect people, and you did the opposite when you bit Sonya in."

I braked a bit hard when I pulled into one of the few vacant parking spots in the large lot of cars behind the south wing of the main house. The bumper of the red Corvette in front of me lay only inches away.

"I know you won't believe me, but I did what I did to protect people. I just...did it all wrong." The last came out as little more than a growl. I hadn't meant to say anything defensive. It could lead to questions, which could lead to things I didn't want to discuss. But dammit, this woman got under my skin and made herself comfortable there.

I flung my door open and barely missed a yellow XR7. The anger drained right out of me. I hadn't seen that car since the night I was detained after biting in Sonya. If that bastard was here, I was going to beat the shit out of him, damn the hierarchy ladder to the molten planes of Muspelheimr.

My vision narrowed as my heart rate increased. I jumped out, slammed my door, and wove through the hundreds of cars all neatly parked on the cobblestone lot. Smell and instinct guided my movements more than sight. Boot heels clicked on cobbles as Elexis rushed to catch up with me.

"Whatever. You don't have to get all pissy about it. The truth is what it is," she said.

I ignored her and kept moving. Nose in the air, I checked for his scent. Hundreds of werewolf scents filled the air. It smelled like the entire pack was here. They didn't all show up just for my daily fights. This had to be because of Elexis. I didn't smell *him*, but I smelled the next best thing. Legs stretching out to their full length, my bare feet ate up the cobblestones. Elexis's vanilla essence blew to me as she jogged up to my side.

"You don't have to leave me behind just because I hurt your feelings. Some Viking descendant you turned out to be," she said in a mocking tone.

We made it to the enormous backyard—a long, wide stretch of open grass dotted with huge spruce and hemlock trees and over fifty gathering areas sprinkled throughout with fire pits at their center.

Elexis gasped. "Damn."

I kept walking. My nose led me to a group of about twelve people sitting on the circular stone bench surrounding one of the closest fire pits. At the edge of the group, a blond woman stood, arms folded, hands holding her elbows. She hunched in on herself and watched the conversation rather than took part in it. A pang of sympathy threatened to throw me off my game, but I squashed it.

"Tamara," I called.

She looked up at me and her eyes widened. Little red dimples formed beneath her fingers where she gripped her arms.

"We need to talk," I said.

She looked everywhere but at me. "Hi, Raul. I um..." She moved a step closer to the fire pit, but those around it ignored her just like they ignored me. A few of them glanced our way out of their peripheral, but none would actually look at us.

"I don't..."

I was beginning to wonder if she'd lost her wits when she disappeared a few weeks ago. The pressure of Elexis's power told me my time was up. *Shit*. I couldn't let her screw this up. If Tamara took off and I chased her down, the whole pack would be on me. And they wouldn't care about my reasons. I smothered the urgency rising up, trying to make my fangs spring, and projected a sense of calm I didn't feel. Tamara's grip on her arms relaxed enough her fingers stopped digging into her flesh. Her gaze flitted past my right shoulder to where I felt Elexis approach. I turned slightly and motioned in Elexis's direction.

"This is my *nemi*, Elexis Sandalius. Elexis, this is Tamara. She is James Jóndórson's girlfriend."

Elexis's energy popped for several seconds before she got it under control. Tamara's eyes widened. "Not anymore. Not since..."

An almost giddy, cheerleader-like happiness suddenly exuded from Elexis. I had to fight the urge to turn and see if she had plastered on a cheesy smile. "Hi, Tamara. It's nice to meet you."

Tamara's shoulders relaxed a bit as she accepted Elexis's hand and shook it weakly. Now that Elexis stood at my side, I saw she was smiling, but it looked genuine. "It is okay if we chat a bit?" she asked in a voice so sweet it sounded like a completely different person.

The feel of her energy changed, became gentle, nurturing. It was like watching Hyde turn into Jekyll.

"Just a bit, I promise," Elexis pressed.

Tamara lifted a shoulder in a non-committal shrug. Elexis smiled and made a motion with her head as she turned. Tamara followed. I fell into step beside Elexis. At a leisurely pace, she led us away from the group—all of whom were now watching us out of the corners of their eyes. Though their conversation continued, distraction was obvious in their voices.

"I already told the chief I don't know where James is," Tamara said.

Elexis sighed long and deep. "Oh, I know. But new girl on the force and all, emphasis on the girl." She rolled her eyes. I had to look away to hide a smile. "He wants me to go through the motions. Good training or some crap like that," she went on in an exasperated tone.

Tamara made a little laugh of sympathy. "Yeah, I get that."

"When did you see him last?" Elexis pressed gently.

Tamara's eyes glistened with sudden tears. "Just before he kidnapped Sonya and Ayra. We had a big fight 'cause he wouldn't tell me what was going on."

Elexis touched her arm. "Always keeping us in the dark, it's a man thing. Makes them feel more powerful." She paused and chewed her bottom lip as if she didn't want to go on. But she did. "Did he ever raise a hand to you?" The last was gentle, encouraging in a companion-like way.

Damn Elexis was good at this.

Tamara looked away and shrugged. "Only when I did or said something he didn't like, which seemed to be more and more as time went on." Her voice trailed off on the last part.

"Bastard," I mumbled.

"He wasn't like that when we were younger. He was sweet, thoughtful," she protested in a small voice.

After a few seconds of walking in silence, Elexis asked, "When he started to change, was he hanging out with anyone new?"

Blond brows pulling together, Tamara thought long and hard. "Well, yeah. He had just moved up to *verndari* in the Arnoddr pack, so he started hanging out with Calder all the time."

"Arnoddr pack, hmmm..." Elexis seemed to take a mental note.

Tamara cocked her head. "Yeah, I thought it was an odd choice, since Bain was like a mentor to him when he was growing up. But I was happy. I thought Arnoddr would be better for him than Draupnir, since he was dead set against choosing my pack." She huffed a bit at the last.

If this news shocked Elexis, it didn't show. Hel, it shocked me. The way she had drawn the info out of her was nothing short of brilliant.

"Has he reached out to you at all?" Though Elexis's tone remained gentle, it had that cop undertone of demand to it. I liked it. Too much.

Tamara's bottom lip quivered a little. "No, and after our fight, I'm not sure he will." She stopped walking, turned to Elexis, and grabbed her hand. Her eyes flicked around us. She leaned in. "But you have to find him. I think he's in danger," she whispered, so quietly I could barely hear her.

Every molecule of Elexis's energy sang with tension, but she showed the woman nothing but gentleness and a smile. Little did she know, Elexis was part of the danger to him. "I will, don't worry. But why do you think he's in danger?"

Again, Tamara looked around before she answered. "I don't think things went the way they were supposed to. And I think the guy behind it is pretty pissed about that," she whispered.

"Calder you mean?"

"No. It wasn't just him and Calder."

"Well it definitely wasn't Dustin," I pressed. Dustin, who had taken part in the kidnapping, was a low pack member who wouldn't have been up to orchestrating any of it. And he had cooperated completely with authorities, mostly out of guilt for betraying Ayra, his childhood friend, which he had said he'd been blackmailed into doing for her safety.

Tamara made a face. "No. Sometimes James would get a message when he and Calder were both together. Then they'd take off to do something and I wouldn't see him for days. It was like whoever was messaging him was giving them orders."

"Did you ever see who the messages were from?" Elexis asked.

Eyes widening, Tamara drew back a little. "No way. James never let me get near his phone. You have to believe me, though. I could tell both him and Calder listened to whoever the messages were from."

Elexis patted her hand where it gripped her arm. "I believe you."

"Thank you. I'm so worried about him, and I don't think the chief wants to find him," Tamara said.

Elexis played it up, giving her a sympathetic look. "*I* definitely do, and I will. Did James have anywhere he liked to hang out, or anywhere he went when he wanted to be alone or get away?"

"There's a strip club near Kalispell he liked."

Elexis leaned in close and kept her voice low as she asked, "Somewhere else. Somewhere he would go if he was in trouble or wanted to get away for a while."

Seconds ticked by as Tamara thought long and hard. The way she scrunched her face up and hunched in on herself made it look like thinking was difficult. She shared a long look with Elexis, then whispered in her ear, cupping her hands around her mouth. I heard, but only because I stood so close.

"Ram's Horn. He hiked and sometimes camped there when I messed up real bad or the big stuff got to him too much." The way she talked about James made me want to find him and pummel him. He had hit this woman, a lot. I could tell by the way she held herself, all hunched in like she was trying to tuck her tail in and was waiting for a blow. And she wanted him back.

Voices drifted to us, boasting male voices. Three men strode toward us from the backyard. People had begun to gather there around the huge patio against the house while we'd been talking to Tamara.

At the sound of the men's voices, Tamara took a quick step away from

Elexis. She cleared her throat. "Like I said, I don't know anything and I don't want to. He's a traitor to our kind."

Her pleading eyes said something completely different. Elexis nodded to her and gave her a wink. "All right. Well thanks for nothing," she said, making a show of it.

Tamara's shoulders sagged in relief. The men were too busy giving me the stink eye to even notice her. The biggest of them—a six-foot-four guy with so much brown facial hair he looked like he was in the middle of shifting—called out. "There you are, Raul. Hanging out with the bottoms where you belong. Did you come to fight or hit on someone's leftovers?"

I ground my teeth against a reply, determined not to let them get under my skin. The other two guys sneered at me from out of long faces with prominent noses and wide brows. Brothers. I searched my memory for their names.

Elexis took a step toward them. Head high, chest out, she looked ready to take them on. "Who the hell are you to call him a bottom?" she demanded. Her words blew me away, taking my breath and any response I had been about to make to them.

The three men laughed as they walked up. Behind us, I felt Tamara slip away. Ah, she had done it for her, not me. That made sense.

"That's Hati," I told her, thrusting my head in the direction of tall and hairy.

Her top lip rose, exposing fangs. "Your parents had high expectations—the wolf who swallows the moon—which you clearly won't reach."

The barb she shot him made me smile, for two reasons. To say she had read up on our religion was one thing, but to actually demonstrate it showed she had paid attention to her reading.

Hati whistled as his gaze crawled over Elexis. "Damn, new wolf is fine." His nose wrinkled as he looked to me. "How the hell did you get her for your first *nemi*? That shit don't seem right."

Elexis stepped in between Hati and me, her power crackling. Despite the fact the top of her head barely came to our noses, she stood tall and defiant. "Hey, hairy cliché, I asked you a question," she snapped as she poked him in the chest.

Eyes widening, he looked down as if he'd forgotten she was there. His lips spread into a leer. "Hot and feisty. I didn't mean you were a bottom. Unless you like it on the bottom, nothing wrong with that."

Elexis put one hand on a hip. "That's something you'll certainly never find out."

Hati put his hands up. "Hey, come on now. I meant no harm. Not to you, at least." His swampy green eyes lost their playful look as his gaze shifted to me.

But Elexis wasn't done with him yet. She put a hand on his chest and pushed him back enough she didn't have to crane her neck to look at him. "Too late. The harm is already done. You will deal with me before you get to talk to him."

Hati smiled. "You're welcome to cuff me and frisk me. And hey, I don't mind if you want to be on top."

"Are you this disrespectful to all the women you talk to?" Elexis asked in a dangerously calm tone.

"Whoa. I meant no disrespect, *lögreglu*. Just meant to rile up Raul here, not you."

"What'd you call me?" she leaned in, fangs flashing when she talked.

I laid a hand on her shoulder. "Easy, it just means police."

She made a sexy little growling sound and stepped back. "Good. In that case, you're free to harass him," she said as she moved aside.

For a second there, I had almost liked her a little.

Hati's already narrow eyes pinched even more. "Didn't think you were coming today, Raul. Thought the teaching life might have made you soft already."

I laughed. "Does she seem like she could make a guy soft?"

Hati and his two friends joined in my laughter. It reminded me that once upon a time Hati had looked up to me. The sting of the memory cut my laughter short. Elexis's energy burned against my side, warning me I'd regret that comment later. Hel, I already regretted it. The woman's power was strong enough to make me wince.

Hati's humor disappeared as quick as a switch flipping. "You here to fight?"

"You know I am."

He clapped his over-sized hands together. "Then let's get this party started!"

He turned and strode off, his two friends in tow. I started to follow, but Elexis grabbed my arm in an iron grip.

"You really came here to fight?" she hissed between her fangs.

I twisted against her thumb and pulled free. "Yes."

I started walking. She caught up to me in two impressive strides. "What the hell does that have to do with our investigation?"

"Nothing."

She grabbed my arm again, this time hard enough to hurt. "I get that you have this thing you have to do." She leaned in close, whispering the next part in my ear, so quiet and close it would be tough for even werewolf hearing to pick it up. "But we've got a lead. We need to go."

I gave her a hard look. "Not yet. This has everything to do with stopping the person behind it."

She let go and I strode after Hati.

"Fight!" someone yelled with gusto.

Staying right beside me, Elexis shot me a look as sharp as needles. She didn't protest or grab me again, which I took as progress. People flowed in like the tide, all gravitating toward a platform standing just off the back of the huge patio of the main cabin. A few nodded to me, but most shot glares my way or ignored me altogether. Those I'd already risen above bowed their heads or found somewhere else to look. Hostility and excitement filled the air like a noxious fog. I bared my fangs at anyone who glared at me for too long.

On the second-story deck overlooking the backyard, two figures radiating power reclined in Adirondack chairs. I bowed my head slightly to them. Hati and I climbed the steps to the platform and went down on one knee before the couple on the deck. The man looked utterly relaxed in nothing but a pair of shorts, his feet propped up on a stool. A full head of dark, tousled hair and the body of a rugby player hid his true age. His lips curved up in a half-smile as he looked past me to a place at the base of the platform. He must have spotted Elexis. Of course he approved of her, I knew he would, blue-streaked hair and all. Deep down he'd know I didn't like her and that would be enough.

Beside him, a woman lounged with her hands crossed over her flat stomach, one leg strapped with the muscles of a runner crossed over the other. Blond hair hung in a plait over one shoulder, down the blue top she wore, nearly reaching her waist.

"Alphas Ander and Gyda, I've come to challenge Hati for his position in the pack, along with Nathan and Jagger after him," I announced in a voice loud enough to carry to the steadily gathering crowd.

Ander's eyes widened. Gyda's lips twitched as she fought a smile. *Oh no.* It wasn't good when she was amused. Ander sat up, resting his elbows on his knees. "Are you so confident you'll defeat Hati?" he asked.

"I am." No sense in lying. He'd smell it and just get aggravated.

A slow smile lifted his lips. "In that case, why not fight all three at once?"

Gyda's brows went up, and her lips pursed as she cast a look Ander's way.

A thrill shot through me. "Challenge accepted."

I stood, nodded to both him and Gyda, and turned to face Hati. Nathan and Jagger sauntered up the stairs, rolling their necks and cracking their knuckles. The crowd—now three hundred strong at least—cheered and jeered. A few voices called out over the others, taking bets and shouting odds. Cheering over them all, I heard Leif's cocky tone. It made me smile to know at least one person among them supported me so fearlessly. I caught sight of his blond head in the crowd, met his gaze, and nodded my thanks to him. He pounded a fist to heart and then thrust it to the sky in solidarity.

I tuned everyone else out and started to stretch. The fact so many took great pleasure in the odds being so stacked against me tried to dredge up my anger, but I refused to give in. At least Leif was a true friend. He gave me strength.

To the right of the platform I spotted Elexis, arms crossed beneath her breasts, a scowl fixed on her gorgeous face. I winked at her. She rolled her eyes and shook her head. Despite the uncaring air she put on, concern hid in her eyes. I didn't know what to do with that, so I looked away. Across the ring from me, Hati, Jagger, and Nathan were working the crowd, flexing for them, joking with them, laughing at the odds against me. I shook my head. Hati caught the motion out of the corner of his eye and turned to me.

"You got something to say, *fallið?*" he asked.

The insult struck like a knife, but I smiled. Fallen, there were worse things to be called. Not many. "Yeah, don't underestimate me."

He threw his head back and laughed with dramatic flair. "Says the guy who just agreed to fight all three of us!"

I shrugged and rolled my shoulders. "Doesn't mean I underestimated you. You've been warned."

Nathan took a step forward, hands balling into fists. "You arrogant son of a—"

"Ah, ah, watch yourself," I said as I wagged my finger at him, then pointed to Gyda watching us from the deck above.

He snapped his mouth shut and bowed his head to Gyda—which saved his ass from a beating by Ander. Fear flashed in his eyes. Hati smacked him on the back of the head, messing up his perfectly styled blond hair.

"Jeez, Nathan. Don't forget who you're talking to," Jagger said.

Out of the corner of my eye, I saw Ander rise. A buzzing hush fell over the crowd. Their excitement tinged the air with a spicy taste. Ander lifted his arms. "Reinhard pack, a challenge has been made and accepted!" he announced.

The crowd cheered and howled. More cheered for the threesome than for me, but I'd grown used to that over the last month. A few friendly faces pushed their way through to the edge of the ring, along with my old fullback Leif, two from my offensive line in college, Oliver Gilmerson and Leo Ragnarson. They thrust their heads up at me, and I did the same in return. A bit of tension eased from my shoulders.

"Fighters ready?" Ander asked in a booming voice.

The threesome and I moved to opposite sides of the ring. I stripped naked, walked to where Elexis stood against the wall of the ring, and held my clothes out to her with a beseeching look. For a tense, uncomfortable second, I didn't think she would take them. If she didn't the crowd would eat it up, and I'd never hear the end of it. The left outer corner of my eye twitched twice. Her look softened slightly, and she accepted them without uttering a word. By the way her mouth gaped and her gaze flicked along my body, I was guessing she was speechless. I gave her a wink.

When I got back into position in the ring, only Hati had stripped naked. That meant my suspicions were right. The other two couldn't shift while fighting. It was a hard-learned skill, so that didn't surprise me. But it did give me an advantage and tell me who I needed to watch out for. I slid into a back stance, allowing me to keep my balls tucked away a bit. Not that any of them should go for a groin hit. It was one of the disqualifying strikes we had. But it was always hard to tell what the mid-level members would be willing to try and get away with. Several of them barely put up a fight at all. Losing meant I rose above them. It didn't mean they dropped to the bottom, so the incentive was low. Unless they hated me and didn't want me to rise, like these three.

Hati moved into a similar stance, while Nathan and Jagger stood there like undisciplined street fighters. I concentrated on my breathing while we waited for the alpha's word. Nathan started to dance around like a nervous boxer, fists pumping at the air. A twitch developed in Jaggar's left cheek. Hati bounced in a screwed-up version of squats. All conversation from the crowd ceased. Still, we waited. My three opponents grew more fidgety by the second. Being used to the drill—and Ander's flair for the dramatic when it came to matches—I just concentrated on breathing.

"Begin!" Ander finally yelled.

Hati stalked toward me while the other two went around to flank me on both sides. The crowd started up again but their cheers, jeers, and howls faded away as I focused in on my opponents. Nathan moved out of my peripheral vision around to my back, but the pressure of his power told me right where he was. Hati rushed me at the same time I felt Nathan's power move in. Nathan would reach me first, so I went for him.

I spun, deflecting his punch and throwing him into Hati's path. The two got tripped up over each other. I put a foot in Nathan's back and used him to launch myself into the air toward Jagger. As I jumped, I spun into a side kick. My foot connected hard with Jagger's chest. He stumbled back several steps. But not far enough. The ledge still lay two feet behind him.

Hati came at me from behind. I threw a back kick at him at the same time I threw a punch at Jagger. Both connected. Neither landed with enough power to do more than stun them. Nathan lunged at me. I spun to him and threw a roundhouse kick into his abdomen. Air blew from his lips in a pained grunt. Out of the corner of my eye I saw a fist flying toward my head. I leaned back and avoided it, but another struck me in the side. Pain pulsed through my kidney. I bent around it out of instinct. Hati moved in for another hit.

Not caring if it landed, I left myself exposed to throw an uppercut at him. It connected hard under his jaw. He flew backwards, his second punch missing me by inches. I threw a hook kick at Jagger's exposed back—throwing my leg out and whipping my heel back toward my target. The impact jarred me so hard my balls slapped against my leg. The sharp pain screamed for my attention, but I ignored it. Jagger went down. I kicked him in the side hard enough to send him flying over the edge of the ring—which he wasn't allowed to re-enter. One down.

A hammer fist strike came down toward my head. I thrust my arms up and blocked. Nathan's wide brown eyes looked at me beneath our raised hands. The scent of fear wafted off him. Without breaking eye contact, I bought my knee up and thrust a front kick into his stomach. He flew back—right off the platform and into the crowd. Second down.

I turned in time to see Hati arch his back and flip to his feet. Not only a waste of energy, but it flashed his half-hard cock to everyone in the most extreme way possible. Which was exactly why he did it. For that alone I wanted to punch him. Elexis was watching and I didn't want her to see that. I shouldn't care, but I did. It fueled my anger even more. I pushed it down into the dark, endless well holding all the rest.

A telltale sign of his intentions flashed in Hati's eyes. He charged and leaped. In mid-air, he shifted to wolf form. I dodged, but not fast enough. Claws raked down my left arm in four burning lines. I landed a punch, but my momentum was all wrong. Not to mention, the bastard was even hairier in this form, and it gave him a lot of cushion.

Preparing to spring, I crouched as he landed and spun around. He jumped at me again, snapping jaws going for my throat. I launched myself at him, spinning as I did so, and shifted to wolf form in mid-air. This brought me under him. My jaws closed around his throat and my spin turned both of us so when we landed, I was on top. I clamped my jaws down a little tighter, getting through all that hair until I felt skin. He froze.

The crowd went wild with howls, yips, and cheers. The old Friday-night football rush from days gone by coursed through me at the sound. In that moment I felt like a part of the pack again.

"Match!" Ander's voice carried easily above the roar of hundreds of excited voices. Was that a hint of pride I detected in it?

I released Hati's neck, spat out fur, and stepped back. In mid-step, I shifted to human form and rose to my feet. Hati rolled over, stood, and shook, but didn't shift back. Tufts of hair floated to the ground. While he didn't growl or bare his fangs, the glare he fixed on me made it clear he wasn't happy.

Power heavy enough to make my breath catch passed over me. The full weight of that power settled on Hati. I could see it as he cringed beneath it, ears wilting a little, tail dropping down to touch the ground. A heavy and immediate hush came over the crowd. The standing hair on Hati's back smoothed down, and his tail tucked between his legs. From above us, Ander fixed a dark gaze on him, but still Hati didn't shift back to human form as was customary. Another flare of breathtaking power scorched the air. Ander leaped from the second-story deck and landed in the fighting ring not five feet from us. His gaze—along with all that power—focused in on Hati. Still, the idiot didn't shift.

"Shift!" Ander commanded in a voice that boomed across the quiet crowd.

With the heat of a furnace, power burned the side of me standing closest to Hati. He yelped. His wolf form blurred, and a second later, he was a man on all fours in the sand. Pain etched deep lines into his face. His chest heaved with labored breaths. Despite the heat from Ander's power, Hati shivered so hard it looked like his elbows might give out. Ander took a huge stride forward to stand towering over Hati's kneeling form.

"You dare to disrespect the customs of our ancestors. To do so is to disrespect me, Gyda, and your very pack." With each word little snaps of heat flared from Ander.

Feet brushed on sand behind me as Nathan and Jagger went to a knee. Hati half settled, half fell back onto his heels. "No sir, I would never disrespect you, our traditions, or our pack," he said through a whimper.

"You just did," Ander said in a calm voice more disturbing than his earlier shout.

"I didn't mean to. I just didn't want to shake the hand of the *fallið*."

Ander grabbed him by the hair and hauled him to his feet. A small whine slipped from Hati. "You have no choice. This fallen has risen above you. You will show him the respect our traditions demand, or you will fall to the bottom of the pack yourself."

Ander thrust Hati in my direction and let go of him—but not before pulling his hair hard enough to yank his head backwards. Hati fell on the ground at my feet and quickly scrambled up. Nathan and Jagger moved to stand on either side of Hati, but they kept their distance as if his disgrace was contagious. I stifled a smile. Ander shot me a glare, as he no doubt felt my amusement.

I straightened and gave the three men my full attention. Nathan and Jagger wouldn't meet my eyes, but Hati did. He stared me down with an intense hatred. I stared right back at him. When he didn't lower his gaze as was appropriate, I called up some of my power and splashed him with it. He flinched and drew his head back as if he'd just walked into a group of bees. Which was how it felt—I knew from experience of having my own father do it to me when I got out of line.

Clearly, Hati had either forgotten what I was capable of, or he thought I'd lost my power when I'd fallen. But that wasn't how it worked. Then again, Hati never had been that smart. His face turned red with anger and still he didn't look down. I splashed more on him. A gasp tore from him, he staggered back a step, and finally looked down.

The corner of Ander's lips twitched as if he were fighting a smile. Pride wasn't something I'd seen him direct at me since I'd fallen. He stepped forward, took hold of my right hand, and thrust it high. "Raul is the winner!"

Many more cheered this time than had last time. With each successful fight, I won them back a little too. Loudest among them was Leif, howling and hollering despite some of the nasty looks shot his way. I caught his blue-eyed gaze and smiled and nodded. Tilting his head in a slight bow, he pursed his lips and raised a brow.

Cocky motherfucker, that look said.

I laughed. His expression turned serious, telling me we needed to talk. I nodded to him.

Ander gave me a slight smile before releasing my hand. I stepped forward and extended the same hand to Jagger. Without looking up, he took it, shook it, and released it. I offered my hand to Hati next. His gaze slowly dragged up to meet mine. After a second of hesitation, he took hold of my hand. His grip surprised me by grinding my finger bones together. I squeezed back equally hard. His grip grew tighter. Keeping my expression neutral, I increased my grip. My strength surpassed his quickly. Pain flashed in his eyes. Finally, just before his bones could break, he looked down. I let go, and he pulled his hand away.

Though his eyes were still lowered, I saw him sneak a look at Ander. Head still bowed, he took a step back. I didn't like that his submission had everything to do with our alpha standing beside us and nothing to do with me defeating him. I offered my hand to Nathan. His handshake was weak and sweaty, and he didn't look up.

"With that settled, let's eat, drink, and give Elexis Sandalius the Reinhard welcome!" Ander announced.

The crowd broke into cheers and started to disperse and filter out to the dozens of fire pits. The announcement made me look to where I'd last seen Elexis. Her blue eyes pinched into slits as sharp as razors. I tilted my head and lifted a shoulder. Gaze going skyward, she shook her head and turned away, but not before that gaze dashed down the length of my naked body. I grinned.

Hati and his friends leaped from the fighting platform and stepped into the retreating crowd. Before they were completely swallowed by them, Hati shot me a look of utter hate. I called my power up until it filled my eyes. He turned and stepped deeper into the crowd. Ander's hand clamped down on my shoulder.

"Well done," he said in a quiet voice. Those two words left me stunned. He gestured to where Elexis stood talking with another woman. "Bring her up. Gyda and I would like to meet her officially."

I nodded. "Of course."

He leaped back up to the second-story balcony without another word. Even though I knew he had to act that way toward me due to me being fallen, his cold attitude stung. The moment of pride had been just that, a moment. It was even possible I had imagined it.

Preparing for an argument, I turned in Elexis's direction, only to find her already deep in the throes of one. I grabbed my clothes from where she'd set them on the stone edge of the platform and dressed quickly. The sight of the petite brunette she was arguing with raised my inner hackles. Gisella.

Elexis's hands were balled into fists at her sides, and Gisella was pointing a finger in her face. Gods, Elexis looked beautiful angry, all fierce and dangerous. I felt the crackle of her power from here.

"Well, you have no self-respect if you're allowing a *fallið* asshole to be your *kennari*."

Elexis stepped closer to her, close enough that Gisella's finger poked her in the chest. "Are you seriously going to question my self-respect? While you're standing there in your red stripper heels and mini shorts? I don't think so, bitch."

"Bitch? Oh you had better step back. You do not know who you're messing with."

Elexis bared her fangs, which made Gisella's eyes widen. "Do I look worried to you?"

It occurred to me Elexis didn't know how rare it was to be able to grow just fangs without shifting. Shit, I'd forgotten to tell her. I jumped down from the fighting platform and landed beside her. "Whoa, ladies. I'm flattered, but there's no need to fight over me."

Gisella turned on me. "You wish, you self-centered ass."

"It wouldn't be the first time you fought over me."

She growled at me. "Fuck off, Raul."

I lifted my brows. "Now you're propositioning me. And here I thought you didn't like me anymore."

Gisella waved a hand, her long, sparkling red nails catching the sunlight. "Whatever."

I took Elexis's hand and gently pulled her in the direction of the main cabin. "Great chatting with you, as always G-string, but I have to take Elexis to meet the alphas."

Thankfully, Elexis didn't resist. But we only went two steps before Gisella got one more jibe in. "Fine, take your latest slut to meet Mommy and Daddy."

I barely clamped down on Elexis's hand fast enough to stop her from lunging at Gisella. I thrust my arms around her. She squirmed in my grip, struggling to break free. And damn if she didn't feel immensely good against me doing it. A wordless roar tore from her. Gisella just laughed. Elexis went still. Like an idiot, I relaxed and let her feet touch the ground. Her butt slammed into my groin as she thrust her arms out, breaking my hold on her. She lunged forward and punched Gisella in the face. It happened so fast I saw nothing but a blur, then blood spurting from Gisella's pointy nose.

Gisella's hands flew up to cover her face. "You bitch!" she yelled in a muffled voice.

Using my size and strength, I shoved between them.

"Get out of the way, Raul. I'm going to beat the bitch right out of that woman!" Elexis demanded. Power weighed heavy in her voice, the type of power that if honed right, could possibly make a person do as they commanded, just like Ander made Hati shift.

"Damn," I murmured, impressed.

"What is going on?" Gyda's booming voice demanded from above us.

Dropping her hands, Gisella stepped around us and bowed her head to Gyda who overlooked us from the balcony. "Sorry for the disruption, Alpha. Elexis and I had a disagreement. But it's squared away now."

Power vibrated so strong around Gyda I felt it from where I stood. Her eyes narrowed on Gisella before turning to Elexis. "Do you agree the matter is settled, Miss Sandalius?"

Elexis took several deep breaths before turning to face Gyda. Her top and bottom fangs were extended and her eyes shone with the rising of her wolf. "For now," she growled.

"If she has offended you, it's within your rights to challenge her," Gyda said. I didn't like the official sound to her voice. I knew what it meant, what she was trying to do. I glared up at her.

The look on Elexis's face told me she was thinking about it. I caught her eye and gave her a small, subtle shake of my head.

Elexis inclined her head slightly to Gyda. "Thank you, but no."

Huffing like a child, Gisella plopped a hand on her hip. "And my rights, Alpha?"

Eyes narrowing, Gyda gripped the deck railing so hard I heard it splinter. "You have no rights in this matter. You have upset an honored guest and therefore forfeited your right of challenge." Her gaze softened as it turned to Elexis. "I do hope you'll forgive our *verndari's* poor behavior. Sometimes her mouth outpaces her mind."

Elexis smiled and nodded.

"Good then. Do come up so we may welcome you properly." With that, Gyda turned and walked back out of sight. Not once during it all had she looked my direction, though I know she'd felt my glare.

Ander paused a moment longer to shoot a warning look at Gisella. She shrank in on herself and took a step back. The moment he turned to join Gyda, Gisella let out a little half-growl and stormed off. Those gathered around the nearest fire pits who'd begun to stare found something else to look at. The few who didn't, I fixed with a glare that made them look away. I let go of Elexis when I felt the first tiny tug from her. We started to walk back toward the stairs.

She cast a wide-eyed look my way. "Did a pack *verndari* seriously just try to pick a fight with me?"

"Yeah, sorry about her. She's a raging bitch. And she probably did it because of me."

"An old girlfriend, or one-night stand?"

I shuddered. "Hel no. She tried, a lot, but not only is she not my type, she is my sister's best friend."

She made a surprised humming noise. "Morals, who knew?"

For a second I had almost liked her. "Don't tell anyone. You'll ruin my carefully crafted reputation."

She snorted.

Once we started up the stairs, I leaned over to her. "Be careful of her from now on. You embarrassed her. She won't let that drop."

"She'd better be careful of *me*," Elexis said in a cold, calm voice that did anything *but* chill me.

"Meeting my parents should be a breeze after that."

Her eyes shot open wide and her mouth gaped a bit. "Your parents? You didn't tell me you were the son of the alphas."

"You didn't ask, and it didn't seem relevant. Besides, thought you would have learned that in your research."

By the time we reached the top of the stairs an almost serene sort of calm had come over her. She'd even managed to retract her fangs, something she hadn't been able to do all day. I kind of missed them. Something about her lack of control had been a bit hot. We stepped onto the huge deck spanning nearly the length of the second story. A breath eased from me at seeing Ander and Gyda were the only ones on the deck. They rose from their Adirondack chairs next to a fire pit that reeked of natural gas. I smiled at my mother, and her eyes twinkled just a touch.

I inclined my head to them both. "Alphas Ander and Gyda, this is

Detective Elexis Sandalius, formerly of the Jackson Hole Police Department."

Ander took Elexis's hand and placed a chaste kiss on the back of it. The way her eyes popped open made me smile. "It is a pleasure to meet you, Miss Sandalius," Ander said.

Elexis tried to respond and crumbled into a stuttering mess. The second Ander released her hand, Gyda swept in. "Do forgive my husband. He is a bit old-fashioned, as we grew up in a different time. Welcome to the Reinhard Den. We are pleased to have you as our guest today. May we get you anything? A glass of wine? A pint of ale?"

Elexis's shoulders relaxed a bit. "Um, sure. A glass of wine would be nice."

Smile growing, Gyda called over her shoulder. "Eva, dear, will you bring us four glasses of that Chateau St. Michelle Pinot Gris?"

Soft footsteps padded away from the French doors leading out of the house onto the deck. Gyda motioned to two chairs to her right. "Thank you for accepting. I needed a reason to get Eva out of hearing range. I trust her, of course, but now we can speak freely."

Elexis sat in the chair closest to my mother, while I took the one on the outside. Her stiff posture gave away her discomfort, and each movement she made was cautious. Her energy crackled. Whether it was a cop's discomfort over being in the middle or a distrust of my parents, I couldn't tell.

My mother leaned over Elexis and patted my leg. "That was a superb fight, son," she whispered.

I gave her a warm smile before shooting a glare at my father. "Thank you. Speaking of which, three on one, Father, really?" I said.

Ander smiled as he pushed a plate of sweet potato fries down the table toward us. "I knew you could handle it, and I wanted to spend the morning getting to know Miss Sandalius rather than watching fights."

"And if you'd been wrong?" I asked through a tight jaw.

"I was not," he said with complete confidence.

I shook my head and took a few fries. Out of habit, the kronur I kept in my pocket found its way into my hand, and I began weaving it through my fingers. My father's gaze flicked to the coin for a moment, but he didn't say anything. The coin reminded me that one had to work hard if they wanted something, and be patient. Remembering soothed the anger. Reasons or not, I deserved the contempt of this pack, of my parents, after what I'd done.

Elexis shot me a dark look. "You are the one who insisted on coming here and fighting today." Even being in their presence, she showed no hesitation. Ouch. I swallowed the mouthful I'd been chewing before responding. "You didn't have to come along."

Gyda smacked my arm. "Mind your tone with our guest."

"Sorry, Mother."

The nervous feel of Elexis's energy mellowed, and she smiled. "I like her," she said to me.

"Of course you do," I mumbled under my breath.

Mother smacked me again. "I do hope Raul has been a good host to you," Gyda said in a sweet voice that held an edge of warning.

Elexis surprised me with her answer. "Actually, he's been quite gracious. A gentleman even."

Gyda patted my leg, an improvement from the smacking. "Dear, do close your mouth."

Heat tried to rush to my face. I covered it with a question to lead things in the right direction. "Where did you find Tamara?"

"Leif found her at her mother's house in Bozeman," Gyda answered.

Elexis leaned forward, elbows resting on her knees, hands coming together to clasp each other. "Do you believe her about not knowing James's whereabouts?"

Ander nodded. "Pack members have a hard time lying to their alphas. We can smell it on them. Tamara is too low in the pack to be able to disguise such a thing."

"Did she tell you anything about where he might have gone, who he might be with, if anyone?" Elexis pressed.

I held a hand up to her, not quite wanting to touch her but needing to halt her words. "Whoa, Sandalius. You can't just grill alphas like that."

She shot me a look halfway between pissed and confused. "Why not?"

Ander laughed long and deep. "Oh, I like her."

My mother grinned and patted Elexis's knee with no less affection than she had mine. "Why not indeed, my dear? You have the right attitude. Too many are afraid to speak to alphas in such a manner. It complicates things."

Ander nodded. "You are the *lögreglu*. You can ask us anything you want. Unfortunately, Tamara didn't know anything helpful. We questioned her extensively. I am sorry James is missing. He needs to do penance for what he did to you. But I am glad he is away from Tamara."

"You care for her?" Elexis asked. She sounded surprised. It reminded me of all I had to teach her, as did the glare my mother shot my way.

"Of course. She is part of our pack. We want the best for each of our members," Ander said.

Gyda took his hand. She gave Elexis a warm smile. "You have not chosen a pack yet, have you, dear?"

"Well...uh...no. I've only just arrived and I..." The strangled look on her face made me spring to her rescue without even thinking about it.

"Mother, please. We're not here so you can recruit Detective Sandalius. Give her a break. She's been here two nights."

My mother's expression sharpened. "Now, Raul, it is never too early to make a lady feel welcome." The gentle expression returned as her attention moved back to Elexis. "And we do want you to feel welcome."

I knew they did. But they didn't know about Elexis's past, her lack of a family, her discomfort over the fact. I shouldn't care, not with the way she acted toward me. But I did.

"Thank you, Mrs.—"

"Please, call me Gyda. And you go right ahead and ask anything you want, like Ander said."

The French doors opened and out came Eva with a carefully balanced tray filled with wine glasses. As always, she looked the very picture of poised, her golden hair—with only a few streaks of gray—wrapped up in a plaited bun at the back of her head, her simple brown linen dress pressed to perfection. Crow's feet formed at the corners of her eyes as she smiled at me. I jumped up and relieved her of the tray before her bare feet could get two steps out the door. I gave her a quick peck on the cheek and whispered in her ear, "Thanks, Eva. You're a lifesaver."

She smiled and patted my cheek, inclined her head to my parents, and returned to the cabin. It stung that she wasn't allowed to speak to me, but the touch said enough. The staff to the alphas were too high to speak to a fallen, even if she had changed my diapers. She wasn't supposed to look at me, let alone touch me. Until I regained my prior standing in the pack, I had to be all but invisible to them. Hiding the pain behind a grin, I delivered the drinks, offering Elexis one first.

The remainder of the day wasn't any less painful. We spent it introducing Elexis to select pack members, eating, and drinking. The wine helped ease the endless stream of cold shoulders, but only so much, and only until I stopped drinking a few hours before sunset. Two hours of being clear headed and taking people's shit, and I was done. When the eighth *verndari* my parents introduced Elexis to took his leave and glared at me as he walked away, I spoke up.

"Thank you, Alphas, for welcoming my *nemi* so warmly today. We have lessons we must get back to." I kept my words formal, partly because dozens of others were still in earshot, and partly because my parents' welcome had barely been warmer than anyone else's. I knew they had to treat me this way for appearance's sake, but it was more than that. They were disappointed in me for what I'd done. It killed me that I couldn't tell them the truth.

My mother clasped one of Elexis's hands in both of hers. "You are welcome at our den any time. We hope you'll consider joining Reinhard. We feel you would be a good fit," she said in a sweet voice filled with sincerity.

Ander took her hand next and kissed the back of it. "Yes. And I imagine you would qualify for the *verndari* ranks immediately, if that were your wish."

A bit of a blush colored Elexis's cheeks. It looked good on her. "Thank you. I'll definitely consider Reinhard. And thank you for letting me question so many of your members. You've been wonderful."

Ander nodded to me. Gyda met my gaze but didn't say a word as she took Ander's hand and they turned for the house. Not trusting myself to speak without growling, I started back to the parking lot, leaving Elexis to follow. I wove my way through the multiple seating areas on the lower patio. Glares and sideways glances from those gathered came my way. To my surprise, a few friendly looks were scattered among them. Most of those came from old classmates from high school and my old football team members.

"Lessons, really? Since when?" Elexis asked as she sped up to walk alongside me.

"Yeah. Lesson one: don't pick fights with *verndari* unless you want to take their place."

"Hey, she picked the fight. Wait, what do you mean 'take her place'? I thought you had to fight your way up."

Soft grass beneath foot turned to cobbles as we reached the parking lot. "Fallen do. New challengers don't, unless they want to start at the bottom and work their way up," I explained.

"Hmm, good to know."

I sped up a bit and opened the passenger door of the Cherokee for her. She raised her eyebrows at me but got in without a word. As I started to walk around to the driver's side, I noticed Leif leaning against a tree at the edge of the parking area a few yards away. I held a finger up to Elexis. She nodded and looked down at her phone. I jogged to where Leif waited.

"What's up?"

Lips pursed, Leif gave me a crooked grin. "I should be asking you that," he said with a chin-thrust in Elexis's direction.

I blew air out through my lips. "It ain't like that."

"Sure it isn't. Yet."

Considering how painful the subject was, I wasn't about to go into how she hated me. "What've you got for me, bud?" I asked instead.

"You talk to Tamara?"

"I did. You had something to do with her being here from what my mother says."

He nodded. "Karman and I encouraged her to come back and convinced her to come today. It wasn't easy. That asshole did a number on her."

"He did," I agreed. "And he'll pay for it when I find him."

"She have helpful information?"

"Possibly. Thanks to Elexis's smooth talking, Karman gave us the first lead we've had since this mess started."

Leif let out a long breath and nodded, his furrowed brow relaxing. "Good, I'm glad. You going to the AVW meeting later this month?"

"Definitely."

He clapped me on the shoulder. "Good. See you there, buddy. If there is anything else I can do, just let me know."

"Of course. Thanks, appreciate it."

We clasped hands palm to palm, slapped the backs of them together, and bumped fists, our signature handshake since grade school. Leif worked his way back toward the closest gathering. When someone shot him a dirty look, he threw his arms out wide and gave them a challenging growl. The guy shook his head, cast his gaze down, and turned away.

Smiling, I got in and started the vehicle. Elexis looked up from her phone.

As I backed out I said, "I'm sorry if Gisella gave you crap because I'm your *kennari*." I sneaked a glance at her out of my peripheral to see her reaction.

A lock of blue hair slid over her shoulder as she shrugged. "She's a bitch. Don't worry about it."

Tension eased from my shoulders as I started down the tree-lined drive. "Wait, did you defend me?" I teased.

She made a huffing noise. "No."

"You did!" I laughed, and for a moment, I almost thought she was going to smile. Then a wistful, sad look came over her.

"Your parents are kind of harsh with you," she said.

I shrugged as if it didn't feel like daggers digging into me each time they gave me the cold shoulder. "They have to be. They're alphas. And I disappointed them in a huge way."

"Why'd you do it?" The bold question took me by surprise.

We weren't at that place, and I wasn't sure we ever would be. "How about we get back to your lessons."

"Again with the lessons," she scoffed.

"Yeah, let's start with your control of your fangs and claws."

She rolled the window down and turned to look out it. "Let's not."

"No, let's. Listen, it isn't totally a bad thing. Only the strongest can partially shift."

Though her arms didn't uncross, she turned to look at me. "Partially shift?"

"Yep. Only those with a *verndari* or alpha's strength can do it. Well, and the seeker and reaper, of course. Hell, even a lot of *verndari* can't do it."

Her dark brows furrowed. "I thought it meant I needed better control."

"It does. But only because you can do more than most. They call it Loki's touch."

Her face scrunched up in that way it did when she was thinking hard. "He's the...trickster god, right?"

"That's one of his titles."

"Isn't he supposed to be the one who brings about the end of the world?"

"It's more complicated than that."

Pink-stained lips pushing into a half-pout, she gave me a look. "Great, I'm touched by the God who brings about the end of the world. Why am I not surprised? So does that mean this ability is viewed as a bad thing?"

"Only by those who don't have it and want it."

She leaned back and put her bare feet out the window, crossing one over the other. All that long, limber flesh drew my gaze. A rhythmic thumping sounded as I crossed the center line and ran over those damn rumble strips in the road. She laughed, a fantastic, carefree, confident sound that made my blood pump hotter. With a smile on her face, she leaned back and closed her eyes, lifting her chin into the wind. I liked seeing her relaxed and happy like this. After a quarter mile of comfortable silence, I turned down the driveway to my house.

"I'm sorry my parents ambushed you and tried to recruit you."

"Don't be. They're all right, and so is your pack, for the most part."

I liked the sound of that, a little too much. The last thing I needed was a complication when it came to working my way back up in the pack. And I had a feeling she'd be a big one.

"Does that mean you——" A stench blew in the window and cut my words clean off. It was sweet and terrible at the same time, with a musky undertone. I gagged, coughed, and covered my mouth.

"Damn, what is that?" Elexis asked, rushing to roll up her window.

"Something dead," I answered as I stopped the Cherokee along the side of the house.

She paused with her hand on the door handle. "But it smells like..."

"Wolf," I finished for her.

We jumped from the vehicle at the same time. I followed the scent to the front door of my house. The pelt of a wolf lay spread over my threshold. A breath eased from me when I saw it was too big to be the pup's, but it was definitely a normal wolf, not *varúlfur*. The distinctive lack of blood on my step made me realize the carcass was at least a few days old.

"Oh no! That isn't one of the North Fork pack is it?" Elexis asked in a muffled voice. She had a hand over her mouth and nose.

"No. It's one of the South Fork."

Her eyes narrowed. "Someone got it out of evidence and brought it here. Why would they do that?"

I took a shallow, shuddering breath. "To warn us that someone in this house is marked for death."

CHAPTER SEVEN

ELEXIS

After a night of helping Raul bury the wolf pelt, scrubbing the front step, and endless hours of going over possible suspects, it felt good to be out in the warm sunshine. I wiggled my toes in the breeze flowing through the Cherokee's window. I tried not to steal glances in Raul's direction, but it was difficult. The image of him naked, fighting like a Viking of old in the circle against three opponents kept replaying in my head. All that rippling muscle, his swinging—no! Death threats, I was supposed to be thinking about death threats.

"So plenty of people could want you dead, I get it. But what if the threat is against me?"

He scratched at the day-old shadow of hair on his chin. Yet again, it made me think of him in ways I didn't want to think of him—rugged, sexy. And it wasn't just about his body. After seeing how gracefully he'd taken the shit from his pack members yesterday, how cold his own parents had been toward him, it was hard not to feel a little bad for him. It softened me in other ways to him too. Though he hid it well, I could tell their attitudes hurt him, a lot. A man who cared that much about what people thought of him didn't seem like someone who would do something to upset so many of them. I was beginning to think biting in Sonya hadn't been his idea, and maybe not even something he'd had a choice about. It dropped him to the bottom of my suspects for the crime of the bitings.

"But why would someone threaten you? You're too new in town to have made enemies yet," Raul said after a while.

"Because of what I'm investigating. Maybe it's this Bain."

Raul shook his head. "Bain wouldn't make a reckless threat, not against you."

"But he would against you?"

"No. It has to be someone else, maybe Hati, or my ex-fiancée."

My whole train of thought took the express track out of town. "You were engaged?" I didn't mean for the words to come out with a laugh.

Hurt flashed in his eyes. "Is that so hard to believe?"

"You don't seem like the marrying type."

"Another thing you're wrong about. I am, or I was."

Now my curiosity was stirred. "Really? What changed?"

His fingers tightened around the steering wheel. "I found out she was banging Calder, and then I bit in Sonya so..."

"Ah."

He shot me a sharp glare. "Ah, what?"

"It makes sense why you want to stop him."

He took a hard right turn at far too high of a speed, slamming me into the door. "That isn't why I want to stop him, or why I want to beat him until he shits himself. I want to stop him and everyone working with him because I care about this town, about our kind. I don't want the mobs with pitchforks and torches to descend on us again." The sincerity and conviction in his voice convinced me, and cracked my perception of him even more.

"Okay, I'm sorry."

He gave me a sideways glance. "That was too easy."

"Hey, when I'm wrong, I'm wrong."

His wide eyes looked impressed, and a little...interested.

I liked the second look more than I wanted to. Which meant I had to approach the elephant again. "Is that why you bit Sonya? So there would be someone to find the newly bitten and stop them from exposing us?"

His eyes went cold and distant. "No. But it's why I would have told her about her bloodline and given her the option if we'd had time."

It wasn't a reason, but it was the most I'd gotten out of him on the subject so far. I knew I shouldn't push, but I had to. "Were you rushed because you wanted out of the engagement to your cheating fiancée?"

He took another corner faster than necessary, and another. The speedometer climbed. "No." It was more of a growl than a word, but I got the meaning.

Still, I couldn't help myself from pushing a little more. "Who was she?"

"Abela Aronsdöttir, niece to the alpha of the Arnoddr pack."

I whistled. "That kind of engagement would be hard to break." I couldn't help it. Shutting up wasn't my strong suit when I had something on my mind.

He didn't answer. The hum of the Cherokee's off-road tires flying down the road at eighty miles an hour became a roar that filled the silence. His power flooded the cab, making it stifling. It didn't take long for the tension to become too much. But I wasn't done. "We should question her."

"We already have."

My proverbial hackles rose. "No, *we* did not. I want to question her."

"Well that will be a long flight."

"Flight?"

His jaw clenched and unclenched before he answered. "She's been taken back to Iceland to be re-educated in the temple of Frigg."

"Sounds...archaic. Do I even want to know what that means?"

One of his eyebrows lifted. "Probably not." After a moment, he added, "I can get you the recordings of her interrogations. And if you really want to, we can go to Iceland so you can question her."

"The recordings will do for now. I'd like to question Bain today," I said.

"No." The finality of his tone pissed me off.

"Why the hell not? He's our main suspect in the bitings and is a suspect in the death threat against one of us."

"That's exactly why. I don't want to tip him off. He'll be easier to catch if he doesn't think we suspect him."

Such logic was hard to argue with. I sighed. "Agreed. In that case, tell me why you suspect him—aside from what he did to become alpha."

The Cherokee slowed to a more reasonable sixty-five miles an hour. We drove through an unending stream of tall evergreens. It should have been a peaceful drive, but I was too keyed up.

"When he became alpha, it got him a position on the Alpha Council, which gives him a say in town decisions. He didn't stop there. He has spent the last three years politicking and worming his way into the graces of Brigid Thomasdóttir, the *varúlfur* Shifter Council member."

"You think he's trying to make her his mate?"

Raul nodded. "She recently gained the position when the previous councilor died under suspicious circumstances, away from home and pack."

"What made it suspicious?"

"He was old, five hundred and thirty-one. *Varúlfur* who die of old age, like he supposedly did, know when their natural time is coming. We return home, to our pack, for a death ritual. It's very rare for an elder to die of natural causes off on their own."

Chills danced up my spine for multiple reasons. "We can do that? How early ahead of time do we know?"

"Within the year. Maybe a month or two out we pin it down almost to the day."

I thought about it for a moment. "He killed his alpha—his own brother. An elderly council member isn't a stretch from there. I'm on board. So what do we have to tie him to Calder?"

Raul's upper lip curled into a slight snarl that revealed his fangs. It was a sexy look on him, even sexier now that I knew the fangs were a sign of a powerful werewolf. "Circumstantial evidence, unfortunately. Calder's parents won't allow us near his house without a search warrant, and it's on their property. They support him, claiming he's misunderstood and innocent until proven guilty."

I pulled my feet into the vehicle and sat up straight. "He kidnapped not only Sonya but his own sister, their daughter. Don't they care?"

"They claim it's a family matter, not a *lögreglu* one."

"So they could be in on it."

"Definitely."

Everyone's lips being sealed made it more suspicious. The list of suspects was only growing and complicating matters, like a giant community web. The deeper I dug into this, the more I understood why the chief wanted an outsider for the job.

We passed a gym, a park, and a few shops before Raul had to stop at a heavy-duty, black, iron gate. From this road, the gate was the only way through the ten-foot-high stone wall surrounding the back of the circular main street of businesses. It was a clever—if excessive—way of keeping visitors corralled and away from the "real" town. Raul punched a code into the box and leaned out to put an eye up to the retinal scanner. Hydraulics hissed as the big gate slid open. Raul drove through the opening into the public part of town.

Main Street wrapped around a circular park in the middle of town. All the businesses open to the public surrounded it. They butted up against one another in a seamless manner that camouflaged the ten-foot-high wall behind them. It was no accident the street wrapped back around to itself as the only entrance and exit into town. Three other streets like the one we'd come down led out of the public section into the packs' parts of town. The design had both impressed and freaked me out a bit. Visitors would never know what they'd stumbled into. On the surface it looked like a quaint mountain town.

After the gate closed behind us, Raul pulled onto Main Street.

"James is the connection we need," I said. It burned down to my soul just to say his name. While I was adjusting to being a werewolf, I hadn't chosen it. And anyone who took someone's choice away knowingly and maliciously deserved to pay just as high a price. So why was it getting increasingly harder to feel that way about Raul? My gut told me he may not have had a choice in what he'd done. I just wished he'd be honest with me about it.

"Possibly." His guarded tone put me on edge.

"I'm not saying that just because I want to catch him. He helped Calder, according to what Ayra told the chief. We need to find and question him."

"I agree."

Eyes going wide, I turned to him. "Finally, something we agree on. So we should follow up on this lead about Ram's Head."

"Yes. Just not today."

Just like that, the moment of seeing eye-to-eye was gone. "Why the hell not? Waiting could make the trail go cold."

Unfazed by my biting tone, Raul maintained a cool face as he pulled into the parking lot of the Crescent Coffee shop. Their clever iron sign hanging over a ski chalet-looking building drew my eye—a full moon with a steaming cup of coffee on it, flanked by a half-moon on each side, one with the word "Crescent," the other with the word "Coffee."

"Because that's Draupnir land and they won't let us on it without a warrant," Raul said.

"Shit."

Raul parked between a blue Maserati and a green Mustang. These rich werewolves liked their fast cars.

"Yeah. But don't sweat it. I'll pull a few strings and get us permission. It just may take a few days," he said.

I sighed. "That'll have to do."

Raul shook his head. "Well excuse me if I can't pull an invite out of my ass."

"No."

"No what?"

I opened my door and jumped out before answering. "I won't excuse you. Though I really don't want to see you pull anything out of your ass."

He let out a frustrated sound that made me smile as I shut the door on his reply.

On the other side of the parking lot sat a news van. A brunette in a suit leaned against it, looking down at her phone. At the sound of our steps, she looked up, eyes going wide. She stuck the phone in her pocket, straightened her jacket, and rapped on the window of the van.

"Shit. The press," I said.

Raul's forestry van and my Hemlock Hollow PD uniform attracted her like a fly to a corpse. I knew I shouldn't have worn the damn thing, but my business-casual detective wear was all either packed or dirty.

"I'll take the lead," Raul whispered to me.

The charming smile he turned on the pretty young woman could have melted an iceberg. She took one look at it and gravitated toward him. A cameraman hopped out of the van and dashed up, camera in hand. The woman gave him a signal I took to mean "start recording," which he promptly did.

"Officer, what can you tell us about the latest wolf attack?" the brunette asked.

Raul's sweet smile faded, replaced by an innocent—though clearly faked—confusion. "You mean the attack on the wolves on our preserve?"

"No, Officer, I meant—"

"Because that's the only attack I know about. An entire pack was slaughtered, all except for one member. A wolf cub, who is now an orphan thanks to poachers jumping to conclusions about alleged 'wolf attacks' in the surrounding area," he cut in smoothly.

"Are you saying the attacks all over Montana aren't by wolves?" she said, not missing a beat. Interest flashed in her eyes.

"We need to consider the possibility it could be someone trying to make it look like wolf attacks. It is best if people don't have a knee-jerk reaction and go around killing innocent animals." The passion in his voice stirred me.

"So you are suggesting we could have a serial killer on our hands," the woman said with far too much excitement for my liking.

"No, that's not what I meant," Raul began.

"But it is something the Forestry Department is considering."

"No, ma'am. That is not what I said. And besides, the investigation into the attacks is police jurisdiction. The Forestry Department is only concerned with keeping both the people of Montana and the wolves, safe."

It was a decent recovery, but I saw by the fervor written all over her face it wouldn't be enough. Eyes widening with an eagerness that made me ill, she turned to me. Her gaze flicked across the name tag sewn onto my blue uniform shirt.

"Officer Sandalius—"

"Detective," I corrected in a cold tone.

She smiled, but it wasn't a friendly look. "Detective, what can you tell us about the investigation?"

"Nothing. You'll have to talk to my chief." I grabbed Raul's hand and hauled him away from her. The moment she turned her attention toward her cameraman to do a bit of monologue, I let go of Raul.

Out of the corner of my eye, I caught sight of a man without an ounce of fat on his tall body. Hair the hue of honey, with enough body to make a shampoo model envious, wafted in the breeze. He shot Raul a charming grin that made things low in my body clench. If the full force of it had been focused on me, I kind of think my legs might have gone weak. He tipped an imaginary hat at me before intercepting the camera woman, who took a step in our direction.

"Howdy, ma'am. What brings such a lovely reporter to our charming little town?" he asked her.

Under his breath, Raul muttered, "Thanks, Leif."

Leif gave an almost imperceptible nod as he shot Raul a sideways glance.

Ah, so that was Leif Jörgensson, husband to Karman, the coffee shop owner who helped with the wolf pup.

I set a fast pace toward the shop, but Raul caught up to me in only two strides. Damn those long legs of his. Long, fit, and leading right up to a nicely hung package—the sight of which, naked and hanging, was burned into my brain. No matter how hard I tried, I couldn't forget. I walked faster. He outpaced me easily, reached the glass door first, and opened it for me. The chivalry didn't fit with my asshole image of him, so it only annoyed me. I entered the coffee shop without a word or a glance toward him. The smile twitching under the surface of his detached expression made my cheeks burn.

Anger worked at the edges of my control, but I fought it. I didn't want the whole coffee shop seeing me with my fangs out. It wasn't much consolation that the ability was rare and meant I was stronger than most, the opposite if anything. It was better when people underestimated me.

Six people occupied the coffee shop: two men at a corner table, their backs to the wall, a couple at a table on the left wall, a lone woman at another table, and the young barista guy behind the counter. Most of them let off a mid-level pack member vibe. But one of the guys in the corner radiated power like an industrial shop heater. He was slim and trim, like a marathon runner. Tousled, dishwater blond hair with a bit of a curl to it framed a face that looked thin to the point of being sharp angled. Calculating pale green eyes stared at me down a hawkish nose. Just like the rest of him, those eyes were so sharp they made me feel like a butterfly he was trying to pin down.

Raul's hand touched the small of my back and gently pushed me forward. He stepped up alongside me, breaking the man's almost hypnotic stare. The warmth of Raul's hand remained on my back as we walked to the glass counter filled with baked items loaded with sugar. His touch felt good, too good. I sidestepped out from under it as I pretended to peruse the menu overhead. Once I saw the extensive smoothie options, I didn't have to pretend. The little star next to several items that said "no added sugar" made my day—hell, maybe my week.

The dark-haired young man behind the counter gave me a huge smile. His badge said Brian. "Hi! You must be Elexis Sandalius! It's so good to meet you. What can I get you, darling?" he asked in an over-caffeinated voice with a gentle lilt to it.

His warmth made me smile back at him. "I'll take an almond strawberry smoothie with an extra shot of protein please."

"Coming right up!" He spun away, grabbing ingredients from behind the counter as he went.

Raul leaned closer. "A health nut, hum?" His warm breath brushed my cheek, making heat shoot through me.

"So I care about what I put into my body. Nothing wrong with that."

He smirked, eyes reflecting the dirty thoughts behind them. I'd never wanted to take my words back so much.

The barista called out, "The usual for you, Raul?"

"Yep," he answered.

The radiating power I'd felt from the corner of the room approached us. The sharp-featured man moved with a grace that reminded me of a snake, his expensive-looking boots barely making a sound against the wood floor. The black leather jacket he wore made me think of the two Harleys I had seen parked outside. Skinny blue jeans hugged his legs—a look I had trouble liking on guys—and a black tank covered the fit-looking chest beneath his jacket. He smiled at me, but the hostility rolling off him made me not trust the expression.

The way he slid around Raul reminded me of a snake again. Before I could think to react, he took my hand in his. Shock left me unable to speak as he raised it to his lips and kissed the back of it. Bumps rose along my skin as it literally tried to crawl out from under him.

"Elexis Sandalius, it is a pleasure to meet you. The chief didn't tell the council you were such a beauty," he said in a slightly gravelly voice.

I pulled my hand back the moment he let go. "And you are?" I kept my tone as light as possible and even managed a smile.

Somewhere behind me, Raul growled, low and quiet. The sound turned into him clearing his throat—a poor attempt at covering his anger.

The man made a humming noise that set my nerves on edge. "Direct, I like that. I'm Bain, Alpha of the Draupnir pack." He said it like his title should have me melting at his leather-clad feet.

He wanted me to like him. I could use that. With a bat of my lashes, my smile turned coy. Well, as coy as I could manage. Being girly wasn't something I was good at. "It's nice to meet you, Bain."

His gaze didn't move to the low V-neck of my tank top like I expected it to. So he liked attention more than he liked to give it. Fine by me. I didn't want him looking at my tits anyway.

"The pleasure is all mine," he said. The dullness in his eyes told me he didn't mean it, but his tone told me he wanted me to think he did. "Welcome to our fair little town, and to Montana. The word is you're from Wyoming."

I leaned against the counter in a casual pose, one hip stuck out, accentuating my long legs. Finally, his gaze moved over me, calculating, methodical, like someone considering livestock. Not exactly the attention I was used to from men, but it would do. "The word is correct. But I'm sure you know all the boring details about me. You're an alpha. Now that's interesting." I leaned a bit closer, widening my eyes. "You must have such a big..." I forced my eyes to drift down his body, "...stretch of land."

Raul made a disgusted sound but didn't interrupt.

Bain wasn't exactly bad looking. It was more of a feeling he gave off that I didn't like. My cop's gut instinct wanted nothing to do with him.

True joy authenticated his smile at last. "I do. Ten thousand acres on the east side of the hollow, gorgeous forest land."

Since we were getting warmer, I didn't have to fake my enthusiasm. "Wow, I'd love to see that."

Something devious flashed in his eyes. For just a second, I wondered who was manipulating who. "Come by any time. It would be a pleasure to show you around and introduce you to the pack. They'll love you, I'm sure. And I cook a mean filet mignon."

Ah, so that was it. Smallest pack in town, he wanted to add to his numbers. "Thank you, I definitely will. I look forward to meeting them, and to dinner."

Grin still in place, he handed me a card. A large B written in a scrolling font in blood red dominated one side of the otherwise all black card. A phone number in the same font was printed on the other side. I slid it into my bra. Eyes following the card in a slow, mechanical way, he nodded and turned. His smile fell away as his gaze passed over Raul. On the way by him, Bain's shoulder collided with Raul's, hard. Raul growled but didn't say anything.

The man who had been sitting at the table with Bain rose and went to the door. From beneath artfully messy brown bangs gazed gentle brown eyes. He gave me a weak smile that hid something. Was it sympathy? I couldn't quite tell. He opened the door for Bain and followed him out. The soft features of a youthful twenty-something gave him a boy-band look. The doe brown eyes only added to it. His power had a gentle feel, like a low-level pack member. And yet here he was having coffee with the alpha. I filed him away in my memory for later.

"Elexis and Raul," Brian called from the counter. He placed two tall metal mugs with lids on the counter.

"Oh, I'm sorry, I wanted that to go," I said.

He gave me a big smile and waved a hand. "It is, honey. Raul bought the cups. You bring that back on in next time and you get a discount."

"Thanks. I will."

I picked up the black metallic mug with the store logo on it and started for the door. Thankfully, the news van was gone.

Once outside, I asked Raul, "So what's up with the cups?" I did *not* want him buying me things.

"You won't find disposable cups in Hemlock Hollow unless they are the biodegradable kind, which are only meant for the tourists. Every business in town is as green as possible."

Brows rising, I nodded. "I get that. Werewolves being tied to the earth and all. I like it." I thrust my head toward his cup. "So what's in your usual, some triple caramel macchiato type of thing?"

He gave me that disarming smile of his, and I knew I wouldn't like the answer. "Almond cherry smoothie."

"Whatever."

"Don't believe me? Smell it." He held it out toward me.

I didn't have to get very close to smell he was telling the truth. "So you have good taste in smoothies." I wasn't about to admit I'd asked because I suspected it was the same as mine. Good taste in smoothies didn't redeem him, not by a sniper's shot. Neither did him buying me a cup. "How much do I owe you for the cup?"

"Nothing. Don't sweat it." Was that amusement in his tone?

"Seriously, how much do I owe you?"

Too late, I realized he was walking toward the passenger side of the vehicle. He opened my door for me and stepped aside. My cheeks burned with indignation, and something else. "I'm capable of getting my own door, thank you." It came out sounding harsh, and I didn't care. I hated that I had to look up to meet his golden eyes. They caught me, pulled me in, and held tight like quicksand. The mirth in them pissed me off even more.

"I know. But Montana country boy and all. Raised up right. My mother is over a hundred years old and is very serious about this kind of thing."

Shock ratcheted my voice up an octave. "Seriously? She looks like she's in her late twenties."

"Well, yeah. She isn't even middle-aged," Raul said, a touch of humor in his voice.

I climbed into the vehicle without argument. I couldn't imagine what it would be like to be raised by someone who had been born over a century ago. Raul closed my door and went around to his side. Once he climbed in, he asked, "So what'd you think of Bain?"

I swallowed the drink of my smoothie I had taken before answering. "He's self-centered, arrogant, and definitely calculating. I don't trust or like him."

Eyes widening, Raul looked surprised and impressed. A surge of triumph—and pride—washed through me. I didn't want to like impressing my partner, not this one, but I did. Dammit.

"Then why'd you accept his invitation?" he asked. Was that a hint of anger in his voice? Oh for the love of all that remained sane in the world, no—it was jealousy. Part of me thrilled, and I hated it.

I hid it with a big grin, delighting in the triumph of my cleverness. "Because now this Loki-touched wolf has permission to go onto Draupnir land."

CHAPTER EIGHT

RAUL

The fifteen minutes it took to get from my house to Hemlock Hollow PD became agonizingly long with Elexis behind the wheel. It wasn't that she drove the unmarked Charger slow. It was the silent treatment she gave me the whole way. Antagonistic energy crackled from her, filling the cab. It made it hard to even think about speaking, which I didn't. If she was going to give me the silent treatment, she was going to get it right back. Ignoring her wasn't easy when she looked so hot and her power felt so fierce and amazing, but I managed.

Yesterday had been a bust. We'd spent the entire day hiking around Ram's Head, both in human and wolf form, and came up with nothing. No trails, no clues, no James. It had put both of us in a foul mood this morning. Of course, crashing on the couch to keep an eye on her sleeping outside on the patio furniture hadn't helped matters. And for some reason, being in wolf form pissed her off.

As she pulled into the parking lot, I thought I'd give smoothing things over one more try. "Look, Elexis, I didn't mean to question your methods. It's just that Dustin has already been questioned by his old alpha, and the chief. He's a bottom level pack member. He wouldn't be able to lie to his alpha."

She gave me a hard look. "Was that before or after his alpha kicked him out of the pack for being involved in Ayra Valdísdöttir's abduction?"

The response I'd prepared died on my tongue, and I had to force my gaping mouth shut. After a few seconds, I said, "Good point."

We got out and walked into the police department. Hostile gazes turned on me as I entered the squad room. Just my luck, Sandalius had chosen to do this on a day not one of my friends was on duty. I strode through and let the three officers' hatred roll off me. One was a member of my own pack. The other two belonged to Arnoddr. I smiled and waved as I walked by.

I followed Elexis into the chief's office and shut the door behind us. The extra sound dampening insulation in the walls and solid oak door would help keep anyone from hearing us. If they wanted to eavesdrop, they'd have to have a listening device in the room or literally put their ear against the door with one. While they were assholes, I felt confident they wouldn't be that bold.

At our entry, the chief looked up from his computer with a warm smile. He motioned to the two chairs in front of his desk.

"Detective Sandalius, Ranger Anderson, good morning. Please, have a seat. What have you got for me?" he asked in a jovial tone which warmed a bit of the cool shell I'd donned thanks to Elexis's silent treatment.

His power filled the room with a soothing presence that made the place inviting. It didn't hurt that he was one of the handful of people left in this town who didn't think I was a complete screwup.

Returning his smile with a warmth I envied, since it wasn't directed at me, Elexis sat down. "Good morning, Chief." The sweet, companionable way she spoke to him irked me even more.

With a soothing breath, I managed a smile as I sat down next to her. She did most of the talking, detailing our investigation so far, telling him of our leads. The way she included me and the ways I had helped—though they were small—impressed me. From her professional manner one would never guess she could barely stand to be around me.

The chief asked a lot of clarifying questions, including me in the conversation as if I were a respected colleague instead of *fallið*.

"It sounds like I made the right choice pairing you two together. This is more progress than we have been able to make on this case in months. I'm impressed," he said.

A tone sounded from his desk phone. He clicked a button on it. "Go ahead, Helga."

"Hey, Chief. Dustin Magnússon is here to see Detective Sandalius."

"Thank you, Helga. Go ahead and send him into suite one."

I raised a brow at him. He grinned so big, dimples formed. "Our interrogation room. You'd know that if you came around more Anderson. Which you are always welcome to do, you know."

Uncharacteristic heat worked its way up my face. "I...um...well, yeah, I know. It's just—"

Elexis stood up and interrupted, taking mercy on my bumbling. "We'd better get to it before he changes his mind about talking to us."

Chief nodded and rose like the gentleman he was, hurrying around to open the door for us. "Thank you for the briefing. Keep up the good work, you two."

"Of course, Chief," Elexis said as she walked past.

I returned the chief's smile.

Thankfully, as we walked out the remaining two officers in the briefing room were so engaged in their own pretend conversation they didn't even look up. I glared a hole through the back of their heads in case they decided to turn around and look at us. They didn't. Elexis reached the interrogation room before I did and heaved the massive, reinforced steel door open. The entire room was of the same metal, designed not only to hold a *varúlfur* in but to be soundproof. Dustin sat in a metal chair behind a metal table that was bolted to the floor. His thin, piano-player-like hands sat folded on the table before him. Nervous energy prickled all around him, contrasting with the serene expression on his face. I smelled sweat and saw the shine of it beneath his long brown bangs.

"Too hot in here for you, Dustin?" I asked.

Dustin gave me a big grin that formed deep dimples in his cheeks, making him look even more like a boyband reject than he had before. "Yes, Raul, it is. Why don't you go out and turn the AC on for us?" His sweet, mocking tone made me want to punch him right in his perfect teeth.

I started for the table. "Look you little son of a—" Elexis's hand across my chest stopped both my forward progress and words. Some serious guns filled out the short-sleeved silky shirt she wore. It sent an unwanted thrill through me.

"No insulting the mother of our witness, Ranger Anderson," she warned.

Dustin's smile turned almost genuine as he shot it Elexis's way.

I let out a bit of a growl. "Have you met his mother? It's warranted, trust me."

One of Dustin's slender shoulders rose in a half-shrug. "He's right about that. Wait, did you say witness? What is it you think I witnessed?"

Elexis sat down in one of the chairs on the opposite side of the table from Dustin. "The abduction of Ayra Valdísdöttir, for one."

"You don't think I'm an accessory to the crime, like everyone else does?" he asked, tone defensive but hopeful.

"In the literal sense, yes. But I don't think you had much choice in the matter."

I had no idea where she was going with this, but I didn't like it. Arms crossing, I remained standing.

He leaned forward a bit. "That's right, I didn't."

I couldn't take it. "Like Helheimr you didn't. Ayra was your friend. You betrayed her," I snapped.

Wrinkles formed at the corners of Dustin's eyes as they narrowed at me. "I tried to save her, and Sonya, who *you* bit in against her will."

My fists slammed down onto the table, denting it despite the fact it was reinforced steel meant to stand up to most werewolves. Dustin let out a whimper and scooted back in his chair. "You don't know shit about that you little cocksucker, so don't you dare go there."

Rather than cower like I wanted him to, he smiled again. "At least I admit what I am."

Before I could raise my fists from the table, Elexis grabbed me by an arm and hauled me back. The fierce look she gave me stopped me in my tracks. A storm flashed in her dark blue eyes.

"I need a cup of coffee. Would you be a gentleman and bring me one, since I'm new to the PD and don't know where it is?" she asked in a carefully controlled tone.

I knew an out to save face when I heard it. And I also knew from the look in her eyes if I didn't take it, things would get ugly—well, uglier.

"Sure, because that's the kind of guy I am," I said through a tight-lipped grin.

The smug look Dustin gave me as I walked from the room almost made me want to brave the storm of Elexis's anger. But I knew she was right. Dustin was pushing my buttons, and it was undermining what Elexis was attempting. I closed the door and stepped into the observation room to watch. A flick of a switch allowed me to listen in on their conversation.

"Sorry about that," Elexis said.

Dustin shrugged. "Don't be. That's just how Raul is. It isn't your fault."

"So I keep hearing."

"All testosterone and good looks, no brains or self-control."

I suppressed a growl before I remembered he couldn't hear me through the soundproof one-way glass. But he probably knew I was here, watching, listening. The words were no doubt meant for me.

"There's bad blood between the two of you," Elexis pointed out.

Again he shrugged. He was starting to look like a tweaker. "Raul just has strong feelings on what he views as betrayal."

"And he thinks you betrayed Ayra because you lured her into James's and Calder's clutches."

Shaking his head, he leaned forward. "It didn't happen like that. When Calder sets his mind to something, he gets it, no matter what. He's mean and cruel, and he would have hurt her badly if I hadn't drugged her and brought her to him." His eyes shone with moisture. "I know how that sounds, but I couldn't stand to see him beat her up again."

"And Calder was your superior, right?"

Dustin's throat worked as he swallowed hard. "Yes. He was one of Isak and Iona's *verndari*."

"Why did you hang around with Calder and James?"

His eyes flicked to the door. "I had a bit of a crush on James, and he hung around Calder."

"Were you two in a relationship?"

He blew air out between his pursed lips. "James's tail didn't swing my way, no matter how hard I tried."

"Did anyone else hang out with the three of you? James's or Calder's girlfriends maybe?"

"No. Calder didn't like having them around."

"No one else, ever?"

He shook his head, gaze still on the door. A drop of sweat worked its way down the side of his face.

"Did Isak or Iona know Calder wanted to awaken Ayra's powers? Or that he was biting in people without permission?"

Dustin's gaze returned to Elexis. "No. Isak would have killed him if he knew. It was all Calder's idea. He'd been working on it for decades, supposedly. I only found out that part after the fact."

"So Calder had no real loyalty toward Isak or his pack?"

"None. Not for them or anyone else. He's loyal only to himself."

"And James?" She managed to keep her tone neutral, something I wouldn't have been able to pull off.

"He was loyal to Calder."

"Not his alphas or pack?"

He looked down at the table. "Not in the end."

"And you?"

Anger flashed on the man's face. "I was loyal to Isak and Iona, but they didn't understand my need to protect Ayra."

"So they banished you."

Elexis reached into her jacket pocket. Dustin leaned back, eyes widening a bit. She withdrew a business card and handed it to him. He reached slowly for it.

"The police will protect anyone who comes forward with information. I will personally see to it that anyone who talks to us is not harmed. If you think of anything else that can help us uncover everyone behind the bitings, call me," Elexis said.

Dustin looked down as he drew the card toward himself. Elexis rose. "Thank you for talking to me, Dustin."

His chair screeched across the concrete floor as he rose a bit too quickly. Nodding, he made his way out of the room at a brisk pace. When the door swung shut behind him, Elexis growled and thrust a fist onto the tabletop. The metal dimpled beneath her flesh. I switched off the sound and returned to the interrogation room before she could destroy the furniture. She whirled on me the second I entered.

Fangs flashed as she said, "He's lying!"

"Only when he speaks," I said.

Black hair flying, Elexis spun in my direction. Power crackled over me like a Taser. "You were no help," she said through a growl.

I held my hands up. "Easy there. I am not the enemy. I knew he wouldn't talk, that's all I meant."

She drew in several deep breaths. Face scrunched with effort, she pulled her power back into her almost painfully slowly, and an eerie sort of calm settled. A smile worked its way onto her lips.

"But you learned something from him, didn't you?" I asked.

Her smile crooked up into a wicked look. "Two things. He said James was loyal to Calder, which means either they had a falling out, or James is dead. Two, James, Calder, and Dustin all share something in common with Bain."

"What's that?"

"No loyalty to their old alphas."

Why I hadn't pieced those things together before, I had no idea. As much as I hated to admit it, this frustrating woman had a brilliance about her that could outshine the moon.

CHAPTER NINE

ELEXIS

I pulled up in front of the four-car garage, put the Charger in park, and shut the rumbling engine off. Now that the vehicle wasn't moving, the new car smell nearly choked me. I couldn't exactly complain, though. The chief had purchased the navy blue, unmarked car brand new when I accepted the job, and he insisted on me using it for work. On the plus side, it didn't have any of the funky smells most cop cars had. Considering how strong my sense of smell had been before I'd been bitten in, I couldn't imagine how bad they would be now. And I was infinitely glad I didn't have to.

As I stepped out onto the artfully stained concrete driveway, I attempted to massage the crook out of my neck. The nights on Raul's patio furniture had not been kind to me. But I'd take the discomfort over sleeping under his roof any day. He'd almost convinced me to that first day, but thankfully I hadn't given in. Though he was polite as a gentleman of old, charming, and kind to puppies, he was still a suspect in my book. And I would not sleep in a suspect's house. Allowing him to be my partner for the sake of his knowledge and keeping an eye on him was one thing, trusting him was another altogether. The sooner I found a rental, the better.

The massive two-story house sitting amidst a grove of fir trees cast a shadow that gave me chills as soon as I stepped into it. Three groups of people sat on furniture clustered about the huge wraparound porch. Curiosity, suspicion, and even some hostility poured from them. Their power reached out to me as if testing the water. I walled myself off from them out of instinct. From around the corner of the house I felt the familiar press of Bain's slick power approaching. It felt heavy, like the air before a storm.

The more powerful ones felt that way, I was starting to notice.

Another walked with him, not nearly as powerful. It was the brown-haired, boy-band-looking guy from interrogation. Dustin stopped at one of the groups of people on the porch and dropped into a chair. Bain continued down the steps toward me, a broad, self-satisfied smile on his face.

I did my best to look friendly, which wasn't exactly a natural state for me, so I had to work at it. Considering all the points of werewolf power I felt—not only on the porch, but in the trees to both sides and behind me—I had to behave myself. Outnumbered and with backup at least fifteen minutes out, coming alone may not have been the best choice I'd ever made. But I had a feeling Bain wouldn't talk to me with Raul around.

"Elexis, I'm so glad you came," Bain said as he approached. He took hold of my hands and raised the right one. His lips brushed the back, firm and cold against my skin.

I was kind of proud I didn't flinch.

"To what do we owe this honor?" he asked as he straightened.

He didn't let go of my hand. I forced a smile as I gently pulled it free, using the excuse of tucking a lock of hair behind my ear. "Business, unfortunately," I said.

His smile didn't wilt in the slightest. "Ah yes, I expected you would want to come by to ask questions, as any good detective would. Shall we go for a walk?" he asked pleasantly as he gestured toward the trees to the right of the house. His smooth words contrasted with his biker-like looks, reminding me he was an older werewolf who had been around more than one block.

"Sure," I said in a casual tone I did not feel.

I wasn't sure which was worse, being surrounded by a bunch of potentially hostile werewolves, or walking alone with one who pretended not to be.

A decorative gravel pathway sprinkled with fir needles led us into the towering trees. Bain walked intimately close, his elbow brushing mine from time to time. Birds sang from the branches above us. Gravel crunched under foot. The feel of the power of others faded into the distance, easing some of my anxiety. The need to fill the silence gripped me.

"Sorry to make my first visit about business, but I wanted to get the questioning of the alphas out of the way," I said.

"The alphas?" he asked, all curiosity, no judging.

"Yes. You know your people best, and you would know better than anyone if they are acting out of character, or if they harbor beliefs that might get them involved in the unsanctioned bitings."

Blond brows high, he nodded. "A wise deduction. I like how your mind works, Elexis."

It bugged me that he used my given name rather than my title, but I hid it behind a smile.

He went on. "Like myself, my pack members believe in the old ways, in preserving our customs and honoring our gods. Gaining council permission to bite anyone in is our custom and our law. No one in Draupnir would risk my wrath by breaking a custom."

"Your pack is the smallest in Hemlock Hollow. Maybe someone wants to help it grow."

Bain nodded, not like he agreed, but like he was thinking. "You're new to our ways, so you don't understand yet. To go against one's alpha is to risk banishment, even death. Very few *varúlfur* would do that, and my pack are loyal to me. We've been through a lot together." The veil of friendliness slipped a bit on the last part, revealing the pain of unhealed wounds.

"You don't wish for your pack to grow?"

"Not really. There are very few packs in existence as large as those in Hemlock Hollow. My pack is big by any standards. And definitely not because of breaking tradition. That's how things fall into chaos."

"A state worshippers of Loki revere, from what I hear."

"You know our religion." He sounded impressed.

"I'm learning," I admitted.

"The outcasts from the Draupnir pack have far more to gain by unsanctioned bitings than our loyal members. To cast suspicion, discredit our pack, and cause chaos would make many of them happy." He lifted a finger. "Then there's Arnoddr, James's pack, the one who bit you. And he isn't the only one from that pack. Calder Valdísson has apparently been performing unsanctioned bitings for decades in an attempt to awake the reaper in his bloodline, which eventually worked." Another finger rose to tick off another point. "Raul Anderson of Reinhard was engaged to Abela Aronsdóttir, niece to Iona, proxy alpha of the Arnoddr pack. Many say Abela was in a relationship with Calder on the side."

No one had said that to me. Except for Raul. I pretended to be shocked.

Bain pressed on as if sensing an opening. "You need to be careful of Raul. That engagement was less than a month ago. He cast his fiancée aside without a second thought to bite in Sonya. Was it because he knew she was the seeker and making her his mate would make him powerful beyond equal, or because he found out his fiancée was fornicating with Calder? Who knows? Neither reason bodes well for his involvement in any of this."

Chills worked all through me. The path we walked arced around through the fragrant trees, heading back toward the house. I slowed my pace. First, Bain had redirected the conversation, now he seemed to want to keep it short. I would not be distracted.

"I trust him as far as I could throw him. You don't have to worry about that." I leaned toward him a bit, flashing cleavage and brushing his arm. Blood darkened his cheeks, and he looked away, fast. "Where can I find this Abela?"

"Unfortunately, she's in Iceland."

Chances were he had told the truth because it was common knowledge and he didn't want to be caught lying. "Hmm." I chose a more direct approach. "Do any of your pack members want *varúlfur* out to the world?"

"Of course," he surprised me by saying. "We all wish we could live in the light. On the other hand, we don't want to be running from the proverbial torchlight. I was born in 1952. I know all too well, as does my pack because I tell them, about the fear and ignorance of this world and what coming out to it would mean."

His fingers brushed my arm, making the hair on it stand up. "But we aren't the only packs in the world. There are many others, some with much younger alphas who don't know any better. And we aren't even the only shifters."

Unable to answer, I stared straight ahead. News to me. Not overly surprising but still news. We were nearly back to the house. I had more questions, but I couldn't remember them. All I could think about was how big the world suddenly seemed. I had expected there were more of us, and I'd figured there could be other shifters. But now it was a reality, and it floored me.

Bain took my hand, holding it between his. "We're going to put some steaks on the barbecue. We'd love to have you if you can stay," he said in a smooth voice, as if he didn't realize he'd just thrown me for a loop. But he did. He knew exactly what he'd done. I felt the smugness in his power, saw it in his smile.

I gestured to the badge clipped to the belt of my black BDUs. "Thanks, but I'm on duty. I'll have to take a rain check." I sounded distracted. Not what I wanted him to hear.

Instead of continuing on to the house, he escorted me back to my car. That had been entirely too easy. He opened my door for me, his smile holding all the warmth of a serial killer's. Okay, maybe it wasn't that bad, but the whole encounter had thrown me off kilter, something I wasn't used to.

"I hope you cash that check in soon. I'd love to visit with you on a personal level instead of business," he said in a suggestive tone.

I got in the car and shut the door. Resting an arm on the windowsill, I forced myself to smile up at him. "Soon," I said.

He nodded and stepped back from the car door.

I fired up the engine, put the Charger in reverse, backed out, and turned around. The engine rumbled as I started down the concrete drive. The souped-up undercover car sounded as restrained as I felt. In the rearview mirror I watched Bain. The smug feel of his power made me ill. He had taken control of my questioning with barely any effort at all. In my defense, the man was over sixty years old and had well over twice the life experience I did. But in his arrogance he didn't realize I'd discovered something important. He wasn't just hiding something, he was protecting someone.

CHAPTER TEN

ELEXIS

After a fruitless day of chatting up the locals to see what they knew about the bitings, I'd had it. No one seemed to know anything, and I felt like we were talking to all the wrong people. Problem was, we didn't know who the right people were or they weren't in town.

The only useful part of the day was when Raul had taken me to the loft of an old barn where Calder—sadistic brother of the reaper—used to hang out. The sicko had plastered the walls with news clippings of "animal attack" crime scenes from the last thirty years. From what Raul told me, the guy had a journal listing those he'd bitten in over the last three decades. But the reaper—or *uppskera* as he called her in a derivative of Icelandic—had taken it when she'd gone off to hunt Calder down.

Nothing but dead end upon dead end. Calder's parents had refused to talk to us, so no progress there either. By four o'clock I'd had all of Raul's charm and snappy wit I could stomach.

"I have to swing by the ranger's station. You wanna come, or you want me to drop you at the house?" he asked as we pulled out of Calder's vacant place.

"Neither. Does Hemlock Hollow have a library?" I asked.

He cast me an odd look through his artfully tousled brown-black hair.

The way his golden eyes peeked at me from beneath those almond locks made my stomach flutter. "A library?" he asked.

"You know, those places with printed books you can check out?"

He let out a little laugh. "Yeah, we have a library."

"Great. Can you drop me off there instead?"

"Sure."

He took a left and brought us around the west side of town via the backroads. A mixture of spruce and aspen trees lined the road, making it look like golden splashes of color spotted the thick forest. From out of all that gold and green rose a massive two-story brick building. Behind it stretched an extensive green space flanked by the steel uprights of a football field goal post. Beyond it I could just see the edge of a running track going behind the building. Above two double doors on the front of the building, tall metal letters proclaimed "Hemlock Hollow High School." And above was a copper silhouette of a howling wolf.

I turned to get a longer look at the building as we passed. "That's where you went to high school?"

"Yep."

My mind conjured up images of him playing football on that field, climbing those steps wearing his letterman's jacket, surrounded by girls and his team members. It made me ache for the type of childhood I'd never had. Worse, it made me ache for what he'd lost. What the hell? I shook it off.

"Quarterback, alpha's son, sounds like a great childhood," I said.

Raul's smile fell a bit. "Sure, if you don't mind constantly fighting to prove yourself, pressure from home and school, high expectations from everyone around you," he said in a bit of a dark tone.

"You had to fight a lot as a *kid?*"

"All the time, both to reach my place in the pack and to keep face from outside challengers at school. Being a young werewolf with aspirations isn't easy."

"Are you born into packs?"

"No. We belong to the pack of our birth until we come of age, then we choose. Usually it's at eighteen. I was sixteen though."

"Did you come of age so early because you're the alpha's son?"

He shrugged. "Partially. It has to do with how strong we are."

"What about newly bitten?"

"You get to choose when you're ready. Until then, the packs will be trying to convince you to join them."

"Do they do this with every newly bitten?" I asked.

"No. Just the powerful ones."

I grunted. "Just because I can grow fangs and claws without shifting doesn't mean I fit that bill." I didn't want the packs trying to convince me to join them. Two much darkness stained this place at the moment, and I didn't know who was involved. I didn't want to choose wrong.

"It does, actually. But it's more than that. You radiate power, a lot of it," he said.

"No, I leak power. There's a difference. It's a lack of control, which you should be teaching me, by the way." I tried to make my tone light, to put a bit of a laugh in it, but it still came out dark.

"It isn't, trust me. And you have more control than some mid-level pack members."

That didn't make me feel any better. As a kid trying to beat the system, then a woman trying to work in a man's profession, I'd never been able to be satisfied with anything mid-level or out of control. Being a werewolf made me feel like both.

Raul went on. "This month's full moon festival will be all about the packs trying to recruit you, so be prepared."

"Great," I grumbled.

Maybe I could find a way out of going. I had five days to do so, plenty of time.

We passed another brick building. The sign on this one read "Grade School." On the same side of the road lay another building, this one a smaller two-story. "Wow, that's a good-sized library," I said upon seeing the sign.

He pulled up to the doors and stopped. "We're serious about preserving our books. A lot of our history is only in printed books because we can't trust digital platforms in case it were to leak online. And as you might have noticed, internet is spotty in Hemlock Hollow, so people read more."

"Spotty is a kind word for the complete lack of any satellite signal."

He almost smiled. "That's because of the sat net we have over our town and the surrounding forest."

Hand in mid-click on my seatbelt, I gave him a look. "Sat net?"

"Tech designed by one of ours to scramble any satellite feed that might be looking at us."

"That kind of tech doesn't exist outside of the government."

He pointed to where my phone bulged in my front pocket. "Tell that to your phone."

My mind blew a little. "Wow, okay."

I opened my door.

"When would you like me to pick you up?" Raul asked. The low rumble of his voice vibrated along nerves leading straight to my core.

I hated it. And if I told myself that enough times, I'd believe it. While he didn't act like the type of guy who would bite a woman without asking her permission, he was that type of guy. I shouldn't have to remind myself. "I wouldn't. You picking me up…just no. Don't phrase it like that, ever."

He gave me a sly grin that made heat spread out from my middle. Why did the man have to be supermodel sexy *and* charming? It wasn't right.

One of his brows rose in a display of muscle control I would never possess. Which led me to wonder how much control he had over other muscles. "Okay then. Would you like me to drive back here so we can carpool to my place?"

Pinching my eyes shut tight, I shook my head and got out of the vehicle. "Not better. I'll walk. It's only two miles, and I'd like the exercise anyway."

The cute smirk on his face made me want to smack him. "Suit yourself."

I slammed the door and stormed toward the library. As he pulled away, I muttered a mantra. "Syphilis, gonorrhea, herpes, crabs. A guy like him gets around." Although I was believing that about him less each day.

I needed away from him just as much as I needed to do this research, maybe more. If he could just be rude like a proper asshole was supposed to be, I'd be fine. A little bit of tension eased from me as I heard the Cherokee pull back out onto Main Street. The longer I was around him, the more my defenses dropped, and I hated it. I wasn't ready to trust anyone yet, let alone him. Not after what he'd done to Sonya.

I opened the library door and stepped into the comforting smell of books. Row upon row of shelves stretched out in all directions. The sight and smells took me back to my college days and nights spent bent over law books. So did something else. The sound of hard rock music turned low drifted to me from the right. The words were foreign, probably Icelandic, but the sound of an electric guitar and booming drum riff were unmistakable.

Up against the outer wall sat the librarian's desk, a huge, solid wood thing stained dark cherry. Behind it sat a woman not much older than me —or at least, she didn't look it. One couldn't be sure with werewolves. Her white-blond hair was pulled up into two pony tails on the sides of her head. The tip of one pony tail was blood red, the other bright blue. She popped gum while bobbing her head to the music leaking out of her ear buds. In her hands she held an open copy of the latest Alice Worth novel. On the desk in front of her sat an open sketchpad with an amazing pencil-drawn portrait of a woman. Graphite smudges along the side of her right hand and pinkie finger told me she was the artist.

The rest of the day's tension eased from me and I smiled.

The librarian's nose twitched, nostrils flaring. Her eyes opened a bit wider. She lay the book down and met my gaze. She tapped something on the desk and the music shut off.

"Detective Sandalius, welcome to the Hemlock Hollow Library. Looking for a book?" she asked. Her low-pitched, easy-going voice was filled with confidence.

My smile grew as I approached the desk. I listened for anyone else in the library. Nothing. Considering I could hear a heartbeat a half a mile away when I tried, I was confident we were alone. "Not exactly," I said.

A bank of computers lined the wall down from the librarian's desk, and in the far corner I could just see a microfiche machine poking out past a shelf. Bingo. "I came to do a bit of research on the prominent people in town," I said in a quiet tone.

The librarian's blue eyes sparkled as she leaned forward. "Then you don't want that ancient pile." She opened a drawer, took out a little sign on a chain, and stood.

Popping a bubble, she winked at me as she walked past. She hung the sign—which I now saw said "Closed"—on the front door. A quick dig in the bejeweled back pocket of her jeans produced a key, which she locked the front door with. She walked down an aisle, blingy cowboy bootheels clicking, beckoning me to follow with a hand gesture. My gut didn't give off any warnings, so I followed.

"I'm Iris," she said.

"Nice to meet you, Iris."

She took us around behind a staircase that led to an upper level. Another key from her ring opened the small door under the stairs. Once inside, she waved for me to follow. The sight of the tiny storeroom almost made me step back. Air movement from under the back wall stopped me. Iris did something to the shelf on the wall, and it swung toward her and out of the way. The wall behind it didn't look unusual, just white stucco over cinder block. Iris pressed her thumb against one of the cinder blocks.

Leaning close to the same cinder block, she said, "Iris Vicktorsdóttir."

Something clicked, and an electronic hum followed. With only the sound of smooth hydraulics, the brick wall opened inward. Beyond it lay a hallway with a concrete floor, walls, and ceiling. Iris stepped into the hallway, hesitating when I didn't follow.

"Where are you taking me?" I asked.

Her red-tipped ponytail touched her shoulder as she dipped her head. "To the real archives, of course."

While my cop instincts told me I could trust her, I couldn't forget about the death threat.

"You can trust me," Iris said, as if reading my mind. "I'm *útrýmt*, outcast. I have no pack, no allegiances, and I'm not involved in the bitings," she said. Her serious tone clashed with her playful looks and demeanor. But her eyes told me she meant it, and her words rang with truth. She had a few inches and few pounds of muscle on me, but being no stranger to fighting, I thought I might be able to take her if I had to. I gestured down the hall. "Lead on."

A second after I stepped through the door, it closed. A hiss of air sounded. The bounce returned to Iris's steps as she walked down the hall. We rounded a corner and came to another door, this one thick, heavy-gauge steel with a hand scanner beside it. She placed her hand on the scanner and it lit up with blue light. Her blond brows wiggled as she looked at me.

"Checks prints and pulse. Most aren't allowed down here, and none without a librarian to accompany them."

"Fancy device."

The light behind her hand went green. A lock in the door disengaged with a heavy "thunk," a big one.

"Yep. Even *varúlfur* have their tech heads," she said.

The door opened to a staircase leading down. Unlike the hall, the stairs looked old. A closer look showed they weren't just old, but actually chiseled out of stone. Iris flipped a switch on her way and sconces to both sides of us lit up all down the staircase. The soft light revealed a long staircase going deep down below to the basement library. The heady scent of very old books wafted up the stairs. My hand itched for the feel of the gun holstered at the small of my back, but I had no reason to draw it. In the academy, it had been drilled into me not to draw it unless I was going to use it. And as good as it would feel in my hand, there was no threat. Though it probably broke the same rule, I let my claws extend a bit.

By deductive reasoning, I took a stab at Iris's history. "Did you belong to Bain's pack?"

A small growl sounded from her as we walked. "You mean Didrik and Lísandra's pack, Draupnir. Yes, I did."

"I'm sorry. I would have mention their names, but I notice a lot of people avoid saying them."

"That's because it's forbidden to say their names in public, which is bullshit."

"It is," I agreed. "I'm sorry about Didrik. It sounds like he was a good alpha."

"He was the best." The anger in her voice made her power spike until the stairwell felt like a furnace.

I was about to say more, but we reached the bottom and the sight of the secret library blew me away.

Row upon row of fine, wooden shelves lined a room that could have come straight out of a castle with all its richly colored woods and tapestries. Metal, stone, and wood artwork perched on marble half pillars and in cubbies, most either of wolves, trees, ships, or dragons. All of it contained elaborate knot work that reminded me of the tattoos on so many of the towns' people. The scents of old books, cloth, and oiled metal mingled in a pleasant way reminiscent of college.

"Wow," I murmured.

Iris did a little spin at the bottom of the stairs, arms out. "Welcome to the Hemlock Hollow archives. You'll find everything on the history of each pack here, dating all the way back to when we immigrated from Iceland."

"Wow," I said again like a skipping record. "I have no idea where to start."

"What are you looking for exactly? I'll steer you in the right direction."

I'd trusted her this far, so I had to take a chance. "I want to know all about the powerful and influential citizens of Hemlock Hollow."

Her eyes widened. "You're trying to figure out who's behind the bitings, and you think it's someone in town." The surprise on her face struck me as odd. Surely everyone knew that was why I'd been brought here. "And you don't think one of the *útrýmt* did it."

Ah, now I got it. "Why would I think that?"

"Everyone else does, except Raul. They think we're vengeful, angry."

"Are you?" I asked.

"Thor's balls, yes. But we'd never disrespect the memory of our alphas by doing something that goes against the most sacred laws and could harm our entire race."

"Do you all keep in touch enough to know what the others are up to?"

Her eyes shifted to the side, long blond lashes practically sweeping her cheeks. "We're not supposed to, but yes." The last part was the barest of whispers I didn't so much as hear but saw from the movement of her lips.

"Why aren't you supposed to?"

"If the new alpha starts to think we're organizing to move against him, he is allowed by law to attack us."

"That's messed up."

She shrugged.

"Who are some of other *útrýmt?*"

"Tyler Viðarrson, the seeker's *kennari*, and Vidar Balderson, a monk of the Order of the *Verndari* who is traveling with the reaper, are two you might have heard of."

"Evidence suggests they're trying to clean up this problem, not exactly suspect material."

A huge smile spread across Iris's face. "We're going to get along great." She started down the aisle to our right at a brisk pace, making me rush to keep up. "I know right where you should start."

When the shelf ended, we took a right. Above the next aisle hung a hand-carved sign that read *Draupnir*. Iris retrieved the sliding ladder attached to the top of the shelf halfway down the aisle, pushed it to the beginning, and climbed up. Her fingers brushed over old leatherbound volumes for a minute. She finally grabbed a book from the top shelf and descended. I took it when she handed it to me.

The title read *Alpha's Journal, Didrik Kristoferson.* "An alpha's journal. Am I allowed to read this?" I asked.

Iris nodded, colorful ponytails bouncing. "Of course. You're *lögreglu*. Nothing in the vaults is off-limits to you. Every alpha writes one of these. They contain all the pack members' names, standings, mates, as well as personal notes from the alpha on many members, financial matters, property, that kind of thing. This is the second to the last one Didrik wrote."

Suspicion tingled through me. "Second to the last?"

She leaned in a bit closer. "They never found the last one."

"Is that unusual?"

"Everything that happened to my pack was unusual." She turned around to the shelf behind us and grabbed another book. This one was titled *Alpha's Journal, Bain Robertson.* I met her intense gaze and held it. Her blue eyes contained a world of hurt and anger, but also hope. She started to walk off and made a beckoning motion with her hand.

"I'll show you to one of the reading areas."

Around another few aisles, we came to a solid oak writing desk tucked into a corner, with a plush wingback chair at it. Shelves of even more books covered the walls beside and around it. I set my books down on the desk and sank into the big chair.

"Thank you."

"You're welcome. I think you'll find the comparison of those two... enlightening. There are a few more books that might be helpful. I'll grab them. If you think of anything else, just holler." Another pink bubble formed between her lips and popped before she spun and walked off.

I pulled my phone from my pocket, opened my notebook app, opened Didrik's journal, and got to work. Hours later I had six books open on the desk before me, a ton of notes, and a far better understanding of the powerful members of Hemlock Hollow. I knew which werewolves descended from which, who had immigrated to this country—only three generations back, which explained the accents—who was the wealthiest, the most politically influential, and more. What I didn't know was who was involved in the bitings, or even who our main suspect should be.

From Bain's journal I gathered he was wealthy, arrogant, and power hungry. But none of that tied him to the crimes. The less I found on him, the more suspicious I became. He had not only killed his brother, Didrik, to take over the pack, he had also killed the prior alpha—his own father—Kiljan, who had challenged him shortly after he had killed Didrik. There was no mention of what had happened to his mother—and Didrik's—Pálína. I was reading over the names of the members Bain had banished from the pack when Iris came back again.

"Hey Elexis, I hate to disturb you when you're neck deep in it, but it's time to close for real now. I'd close late for you, but they keep close tabs on us *útrýmt*," she said.

"Sorry, Iris. I didn't mean to keep you from going home."

She waved a hand. "No problem. No one there waiting for me anyways. My asshole ex swore loyalty to Bain when he took over, so it's just me."

From the hours I'd been here, I'd learned she wasn't an over-sharer so much as she was just brutally honest. I liked that about her. Hell, I liked a lot about her.

"Still, your time is your time, and I don't mean to suck it away." A thought occurred to me as I closed the last book. "But I do have a question."

"Fire away."

"How can I get ahold of Lísandra?"

Iris went white as milk. "We aren't supposed to speak of the *ósigur*. It's forbidden."

"The *ósigur*?"

"The defeated." She sucked in a deep breath. "But you know what? That's bullshit." She grabbed a second chair and sat down across the desk from me. "You can't get ahold of her. No one can."

"Why?"

Elbows coming to rest on the desk, she leaned in close. "Good question. We've tried, the outcasts, and none of us can reach her. She supposedly left one day and fell off the face of the planet."

"The pain of her husband being killed was too much maybe?"

Iris shook her head. "It wasn't that, though she definitely loved Didrik more than anything. They had one of those fairytale marriages we all envied." Her voice lowered. "She wouldn't have left. Lísandra was a fighter. Even though she wasn't able to challenge Bain, I know she would have wanted to stay and undermine him in every way she could. And she wouldn't leave us—the outcasts—alone to fend for ourselves. She loved us like her children. Running away, leaving us, wasn't in her nature."

Again she paused, this time to dig in her pocket. She took her phone out, clicked on a few things, and turned the screen toward me. The blond couple on her screen were embracing and grinning like two people sickeningly deep in love. The woman had a hand against her breast, fingers just touching a knot work necklace of Odin's triple-pointed triangle with a heart woven into it. Diamonds shone on the silver-hued metal. Iris pointed to the picture. A wistful, sad smile turned the corners of her deep red lips up.

"That's right after her one hundred thirty-eighth birthday, when he gave her that necklace."

"You loved them," I observed.

"Very much. They were like parents to me." She withdrew the phone and met my gaze. Tears shone in her eyes. "Lísandra wouldn't leave, and she wouldn't ignore our calls. She was furious when Didrik was killed. She vowed to take Bain down. Then she disappeared and texted a few of us that she'd decided to move back to Iceland with her aging mom, who was close to her time."

"Has anyone spoken to her mom?"

Iris's eyes grew dark and her power crackled. "We couldn't reach her. Then we found out she had died."

I twirled my pen through my fingers as I contemplated this. Movement helped me think a problem through. "How old was she? Was her death suspicious?"

"She was of age, over four hundred and fifty."

"How well would you say you knew Lísandra?"

"Extremely. I was one of her *verndari*."

The pen fell from my fingers. I leaned forward. "Do you have any idea where she'd go if she were running from someone?"

Her power grew so hot I had to sit back in my chair. "She would never run from anyone. Something has happened to her. I'm sure of it. It's why I stayed in Hemlock Hollow, to try and find out what."

"You suspect Bain."

"Of course, but I haven't been able to find any proof. But then, no one in the pack will talk to me because I'm outcast."

A thought occurred to me. "If Bain did kill her, are there any pack laws protecting him?"

She shook her head. "Not unless she attacked him and it was self-defense. But if that were the case, he would have reported it. She wouldn't have just dropped off the map."

I stood and picked up the last of the books. Together we carried them to the shelves and returned them to their appropriate spots.

"I can't promise I'll find her, but I'll damn sure try," I said as we started for the stairs.

She gave me a small smile. "Thank you."

At the last shelf, she stopped, skimmed her fingers over the spines of several books, and pulled one out. She handed it to me. "This should help. Just don't let anyone see you with it. Books like this aren't supposed to leave the vault."

Embossed into the cover were the words "Pack Law." I lifted my shirt and tucked it into the waist of my jeans. "You got it. And thanks, this will help a lot."

We started up the stairs. Iris didn't speak again until we reached the hall. Once we were able to walk side by side, she gave me a serious look that clashed with her multi-colored hair and carefree attitude. "Be careful, Elexis. Someone killed her. They'll be willing to kill you too."

I thought about the wolf carcass left on Raul's threshold. "I know, and I will." Her forthright manner encouraged me to ask one more thing. "Have Bain and Raul Anderson ever been on friendly terms?"

A sort of snorting laugh came from her. "Definitely not. Raul hates him as much as we outcasts do."

"Was him biting Sonya in out of character for him?"

She gave me an impressed look, lips almost turning up into a smile. "It was. I've only ever known him to be the dutiful, respectful heir to the Reinhard throne. Something had to have happened to make him do that because he would never do anything to displease his father. Besides, he's just never been the type of guy who would do something like that. He has a player rep, but..."

"But you think it's a false reputation?" I asked when she trailed off.

Lips pursed, she nodded.

We reached the door into the closet, and she had to scan her hand again to let us out. "It must be tough having your *kennari* be a *fallið*. That sucks," she said as we stepped into the supply closet.

I lifted one shoulder in a half-shrug. "It's his penance. If not me, it would have to be someone else." I did mind, a lot, but I wasn't going to be a diva about it. Besides, I had a feeling the mystery of why Raul bit in Sonya had something to do with all this.

"True, but after what happened to you...it sucks is all."

The still library greeted us with its scents of new ink and plastic/paper blend book covers. "Yep, that's life. It often sucks," I said.

Iris laughed. "No shit." She held her fist up, and I gave her a fist bump.

Rain pattered against the solar panel covered roof. The cloud-choked sky outside the glass entry doors brought on an early dark, making it feel far later than it was.

"Speaking of sucking," Iris said with a long, drawn-out sigh as she looked outside. Keys jingled in her hand as we approached the door. "Sorry. I'd offer you a ride, but I'm only allowed on neutral property."

"Neutral property?"

"Property not owned by one of the packs, which leaves the town and the holy ground."

"The holy ground?"

"The hollow where the bridge spans. It's a place of power, so it belongs to everyone, though they really don't even like my kind there."

"That's bullshit. Just because your alpha was defeated and you stayed loyal to him. Loyalty is a good thing." Some of their ways pissed me off.

Her red lips turned up. "You're all right, Elexis. I think we're going to get along great."

"Damn straight," I said.

She paused before opening the door. "Be careful. The people who betrayed Didrik and Lísandra, who stayed and pledged loyalty to Bain, they're dangerous."

"Thanks for the warning."

She opened the door, and I started to step out. "Hey, will you be at the full moon festival?" I asked.

Her mascara-laden lashes rose high. "I'm allowed on the holy ground, but I'm not exactly welcome."

"Well, you would be by me."

It might have been moisture I saw in her eyes, or it might have been a trick of the premature dark and rain. "Noted," she all but whispered.

Zipping my jacket up more to protect the book than myself, I stepped out into the pouring rain.

CHAPTER ELEVEN

ELEXIS

Thanks to the pouring rain, I couldn't hear or smell them, but I knew someone was following me. I felt it deep down on an instinctual level. For the millionth time, I fought the impulse to look over my shoulder. The tall evergreens lining the road combined with the rain to make it dark as night. The constant downpour dampened all my super senses until I was reduced to a normal person. It made me feel blind and vulnerable. Until that moment, I hadn't realized how much I'd come to rely on those heightened senses.

No cars traveled the road. The town was too small for steady traffic on the backroads. And on a night like this, no one was out walking besides me. In my on-duty detective clothes—black BDU pants and a gray silk top with a gray and black jacket over it—at least I blended into the dark. But I still felt entirely too visible out here on the road alone. The Sig Sauer .45 holstered at my back brought little comfort. Lead bullets wouldn't do any good against werewolves unless they were incredibly young or old. If someone was following me, I'd have to handle this the old-fashioned way, with my fists. Considering foster care and years of law enforcement martial arts classes had me well prepared, I was fine with that.

Finally, I started to recognize rocks and trees along the road. Raul's driveway couldn't be more than two miles away. Power suddenly pressed in on me from three sides. I grew hot despite the rivers of rain running all down my body. No need to see, hear, or smell them. I could feel my stalkers now. *Yes, plural.* One approached from behind, another from my left, and another on my right. By the pressure of their power, I could tell they were maybe fifteen feet away and closing in fast. The feel of that power told me they were werewolves, one of them at least pretty powerful. Running would be the smart thing to do, but it wasn't in my nature.

I bent my knees, balled my hands into fists, and waited.

Eyes shone in the dark to my left and right at about chest level—wolf's eyes. Shit. If I shifted, I'd just end up ruining my clothes and then getting tangled in them. My control slipped a bit, forcing me to open my hands as my fingernails grew into claws that extended beyond my fingers a good two inches. A low growl rumbled through my growing fangs. Dammit. I could not afford to lose my shit now.

Teeth gnashed and a golden-brown shape flew at me out of the liquid darkness to my left. I side-stepped and drove a palm-heel strike into the side of the wolf's face. The size of it made me think it was either a young wolf or a female. Now that it was this close, I realized it smelled like the latter. Nothing cracked—to my disappointment—but her head did whip to the side. I threw a kick at the wolf charging me from behind. My hiking boot connected with a shoulder. The brown wolf dropped with a wheezing sound. I threw another kick at its face. The momentum of the strike sent it rolling. Not it—him. I ducked low beneath the leap of the third one.

The rhythm of the fight carried me along, block, strike, dodge. They landed a few, but I landed more. Adrenalin or werewolf constitution kept me from feeling any pain. They were good fighters. It quickly became clear I was better. In seconds, I'd drawn blood from two of them and they had only grazed me with a claw here or there. But they were smart. They started to take turns attacking, saving their strength. The chances of me outlasting them went down with each strike. Minutes ticked by, feeling like hours. I didn't tire as fast as a human, which was why I knew it had been a while when I finally got winded. One of my attackers lay writhing on the wet pavement from a broken back leg. Being down one helped, but not enough. Claws raked along my arm when I dodged too slowly. The second wolf—a male from the smell—darted in and got a lucky stab of claws into my side.

I pulled back fast enough the claws didn't go in more than an inch or so. The pain still took my breath away. I punched the male wolf in the throat for it. Pain seared into me as my own claws dug into my palm. The strike only landed hard enough to push him back. I'd been hoping to collapse his trachea so it stuck to itself and choked him to death. No such luck.

Growling, I lashed out with my claws at the face of the golden-brown wolf. I grazed her cheek, taking fur and a bit of skin. I kicked her in the shoulder. She went down. Grabbing her by the scruff of her neck, I pinned her to the ground. My first instinct was to go for my cuffs, but how did one cuff a wolf?

The rev of a souped-up engine made me look up. Headlights low to the ground blinded me. Breaks squealed on asphalt. The wolf wriggled out of my grasp and scrambled to her feet. I reached for her and missed. I just caught sight of the tails of the other two wolves as they disappeared into the trees. I started after the female, but the movement caused three sharp pains to stab into my side. It took my breath away and nearly sent me to a knee.

Those punctures had to be deeper than I'd thought. I pulled my gun, hoping to at least slow her down. Despite the headlights rendering me blind, I fired two shots toward the woods. The lack of any yelp was not encouraging.

"Dammit!"

The gun became too heavy to hold up. My arms sagged. Hot blood ran down my right arm. I took another step in the direction my attackers had fled. This time I did fall to a knee. My gun clattered to the asphalt and into a puddle. "Shit!" I fished it out and holstered it with a shaking hand.

The night swam, but that could have just been the rain and headlights. A car door opened. Feet splashed across the wet road.

"Elexis, by Odin! Are you all right?" came Raul's voice.

I tried to rise, but my legs shook too much. "Aside from the whole bleeding out thing, sure." My voice sounded as weak as I felt. "Go after them!"

He ignored me and ducked a shoulder under my left arm. When he lifted me, the torn skin over my ribs stretched and burned like fire. A hiss of pain slid between my gritted fangs.

"I'm not leaving you here for them to circle back and attack again," Raul said.

"We can't just let them go!" I tried to pull free, but he held me far too easily.

"I'm not leaving you," he insisted. The desperation in his voice made me really look at him for the first time. Guilt darkened his eyes and dug deep lines between his brows. Seeing it took the edge off my anger.

He pulled his shirt off and tore it in half. My eyes fixated on the rain running in rivers down his hard, bare chest. I must have taken a blow to the head. Or maybe it was blood loss. He tied part of his torn shirt around my wounded arm and hand. The pain it caused cleared my head, wiping the attraction away. He balled up the rest of his shirt and pressed it against my side. It felt like being punched.

"Hold this against your wound. Keep good pressure on it," he instructed.

I tried to walk with his help, but my knees gave out. He gripped my arm tight to keep me from falling.

"Shit, how much blood have you lost?"

"Wasn't keeping track, too busy fighting," I slurred. Each word was a chore.

The night felt like it was getting darker, the rain colder. The world swam, despite Raul holding me upright. It swam even more when he scooped me up in his arms and cradled me like a child. Or a lover. I started to protest but his chest was so warm. Instead, I snuggled in against it, desperate for that warmth. His power engulfed me with an otherworldly heat all its own. It fed my own power, reviving me to the point where I could lift my head.

He sat me down in a seat and leaned over to put my seatbelt on. He smelled so good, like pine, musk, and nuts. That thought took me to dirty places. His groin brushed my arm, plunging me deep into that dirty place. But a second later he retreated, taking the warmth of his power with him. Cold set in, seeping into my bones. It made me realize I was probably bleeding all over his seat. Which I now saw wasn't the Cherokee. The soft glow of the dash lights of a Porsche lit up the interior of the vehicle. Beneath my blood, I smelled genuine leather and the faint scent of some kind of dashboard conditioner.

"Dammit," I mumbled as I pressed the remains of his shirt harder against my side.

"Are you all right?" he asked as he sat down in the driver's seat.

"Oh yeah, fine, just bleeding all over your six-digit car."

A small laugh came from him. "Don't sweat it. My father and I bought it as a wreck and rebuilt it. Besides, the leather is well-conditioned. Blood wipes right off."

"Why does it sound like you're speaking from experience?"

"Daily fights, remember?" he asked with a shrug.

I made some kind of humming noise in response. It was all I could manage.

The engine revved and we flew backwards, hydroplaned on the wet pavement, and spun in a half circle. Without missing a beat, Raul slammed the pedal down and took off. Pressed back into my seat by momentum, it was a minute before I could say anything else.

"Drive like this often?" I asked, only getting out half the words I'd meant to. Speaking was difficult. I had to concentrate on the words.

He laughed, but it was filled with more concern than humor. "I own a Porsche, after all."

I rolled my head to the left. Dash lights played across his half-naked body, pooling in the valleys of his muscles. Knot work tattoos snaked around his arms from his back. Locks of brown hair clung to his face, reaching down to his cheekbones. He looked like a dark Viking from an era long ago—behind the wheel of a very fast ship. And damn if he wasn't hotter than any hell imaginable.

My body craved his heat, needed it. The power lying beneath my skin pulsed. It reached for him. I hated that part of me wanted him—even if it was just for his warmth. He still hadn't told me why he bit Sonya, which made him a suspect and an asshole in my book. I wasn't ready or willing to rewrite that chapter any time soon.

He put a hand on my arm, which made me uncomfortable for many reasons. One of which was the speedometer reading ninety-some miles per hour. I opened my mouth to protest, but then heat seeped from his hand into me. It spread from my skin down deep, then moved throughout my body. The pain in my arm started to dull.

"What are you doing to me?" I asked. While it felt good, I didn't trust it.

"My power will help heal you," he said.

"Why? How?"

"My energy feeds yours, strengthens it. That helps you heal. It's how we're wired."

A little of the tension went out of me. I looked up as we started to slow. Raul turned into his driveway. I sat up a little straighter.

"Why aren't you taking me to the hospital?"

"Because our doctors only treat potentially fatal wounds. Instead, you would be treated with energy sharing."

"Bullshit. Take me to a hospital."

"They'll bring in at least four staff members who will all lay in a bed with you, touching your body as much as possible, and you'll have to sleep that way overnight. Is that really what you want?"

I let out a long breath. It hurt my side so bad I sucked it right back in, which only hurt more. Him figuring out my dislike for physical contact with random people bugged me on a level I didn't want to think about. The idea of him knowing me at all rubbed me like bad polyester and wool put together. "I take it I have another option?" I wheezed.

"I'm strong enough to heal you. But if you prefer to go to the hospital and have a group do it, I'll take you there." No judging, no snark lay in his tone, just honesty.

Though the garage door was already opening, he stopped the car before going in. My skin crawled at the thought of four strangers sleeping in the same bed with me, touching me. I wouldn't be able to do it no matter how bad I was hurt. On the other hand, the idea of having Raul snuggled up to me in bed sent a thrill through me that made me want to vomit. I turned the thrill into anger.

"You will be a complete gentleman, or I will cut your balls off."

"I will. You have my word." He sounded sincere enough, but...

"I have no idea what your word is worth."

"It's priceless, I promise."

When I didn't answer him, he went on. "You can sleep with a knife under your pillow, or your gun, if it makes you feel better."

"It does and I will," I answered before I realized I'd even decided to do this. The danger I knew was better than the danger I didn't. Three people had attacked me. I didn't know who they were or who else might be aligned with them. I could handle Raul better than a bunch of strangers. Besides, as much as I hated it, the wolf in me wanted to trust him.

He pulled into the garage, and the door slid closed behind us. When he got out I closed my eyes to rest for just a second. When I opened them again I was sitting on the edge of a bathtub while Raul gently cleaned blood from my arm. The lost time made me jump and sent a shot of adrenalin through my system. Two red towels lay in the tub beside us. They reeked of my blood.

"You're awake," Raul said in a long, drawn-out breath, tone filled with genuine relief. It wasn't the sound of a man who would bite a woman in without asking her. Or was my brain trying to justify my body being attracted to him? The man perplexed me at every turn. "Do you feel strong enough to sit up on your own?"

I didn't, but I nodded anyway. He let go of me slowly. I gripped the side of the tub to steady myself.

"You'll have to take your shirt off so we can clean the wounds on your side. You okay with that?" he asked.

At this point, I was too hurt, tired, and cold to care. Besides, the gentle way he handled me and the fact he had asked, put me at ease. It shouldn't have. I chalked it up to blood loss. "Yes. Let's just get this done. I'm freezing."

He took hold of the bottom of my shirt and met my gaze. The concern in his golden-hued eyes tugged at me. None of my cop alarms went off, so I lifted my arms. He removed my shirt and quickly pressed a warm, damp towel to my side. It both hurt and felt wonderful for the heat it brought.

"I'm sorry," he said when I flinched.

Pain overrode the comfort of the warmth as he started to wipe the blood away. I did my best not to cringe as I sat and shivered. Blood had soaked into the bottom left side of my black, lacy bra, making it crusty and hard. And my jeans were a mess. I'd never be able to get all the blood out. The wounds were deep. One of them cut through all layers of skin and exposed muscle. They'd stopped bleeding, thankfully. Not even Raul's gentle swipes over them triggered more blood.

126 | HEATHER MCCORKLE

"Should they have stopped bleeding? You don't think that means something is in them, do you?" I asked.

Raul shook his head and gave me a smile. "No. Your *varúlfur* healing has kicked in and stopped it."

I winced as he brushed across one of the deeper gouges. "Then why does it still hurt so damn much?" I hissed.

"Because your body is so damaged, it's concentrating on healing the big issues first."

"Yeah, well, it sucks," I complained.

Raul pointed at the book tucked deep in my front waistband. "At least you didn't lose your reading material."

I took the book from my jeans and laid it face down on the counter. Surprisingly, only a little blood had dripped onto the leather cover. Raul only gave it a quick side glance. "Iris took you to the archives. Good. I was hoping she'd find you worthy."

He put the towel down and picked up the bottle of peroxide from the counter.

"Find me worthy?" I asked, a bit of bite in my tone.

He wetted a cotton ball with the peroxide and pressed it gently to one of my wounds. The burning pain drew a growl from me.

"Sorry." The soft tone of his voice made me think he truly was. "Iris won't take just anyone to the vault. I was hoping she'd take you."

"Doesn't everyone have access?" I asked.

"They used to. But with theft, vandalism, and idiots not respecting our history, we can't be too careful anymore."

I breathed a sigh of relief when he threw the cotton ball into the trash.

"Sounds like she's more of a guard than a librarian," I said.

With light fingers, he placed a huge bandage over the wounds on my side. "Hold this," he instructed.

When I did, he started to wrap gauze around my torso to hold it in place. "She is. That's why the council chose a former *verndari* for our librarian."

"You say that like she didn't lose her position when she was outcast."

His jaw tensed and his teeth ground. "She did, but it was wrong. Everything that happened to that pack was wrong."

"Sounds personal," I said in a soft tone. And familiar. Iris had said almost the exact same thing. The two of them being like-minded struck a chord in me—a good one.

He picked a new cotton ball up and started on my arm. "It is. Didrik was my high school football coach. He was my mentor, my friend." The pain in his voice eclipsed any I was feeling.

I touched his arm. "I'm sorry. I didn't know."

He shrugged as if it meant nothing, but the look in his eyes told me it meant everything. It made me wonder how much more I didn't know about this guy.

He traded the cotton ball for gauze. "Can you lift your arm?"

I tried. The limb wouldn't obey. Exhaustion weighed on me. I swayed from the effort of trying. Raul held me with a hand around my back. Though I'd stopped moving, it felt like the room hadn't. I leaned back against his hard, bare chest. Delicious warmth soaked into my skin from his. A sigh slid from me.

"Easy there, don't pass out on me yet. We need to get you into some clean clothes," he said.

I didn't want clothes between me and all that soothing heat. Yep, I must have gotten kicked in the head, by something like Odin's six-legged horse maybe. Or I needed to be.

"You've gotta lift your arms for me, Elexis," he said. His deep, gentle voice vibrated along the skin of my neck—and shot down between my legs.

I squeezed my eyes shut and concentrated on my breathing. In...hold, two, three, four. Out...hold, two, three, four. It helped me shove the attraction, the need, down into the deep dark hole it had emerged from. Raul moved behind me and helped me take my bra off. I dropped the crusty ruin of silk and lace into the tub. He gently lifted my arms and slid a sweatshirt onto me. Warmth and fresh laundry smell wrapped around me in the form of blue cotton. He must have gotten it out of the dryer. On the front was clipart of a wolf's head with a full moon behind it. The words "Hemlock Hollow" arched above it and the word "wolves" was printed below. The well-worn design made it look several years old.

"I hope my football sweatshirt is okay. It's what I had in the dryer," Raul said.

I wrapped my arms around myself and snuggled into the cozy, soft fabric. "It's warm and perfect," I murmured.

"We're going to stand. You ready?" he asked.

I nodded, even though I wasn't. He lifted me. His sweatshirt fell halfway down my thighs. The room swayed enough to make me queasy. Raul's arm slid around my waist, steadying me.

"Do you want a pair of my sweats?" he asked.

I shook my head, which made things swirl like a vortex was opening. "Shirt's enough." I wanted to say more, but those were the only words I could get out.

"We have to get your pants off. They're soaked and bloody. You okay with that?"

I nodded once, and the small motion almost made me lose my balance. Gathering up the last of my strength, I unbuttoned and unzipped my jeans. I pushed them down past my hips and stopped, afraid to bend over. The pain of the motion sent white-hot shards shooting through my gut. Raul turned me around and sat me on the toilet. The porcelain chilled me right through my lace panties. He grabbed the cuffs of my jeans and pulled them the rest of the way off.

"Did you recognize the wolves who attacked you?" he asked.

"No. Too dark, too rainy."

"Two wolves?"

"Three. Female, two males."

Raul whistled. "Damn Sandalius. You fought three? No wonder you got hurt so bad." He sounded impressed. It made me smile.

He scooped me up and carried me out of the bathroom. I tried to protest, but I must have blacked out. The next thing I knew, I was lying in a big bed and he was climbing in next to me. Anxiety tried to flare, but I didn't have the energy to give it any attention.

"You don't have to worry. I'll be a gentleman," he said. That delicious, deep voice hovered over my shoulder.

His power trickled over me like warm water. I wanted to sink deep into it and not come up for air. I'd never been attracted to bad boys before. I didn't know what the hell was wrong with me. My alarms should have been going off, making me freak out. Since the attack that had turned me, I'd barely been able to handle people touching me, let alone this. But something about his power, his demeanor, comforted me instead.

"Damn right, you will," I murmured for good measure.

"I need to touch you to share energy. Are you okay with that?" he asked.

Him being a gentleman only confused matters more.

"Yes, already," I snapped with such vehemence, the muscles in my side tightened. Pain shot deep into my wounds.

His hand settled on that side. Heat poured from his palm into me, soothing and relaxing my muscles. It felt like a warm bath stepping into me rather than the other way around. Longing for more relief, I leaned toward him. His chest touched my back. Along with heat came his power, trickling into me as if reluctant and still waiting for permission. That small trickle dulled my pain enough I could breathe normally in only seconds. The power waiting inside me craved more, desperately. Before I knew I had done it, I'd scooted back to Raul until we were spooning. I didn't want to think, to chance rationalizing and rejecting all of this. Now, I just wanted to stay lost in it. For the first time, I let my wolf side take over and gave into the instinct. Lost in a cocoon of his warmth and power, I drifted off.

CHAPTER TWELVE

RAUL

The pale light of pre-dawn peeked around the edges of the thick sapphire curtains of my bedroom. Seeing it raised an urgency in me. Careful not to disturb her, I unwove my arm from Elexis's and scooted back. She stirred and I froze. A small, sleepy sound of protest came from her, then she snuggled her head back into the pillow and went still. Her breathing evened out. Black hair with the occasional blue highlight spilled across my midnight blue pillowcase like silk. Not a single wrinkle of stress marred the skin between her naturally arched black brows. A slight smile turned up her lips. It made me long to touch them.

In fact, every part of me longed to touch every part of her. Moving had been the last thing I had wanted. But a dream of a frozen land filled with giants had my heart rate up. I'd awoken with a start. As always, the dream had been vivid as real life, so much so, it was disturbing. A foreign landscape dominated by two moons had burned into the back of my eyelids. If I went to sleep I'd fall right back into the dream. It would only be a matter of time before I started tossing and turning and would wake Elexis up. Peaceful as she looked, that was not an option. Besides, she would wake up healed and mad as a badger if I was still touching her.

And there was something I had to take care of.

I tucked the covers up around her, grabbed my phone off the

nightstand, and crept from the room wearing only sweatpants. Fingers dialed before my bare feet touched the back deck. Gripping the railing with one hand, I launched myself over it. I dropped the two stories of my split-level house and landed lightly on the flagstone path below.

"Hello," Iris's voice came through the phone.

"Iris, it's Raul. Sorry to call, but there isn't anyone else I can trust."

"Not even your sister?" came her bitterly amused reply.

"Not when she could be sleeping with the enemy. You know that."

She sighed. "What do you need?"

"Can you come over and stay with Elexis for a while today? She was attacked last night. I don't want her to be alone."

"Shit! What happened?"

Keys jingled through the phone.

"She was jumped on her way home by three people."

"Who?"

As we talked I wandered around the side of the house, looking and smelling for any signs of intruders. The skin on the back of my neck crawled with the desire to raise hair that wasn't there in my human form. My fangs started to extend.

"That's what I'm going to find out," I said through a growl.

"I'll be there in five." The line went dead.

After a complete check of the grounds, I returned to the house—via the front door so I wouldn't wake Elexis. She needed her rest, and I didn't want her to see me go sideways on the alphas, because gods knew, if she woke up, she would insist on going with me. I grabbed a T-shirt and a pair of shorts from the dryer, and a protein shake from the fridge. My shorts were only half buttoned when I heard a car pulling up the drive. Iris's blue VW Jetta rolled to a stop next to my garage. I downed the protein shake in a few drinks and sat the tumbler on the counter before I stepped out. Turning the knob so it wouldn't click, I eased the front door shut behind me.

Iris met me halfway up the walk. With one blue braid and one red, wearing a form-fitting tank crimson as heart's blood, she looked like a psychotic comic book writer's idea of a mad shieldmaiden. That was Iris, colorful and a touch crazy.

"Thanks for coming. She's still asleep."

"How bad was she hurt?"

"Deep claw wounds to the side and down her right arm. I gave her a lot of healing energy. She'll probably sleep a few more hours. There's a crossbow in my study with silver-tipped arrows. Study is the second door on the left down the south hall. Elexis is in the bedroom down the north hall, first door on the right."

With one brow raised, she nodded. "Don't sweat it. No one is getting into this house but you." She patted my shoulder as she passed. "You calling for an alpha meeting?"

"Damn straight," I said.

"Good. Catch these bastards."

I lifted the cover to the keypad on my garage. After punching in a series of numbers, the door glided open. I jumped in the open window of my Porsche, dropped the keys from their spot over the visor, and fired the car up. As soon as my phone connected to my car, I told it to call my father.

"Hello, Raul," he answered.

"Father, Elexis has been attacked."

Teeth clenched as hard as my fangs would allow, I stormed up the steps of the A-frame style log City Hall building. The two brow-pelted *varúlfur* in full wolf form, standing to either side of the solid oak double doors, bared their teeth and growled. I bared my own fangs and growled right back. The wolf on the left—a male whose scent I recognized as a member of the Reinhard pack—took a step toward me. Leif's blond head came bobbing around the corner of the building. In nothing but running shorts—not even shoes—he looked ready to shift and throw down. If I weren't so pissed, I would have grinned like the Cheshire cat.

I'd given him a call on my way here. Most crazy shit we did, we did together, so of course I had to let him know.

He acknowledged me with a chin thrust. "'Sup? You here to crash the alpha meeting?"

"Yep."

He raised one shoulder. "Thought you might be. Could get bloody."

"Yep."

A shit-eating grin split his face. "Let's do this."

I continued for the door. Both wolves lunged at us. The left one reached me. I caught him by the throat and threw him to the bottom of the stairs. After growls and a yelp from my right, the other tumbled down shortly after.

Leif pitched the huge, heavy doors wide open and stepped aside to let me through first. They slammed against the walls so hard the frame shook. The receptionist sitting behind the solid-slab hemlock desk in the waiting room looked up with wide eyes. Her over-plucked brows rose high into her brown bangs.

"Leif, Raul, you can't just barge in here. Raul, especially not now that you're *fallið*," she said as she started to rise.

Lifting the left side of my upper lip, I bared two fangs at her. "Clearly I can, Nora."

She sputtered over another protest as she rose to her full height. In one sweeping step, Leif stood before her desk, his broad shoulders blocking her view of me. "Nora, darlin', it's just investigation business. They'll want to hear what he has to say. And who are we to stand in the way of justice. Surely, you don't mean to stand in the way of justice," he said in his most charming, good ol' country boy tone.

Leaving them to it, I stormed past to the next set of double doors.

I had the second set of doors opened by the time she started arguing with Leif about the need to warn them of my intrusion. Thanks to his intervention, she became too distracted to phone them ahead.

Five people sat at a triangle-shaped wooden table with a wolf's head formed of intricate knots carved into the top of it. My father cringed as he looked at me from across the room. Though my mother's expression remained neutral, her eyes were laughing. To their left, Isak and his mother, Iona—stand-in female alpha until Isak found a mate—only gave me a curious look. From the final wing of the table, Bain glared with a ferocious heat I felt from across the room. I walked up the few steps to the raised dais where the table of alphas sat. Bain's eyes widened further.

"You have no right to enter this hall. What are you doing here?" he snapped in a loud voice, teetering on the edge of control.

Power crackled from my skin, spilling out and splashing over Bain. He flinched and hid it badly.

"I'm here to find out who attacked Elexis. She is my partner and my *nemi*. I have a right to know."

I forced my rage down and looked at him, really looked. Elexis said she'd slashed one of the wolves across the face and broke the leg of another. We didn't heal fast enough for things like that to disappear in a day, not even alphas. No mark marred Bain's face, and he had leaped to his feet too smooth and easy to have an injured leg. But of course, he wouldn't do his dirty work himself.

"You have no rights in this hall, *útrýmt*," Bain snapped.

My mother slapped her hand down on the table hard enough to make the pens and paper on it jump. "Watch your words, Bain. Raul Anderson is *fallið*, not *útrýmt*. He has the same rights as any mid-level pack member in our society."

"I think you mean bottom level," Bain said through a sneer.

Mother's chin rose. "I do not. Just this week he has risen to mid-level and has been steadily climbing through those ranks."

Bain paled a bit and tried to hide his reaction with a wave of his hand. "No matter. Mid-level members have no place in this hall either," he said, voice rising. The cold way he looked at my mother made me want to rip his arms off.

"And those who turn against their own kind have no place in Valhalla," I said.

His attention whipped back to me. A growl rumbled through his bared fangs. Scalding power washed over me and continued on to Bain. Isak—alpha of the Arnoddr pack and the source of power—rose to his feet. The man's broad, six-foot-six form towered over even me. "Enough!" he bellowed.

Bain flinched. Isak fixed the man with the coldest green eyes I had ever seen. "Bain, sit down and act like the alpha you are." That gaze turned to me. "Raul, you do have the right to know our findings, but you do not have the right to enter this hall unannounced and without admittance." He looked to my parents and then to his mother at his side. "Since he is here, we may as well inform him. Unless anyone has any valid objections?" At the word "valid" he shot a look at Bain.

My parents and Iona said they had no objections. After a long few seconds, Bain mumbled the same. I nodded to my parents and the alphas of the Arnoddr pack.

"Thank you, Alphas."

Out of respect for them, I took several steps back until I moved down to the lower floor of the room's entrance. Looking up at anyone always made my skin crawl. Bain made it nearly writhe. But the others deserved my respect. This hall and its laws deserved my respect. Everyone looked to Iona, as she was the eldest female alpha. She swiped a lock of graying blond hair from her brow and nodded to me.

"We have a dozen wolves with minor wounds from sparring. None have any facial wounds, nor signs of a broken or injured left leg. Every member of our pack has been accounted for. You are, of course, welcome to visit the Arnoddr den to inspect them for yourself."

I inclined my head deeply to her. "Thank you, that won't be necessary. I trust your report."

I looked to my mother.

"Seven of our pack members have minor injuries. None of them match those you've described. Every member has been accounted for," she said in a formal tone, all traces of the supportive mother gone.

"Thank you," I said, knowing I had caused several of those minor injuries during my daily fights.

Doing my best to keep my expression neutral, I looked to Bain.

"We found no injuries among any of our members matching those Elexis described," he said.

"Why is my sister not here to give this report?" I demanded. As his female alpha stand-in until he found a mate, she should be here. "If you've done anything to her—"

"Of course I haven't done anything to her. She's questioning members of our pack to see if anyone knows anything about the attack. Call and ask her yourself if you don't believe me," he said, crossing his arms as he spoke.

While he gave off plenty of hostility, he didn't reek of lies. And it sounded like something my sister would do. Bain laughed when I didn't respond.

"That's right, she isn't taking your calls. A smart man would look to the *útrýmt*. They are the most likely suspects behind the bitings, and therefore

Miss Sandalius's attack," he said. Sneer turning into a serious expression, he looked to the other alphas. "If Raul isn't capable of protecting Elexis, it may be best to assign her a new *kennari*. My pack happens to have several excellent candidates."

Bristling, I ground my teeth until I could respond calmly. "Elexis should be the one to make that choice."

Bain laughed. "Oh, the irony of that coming from you!"

A fierce growl tore from between my clenched fangs.

Iona let out a small laugh, defusing the situation with ease. "Enough posturing. I do not think a reassignment is at all necessary. Miss Sandalius fought off three *varúlfur*. And Mr. Anderson here is not her protector, as he said, he is her *kennari* and her *lögreglu* partner."

"Agreed," Isak said.

My parents echoed his answer.

My father looked at me. "We will question our pack members and report any findings to you and Miss Sandalius. Aside from that, it will be up to the *lögreglu*. May Odin's wisdom guide you to find the attackers."

I dipped my head. "And may they fall to Forseti's axe."

Several in the room repeated the ancient mantras. Forseti, God of justice, would be a mercy compared to what I'd do to these people if I caught them.

CHAPTER THIRTEEN

ELEXIS

The cold sheets woke me when I rolled over. Disappointment warred with relief as I realized Raul wasn't in bed anymore. The disappointment made me angry, which woke me right up. I hated being drawn to this man who I knew so little about, and what I did know was bad. Being a slave to hormones wasn't my thing. So why was he getting under my skin?

I realized I was lying on my wounded side, and it didn't hurt. Neither did my arm. I sat up and unwound the gauze. Three red marks were all that remained of the deep gouges. I made a fist. It didn't hurt.

"Wow."

Raul had skills, though I'd never tell him that. Thinking it was bad enough. What was worse, he'd been a total gentleman all night. He hadn't groped me once, or even attempted to grab a feel. It made me wonder how wrong about him I might be. But just about anyone could restrain themselves for a single night. Still...

Where was he? I listened hard but couldn't hear anyone in the house. A note lay on the nightstand.

Gone to talk to the Alpha Council. Iris is outside keeping an eye on the place. Don't shoot her.

-Raul

A smile pulled at my lips. "Perfect!"

I needed to know more about this guy, and since he wasn't forthcoming with answers... I leaned over and opened the nightstand drawer. Careful not to disturb things too much, I perused the contents. A box of .40 caliber bullets sat next to a paper tablet. Beside those lay a large hunting knife that smelled of silver—metallic and harsh to the point of hurting my nose a bit. Behind it all sat an unopened box of condoms, size large.

"Ew."

After flipping through the tablet, I got up and moved on to the dresser. Nothing unusual there either, not even in the underwear drawer, unless I counted how organized everything was. The guy liked things even more orderly than I did. His clothes were not only neatly folded, but arranged by color. I tried to focus on that instead of how he was a boxer-brief kind of man and how good those would look hugging his nasty bits. Not that he wore them, as he proclaimed.

Unable to get the image out of my mind, I moved on to the walk-in closet. The thing was big enough it had a window and a bench seat in it. Evergreen treetops stretched as far as I could see beyond the framed windowpanes.

"Hell of a view for a closet," I grumbled. A secondary closet, I reminded myself, recalling him coming through the guest bathroom to access the closet there. The man liked his designer clothes. I started toward the guest bathroom. Most of my life I'd spent shopping at second-hand stores.

The framed art canvas over the bed made me stop. Earthy colors in rich, deep hues splashed across a foreign landscape of mountains with three moons in a purple-blue sky. It was gorgeous—if a little strange. I pulled it away from the wall, checked behind it and around the edges. Nothing. My determination to find something to substantiate my suspicions about Raul being involved in the bitings grew.

I moved on to the next room and the next. The house was big for just one man, easily over two thousand square feet. He had a home gym bigger than my apartment in college. I spent several minutes searching the thirty-foot-long wall of mirrors for secret panels. Part of me felt like I should have been able to feel air movement around a secret panel, smell it, or something cool and supernatural like that. But I was too new at this werewolf stuff, and if I used a bit of power, I was afraid it would spiral out of control.

The expensive exercise equipment revealed nothing unusual—aside from Raul's meticulous upkeep of them. Chrome parts shone, and I could tell it was from cleaning, not lack of use. I checked around several large football-related art prints on the walls. They were printed on glass, modern, and expensive looking. Being a big football fan myself, I enjoyed the ambiance of the room, but that wasn't what made me look closer at the prints. One was a photo of Raul in a college uniform, arm cocked back in the midst of a throw. Another was of an entire team wearing the same uniform, a third and fourth of other young men playing. I recognized two of the men, a considerably more clean-shaven Officer Gilmerson hustling down the field, and a teenage Leif reaching up for a football flying at him.

If the two were old football buddies, why had Gilmerson wanted me to see Raul with Karman and get the wrong impression? Because I was sure that was why he had taken me out there. Maybe he didn't want Raul and I to work well together. But again, why? It was something, but it wasn't the something I was looking for. I kept searching. All throughout the house I came across canvas prints of alien landscapes of different types. Some were frozen mountains with tall people who had whitish-blue skin, others were scorched planes with tall, thin, dark-skinned people with pointed ears, and yet others portrayed muscular, bearded people.

At first, I thought all the wall art was just a sign of Raul being a sci-fi or fantasy buff. But then I started to notice similarities, like the knot work around the frames, the Norse tattoos on many of the alien people, the Viking swords and axes. Finally, I opened a door into a room with a massive desk of wrought iron and glass. Glass shelves lined the walls to either side of the current painting drawing my attention. The shelves held a variety of things, from books, to wolf carvings, to knives. His office.

"Jackpot," I whispered as I stepped inside.

Sandwiched between two pieces of glass making up the desktop lay an art print of nine worlds lined up like a cross. Each was a different color, as if they had different atmospheres. Some had rings. The names of each were printed beside them on the celestial background, Asgard, Niflheimr, Muspelheimr, Midgard, Jötunheimr, Vanaheimr, Álfheimr, Svartálfheimr, Helheimr. The nine worlds of the Norse. I knew them from Ancient

Religions class in college. Now the paintings throughout the house made sense.

Above the bookshelves on one wall hung a huge, framed map of Hemlock Hollow. It included the pack territories beyond the public part of town. On the opposite wall hung a world map riddled with green and red pins. Almost every country had at least one red pin in it, while only Iceland, Montana, Idaho, Wyoming, and Canada had green pins. Maybe they were places he had gone and wanted to go. It tugged at my own desire to travel. For all I knew, it could be places he wanted to conquer.

Focusing on that, I stepped behind the desk and opened a drawer, careful to use the sleeve of Raul's sweatshirt so I didn't leave my scent behind. A notepad with the forestry logo lay tucked in the upper right-hand corner. A few pencils, one ink pen, and a container of push pins all sat in their little cubbies, nice and neat. This guy took tidy to a whole new level. I checked the other drawers. In the last one, I found a tablet. I took it out and turned it on. Once it was up, it asked for a password.

"Damn."

I tried the name of his Porsche, and the South Fork Pack. Denied. Knowing I likely only had one shot left, I switched tactics and finally got in with a combination of his football number, pack name, and birth date. I smiled, pleased to put to use the hacking skills I'd learned in the foster system. I snooped through everything in the tablet, from case files to his internet history. Despite a suspicious lack of porn for a single guy, I found nothing useful. He emailed a cousin in Iceland a lot, a few of his football buddies—Gilmerson included—and work from time to time. Leif Jörgensson's name came up a lot. They seemed to be good friends. Nothing revealing lay in any of it, though. His search history on Stockholm Syndrome piqued my interest.

"Why the hell would you be researching that?" I murmured.

Prickling sensations crawled up my spine. I erased my tracks, shut the tablet down, and carefully placed it back exactly where I'd found it. When I sat it down, the drawer bottom made an odd sound—as if it wasn't quite solid. I removed everything from the drawer and felt around the edges of the bottom. A chipped corner allowed me to slip a fingernail under it. The entire bottom lifted with ease. Beneath it lay a leather journal with an antique-style map of the world embossed into the cover. Using the sleeves of his sweatshirt again, I carefully picked the journal up and set it on the desktop. Leather had a way of absorbing oils, and with it, smells. So I wasn't about to take any chances.

A lot of the first forty pages or so were about the investigation: suspects, motives, profiles, witness testimonies. Halfway through I came across something that snagged my attention.

To whom it may concern,

Should I meet an early death, or disappear like Lísandra, it needs to be known I was blackmailed into biting in Sonya Michaelson by Bain Robertson. He promised to banish my sister from the Draupnir pack if I bit in Sonya. He made it clear not only was my sister in mortal danger from him, but she would be neck-deep in the controversy of bitings and he would fabricate evidence marking her as the main suspect if I didn't do this.

I didn't want to hurt Sonya or force this life on her. I would have asked her and made it her choice if Bain had given me time. For what it's worth, I believe she would have said yes. I was going to Hemlock Hollow to ask the council's permission, but at that point, Bain made it impossible for me to wait.

I have nothing but my word against Bain's. Whoever is reading this, if I'm dead or gone, please protect my sister and Sonya Michaelson from him.

Raul Anderson

"Sister." That's right. I'd forgotten he mentioned having a sister. Not that I had asked. And blackmail. Considering Bain's cold, calculating manner, it wouldn't surprise me. "That son of a bitch."

Bain was worse than I thought. I wasn't sure why I believed Raul's journal entry, but I did. Cop instinct again, I guess.

A howl quieted by distance and obstacles of walls and glass made me look up. Angry yips and growls followed it. They sounded far off, but not far enough. Anger rose in me, part territorial, part something else. I put the journal back, replaced the drawer bottom and all the contents of the drawer, then closed it. Careful to make sure everything was as I had found it, I looked the room over before stepping out.

Barely audible growls drew me to the massive windows overlooking the hollow with the bridge spanning it. Dusk made it hard to see anything beyond silhouettes of trees and rocks. The shape of three wolves running across a distant hill caught my eye. Distant, but still on Raul's property. A pink and dark blue sky outlined them for a second as they worked their way in the direction of the bridge. The hair on the back of my neck tried to rise, not in an eerie way, but a pissed one.

It could be coincidence there were three, probably was. Admitting that didn't cool my rage any. I started for the door. One way or another, I had to make sure. If they were my attackers, I couldn't let this opportunity slip by. Not even if it was a trap. Who else would be trespassing on Raul's property? I'd seen the guy fight. Bringing down his wrath didn't seem like a smart idea.

On my way out, I stopped in the bedroom and retrieved my gun off the nightstand where Raul had put it for me. A neatly folded pile of my clothes lay beneath it. From the pile, I only took the time to put on a pair of cut-off jean shorts. I racked a round into the chamber of my gun before tucking it and my concealed carry holster into the back of my waistband. As I approached the front door, I heard a heartbeat growing closer to it from the other side. I opened it with claws and fangs extended.

Iris the librarian stood on the threshold, hand raised as if going for the doorknob. One blue braid of hair hung over one shoulder and one red braid hung over her other. In a black half-shirt with a pair of lips on it dripping blood, and a pair of shorts, she looked like a comic book geek's wet dream. Maybe not, considering her arms and legs were more muscular than some guys I knew and covered in Norse knot work tattoos. But the best guys, guys who were confident enough to like a strong woman, were into that.

"Are you okay? I heard the slide of a gun rack," she said.

"Peachy. Is my book overdue?"

She laughed. "Naw, I'd be knocking down the door if that were the case. Raul had to go talk to the council. He didn't want to leave you alone, so I've been hanging out."

That made me smile. "How creeper like," I teased.

She shrugged. "Yeah, a little."

As I took a step outside, she moved out of the way. I started around the side of the house and she kept pace with me.

"I saw someone trespassing," I said.

"I heard them too, that's why I was coming toward the house. Do you think they're the three who attacked you?"

"Don't know. But I'm going to find out."

"Sweet. Let's kick their asses." Her cheerful tone made me smile wider.

"Let's."

"What direction were they going?" she whispered.

"Toward the bridge," I answered in a low voice.

"Good. They'll be upwind of us," she said with a sly smile. "I do love having the element of surprise."

"Hell yeah," I agreed.

She started to strip, and before I could protest, the air pressure built with her preparation to shift. No sooner had her clothes hit the flagstones, she was a wolf—a blond one with streaks of red and blue through her hair around her head. The streaks made me smile. Taking my time, I stripped my clothes off and piled them neatly beside hers, tucking my gun inside the pile. Dread filled me. I did not want to do this, did not want to have to fight my instincts for control in front of her. But to refuse would only show my fear, and I wanted that even less. My body temperature rose as the shift came over me. The moment my black paws touched the ground, we set out again.

The instinct to give chase, to hunt them down and tear into them, reared its ugly head just like I had feared it would. I fought against it to keep my pace slow. It was as hard as a fifty-yard shot with a handgun.

Once we rounded the front of the house, I saw the wolves in the distance, nearly at the bridge, maybe two hundred yards away. I worked my way to the tree line along the hollow, and Iris followed. As much as I wanted my gun, running as a wolf was easier and safer. Most importantly, I would need a close-up look to determine if it was them. Fast as we healed, the wounds I had inflicted would still leave a mark at this point. Though the three wolves were some distance away and moving in and out of shadows, none appeared to limp. Doubt set in, but curiosity kept me moving. At least, I tried to tell myself it was curiosity and not the burning need to hunt.

Iris and I stalked along the trees, keeping the three wolves in sight. Her steps were nearly silent, and she moved with an effortless grace that made me think she'd done this before—a lot. Then again, she'd said she'd been a *verndari*, so that made sense. Her stealth was impressive enough to make me think she'd had training of some kind as well. Not one twig snapped beneath her paws. Me, I had trouble not tripping over my own paws. We hung back far enough that they wouldn't hear or see us.

A slight breeze blew their scents to me. The musky scent of wolves mingled with the telltale spice of *varúlfur*. Beyond that, I couldn't tell if they were my attackers. It had been raining too hard that night, and my sense of smell had been shot.

As we drew closer to the bridge, I realized two people stood on it, near the center. They were so far away it was hard to tell who they were. And I wasn't sure, but I thought they might be naked. The sun setting behind them didn't exactly help either. They stood beneath the stone arch over the middle of the bridge that looked like something out of an old sci-fi movie. The three wolves shifted to human form as they joined them. One of the five stood with arms held to the sky.

Keeping a few trees between us and the bridge, Iris and I crept closer. I focused my hearing, letting all my other senses fall away. My eyes slid closed. A man chanted in Icelandic. The deep, gravelly voice was unmistakable—Bain. A female voice joined in. I had no idea what they were saying, but it had a sing-songy ring to it that made me think of a prayer or a hymn. It reminded me of the Sunday school one of my foster parents had forced me to attend. They had hoped it would scare the devil out of me. If only they could see me now.

The chanting changed, became more intense. My attention snapped back to it. The three figures who had been wolves seconds before danced around the chanting pair, now in human form. Hands brushed across Bain and the woman. The touches started out reverent, adoring, but quickly changed to lingering and groping. The figures all moved together, bending around and over one another. I couldn't see who was doing what, and I didn't want to.

A quiet sound that I took as a wolf's version of disgust came from Iris. She and I shared a look and moved back deeper into the trees. The chanting from the bridge behind us turned to moans and cries of pleasure. I dialed my hearing way, way back, and focused on the ground beneath my feet. We put the orgy at our backs and started for Raul's house. My paws did not want to carry me away from what my wolf side had been anticipating as a fight. I had to force each step, stumbling a few times because of it. When Iris sped her pace up, I had to grit my fangs and fight my instincts to lengthen my stride and stay beside her. The feeling of being on the edge of control pissed me off to no end.

The growing shadows of the forest concealed us, but I had a feeling we didn't need to hide. The group on the bridge was too busy to care about a few voyeurs. A shudder moved through me. The idea of Bain, a potential mass murderer, having an orgy with anyone just did not sit well with me. Thinking about it only strengthened my instinct to fight, so I tried to focus on the forest around me instead.

When Raul's house came into view, I breathed a sigh of relief. We shifted back to human form and grabbed our clothes. The instincts pulling at me eased, and I breathed a sigh of relief.

"Apparently, not everyone finds Bain as repulsive as I do," I said.

Iris bared her teeth. "He's alpha. Some find the power alone attractive."

"Disgusting."

"Seconded, sister."

Not wanting to be enclosed at the moment, I went for the back deck. Iris followed, and I was glad for the company. We sat down on the plush chairs beneath the covered patio. I pulled Raul's sweatshirt on along with my jean shorts. Raul's spicy, pine scent wrapped around me, easing my anxiety and helping me breathe easier. It should have done the opposite, but right now I'd take comfort any way it came. Besides, he wasn't who I had thought he was. The journal made that even more clear.

"Who were the rest of those people?" I asked as we sat down on the patio furniture.

"Morene, the stand-in female alpha, Dustin, Lars, and Ada. You didn't recognize any of your attackers among them?"

I shook my head. "Too hard to tell. But I can't see why my attackers would trespass on Raul's property and make enough noise for me to catch them, just to go to an orgy." I cringed. "That's disgusting. I hope orgies aren't a werewolf thing. And do they usually like an audience for them?"

Iris laughed. "Not a werewolf thing, no worries. What we saw was more than that anyway. It was a ritual."

Prickles of dread worked their way up my arms. "What kind of ritual?"

"Not sure. Sexual rituals can be for fertility, honoring Frigg, or for raising energy. Considering those alphas aren't a mated pair, and there were other participants, I would have to go with raising energy."

"Why would they want to raise energy? And why on that bridge?"

Iris leaned forward as if I'd said something interesting. "The bridge is built over a place of great power, and Bain was one of the biggest lobbyists for building it. Said it was to honor the memory of his brother." Her words degraded into an unintelligible growl, but they started off sounding like a curse.

The dread working through me spread. "Either they didn't care if they were seen, or it was worth the risk to do the ritual there. Both maybe?"

She shook her head. "The alphas wouldn't want to be seen. One, they aren't a mated pair. Two, raising power like that can be construed as threatening toward the other alphas. Three, an orgy could be seen as a tribute to the God of Chaos, Loki."

"Shit," I murmured.

"Triple shit," she agreed.

"One of those three who passed by wanted me to see. One had howled. The others had snapped at them as if pissed about it."

"Or maybe they were just horny and in a hurry."

"Maybe." But I wasn't convinced. My gut told me I was right. Maybe one of them had sights on being Raul's mate and wanted to discourage me from the same. He had made it publicly clear he was interested in me for the slot. Or maybe someone in the pack wanted to expose Bain.

"You hungry? Raul has a stocked fridge, and I could use something to eat," I said.

Iris brightened. "Sure. I could eat."

I opened the door to the house and we both paused. While I listened for any intruders, she sniffed the air. A relieved breath eased out of me when I didn't hear anything. We walked inside, and I closed and locked the door behind us. I grabbed the eggs and bacon from the fridge and got to work. I had a lot of heavy thinking to do, and I needed food to accomplish that.

My explorations of Raul's house hadn't uncovered what I'd expected. The opposite, in fact. I was more confused about him than ever. But one thing was becoming clear: he might not be the complete asshole I'd thought he was. The morning had left me with more questions than answers. And when Raul came back, I wouldn't be armed with the shield of hatred I'd been clinging so tightly to.

CHAPTER FOURTEEN

RAUL

By the time my wheels touched my driveway again, it was dark. After the alpha meeting, I'd had to stop by the PD and tell the chief about the attack. Anger had boiled beneath his trademark Balderson calm, evident in his eyes and the burn of his power. But he'd been surprisingly pleased about how I'd helped Elexis heal. In fact, he seemed downright chipper, almost as if he had hopes of the two of us hitting it off. I wasn't about to break it to him that those hopes were not only likely to be dashed but likely burned to ash in the fires of Muspelheimr.

The sight of Iris's blue Yamaha YZF-R1 motorcycle in my driveway let me breathe a bit easier. When I clicked the garage door opener, Iris emerged from the front door. She waved goodbye before I pulled inside. I waved back. The garage was only halfway closed before I had the Porsche shut off, leaped from the car, and was almost to the door to the mudroom. Knowing Iris had been here was comforting, but I needed to see Elexis to make sure she was safe.

A partner's sense of responsibility, that was all.

I burst into the house and called out, "Elexis?"

The beat of her heart—steady and relaxed—drew me to the kitchen. She stood at the stove, the long sleeves of my sweatshirt pushed up to her elbows, blowing on a spoonful of something. Those full, pink lips, pursed into an O, made my blood rush south so fast it left me dizzy. She'd twisted and pulled her blue-streaked black hair up into a clip that made a fan of it standing up like a crown. It left her long, beautiful neck bare. I wanted to kiss and lick all her exposed skin.

The relief at seeing her safe was so powerful, I'd strode into the kitchen before I realized what I was doing. My instincts screamed at me to take her in my arms, hold her tight, make sure she was solid and in one piece. But that was ridiculous. Just because she'd let me hold her last night didn't mean she'd want me to now. Then there was the fact she was a badass fighter, and a cop. She could take care of herself. All that only made the desire that much stronger.

I stopped, hands gripping the counter to keep from touching her. She sat the spoon down and gave me a curious look.

"What's up? Why do you look panicked? Did something happen?" she asked.

"No, I uh...was just...worried." Shit. I hadn't wanted to say that.

She blushed, almost making my awkwardness worth it. "Makes two of us. You're late as hell. So I started cooking." Her easy, flippant tone drained the last of my tension away. "I hope you like spaghetti. But then, why wouldn't you? It was in your cupboard," she rambled on, seemingly unable to stop herself.

It was cute. Almost as cute as her in my sweatshirt. The blush in her cheeks turned a deeper red. I took pity on her. "I love it, thanks. And sorry I'm late. I had to stop by the station."

Needing something to keep my hands busy, I grabbed the garlic and butter from the fridge and started working on garlic bread. "How are your wounds?"

"Healed," she said.

"Completely?" I couldn't keep the shock from my tone.

She lifted my sweatshirt enough to expose her side where the wound had been. All that remained were red marks on her tight skin. I wanted to brush my fingers across all her bare flesh, but she dropped the sweatshirt before I could move and embarrass myself.

"Yep. Why, aren't they supposed to be?"

"Usually not. Only *verndari* and—"

"Alphas heal that fast," she finished for me.

"You sound like you're not happy about being so powerful," I pointed out.

She sighed as she pulled the sourdough bread from the bread box. "It isn't that. It's just what you said about the packs wanting me to join them, and your parents' invitation. I've always wanted to belong somewhere, but following isn't my thing."

"Then lead. You could be an alpha of your own pack somewhere." I kept my tone casual, despite the pedal of dread that dropped on me and slammed adrenalin into my veins. There was one pack in town that needed a female alpha. I realized I did not want her to be their alpha any more than I wanted my own sister to be. Imagining Elexis's fearlessness, straightforward no-bullshit personality being smothered by Bain made my fangs ache.

She began searching through the drawers. I pulled the knife drawer open and handed her the bread knife. I had to concentrate hard on my patience while I waited for her to answer. It had never been a strong point of mine.

"Sure, maybe, but not here. The only choice in town isn't a choice at all." She shuddered.

I wanted to kiss her. Odin, what was wrong with me? This woman couldn't stand me. She thought I was an asshole. But she didn't know the truth. Maybe it was time I told her.

"I saw something disturbing today," she said before I could speak.

I froze. She had woken up in my room. That statement could mean a lot of things. "Oh?" I asked noncommittally.

"Three wolves cut across the property to get to the bridge. Iris and I followed to see if they were the ones who attacked me."

"Were they?" I tried to keep the desperation from my tone and only half succeeded. A protective instinct reared up in me again, taking me by surprise.

"It was too hard to tell, since it had been dark and rainy that night. But seeing the trespassers wasn't the weird part."

She started stirring the spaghetti sauce again, and I got the distinct feeling it was so she wouldn't have to look at me.

"What was?" I pressed.

"They were doing some kind of ritual on the bridge, the three of them and the Draupnir alphas. They were chanting in Icelandic. Iris said it was something about opening the way. She heard something about the nine worlds and a key."

I shrugged and started slicing the bread. "Could be any number of rituals to honor the gods. From the sound of it, probably Heimdallr, since he guards the gateway across the real *Bifrost* into Asgard."

"Do people normally have orgies to honor Heimdallr?" Elexis asked.

I brought the knife down right across my finger. Thankfully, *varúlfur* skin of someone my age is too tough for something like that to cut. "What? No, Gods no. Are you sure that's what they were doing?"

"Unequivocally," she said through a grimace.

"And both alphas were participating?"

"Yep. And to think that asshole hit on me." She shuddered. "Oh... wait..." The revelation in her tone pulled me out of the undertow of rage threatening to drag me under.

The handle of the knife I held creaked in my grasp as the wood came close to cracking. I put it down carefully, deliberately. Elexis had pulled one side of her bottom lip between her teeth, and her dark brows were scrunched beneath her blue-streaked bangs.

"I know that look. What did you just work out?" I asked.

"When the three wolves cut across your land, one of them made a noise, almost like they wanted me to hear. I got the feeling that wolf wanted me to see the ritual, and I think it was so it would turn me off Bain."

"And did it work?" I asked before my brain could catch up to my mouth.

Shit, too eager. I shouldn't care. But the memory of her in my arms last night made me care, a lot. And it helped curb my anger and made me stop thinking about one of the many elephants in the room.

Elexis scoffed. "I did not need to see that to turn me off of him."

My mind reeled with what she had said, all of it, not just the part about not wanting Bain. I gripped the marble countertop as I stared down at the bread. I had to get some air. "We need parsley. I have some in the cellar. I'll be right back," I said, forcing a cheerful tone.

I started for the hallway.

"Hey, Raul," Elexis called after me.

Pasting on a half-smile, I looked back at her. Worry filled her eyes.

"You okay?" she asked.

I let out the shudder that had been working at me. "Yeah, just grossed out."

Her upper lip curled away from her teeth, and she nodded. "Yeah, I get that. It took me several hours and the rest of the bottle of wine in the fridge to wipe my mind clean. Speaking of which, can you grab another bottle while you're down there?"

The depth of my disturbance was so fathomless, I had to force a smile. "You got it."

I should have been thrilled she was so relaxed and friendly. This side of her tugged at something deep in me. But at the moment, those thoughts were buried beneath an ocean of fear and disgust. No matter what the Draupnir alphas were up to, the fact they were having sex—even if it was group sex—killed the hope for my sister that had sprouted in me.

CHAPTER FIFTEEN

RAUL

The flow of questions from Elexis didn't stop the entire way to Didrik and Lísandra's old house. I didn't have answers for most of them, which was why I had agreed to take her. As *lögreglu*, we didn't need permission to go onto the property. I had my reasons for not going there until now. What answers I did give her were half-hearted. My thoughts were occupied with my sister's safety. She hadn't answered my calls last night.

Thankfully, Didrik and Lísandra's place lay on the edge of Draupnir property, so I was able to drive around the back side through neutral territory to get to it. Pulling up the pine-tree-lined drive brought back so many memories of post-football barbecues and team get-togethers, it felt like a sucker punch to my gut.

"Raul, you okay?"

The concern in Elexis's voice reached me through my haze of worry. Her attitude toward me had altered since yesterday. She was softer now, almost kind. We hadn't shared a bed again last night—no need, she was healed. That hadn't stopped me from half-teasingly offering. But she had slept on the couch, which was progress from the patio furniture.

"Yeah, fine," I said.

The sight of the huge A-frame mansion stabbed me like an arrow. The half-dozen windows of the second story and huge picture windows of the first yawned like the dark, vacant eyes of a corpse.

"I'm sorry. I shouldn't have asked you to bring me here. If this is too hard for you—"

"I'm fine," I cut her off, tone far harsher than I meant for it to be.

"Good, because we have to do this for the investigation. And if you can't stomach that..." The last part was far gentler than the first, as if she couldn't keep up her hard front for long.

"I said I'm fine."

She fell quiet for the first time all morning. I opened my mouth to apologize but got distracted by the state of the landscaping. The tiered beds flanking the steps to either side of the front porch were literally overflowing with flowers of every color. Not so much as a single weed poked up through the fresh mulch around the base of the plants. The shake siding on the house looked freshly stained and treated. Seeing it like this hit me almost harder than seeing it decrepit and run down would have. It was like Didrik and Lísandra were still here.

"Wow, looks like someone has been taking care of the place," Elexis said.

I stopped the Cherokee at the steps. "The *útrýmt*—outcasts. They must be sneaking back to do it." Because I knew for certain Bain wasn't doing it.

"According to what I read, that's against pack law. Isn't it?"

"Yes," I said before getting out.

She joined me on the front steps. "That's very brave of them. I think I'd like these outcasts."

I gave her a long look—mostly because I couldn't look away. She returned it. Something burned in her eyes I couldn't quite name. Her cop mask was too good. Her power had a comforting, nurturing feel to it, though. "You would. Are you sure it doesn't bother your cop side that they're breaking the law?"

She shook her head. "State and federal laws are one thing. I understand those and agree with them for the most part. But this pack law, some of it, I just can't wrap my head around or agree with. Does that bother you, or offend the gods or something?" The last part almost had a vulnerable sound to it, as if she genuinely cared about the answer.

I nearly smiled. "Not at all. In my experience, I've found questioning authority when you don't agree with it to be a good thing, and so do our gods."

Her eyes widened in an impressed look.

We walked side by side up the steps. I kept my pace slow to stay beside her, and because each step was hard as hell to take. Memories assaulted me with each one: celebratory team parties hosted here, playing catch with my teammates on this huge porch, listening to Coach and Lísandra laugh and joke. I could hear it, see it, and smell it as though it were happening right now. The memories stung like the slap of a barbed whip. I cleared my mind forcibly, walled off my emotions, and focused on the task, because Elexis was right. We had to do this.

"So this is still Draupnir land, but Bain hasn't taken it over. Why?" she asked.

"That's a bit of a mystery, but I suspect it's because it backs up to neutral territory, and that would make him vulnerable. And who knows, maybe the guy has one remorseful bone somewhere in his body." Hatred and doubt darkened my tone.

"Seems unlikely," Elexis said as we reached the door.

"Highly," I agreed.

Elexis eyed the fancy, bronze-looking keypad below the old-fashioned pull handle doorknob. I punched the date of Hemlock Hollow's last football state championship in, and the lock disengaged. I blew out a breath.

"I wasn't sure that would still be it," I murmured more to myself.

The air of the threshold felt thick as sand, painfully difficult to cross. The perfectly preserved monument I stepped into only made it worse. Cases filled with trophies and team photos lined the walls of the huge foyer. Past that, a wide staircase with a log banister led up to a balcony overlooking the open floor of the great room with its four L-shaped couches. A hallway led off to the left and right at the top of the stairs, each to opposite wings of the massive lodge. Sheets covered the furniture in the great room.

"Wow, this lodge is amazing," Elexis whispered. "I mean, damn, cabin just doesn't seem like an adequate term." She walked into the great room and did a slow spin, wide eyes taking it all in. "I can't believe Bain hasn't moved into it."

"He has good reason to worry about putting his back to neutral land," I said with a bit of growl in my tone.

Elexis turned to me, the wonder on her face giving way to guilt. "I'm sorry. I know this must be hard for you. I didn't mean that the way it sounded."

Where was the snarky woman who jumped at the chance to rile me up? She didn't seem like the type of woman to be swayed by one night of spooning.

"I know. It's just that you're right. Bain's house is half this size, without even enough room for his *verndari*, yet he hasn't moved in here. Despite the risks, it is odd. He could surround himself by pack here. It would balance out the danger," I said.

She made a humming noise low in her throat. "Curious."

She moved deeper into the house. I let her lead the way. Her cop instincts were far more reliable than any help I could give her at the moment. I followed as she started up the stairs. Without hesitation, she took a right and went down the hall toward the alpha's wing of the house. How she knew without knowing their scent, I had no idea. But her sure steps made it clear she held no doubt. Even the natural born *varúlfur* I knew who were cops didn't have her impressive instincts. She navigated the maze of hallways easily and went straight to Didrik and Lísandra's bedroom.

Sheets covered the dresser, nightstands, chaise, and the bed—which looked eerily skeletal without a mattress or blankets. Elexis carefully lifted the sheet off the dresser without even disturbing the framed photos standing underneath. Her fingers traced over the picture frames.

"They look so in love." Her voice had an almost forlorn tone to it.

My feet carried me to her, drawn by something I couldn't control. Each of the pictures was like a small sliver driving into me—Didrik and Lísandra smiling, embracing, laughing, hiking, and swimming. And my favorite, the one where he held her in his arms and she touched that necklace he had given her on her birthday while looking up at him. "They were, very much so," I whispered over her shoulder.

A shiver ran through her, and she leaned back toward me slightly. It took me by surprise, so much that I froze. Her hair smelled amazing, like subtle lavender and mint. I wanted to bury my head in the silky black locks. A small laugh came from her, a sexy, low sound that I didn't think she intended to sound that way.

"Careful, Raul, you sound like a romantic." Her soft voice stirred me.

"I am," I admitted.

How this woman could frustrate and attract me so much at the same time, I had no idea. She turned to face me. The polite thing to do would have been to step back, but I couldn't. Now I knew what drew moths to fire. The rare softness in her eyes only made me want her more. Her power flowed around me, warm and welcoming.

"You seriously make me question my intuition," she said in a breathy voice that made blood rush to my groin.

I put a hand on the dresser to either side of her—mostly to force me to keep them to myself.

"Why is that?" I asked, my own voice having dropped an octave.

She cocked her head to the side a bit. "Because my first impression of you was wrong in so many ways." The look she gave me was serious, like I was a mystery she couldn't figure out.

Only a foot of space separated us, and it was too much. I leaned a little closer. Damn, she smelled good enough to eat. "Most people get the wrong impression of me at first," I said.

She leaned so close our chests almost touched. I ached to pull her against me, to feel the soft curves of her body molding to mine like they had last night. Only this time, I didn't just want to be up against those curves, I wanted to be inside them. It wasn't just her curves, or the way her dark hair made her blue eyes stand out, or her feisty spirit. Something deep inside drew me on a visceral, instinctual level. Her pink tongue darted out and moved slowly across her full lips, making them glisten. It was almost too much.

"Maybe because you don't let them see the real you. Or..." She leaned closer, gaze on my lips. She put a hand on my chest. It scorched through my brown silk shirt, branding me. "Maybe it's because you don't tell them everything." She ducked under my arm and stepped away.

The desire that had been building inside crashed like a wave against a dam. She cast a reprimanding look over her shoulder as she walked away. I clamped my teeth against a reply. I had no ground to stand on. She was right. Before I could decide whether or not to tell her about Sonya, she had left the room. I drew the sheet back over the dresser and followed her.

Elexis took us to Didrik's study. I'd only ever seen it from the doorway. I could see Didrik sitting behind the big desk going over a playbook like it was yesterday. Once again, crossing that threshold was like walking through sand—slow and difficult. Framed prints of some of pro football's greatest coaches and players dotted the walls between shelves lined with playbooks and books on everything from the game to leadership. I perused the shelves, lost in memory as Elexis explored the room. She didn't go straight to Didrik's desk like I expected. Instead, she went to the window overlooking the acres and acres of green space behind the house. For a while, I watched her out of the corner of my eye.

Partly, I did it because she was hard not to watch, with that smoking combination of soft curves and hard muscle. But another part of me watched out of a protective feeling for Didrik's memory. The gentleness with which she handled the few things she touched quickly made it clear I had nothing to worry about.

Letting her do her thing, I lost myself in the memories the trophies stirred up. A lot of them were from the years Didrik had coached my team. It took me a minute to realize Elexis stood staring at the huge map of Iceland on Didrik's north wall. Green dots covered where each pack was located, blue indicated the founding packs. She started to feel around the edges of the framed canvas.

"What are you doing?" I asked.

"This is the only thing in the room that isn't football related."

"It's a map of where the current and founding packs of Iceland are located." I pointed to one of the green dots. "Green is for current packs. Blue is for where the founding packs of Hemlock Hollow originated."

She only made a humming noise in response. "Aha!" Something near her finger clicked. Electronics hummed as the entire canvas slid upward and disappeared into the ceiling. In a recessed area in the wall behind it was a map of the US with similar dots. On a ledge bellow the map sat several journals.

"Holy shit," I said through a breath. "How the hell did you find that?"

She indicated herself with a flourish of her hands. "Detective."

Smiling, I crossed the room to join her. "Well you have mad skills. I never even knew that was there."

She wiggled a brow at me as she picked up one of the books. I reached over her shoulder to pick up another. She didn't move away, not even when my chest touched her back. The heat of her body distracted me until I looked at the book in my hand. The black cover had nothing on it. I opened it and found Didrik's handwriting on the first page.

"Didrik, you clever dog," I murmured.

I lost myself in reading, eventually wandering over to sit at the desk. For the most part, Didrik wrote about pack business: births, mate bondings, finances, *verndari* assignments. After a while, Elexis wandered over and sat on the edge of the desk. I looked up to find her engrossed in a large twelve-by-twelve drawing pad.

"This is odd," she said as she turned it around and placed it before me.

It was a concept drawing of the bridge over the hollow. Didrik's signature was scrawled on the bottom corner of the page. I didn't quite follow. "Why is this strange?"

"Because the bridge was redesigned after Didrik was killed."

"Yeah, but Bain claims he redesigned it to honor Didrik. Maybe he knew about the drawings."

Elexis's eyes narrowed. "Then why were they hidden in a secret compartment? Along with journals that should have been turned over to the library?"

I picked up the drawing pad. "Good point. Anything in there besides drawings?"

"No, but check this out." She flipped to another page. Three people stood on the bridge of this drawing. One had one arm held to the sky, the other extended to grasp the hand of the second figure. Lightning ran in a jagged line from the clouds above to the raised hand of the first figure. The second figure had their free hand extended toward a third who stood under an archway on the bridge. Lightning erupted from the hand of the second figure and shot to the chest of the third. Behind the third figure in the archway lay a scene of stars and a ringed planet.

Chills raced across me. "What the hells?" I stood.

"Glad I'm not the only one who thought that was weird," Elexis said.

Rising at almost the same time, we went back to the hidden alcove. We poured over the other books shelved there.

After a few minutes, Elexis piped up, "Whoa, check this out."

I stepped in to look over her shoulder. The writing was small. I had to lean so close my head hung over her. Her heart rate sped up. The words on the page distracted me from her.

Now that I know what the bridge is capable of with the right combination of varúlfur, *it can never be redesigned. I don't even dare write about it here. Bain's persistent questions about how to redesign it makes me fear that he knows its function as well. And I fear deep down in my bones as to what my calculating brother would do with such a power.*

I sucked in a sharp breath. "That son of a bitch."

"Careful, they have the same mother, and from what I hear, she was a good lady," Elexis said in a half-teasing tone. "What do you think it means?"

"I think it means Bain killed Didrik over the bridge—not because he wanted to be alpha—then used his death as an excuse to redesign it."

"I agree, especially considering the ritual I saw."

A growl added bite to my words, "But we still don't know what it means or what the bridge does."

Elexis sighed. "And this is all circumstantial evidence."

I spun away, roaring in frustration. "Damn it!"

Rage clouded my vision. Soft steps touched the carpet behind me. Power brushed my skin like a soft summer breeze. It raised the hair on my arms, and that wasn't all it raised. It pulled at me, making me want to turn around, step deeper into it. I'd turned before I'd even realized I'd moved. Elexis strode toward me in that confident, smoking-hot way of hers. Something in her eyes had changed. It took her crossing the entire ten feet separating us for me to realize what it was. Those impossibly dark blue eyes looked at me differently now. The scorn and judgment were gone. In their place was a heat that rivaled her massive power. Along with it, concern.

"Easy. Even though we can't use this in a court of law, it's a new lead, which may take us to something we can use," she said.

She stopped in front of me, hand coming to rest on my right arm. It scorched me all the way down to my groin. I dragged my focus back to the task at hand. "I know, thanks."

She gave me a tight smile and handed me the book. "You should hold onto this."

I nodded and tucked it under my arm. She turned back to the alcove and pressed the hidden mechanism that lowered the framed map. Once it settled into place, I took a deep breath.

"You deserve an explanation."

She turned back to me with a heavily guarded expression. When she didn't respond, I went on. "My sister, Morene, was a member of the Draupnir pack when Bain killed Didrik and took over. She insisted on staying, to protect the others who stayed and to try and find a way to bring Bain down."

Elexis sat on the edge of the desk, gaze fixed on me. I paced the room, brushing my fingers over trophies and mementos on the shelves. I knew she considered her a person of interest in the investigation but hadn't been able to nail her down for questioning yet. Not from lack of trying.

"I wanted her to leave the pack, but she wouldn't. Bain wants a powerful mate, one who will attract members to the pack. He approached me, told me he heard of a woman bearing the mark of the seeker. He said if I bit her in, he'd kick my sister out of the pack—which would have made her safe from him." I had to take a breath to keep my fangs retracted. I turned to see her face, to gauge her reaction. That damn cop mask revealed nothing. "I was desperate. I didn't want him to choose my sister as his mate."

The blankness of her expression drove me crazy. I resumed pacing. "I found Sonya, got to know her. I believed she would say yes. I was working up to asking her when Bain got impatient, forced my hand." My hitched breathing forced me to stop and pull my shit together. Gods I wished Elexis would say something to stop me. But she didn't, so I went on. "I didn't want to do it without asking her, and it will always be the biggest regret of my life. I tried to make it right by offering her a place at my side instead, but that isn't the kind of thing you can make right."

I stopped pacing to stand near the edge of the desk where she sat. I searched her expression for understanding, condemnation, anything, but I got nothing. I didn't know why her opinion mattered so much to me, but it did.

"How did he force your hand?" she asked in a tone far gentler than I expected.

I sat down on the desk not far from her. Being close to her soothed something in me, made the words come easier. "I came back to Hemlock Hollow to ask the council permission to bite Sonya in. If I could get their approval, I was going to ask her if she wanted to be one of us. I had a feeling something was wrong with my sister, so I went to Bain's place, knowing she'd be there. We'd been working on infiltrating the Draupnir pack, which meant she stayed as close to him as possible. I found her sleeping on the couch. She was covered in bruises, had a black eye, fat lip..." The words turned into a growl, forcing me to stop. I swallowed my anger and made my fangs retract. Now that I had started telling her, I had to finish. "She wouldn't say what happened, just told me not to mess things up because we'd come too far, and to hurry and bring Sonya to Bain because she was terrified of what he'd do if he didn't get what he wanted."

Elexis's hand came to rest on my arm. Her skin on my skin sucked the anger right out of me. I looked down at her hand, soft but callused at the same time, nails sensibly trimmed, delicate but strong. Heat surged between us.

"The council's decision can take weeks. I didn't have that long. So I went back to Sonya that night. I was going to tell her about our kind and ask her." Memories slammed into me, halting my words.

"But something happened?" Elexis prompted.

"I was there the night he fought and killed Didrik. I know what he is capable of. And I believe he planned to bite Sonya in himself in a way that would mark her as his mate." My entire body vibrated with the need to shift. Letting my mind go there had been a mistake. Elexis's hand covered mine.

"That had to have been horrible."

Her touch brought an unexpected sense of calm. I pushed on. "When I went back to Sonya, I intended to tell her about us and ask her if she wanted the life. I suspected she would say yes because of what she told me about her father's stories of Fenrir and Loki. But Bain tipped off the local *útrýmt* that I was in his territory." My teeth ground together as I struggled to wrestle my anger. "The bastard likes to make things hard on me. He gets off on watching me suffer. The local *útrýmt* came hunting me. Things got out of control." I shook my head hard. "I shouldn't have done it, shouldn't have let him scare me into such a stupid decision. I will regret it for the rest of my life, but the way I bit her in wasn't as a mate, it was in a manner that allowed her to choose a mate without repercussions. Even if she was going to say yes, I know I still took part of her choice away from her."

Elexis stood and moved in front of me. "This is why you don't think Morene is a suspect in the bitings. Not because she's your sister, but because she's trying to stop Bain too." Her dark blue eyes pierced right through me. "We will get this bastard," she said with such vehemence it turned my blood to nitrous oxide.

The intensity of her gaze threatened to throw me into overdrive. Her scent changed, became sweeter and spicier at the same time. I wanted to strip down and rub against her until I soaked it in. Instinct made me stand and move a step closer. She didn't move away. Her tongue slid out and touched her upper lip. Seeing that tender, pink flesh destroyed my restraint. My hands trailed up her arms before I'd realized I'd moved. Goosebumps rose beneath my fingers. Her eyes stayed locked on mine as my hands moved up to her shoulders, then cradled her face. I bent toward her slowly, giving her every opportunity to pull away.

She rose up on her toes and met me halfway. Despite how full and soft her lips looked, they were hard and eager—which made me both. She tasted like raspberries and summer. Her arms went around my waist, one snaking up my back, pressing me to her. Mine found their way into her hair to cradle her head. The clothes between us grew so hot, they were soon in danger of combusting. Or at least it felt that way. I walked her back to the desk, lifted her, and sat her on it. I paused, waiting for any sign that she wanted to stop. Her legs wrapped around my waist, tight as a vise. I pressed against the scorching heat of her center and wanted nothing more than to be inside, to let her heat consume me. Her eagerness—which bordered on desperation—only made mine that much worse.

My power surged up to meet hers. It took me completely by surprise. Of the two *varúlfur* women I'd ever been with, my power had never risen to them, not even during climax. Elexis's hands slid beneath my shirt. The sensation of her skin against mine grounded me and made me feel like exploding at the same time. She molded her body against mine, every hard and curvy inch of her. A slight growl rumbled in my chest. At the sound, her fingernails dug into my back. Her tongue reached deep into my mouth as if trying to lap up the sound.

She pulled back from the kiss so suddenly it left me gasping. "What was that?" she whispered, tone urgent, serious.

I opened my eyes to find her leaning out to look around me. The look on her face made it clear it wasn't a ploy to stop kissing me. Grabbing my hips, she pushed me back and slid off the desk. She started for the gaping door. I opened my mouth to call after her, then I smelled it, another *varúlfur*. The trail was fresh, seconds old at most. Elexis dashed from the room, and I was right on her heels. We followed the trail downstairs. At the bottom, she bent and scooped up a book lying on the floor. I could barely keep up with her as she skipped steps, jumped over handrails, and all but flew. The sight made me picture her in the police academy, fierce, unstoppable—and as a human at that. Now this woman put the super in supernatural.

We grew close enough I heard pounding footsteps pulling away from us. They led straight through the house's great room, into the kitchen, and down the stairs to the basement. Suddenly I smelled not one, but over a dozen *varúlfur*. Many of the scents were familiar, though it had been years since I'd smelled them. Elexis and I both skidded to a halt at the bottom of the stairs.

What had once been Didrik and Lísandra's expansive wine cellar was now a halfway house lined with dozens of cots all laid out in neat rows. Men, women, and children filled the room, some of them on the makeshift beds, others at tables set up in between them. Before Elexis stood a young blond boy with wide blue eyes. He couldn't have been more than six.

Elexis started to sputter as if she wasn't sure what to say or couldn't find the words. I laid a hand on her shoulder. "They are Draupnir's *útrýmt*," I whispered to her.

The young boy with the big blue eyes dashed behind a woman's skirts and peeked out around her at us. "Sorry, Mama. I didn't mean for them to smell me," he whispered to her.

She stroked his hair before pushing him further behind her. "I know, little pup, I know."

Several people stood and walked to the woman's side. The fear in their faces cut me to the core, but the pride and rebellion hiding beneath it stirred my heart.

Tears glistened in the woman's eyes as she met my gaze. "Didrik was your mentor, your friend. Please, out of respect for his memory, don't report us," she begged.

Shaking my head, I strode up to her. Though she shivered, she didn't cower.

"We'll be gone by tonight, you have my word," she continued.

"No," I said. Slowly, gently, I took her hands. "You won't. I won't say a thing. Not out of respect for his memory." I looked at each of their faces. "But out of respect for all of you."

A tear tumbled over the woman's eyelid. She gripped my hands tight as she looked down. "Thank you, Raul. You're a good man and as much a victim of Bain's cruelty as we are. May Frigg and Odin bless you."

A man in a pair of running shorts stepped closer. He locked gazes with me. "You mean it?"

I let go of the mother to place a hand on the man's shoulder. I let him see the truth in my eyes. "I swear it."

Relief broke through the man's mask of bravado. "Thank you. We've heard you've been good to the *útrýmt*. Now I see that's true." His robin's egg blue eyes shifted to Elexis. "But what about her?"

Elexis stepped up to my side. "You can trust me. I'm working with Raul to try and bring Bain to justice, to make him pay for what he's done." The conviction in her voice seemed to be enough for the man. He gave her a weak smile and nodded.

She smiled back and bent down next to the woman with the child. I hadn't realized she was still holding the book until she extended it to him. "I think you dropped this."

The boy peeked out from behind his mother's skirts a little more.

"It's okay," Elexis encouraged.

He reached out and took the book, slowly, as if he expected her to pull it back. "I like stories," he said in a guilty tone.

The look on Elexis's face softened. "Me too. What's your name?"

"Sigur."

"Well, Sigur, I'm Elexis. It's nice to meet you."

A huge smile spread across Sigur's face. "You too."

"Speaking of stories, you all might be able to help me by answering a few questions."

The man lifted his chin. "We'll do anything we can to help bring that monster to justice."

Standing, Elexis clapped a hand on his other shoulder and got to work. She made rounds through the room, talking to each person in turn. But it was more than police questioning. She sat with them, listened to their stories, held their hands, laughed, and joked with them. Seeing it deepened my growing respect for her. By the time we left the basement, a relaxed air had settled over those gathered there. And something else—hope shone in their eyes.

CHAPTER SIXTEEN

ELEXIS

Though Raul kept giving me sidelong glances on the ride home, I couldn't speak. Not only did I have to process what I'd learned, I had to devise a plan. The *útrýmt* told me a lot about Didrik and Lísandra, much of which I'd already learned. But a few gave me an account of what happened the day of the Alpha Challenge. Two of them said Bain had hesitated on the killing blow, looked out into the crowd, then delivered it. They said he had wept afterward. It made me wonder, had he done it for dramatic effect, to instill fear into those watching, or had he been looking at someone in particular?

The sound of Raul's garage door opening finally stirred me from my thoughts. "There's something I have to do," I told him.

He looked at me out of his peripheral as he pulled into the garage. "Your tone tells me I'm not going to like what it is."

I both loved and hated how intuitive he was. The man would have made a great detective. He stopped the car, and the garage door slid shut behind us. I pulled my phone from my pocket as I got out. The number I needed had burned into my memory. I waited until I'd stepped into the house to start dialing. A gruff voice answered on the second ring.

"Hey Bain," I responded, sweet as could be—which for me wasn't very sweet.

I turned to see Raul glaring a hole through me. His *varúlfur* hearing would pick up both sides of the conversation.

"Elexis, it's great to hear from you. I do hope this is a pleasure call," Bain said, voice transforming into a jovial tone filled with sultry notes that made my skin crawl.

"Not exactly. It's business but of a personal nature only you can help with," I said, stroking his ego a bit.

He made an intimate humming noise. I had to repress a shudder. "Can you meet me at Crescent Coffee to chat about it?" I asked.

"Why don't you come by my house?" Though he said it nice and sweet, it held the command of power behind it. The power didn't affect me, but that could have been because it was through the phone.

Just as sweetly, I told him, "Can't have my first real visit to your place be a business one. Shall we say five o'clock? Coffee is on me."

"Five it is." His cheer sounded a bit forced. Maybe the whole alpha voice command was supposed to work through the phone, and he was ticked it hadn't.

"See you then." I ended the call before I could run out of false sweetness.

Raul walked around and stood before me, arms crossed, butt leaning on the couch. "What are you up to?"

"I have to help these people."

His eyes shot open, and he made a negating motion with his hands. "No, Elexis. You can't tell anyone about them. They are trespassing on Bain's property. He would be within his rights to kill them."

Teeth grinding, I started for the bathroom. "That is insanely stupid. But don't worry, I'm not going to mention them."

I felt his power pressing right behind me as he followed. "Then what are you going to do?"

"You're going to have to trust me." No way could I tell him. He would try to talk me out of it, and that would just waste time.

"I do," he said quick enough to shock me. "But let me help you."

I took my gun and badge off and set them on the marble counter. "I will."

A surprised expression came over him that made him look far too cute for my good. He perked up. "Oh, okay, great. So I'm going with you."

I took the hairclip out of my hair and began brushing it out. "No, it wouldn't work if you did. I need you to show up about twenty minutes after to give me a reason to leave." Head cocking to the side, I looked at him. "Does the whole alpha voice command thing work through the phone?"

His face scrunched up. "What? Why? Did he command you to do something? If you're compelled by alpha command, I'm not letting you out the door."

"No, I'm not. He told me to meet him at his house. I told him no, convinced him to meet at the coffee shop instead. So the voice thing should have worked on me?" I asked.

"Since you aren't bonded to another alpha, yeah." He drew the last word out almost into a question. "But it didn't. Hmm, interesting. Still, if he is trying to give you subtle commands, I don't like this."

"Don't sweat it. Clearly, it didn't work." I pulled my sandals off.

Was that a bit of hope mixed with desire in his tone? "Taking a shower so I don't have the *útrýmt* scent on me."

I put a hand on his chest and enjoyed the way he chewed his bottom lip when he looked down at me. I knew I shouldn't. Despite him coming clean about Sonya, he still wasn't completely cleared in my book, not by a long shot. The scent of his desire filled the air. It threatened to distract me. Trust had to be earned, and he wasn't there yet. I gave him a little push across the threshold.

I smiled as I told him, "Alone."

The sun-drenched interior of Crescent Coffee was empty save for the barista behind the counter and Bain. He sprawled across the bench in the corner of the shop, arms stretched out across the back of it, one skinny ankle propped up on the knee of the other leg. His loose, almost knee-length shorts threatened to give me a glimpse of things I did not want to see. A light blue tank hung on the frame of a sinewy chest. The smile he gave me made my skin crawl, but I returned it. He maintained eye contact, which I appreciated but found odd, considering the short shorts and low-cut tank I wore for the occasion. It would be hard to distract him with my breasts if he wouldn't look at them.

The tabletop was empty. Of course it was. I should have known he'd take me up on the whole coffee being on me thing. I waved and smiled before going to the counter. The barista, Brian, gave me a genuine smile that only made Bain's feel that much more fake.

"Strawberry almond smoothie for you, hun?" he asked.

"That would be great. And whatever Bain's regular is," I said.

His smile wilted a little but didn't fall away completely. "You got it," he said, anxiety lacing his tone.

With Bain at my back, I tried to give Brian a reassuring look. His eyes told me to be careful. I paid and turned back to Bain. Despite the fact I knew he'd been raised in the 1950's and 60's with far better manners, he remained seated as I walked up. Fine by me. I pulled out a chair opposite him and sat down.

"Elexis, it's good to see you again. I had hoped we'd get together sooner," he said, tone chiding and slick at the same time.

"The investigation has been keeping me busy."

"You would make better progress if you looked into the *útrýmt*."

"There aren't many of them in town. Makes it hard."

He sat up, his elbows on the table, and interlaced his fingers. "So, you have been looking into them. Any favorite suspects?"

I laughed and shrugged one shoulder. "A good detective never has favorites," I said.

"I am curious, what type of business brings you to me?"

"As I said, the kind only you can help with."

At that, his eyes literally sparkled with a cold, calculating light. His joy over having something I needed made my skin crawl. I pretended to be charmed instead. "You own the house on Birch Street. It is one of the only empty places in town. I want to rent it."

Some of the mirth drained from his face. The barest hint of suspicion took its place.

"That is a big residence for one woman."

I gave him a full, two-shoulder shrug this time. "I like my space, and I like that it backs to the wolf preserve instead of some other packs' territory."

"But it also backs to my territory, sits on it, in fact."

I grinned. "That doesn't bother me."

His cold, blue eyes widened. "Really?"

"Really. Should it?"

"Not at all. Does this mean you'll be visiting my pack often?" I liked the eagerness in his tone. I could use it.

"I certainly hope to." It rolled off my tongue easy, like the truth it was. I had every intention of visiting his pack—to question each and every one of them.

He sighed and leaned back. "Well, it's a big house, fifteen bedrooms, fifteen and a half bathrooms. More of a lodge. Not to mention the dozens of cabins on the back of the property. A place like that might be out of a *lögreglu* budget."

"Yeah, it's a big place that has sat empty for a few years and no doubt needs a lot of maintenance and fixing up because of it. Lucky for you, I have mad skills with a hammer, screwdriver, and paintbrush. Even with my skills, it would take at least a year of severely discounted rent to fix it up. But I'm willing." Now I leaned my elbows on the table, getting closer to him. "And I'm deducing that due to the history of the place, there aren't many people willing to rent it, and even fewer you're willing to rent it to."

Pursing his lips, he nodded. "You're an impressive negotiator. I like that, a lot."

I smiled as if his words charmed the hell out of me. The look in his eyes told me he was almost convinced. "It would also give me a chance to see how an alpha lives, to see if that's for me," I said in a suggestive tone.

His eyes widened and he sat up straighter. "I'll get an agreement drawn up right away. If you'd like to come over for dinner, I'll have it ready tonight."

Giving him a mischievous look, I wagged a finger. "Ah, ah. Remember, I don't mix business with pleasure. But I would like to come by for lunch, say next Wednesday, to chat with you and meet the pack. Besides..." I pulled a folder from my bag and put it on the table along with a pen. "I brought my own." I opened the folder, put the pen on top, and slid it over to him.

As he started to read, Brian walked over and set a steaming coffee mug in front of him and a frosty mug in front of me. Bain didn't look up.

"Thanks, Brian. You didn't have to do that, I would have come get them," I said.

He waved a hand. "Darlin', if you did my job for me, whatever would I do?" he asked.

"Write traffic tickets for me?" I suggested.

We both laughed. After a wary look at Bain, he put on a careless air I could tell he didn't feel and sauntered back over to the counter. During the entire conversation, Bain still didn't even look up. It aggravated the crap out of me that he ignored Brian, but I forced myself to remain calm, heartbeat slow and steady, claws retracted.

Bain took a drink of his coffee while reading. He signed the bottom of the second page. Either he was a speed reader, or he didn't read the fine print. I hoped it was the latter. My smile was genuine when he closed the folder and slid it back over to me. I passed him an envelope.

"Your security deposit. I trust you don't mind if I move in tonight? I am in desperate need of my own place, immediately," I said with a grimace for effect.

His smile broadened and he nodded. "Of course, we can't have the company of that *fallið* dragging down your reputation. Go right ahead." He pulled the hundreds from the envelope and counted them like I knew he would. Once satisfied, he put them back in and placed the envelope in his short's pocket. "Now about dinner—"

The door opened and in walked Raul, just in time. I put on an irritated look to cover my relief. He strode right up to our table, radiating a hostility I knew he didn't have to fake.

"What the hell, Sandalius? This looks more like a social call than a questioning. We're on the clock," Raul snapped.

"I'm on my lunch hour, Raul. Speaking of which," I stood up, glaring a hole through Raul's ruggedly handsome face. "I'm going to spend the rest of it getting my bags from your house so I can get the hell out."

"Good. I can get my fucking patio furniture back."

I rolled my eyes and looked at Bain, who had a confused look on his face. "I slept there so I wouldn't have to go in his house," I explained.

Bain's brows rose. "Why am I not surprised by Raul's lack of hospitality?"

Raul gave a bitter, angry laugh. "My hospitality is great. Hell, I even offered to share my bed."

That was laying it on a bit thick. I had to cut this short before he pushed it over the edge.

"Like that was ever going to happen," I said as I stood. "I'm sorry, Bain. I can't get off this guy's porch soon enough." I looked him in the eyes and gave him an eager smile. "I'll see you Wednesday."

"Of course," Bain said, laying on the good ol' boy charm with a nice twang to his tone and lick of his lips.

I spun away, shoved past Raul, and stormed out.

"Hey Sandalius, that doesn't mean you don't have to work!" Raul called after me, following. "We have people to question and leads to follow up on," he said after the door eased shut behind us.

I continued at my swift pace, and he continued to chip at me until we were a full block away. We came to one of the iron gates leading into the private part of town. After a quick look around, I jumped onto a lamppost support, pushed off it to bounce off the brick wall, and launched over the gate. I dropped a thrilling eight feet, then landed softly in the grass on the side of the road. Being a werewolf certainly had its perks. While I would have been able to pull something like that off before, thanks to my police training, it wouldn't have been nearly as easy, and the landing would have hurt like a mother. A second later, Raul landed beside me.

"My car's at the park just past Lupine Naturals," he whispered.

We started in that direction. I kept up a fast pace, and an irritated look, until I got past Lupine Naturals and reached the edge of the park. Each step along the wood chip path bordering the green space brought the scent of hemlock wafting up to me. The parks in town all had wood-chipped paths. They didn't like to put concrete anywhere they didn't need to. Considering how the scent of tar burned my nose now, I got why. Fir trees big enough to rival the redwoods of Northern California cast their shade across us. The slightly sweet scent cleansed my nose of Bain's musky, slippery smell. I sucked in a deep breath and let it out slowly.

"So what did I just save you from?" Raul asked in a soft voice.

I had to suppress a shudder. "Dinner with the *führer*."

One of Raul's brows rose. "Why do I have the feeling you agreed to much worse?"

"Because I did. Which is why I need your help."

He grinned, but his lips were tight with worry. "Twice in one day. That's not a good sign."

"Nope," I agreed. "But necessary."

"Why me?" He sounded somewhat defensive.

I looked off into the trees as I answered. "Because you're the only one in this town I can come close to trusting."

He moved in front of me, walking backward as I walked forward. The grin on his face threatened to unweave my carefully crafted resistance to him. Damn his smile was hot. Too hot.

"Close?" he asked in a teasing tone.

My lips pursed as I looked him up and down. "Very close."

His smile widened. "And what is it I can do to help you?" His suggestive tone slid across my skin, thick with double meaning.

"I need you to sleep over at my house for a while."

Raul's eyes popped wide open, he tripped over his own feet and fell on his ass. I laughed so hard it bent me over at the waist. Shaking his head, he joined in a second later. Once I could breathe through the laughter, I extended a hand to him. He accepted it and let me haul him to his feet.

"All right, partner. For the good of the investigation, I suppose I can sleep over," he said.

I nodded. "For the good of the investigation."

I saw in his eyes he agreed for reasons that had nothing to do with the investigation. Though I wanted to deny it, my own reasons for wanting him under my roof had nothing to do with the investigation either.

Brows pinching together, his head whipped in my direction. "Wait, what do you mean 'your house'?"

CHAPTER SEVENTEEN

ELEXIS

The mouthwatering scents of bacon, eggs, and potatoes pulled me out of deep sleep. I blinked until my eyes adjusted to the soft light of dawn making the half-sheer shades glow. I looked around at the immaculate guest room, taking a moment to get my bearings. After a long night of pouring over Didrik's journals at Raul's house, I'd decided to stay there one last time. Once I had seen how much care he'd taken to make sure the guestroom was perfect, I was glad I had. All this time I'd been crashing on his patio and couch, and he had gone to so much trouble on this room. It made me feel guilty as hell for being such a bitch about sleeping under his roof.

But then, I had only just recently decided he was no longer a suspect in the bitings.

Part of me had wanted to wake up in his bed again, but with a new lead in the investigation, I wasn't willing to allow myself to get that distracted. Work came first. Always. Lives depended on me staying focused. That, and knowing how Bain had manipulated him only made me want to nail the bastard to the wall that much more. But with Raul doing such sweet things as making me breakfast, I wasn't sure how long I could resist my attraction to him.

Smiling like an idiot, I rolled out of bed. After an abbreviated version of my morning routine, I pulled on a pair of cotton shorts, a snug blue tank top, and started downstairs. The sound of a woman's laugh stopped me on the first step. I knew that voice, but I couldn't quite place from where. I listened for a moment as she and Raul talked. They chatted with the ease of two people well acquainted and comfortable with one another. The topic was Raul's dreams. Finally, it struck me—the woman chanting on the bridge, the female alpha of the Draupnir pack.

What the hell would Raul being doing laughing and joking with *that* woman?

I strode down the stairs fast and quiet, fully intending to find out. I walled my powers off so they wouldn't give me away prematurely. It was easy, like walling off emotions when on a crime scene. Sneaking up on someone was the best way to get an honest reaction out of them. Another of the many gems I'd learned in foster care.

I saw them long before they saw me. Near the stove, Raul bent over a spoon the woman held up to him. A big part of me hated how close she stood to him. Mousy brown hair fell around her shoulders in big, lazy curls, the kind that took a curling iron and an hour to perfect. A black tank top hugged her perky breasts in a way that made it clear she wasn't wearing a bra. Brown yoga pants showed off her slender legs.

Raul tasted the offered spoonful and blew out a breath. "Damn that's hot!"

The woman laughed and slapped his shoulder. I wanted to rip her hand off. The desire to do so infuriated me. "Of course it is, silly!"

Anger boiled my control away into steam. Raul started, eyes darting to me, and nearly knocked the spoon from the woman's hands. Her fast reflexes kept it from hitting the floor. She cast me a look of mild curiosity.

"Elexis, you're awake!" Raul said. I hated the surprised, guilty tone of his voice. But I hated the huge smile the woman gave me more.

"So this is Elexis," she said in a tone far too sultry for my liking. Then again, I wasn't liking anything about this woman so far.

"Yes," Raul said as he hurried from her side to approach me. "Elexis, this is my sister, Morene."

His sister, that made it better, and yet...worse in another way.

The smile Morene gave me flashed perfectly aligned, bleached teeth with slightly pointed canines. Her fangs weren't extended exactly. It was more like she was one of those people who had pointed canine teeth.

"So this is the woman who has been taking up all of my baby brother's time," she said.

I gave her a tight-lipped smile in return. Every ounce of my being tried not to picture her having sex with Bain—and failed. "Yes, trying to solve a crime and keep our kind from getting exposed to the world."

"Hmm, look at that. You've adjusted well, already saying 'our kind.' That's a big step," she said in a tone that tried too hard to sound genuine.

Raul's slight Adam's apple worked hard as he struggled for words. I allowed my look to harden, having no intention of easing up on him. He should have introduced me to her long before now. The way her energy crawled around me as if seeking weak points made it clear why he hadn't. Everything about the woman, from the way she held my gaze just a little too long to how she smiled only when he was looking, made me not trust her. Morene put the spoon down and moved up to the bar to lean on it.

"My position is...delicate," she began. "My brother wanted you to get to know me first, so you could get the right impression. But apparently, someone already told you I was the Draupnir pack alpha." Genuine surprise peppered her words, and her eyes crinkled at the corners like she wanted to glare, but her smile remained. She didn't know how I had figured it out.

Apparently, Raul hadn't mentioned I'd witnessed her little orgy, or that he'd told me about her. I could tell from the way they interacted how much he respected her. But something else hid beneath it, an eagerness to please her, and maybe even a little intimidation.

My anger toward him eased—a little—and shifted toward her. The "woe is me" look in her eyes, combined with her theatrical tone, grated heavily on my nerves. And the way she said she was "the" Draupnir pack alpha rubbed my fur the wrong way. I walked up to the bar and sat down, determined to learn more.

"Yeah, well, I've found you can never form a proper impression of someone until you know everything about them."

Morene flashed her big, cheerleader-captain smile again, full of cheese and fakeness. "Raul said you were a great detective."

Grinning, and making no attempt to make it look friendly, I rested my chin on my fist. "Well, he has said very little about you, so do tell."

In a cheerful tone which sounded like nails on a chalkboard to my ears, she proceeded to tell me all about herself, where she went to college, what she had studied—business, go figure—how much she cared about her pack and worked to protect it. Sometime during her ramblings, Raul placed a plate of bacon in front of me. It went a long way toward his redemption. Morene tried asking about me, but I diverted her questions by turning them around to be about her instead. Her eagerness to talk about herself made it easy. Eventually, my lack of anything more than a grunt or a few words in response had her turning to Raul for conversation.

She started in about the new graphic art she had brought him, a picture of a dark-skinned woman with pointed ears, wearing a cloak that billowed around her in the wind of a desert landscape. It sat on the dining room table. From their conversation, I gathered she was the graphic artist and had brought him all the fantasy-related art hanging in the house. He encouraged her, going on about how beautiful it was and how the setting intrigued him. The doting brother thing looked good on him. Too bad it was over the female alpha of the Draupnir pack.

I watched them cook and talk and laugh with an ease born of routine and comfort. He indulged and praised her, and she ate it up as if it sustained her. Their conversation shifted to his dreams. Apparently, they were what inspired her art—and what gave him his exhausted look so much of the time. Her eagerness to hear about them bordered on obsession. Raul tried to redirect the conversation several times, but she kept returning to the subject.

After we finished eating, I took pity on him and interrupted. "So, you're staying in the pack to protect the other members who stayed."

She nearly choked on her coffee but recovered before Raul looked up from his plate. "I am. Someone has to look out for them."

"What about the members who were loyal to Didrik and Lísandra, and were cast out for it?" I asked.

She looked crestfallen enough to earn an A in theater. My heart thought maybe I was being too hard on her, but my gut disagreed.

"Almost all of them have left town, moved on. There isn't much I can do for them but try to bring Bain down," she said.

"It's been what, five years since Bain took over? You haven't discovered enough to put him away yet?" I pressed. All I could think about was how those poor people had been scratching out a living in secret in Didrik and Lísandra's old house for so long. It fed my anger and mistrust toward this woman. But was that fair to her? She didn't know about them.

She gave me a hard look. "Bain is over sixty years old. He's smart. It takes a long time to earn his trust.

"But you're making progress?"

She smiled weakly and nodded. "I am. It was a huge step for him to name me the proxy female alpha." The humble attitude sat badly on her, like flannel on a beauty queen—out of place, unnatural.

"Hmm, and that was a bit over a month ago. In that time you haven't discovered any evidence."

Morene's cheeks burned a bright red. Power crackled around her. Raul put a hand on her arm. "Easy, Sister. Elexis just can't shut her detective side off." He cast me a look that said to shut it, which made me want to do the opposite.

She gave me a tight smile. "I guess that's what makes you so good at it. That's a good thing." She started to stand. "I need to get going anyway."

I held a hand up and rose before she could. "Don't let me run you off. I need to go get my things and move into my new place. You two visit."

Morene's eyes widened with delight—and surprise. Bain obviously hadn't told her I'd be renting the old alphas' house. "You're moving out?" She tried to sound neutral about it, but the mask was poorly executed.

"Yep. I found a place to rent, and I don't want to impose on Raul's hospitality any longer." I looked to Raul. "You'll stop by later so we can go over that paperwork?"

Confusion wrinkled his brow. "Yeah. Three o'clock. You'll text me the address?"

I gave him a smile for his discretion. It earned him back a shit-ton of points. "Soon as I get there and see what it is."

Raul stood. "I'll walk you to your truck."

I laughed and waved a hand. "Thanks, but I can find it. Enjoy your sibling time."

I turned and left before he had a chance to figure out how to respond. Any conversation we had could be overheard by Morene, and I did *not* want that. Talking to Raul right now was the last thing I wanted to do. Not because I was mad at him for hiding his sister's identity, though I was. A small part of me got why he did it. I needed time to process everything, to think.

Thankfully, my things were already loaded in my truck. The only reason I'd stayed at his house one more night was because we'd stayed up so late going over Didrik's journals, reading all the pack member names so I could compare them with the outcasts living in his house.

My old truck rumbled to life as I turned the key. When I pulled out, Raul stood in the open front door. I wanted to let him know I was all right, but I wasn't. I was sure of two things about Morene: she did not want me living with her brother, and I did not trust her.

CHAPTER EIGHTEEN

RAUL

A s much as I had missed my sister and been worried about her, three o'clock couldn't come fast enough. I hadn't been able to bring myself to ask her about having sex with Bain. Though she hadn't returned my calls for days, she had talked all morning like nothing was wrong. Worse, she hadn't admitted anything about the orgy. If it was out of shame, she hid it well. After exhausting talks about the nine worlds for hours—which only assured I'd dream about them again instead of sleep soundly, dammit—she finally left at 2:45 p.m.

I pulled into the driveway of Didrik and Lísandra's old house at 2:56 p.m. When I stepped out of my car, my spine tingled with the desire to raise my hackles. Someone watched me, several someones. The instinct to shift to wolf form and prepare to fight moved through me. I fought it down. The eyes on me probably belonged to the *útrýmt*. The pressure of two wolves' power came from the towering pine trees just to the right of the house. Young ones, not yet through the *verða* from the feel of their power. They were about halfway up the tree, sitting on one of the limbs. While I couldn't see them, their scent and energy pressure gave them away.

The bursting flower beds to either side of the wide flagstone steps obscured almost all other scents. Almost. Even through the roses and lilacs, I smelled Elexis's alluring scent, along with another that surprised me. The shade of the porch roof provided relief from the hot summer sun as I stepped beneath it. One of the large front doors opened and revealed Iris, multi-colored hair wound into a messy bun atop her head.

"Making house calls for overdue books now?" I asked.

"Something like that," she said as she moved to let me in.

I stepped inside. "What if I'd been Bain?"

She opened her mouth, but Elexis's voice answered from off to her right. "Then my new security system would have seen when you pulled into the driveway, and I would have answered the door."

Barefoot in a pair of cotton drawstring shorts and a dark purple tank with a Wyoming police logo on it, she looked at home, and sexier than Frigg should have made any woman. Sunlight pouring through the huge picture windows to either side of the doors made her black hair look like a silken mantel around her shoulders.

"You look like you're settling in well. You got a couch picked out for me yet?" I asked, knowing the house had half a dozen scattered throughout it.

She smiled, and suddenly I wanted to be the sunlight that draped all across her.

"I am. This place has a great vibe to it. And no, not yet." Her cheeks turned a nice pink.

My lips turned up. It was hard not to smile when she smiled. Besides, she was right. Even after all that had happened to the people who used to call this place home, it did have a good feel to it, especially with her in it.

"So what's this about a new security system?"

Iris closed the door behind me as I stepped in. Elexis started for the huge staircase, beckoning for me to follow. Iris cut off down to the left hall without a backward glance. I fought down the urge to ask where she was going. It wasn't my business. The sight of Elexis's curvy behind ascending the stairs before me commanded my attention anyways. It distracted me so much we'd walked into Didrik and Lísandra's bedroom before I realized it.

The space no longer sat quiet as a tomb. The heavy blue curtains lay open, allowing sunlight to bathe the room. Boxes lined the wall near the dresser, some open and half-filled with carefully packed and wrapped items, others closed and stacked together. The sheets that had covered nearly everything were gone, as was a lot of the furniture. The space looked empty but filled with change and possibility. Elexis's bag sat on a bare bed frame, but not the one that had been in here. This one looked to be queen-sized instead of a king, and it had a brushed bronze headboard and footboard with a decidedly steampunk look to it.

She gave me an uncertain smile. "I hope me moving their stuff out isn't weird for you. This room has the best view, but I couldn't stand the thought of using their things. It felt...disrespectful."

"Not at all. You honor them." I wanted to say more but couldn't.

Her teeth tugged at her bottom lip. "Hmm. That's what Iris said."

"You should have said something. I could have helped you move your bed in." I felt like a bit of an ass for not thinking of offering before.

Flexing her right arm, she shrugged. "Hey, I hit the gym my fair share. A little heavy lifting is nothing, especially with this crazy werewolf strength of ours. Besides, the bedframe is really all I have of my own furniture, and Iris and I made a girl's day of moving it and the rest of my stuff in."

She walked to the far side of the bed frame, bent down, and pressed on the crown molding in the corner. Something clicked, hydraulics hissed, and a four-foot section of the wall pulled back and slid behind itself, revealing another room. The scents of metal and concrete told me the room was reinforced. Elexis stepped inside and flipped the light on.

The room was at least twelve-by-twelve, large for being so well hidden. A plush brown and beige rug covered the hardwood floor. My first steps onto it revealed it to be cushy, like padding lay beneath the wood. An adobe look softened the walls. It would go a long way toward sound dampening. Instead of windows, paintings hung on the walls. One depicted a forest scene, another a winter scene, and another a meadow, all containing wolves. A big brown leather couch with nailhead trim sat beneath the forest painting. On the wall opposite it sat a desk, which stretched the entire length of the wall. Monitors lined the desk as well as a shelf above it—twenty in all.

"Holy shit," I murmured as I approached the monitors.

Elexis spun, arms out. "I know, right? All of this was already here. I just had Luke reprogram it for me."

The monitors showed different parts of the house's perimeter and surrounding property. A few covered the interior of the house.

"Luke?"

"One of the outcasts we met in the basement." She walked up and pointed to the far right monitor. "Check this out."

The monitor showed part of the forest I recognized as where Didrik and Lísandra's property touched the current Draupnir property. A man stood on the edge of it. He paced and ran his hand repeatedly through his blond hair.

"Bain?" I whispered.

Elexis's breath fell hot on my shoulder. "Yeah, he's been there for forty-five minutes, and that's the second time today. And look." She ducked in front of me and messed with one of the camera controllers. It zoomed in on his face. Tears filled his eyes.

"What the hell?"

"I think guilt must be keeping him off the property."

I shook my head. "No way. He must hear the camera, and he's putting on a show."

"I thought so too, at first. But Luke told me the cameras are too far away and are not only hidden but placed inside sound dampeners."

"Weird."

She nodded. "For sure. There's another hidden room downstairs where Luke has been monitoring the cameras so the outcasts know when to hide. Iris is helping him now."

I watched for a while longer. Bain eventually shook his head and stormed off. I turned to Elexis. "So the *útrýmt* have been living here, using the camera system to stay hidden."

"Yep. Most of the lodge runs on solar power, and they said Bain never came around, so it was easy for them. They've been tending a garden in the back and getting a lot of their food from there."

A bit of a growl slid from me. "This is crazy, reckless. Bain may not be able to bring himself to come onto the property, but he could get over his hangup at any time."

She waved a hand in a dismissive gesture. "That's why I had the cameras beefed up, and why I have someone watching them constantly.

And it's why you're going to be sleeping on my couch—well, one of them anyway. This place has a shit-ton of couches." She frowned at the anxious look on my face. "We've been over this, multiple times." The patience in her voice was wearing a bit thin.

I held my hands up. "I know, I know. I just don't like it. You living here is dangerous."

Letting out a long, frustrated sigh, she walked from the room. "Someone had to do something for the poor people here. They need protection."

I followed her, having to stretch my legs out to keep up. The secret door slid shut behind us. "I could talk to my sister—"

She spun on me. "No!" The vehemence in her voice surprised me.

"Why not?"

With a huff, she turned back around and wove through the stacked boxes to go into the master bathroom. She picked up a hot flat iron from the countertop and began running it through her wavy hair. Past a double sink vanity sat a white clawfoot tub big enough for me to lie down in, centered beneath a half-moon window. I wandered toward it and looked out at the forest of neutral territory.

"Plausible deniability. She is already in a dangerous position. If she knew about the outcasts, it would only put more pressure on her. I have it handled. No need to put your sister in more danger."

The idea of Morene in yet more danger wasn't appealing. But I didn't want Elexis in any either. I knew both women could take care of themselves, but even good fighters went down when the odds were stacked against them. I turned from the twilit forest to watch Elexis. She met my gaze in the mirror.

"I can take care of myself. Werewolf cop, remember? And you keep telling me I'm stronger than the average werewolf," she said.

"Yeah, I know. It's just that this isn't a long-term solution."

She snorted. "No kidding. But I plan on taking Bain down sooner rather than later, so it won't have to be long-term."

I shook my head and crossed my arms. "My sister and I have been trying to take him down for years now."

Something flashed in her eyes. Her smile tightened. "I know. But remember, new perspective, mad skills, and Bain wants something from me, which means I can manipulate him."

My reply came out through gritted teeth. "It's what he wants from you that worries me."

Elexis continued to smooth her hair with the iron, her slow, even strokes driving me wild for more reasons than one. "He doesn't want a mate or a co-alpha. He has that already."

I growled, not at her, but at the situation. Again, her eyes met mine in the mirror. "I'm sorry," she said.

I waved it off. "Why do you say that? He's made it pretty clear he's interested in you, and he hinted about needing a mate."

She sat the flat iron down and unplugged it. She turned and looked at me directly. I saw a flash of fang as her teeth worked at her bottom lip again. "Yeah, but he doesn't mean it. I get zero vibes he's interested in me. I think he wants to keep me close because I'm investigating the bitings case."

I crossed my arms, tucking my hands into my armpits to keep from grabbing her. "Then wouldn't renting a house from him play right into his hands?"

A hot little half-grin pulled up her lips. "He'll think so, which will make him drop his guard."

I growled in response. Elexis rolled her eyes and strode back into the bedroom. "Everything anyone has tried so far has gotten them nowhere slow," she began. She unzipped her duffle bag. "Our investigation has only strengthened my suspicion that Bain is our main suspect—or at least our key to unlocking everyone behind the bitings. Drastic measures have to be taken to get results. Our kind live so long they're used to taking their time to do things. But the longer we take to solve this, the more innocent people get bitten in against their will and the higher our risk of exposure becomes, not to mention the outcasts having to live in fear and hiding."

"Yeah, but—"

"No buts. It's done. I am not going to argue about it. You'll be sleeping on the couch, so quit obsessing over me living here."

She pulled out two shirts and held them up against her. "What does one wear to a full moon festival?"

Twilight softened the shadows of the forest and drained some of the heat of the day away. I shifted my eyes only to use my wolf vision. Elexis all but skipped alongside me, jittery as a caffeine addict. I hadn't been able to convince her one went naked to a full moon festival. Disappointing as that was, it was for the best. I'd want to tear out the eyes of anyone who saw her naked for a prolonged period of time. She had settled on what she called a bra-top shirt, a low cut blue flowing thing that apparently had a bra built in. Barefoot, she rocked a pair of black cargo shorts that hugged her ass perfectly. Unfortunately, she had made me leave the room when she changed.

"So what does one do at a full moon festival exactly?" She looked up through the trees, gaze locking on the pale, swollen moon. "Do we howl at the moon? I do sort of feel like howling. Why is that?"

I opened my mouth to answer, but she went on.

"I guess a lot of it will be political, people trying to get me to join their pack and all. But it is a party, right? Like drinking and music, and... Oh man, please tell me there won't be an orgy."

The wide-eyed look she gave me made me want to laugh. Instead, I cocked my head to the side. "Not exactly."

She threw a playful strike at my arm, which stung with the pain of one who didn't know their strength. "You're joking, right? Please tell me you're joking!" she said.

I lifted a shoulder. "The majority of people don't participate in group sex, but there are definitely a few younger, more...exploratory groups that do."

"But aren't there kids at the festival?"

"Not that late. The parents take them home hours before things get crazy."

"Okay, that'll be my cue to leave." She went into a ramble about werewolf parenting.

I took her hand and pulled her to a stop. Despite us being upwind of the hollow, the scent of the bonfire permeated the air. We were nearly there, and she was not ready.

"Elexis, breathe. You don't need to be nervous. They'll be trying to impress you. You don't need to impress them."

She looked down at our clasped hands, fixated on them. I started to let go but she gripped tighter. "The packs are like families. No one has ever wanted me to be part of their family," she whispered.

Oh. *Oh.*

I moved in front of her. Finally, her gaze lifted from our hands to my face. "Okay, listen. Don't fight anyone of *verndari* level unless you both agree it's for sport only, otherwise if you win they are disgraced and you earn the right to their position. Anyone lower, you don't have to worry about. Clothing does come off when higher-level members spar because most who can shift while fighting, do. Other than that, clothes stay on until the kids leave." As I talked, her energy slowly ceased crackling like a live wire.

"So you were kidding about clothing being optional," she said.

I gave her a crooked grin and shrugged. She let go of my hand to strike me in the arm. "Raul! I was actually considering it!"

We started walking again.

Blood rushed to parts I didn't want it to go to. Though she'd been kinder since our kiss, she'd also kept her distance. Every now and then a flicker of mistrust in her eyes made it clear why. I was still the guy who'd bit in a woman without asking her. As much as I hated it, I deserved her judgment. My gaze flicked across her body before I could stop it. "Really?"

"Well, I don't know your traditions!" she said with a laugh. The carefree sound made me laugh too. Her pace slowed a little. "Will people be speaking Icelandic?" she asked.

"Yes, but most won't do it around you, out of respect for the fact you don't speak it."

"How fast do werewolves heal?"

A chill raised the hair on my arms. "Why?"

"So I know if I should watch for ones who limp."

"If they're *verndari* level, the leg would be healed by now. If not, maybe not."

"Good to know."

Soon, sounds that once came only from primordial forests drifted to us on the breeze. Drums reminiscent of something villagers might have heard through the mist as they caught their first sighting of the dragon prow of Viking ships, echoed through the trees. It was a pure sound, clean of any synthesizer or amplifier noise. No guitars or keyboards accompanied, and yet the sound felt complete and utterly moving. I wondered what Elexis would think of such traditional music. Beneath it buzzed people talking and laughing, a lot of people.

"Wow, that's...haunting," she whispered.

The distant look of wonder on her face stirred something deep inside me. "You like it?" I asked, surprised.

"I do, a lot."

Yellow and orange light soon danced through the trees, punctuated by the pulse of dozens of drums. Though we had yet to step out of the cover of the trees into the hollow that stretched out, I felt people all around us. Eyes weighed heavy on every inch of us, making me twitch with the desire to shift. The pressure of each *varúlfur's* power touched me like a breeze, overwhelming, judging. Swallowing the urge, I lifted my chin and walked with a pride that would not be cowed. I was a ranger, the son of alphas, for the gods' sakes. I would act like it.

Moonlight competed with firelight from a few small fires scattered about, bathing the hollow in brightness. The brightness revealed hundreds of people gathered, some dancing around their small fires where groups of drummers tapped out a primal rhythm. Others gathered in groups sitting on logs or rocks. A huge stack of branches made up a bonfire that would be the center of the night's celebration. In front of and to the side of it, pairs of people fought in three rings lined with flagstone. Two pairs were men and the third were women. Their battle had form and beauty, much like martial arts, but also a raw naturalness to it that came more from practicality. People sat on the grass around the rings, cheering the fighters on.

A few dozen wolves moved about or sat among those in human form. Most of the people looked young and in their prime. A few were younger, teens, preteens, but no toddlers or babies. Dozens wore jackets with either the AVW or AVV club rockers on them, and even more bore tattoos of the patch on their backs, like I did.

The moment Elexis and I stepped from the tree line, all sound ceased as if a switch had been flipped. Everyone turned to look our way. The weight of all those eyes and the power behind them made me want to shift and bare my fangs. I resisted the urge. Tension laced the air to the point I could taste it like alcohol hidden poorly in cheap college punch. The tangy scent of fear and mistrust made the skin along my spine and neck crawl as if my hackles were rising. The chances of this night ending in a fight were high and rising by the moment.

I took a deep breath and told Elexis, "Ready or not, here we go."

CHAPTER NINETEEN

RAUL

Six figures rose from the largest group gathered near the stack of bonfire wood and started our way. The crowd parted for them like water eager to flow out of their path. Power pulsed around them like a heat mirage, only this wasn't an insubstantial wavering, it was warm and heavy like New Orleans air in September. My parents' power was among them.

The pair in the center strode hand in hand, one broad and muscled and clearly dark haired, even in the firelight, the other petite with feminine curves and blond hair brushing her shoulders. Though they looked to be in their prime, something about them felt older. Proper and mature though they were, it wasn't their mannerisms so much as it was their power. Or maybe it was just that I'd know the feel of my parents' power anywhere.

To their right walked another man and woman. The man, Isak, also wearing only shorts, was tall and fit, but not overly muscular like my father. Hair a dark brown hung down into bright green eyes. Crow's feet framed the eyes of the lovely older woman at his side, and deep laugh lines dimpled both her cheeks. Proxy female alpha, Iona, was standing in until Isak chose a mate. As my attention fell to the last pair, I had to suppress a growl and clamp my mouth shut to hide my fangs.

Morene walked alongside Bain. I hadn't even realized my feet had slid into a fighting stance until the six stopped and my parents held up their hands in a placating gesture.

"Tonight is a celebration. Please, let us put aside investigations and suspicions, if only for the night," my mother said in a diplomatic tone that grated on my nerves.

But she was right. I retracted my fangs and nodded. "Of course." I turned to present Elexis to them, and them to Elexis. "You have met Gyda and Ander, alphas of the Reinhard pack." I swept my hand toward the older woman and the brown-haired man. "This is Isak, Iona, alphas of the Arnoddr pack." And last I swept a hand toward Morene and Bain, who refused to look at me. "And you've met Bain and Morene, alphas of the Draupnir pack. Alphas, I introduce to you Elexis Sandalius."

They each welcomed her, some with a handshake, others with an embrace, and others with a nod. Bain lifted her hand and kissed the back of it like the traditional gentleman he was not. I glared a hole through him.

My parents took a step back. Isak and the elder, Iona, stepped forward. Isak's green eyes filled with a natural and easy charm. His heart-shaped face and strong brow gave him boyish good looks I hoped didn't charm Elexis too much. While he wasn't actively looking for a mate, he didn't have one either. Until that moment, it hadn't occurred to me Bain wasn't the only single alpha. The gentle feel to Isak's power made people want to be at ease around him. It made him good at placating bad situations, but now I saw how it could also make him charming to women—and men inclined toward men.

He turned to Elexis and like a gentleman of old, took her hand and raised it to his lips. His eyes remained fixed on hers as he placed a chaste kiss on the back of her hand. I tensed but didn't allow even the hint of a growl to slip out. The difference between him and Bain trying this stunt was Isak had the charisma to pull it off.

"Welcome to the fold, Elexis Sandalius. I apologize deeply for what James did to you. He acted without my consent or knowledge. When we find him, he will be brought to you for punishment," he said in a voice as smooth and rich as chocolate.

I had to suppress a growl.

"Thank you, Alpha Isak," she said, remembering the etiquette lesson I'd covered with her.

He smiled at her. It bothered me more than it should have. "You are most welcome."

The elder woman, Iona, took a step forward. "We would be honored if you would join us by the fire so we may answer any questions you have."

Music and dancing started back up, but I could still feel the eyes of nearly everyone on me. The celebratory vibe of the place had become seriously subdued, replaced by a feeling of anticipation.

From a crowd near the bonfire, Chief Balderson's tall, dark form turned in our direction. He met my gaze and Elexis's, smiled, and inclined his shiny head. To each side of him stood one of his eldest sons, both equally as tall. While they shared his facial bone structure, unlike him, they each had a full head of hair. One sported cornrows reaching past his impossibly broad shoulders—Rúnar, an HHPD officer. The other—Friðrik—had dark hair fashioned in the high and tight favored by his employer—the FBI. They both nodded in greeting as well, their acknowledgement more respect than most gathered were willing to offer. Their eyes widened with interest when they fell on Elexis, and they each gave her charming smiles that awoke the green monster in my gut.

The alphas led us to eight Adirondack chairs gathered in a spot far enough away from the fire not to feel the heat or be overwhelmed by the light. Two of the chairs sat closer together and slightly apart from the other six.

Seven chairs, not eight. First, they had barely acknowledged me, then Bain outright snubbed me, and now they didn't even have a chair for me, as if they didn't expect me to be part of this. Elexis frowned as she looked at the chairs, and opened her mouth. Before she could protest, I snagged a log from the unlit bonfire pile. I placed it on its end, close to one of the chairs, and sat down. Elexis shot me a grateful smile. Claws and fangs would have come out before I left her alone with the alphas. Many an uncomfortable look passed among them. It made my night.

Once they all settled, Bain cleared his throat and locked eyes with Elexis. "No disrespect meant, Elexis, but as a *fallið*, Raul Anderson is above his rank here," he said in an official tone that didn't quite hide his disdain.

A tight-lipped smile and narrowed eyes turned her lovely face dangerous. Both their power rose and crackled between them like a storm brewing.

"Raul isn't here as a member of anyone's pack. He's here as my *kennari*. I'm new to all this and need my navigator."

Isak, Gyda, and Ander all spoke at the same time, words of apology tumbling over one another in their haste to placate us. By holding her left hand up, Iona silenced them all without a word.

She turned a glare on Bain that looked as though it stung. "The detective is right. Your past politics have no bearing here. Leave them in the past or leave this circle now. Raul is welcome here as Miss Sandalius's *kennari*."

The prominent Adams' apple in Bain's neck bounced once before he answered. "Of course, Elder Iona, you are right. I shall leave it in the past." His gaze shifted to Elexis. "My apologies, Elexis."

The smile on Elexis's face relaxed, became more natural. "Thank you, Bain. I appreciate your diplomacy," she said.

His thin lips pulled tight into what I think was supposed to be a smile but only turned out looking a bit psychotic. "You are most welcome."

Iona clapped her hands together twice, hard. A muscle in Bain's cheek twitched. Three people came forward, two men and a woman, each carrying a drum and sticks. The traditional drums of deer hide and wood had an ancient smell to them, both thrilling and comforting. Norse runes were carved into the wood of each drum, some to honor Freya, some Odin, and others Thor. The drummers sat on stools near the bonfire pile, the drums between their knees.

One of Elexis's dark brows rose as she looked at me. I let my building smile shine through.

"This is the best part," I whispered to her.

People and wolves started to gather around the bonfire pile. Someone came around from behind it with a flaming torch in hand. With a deep bow, they handed it to Iona. Isak rose and stood beside his mother. Together they walked toward the pile of branches. The drummers started a fast-paced song that pulled at something deep in me, making me long to race through the forest in wolf form. From the look on the faces all around me, I knew it affected all those gathered in the same way.

I glanced at Elexis and wished I hadn't. She swayed to the beat, mouth parted, eyes half-closed, black hair with its blue streaks catching the torchlight. Her power pulsed stronger with each beat of the drum. I could get drunk just on the sight of her.

In a strong, pure voice, Iona chanted above the rhythm, "Hail to thee, Frigg, Goddess of fertility and love, queen of the Æsir. We honor you this full moon and thank you for our new sister." She handed the torch off to Isak.

Isak held the flaming thing aloft, his gaze skyward. "Hail to thee, Odin, Allfather, God of wisdom, king of the Æsir. We honor you this full moon and thank you for our new sister."

They walked together back to where we sat. Iona extended her hand to Elexis. She took it without hesitation and rose. Isak placed the torch in Elexis's hand.

"We light the fire to honor the Æsir, the full moon, and our ancestors. As the newest warrior in our ranks, that honor is yours to perform," he said.

Her hand wrapped tight around the torch. She strode up to the wood pile and touched the flame to it without a second's hesitation. Fire spread across the dry tinder. Cheers rose from all those gathered. People moved in, beginning a wild dance around the bonfire. I rose and went to Elexis's side before anyone else could beat me to it. By the time I took her hand, she was already swaying to the beat. The smile she gave me felt like an adrenalin shot straight to the chest. I pulled her after me in a wild dance around the bonfire. Others joined us, pressing in and moving with us. She didn't let go or allow any of them to cut in. It thrilled me so much it scared me a little. She moved with a natural, easy grace, twirling and swaying with abandon.

And her power, oh Odin, her power! It pulsed and flared with the music, pulling at my own so hard I couldn't move away. Her hand in mine worked like an anchor to this world, keeping me grounded and exactly where I needed to be. The look of pure joy on her face moved me in a way I'd never been moved before. The dark blue of her eyes reflected back the firelight, giving a glimpse of the wolf within. As we spun and gyrated around the fire, I touched her here and there—on the lower back, the hip, the arms. I couldn't get enough. And she leaned into my touch each time.

Though we danced for what had to have been nearly an hour, it went far too fast. All too soon, we were sitting back in the alphas' circle. Letting go of her hand left me feeling disconnected, chilled. Several more times throughout the next grueling hour or so of politicking, I had to bite my tongue and force myself to stay. The alphas each took turns telling Elexis all about their pack, the honor and strength of their members, and every other reason under the moon as to why she should join them. Gyda and Ander were particularly kind to her. Gyda kept hiding a small smile as she looked from Elexis to me. I somehow managed to remain polite to all, even Bain.

Bain and Morene both did their best to charm Elexis. She handled it all very diplomatically, making no promises, as I'd instructed her, yet turning down nothing. She proved an incredibly quick study.

All the while, people danced, sang, drank, and sparred in the fighting rings around us. Though no one approached or spoke to us, I felt their attention on us and knew they listened. The entire time I remained silent, knowing better than to push the welcome extended to me. Finally, just as I reached the end of my tolerance, Iona declared the discussion closed so we might enjoy the festivities.

With a wave of their hands, Ander and Gyda had a few of their pack members bring over food and drink for all of us. To my relief, Bain and Morene took their leave after a formal farewell to myself and Elexis. The way the man's gaze lingered on Elexis with lustful greed made my skin crawl. I did my best to hide my relief. Not only had I tired of politics long ago, but the higher the moon rose, the more I felt its pull. My instincts wanted to take over, to fight through all this tension.

Isak and Iona leaned their heads together and whispered a few words in Icelandic. My *varúlfur* hearing picked it up easily enough. They were eager to start the fighting rings back up. Finally, something I agreed with. The rest of what they said made me want to be in the ring. And it was why they chose to speak Icelandic in Elexis's vicinity. Iona moved into the crowd, calling for two members of her pack and referees. Elexis's eyes narrowed and her lips pursed. Before I could clear up the confusion, Isak spoke.

"We offer a bit of good-natured sparring, both for your entertainment and so you may see our best in action."

I smiled and nodded at Elexis, hoping to communicate that Isak and Iona hadn't meant any disrespect. No, their motives were far different.

The tense lines between Elexis's brows relaxed. "Thank you." It was more of a question than a statement, and I couldn't answer it because my grinding jaw wouldn't unlock. She gave me a questioning look. I nodded to let her know this was normal.

The alphas flowed out around us, leading the way to one of the fighting rings. Though no one spoke to me, they weren't rude either. Many nodded a greeting. I couldn't tell if it was my recent rise through the mid-level ranks or being with Elexis that caused it. Either way, the shift in attitude made me considerably less twitchy.

Isak led us up to the ringside, inviting us to sit in the grass not ten feet from it. I leaned over and whispered to Elexis. "Blood splatter seats, reserved for alphas and their *verndari*. It's an honor to be offered such seats."

Elexis looked at the other alphas sitting cross-legged on the grass around the ring before half-smiling at Isak. "Thanks, I think."

I swept a hand toward the hill around the ring. "See how the hill slopes down toward the ring? Ages ago, the elders chose the spots of the rings based on that, for spectators."

"Our kind puts a lot of thought into fighting," she observed without a judgmental tone.

"We do. Our entire social structure is built around the strong having to prove themselves."

We sat down between my parents and Isak. A member of the Arnoddr pack came by with a tray of drinks. I let Elexis choose before taking a glass of red wine for myself. Something stronger would have helped my diplomacy, but considering I would probably end up in the ring eventually, I wasn't going to chance it. A crowd of people and wolves milled about, filtering in to sit on the hill behind the alphas. *Verndari* from each pack came in to sit around the ring near their alphas. From across the ring, I met Morene's gaze and she gave me a smile. I tried not to think about how close she and Bain sat to one another and what it might mean.

The buzz of conversation took on an excited tone as Iona stepped up to the ring with two muscular, blond men in tow. She gave Elexis a warm smile. "Miss Sandalius, it is my pleasure to introduce to you, Ivar Henrikson of Reinhard and Óli Larson of Arnoddr. Two of our packs' finest *verndari*."

My blood burned, making me acutely aware of every vein in my body.

What Iona didn't say was Ivar and óli were also two of the most available bachelors from those packs. They weren't bad guys. Hell, Ivar was a friend of mine. He'd been the best linebacker I had on my team in high school. But the idea of Elexis with either of them made me itch to be in the ring. Both smiled at her and bowed their heads in a show of respect. óli held her gaze a little too long for my liking. I had to work entirely too hard to suppress a growl.

This was insane. I couldn't be hot for her, and not just because she was my partner. She had judged me just like everyone else. Despite the kiss and the fact she was kinder now, it still felt like she didn't trust me. Then there was the bull-headedness, the fact she was short-tempered and snarky. But she was also smart, smoking hot, and owned several pairs of handcuffs. I focused on the negative, hard. It was the only way I was going to make it through this night.

óli and Ivar faced off as the four referees each took a corner. To my relief, the fighters left their clothes on. It was the polite thing to do, since the guest of honor was so newly bitten and not used to our ways. I should have known Iona would insist on it. I swallowed down the relieved sigh that tried to work up my throat.

Iona moved to the center of the ring. "Fighters ready," she commanded in a tone that sounded far younger and stronger than she looked.

Ivar and óli raised their fists and stepped back into fighting stances.

"Begin!" Iona commanded.

They stalked around one another, muscles flexing for show, fangs extended. They feinted, grappled, blocked, and jabbed, moving with what I had to begrudgingly admit was grace. After a minute or so, Elexis leaned close to me.

"What is this fighting style?" she whispered.

"*Glíma*."

"It's fascinating."

I didn't like the awe in her tone. Was it for the fighting style or the fighters? *Nope, don't care, don't care.* Fangs pricked at my lips as if to prove me wrong.

Fists, legs and blood flew. Soon Elexis was oohing and aahing along with the crowd, shouting encouragement to each of the fighters. Her enthusiasm made me think she might regularly watch fights, maybe even subscribed to a channel that streamed them. It only made me hotter for her. I downed the last of my wine. The fight passed in a blur that I barely noticed. Ivar won, barely. The crowd applauded, none louder than Elexis. Another set of *verndari* entered the ring, this time two from the Draupnir pack.

I knew Iona had planned it that way. If anyone but a Draupnir member fought another Draupnir, it would get ugly and bloody. Few agreed with what Bain had done, and even fewer liked the fact that so many of the pack had chosen to stay.

The Draupnir *verndari* were also two very eligible bachelors. They grinned at Elexis, one openly leering, his gaze lingering on her cleavage. It struck me as odd that Bain would choose two of his single *verndari* to impress her, since he had designs on her himself. Or had it been Morene who had chosen? My gaze shifted to her. She sat at Bain's side, smiling up at the *verndari*, calling out encouraging words to them. Could she have done it because she actually wanted to be Bain's mate?

A cold chill shot through me.

No, that couldn't be it.

One of the *verndari* bowed deeply to Elexis, taking his shirt off as he straightened back up. The other nodded and winked at her before taking his shirt off too. They left their shorts on.

Kicking my feet up on a rock, I leaned back onto my hands and did my best to look like I was watching the fight while instead watching everyone else. Too much flexing and posturing went on between the fighters for my liking. They did bloody each other up a bit, which was a nice bonus. Bain watched Elexis. The calculating look in his eyes disturbed me on a deep level. My sister watched the fight, but like me, I caught her watching others, Bain and Elexis mostly. That disturbed me even more.

The fight came to an end and the crowd cheered.

Power pressed just behind me—or behind Elexis to be more exact. It felt neutral in the careful way power under tight control did. It came from Gisella, one of my parents' *verndari*, who sat right behind Elexis.

"Do you enjoy fighting as much as you enjoy watching?" Gisella asked in a badly faked light tone.

My mother and father's attention—and dagger-like gazes—shot to her. Before they could reprimand her, Elexis answered, "I do." The joy in her voice made it obvious she wasn't just saying it to impress someone. And was that a bit of spitefulness in her eyes? It flashed too fast for me to be sure. What the hell had Gisella said to her back at the Reinhard den to piss her off so much?

"Would you care for a match, then?" Gisella asked, her sweet tone not quite hiding her ill intent.

Elexis's energy crackled with an eagerness that worried me. She started to rise. "Very much so."

My father's back went rigid. "Gisella, Elexis is an honored guest. She is here to relax and celebrate joining our kind, not fight." His warning snapped with a biting power.

Gisella flinched and her fake smile wilted a little. She dipped her head. "Of course, Alpha. I only thought she might like to join in, since she enjoyed the matches so much."

Elexis patted Gisella on the back, a friendly-looking gesture, if a bit hard. Gisella's smile stretched a bit thin. "You're right, I would." She turned to look at Ander. "For sport and fun, not position or power, if it's okay with you, Alpha Ander."

We had practiced that very phrase, just in case. It would keep her from having to take the position of anyone she fought if she won by some stroke of luck. Many in the crowd let out a cheer. I stood fast enough my mother tensed. People started to jostle in closer for a better position around the ring. After exchanging a look, Ander and Gyda nodded to Gisella in unison. She walked onto the sand of the ring and started to stretch.

I leaned in close to Elexis's ear. "You don't need to do this. You have nothing to prove."

Her smile didn't waver. "That isn't why I'm doing it."

"She's a *verndari*, Elexis, a vicious one," I whispered against her ear.

She gave me a hard look. "Don't sweat it, Raul. It's just a friendly match."

A small growl slid from me, and I forced myself to sit back down. The only way to stop her would be to make a scene. I wasn't about to do that. She might piss me off on a regular basis, but she didn't deserve to be the center of a shitstorm caused by me. And with my current popularity level, that was exactly how it would turn out. Thor brought down the lightning, I brought down the shit. That was just how it was now.

I glared a warning at Gisella. At the moment, it was the best I could do. She grinned and rolled her eyes as if I was overreacting. Her power felt light and playful, but I knew better. The woman was a master at hiding her true intentions. She looked away from me with a superior lift of her chin, as if I was beneath her, which I was. My fangs extended, forcing me to pull my shit together before others noticed my aggravation. I could not let her know she'd gotten under my skin.

Elexis stepped onto the sand of the fighting ring. Both she and Gisella stretched while Iona made her way to the ring. Elexis's movements were slow and precise, meant to loosen muscles, while Gisella bent at the waist to show off her cleavage and ass to those gathered.

Iona looked to Elexis. "As the challenged, Elexis, you get to choose what form the fight will occur in: human, wolf, or both."

Elexis's eyes widened a bit. I hadn't told her that part because I hadn't expected her to spar. Her gaze moved smoothly from me to Iona. "Both," she said.

I cringed. She wasn't trained in that style of fighting. What was she thinking? Not to mention, I knew how uncomfortable she was in her wolf form.

Iona nodded. "Warriors, you may remove your clothing, if you wish."

My blood suddenly felt as hot as the bonfire raging nearby. I sat up straighter. My mouth went dry as I waited, trying to act like I didn't care whether or not Elexis chose to take her clothes off. On one hand, I longed to see her naked. On the other, I didn't want everyone here getting to see as well. A possessive streak burned through me. I shouldn't care, I didn't want to care, but I did. When Gisella stripped naked I didn't even look her way. I swallowed a relieved breath when Elexis made no move to remove clothing. But if she wasn't going to strip, why had she said both forms?

Looking at Elexis, Iona explained, "You fight to five points or a blackout. Each successfully landed hit is half a point, unless the striker is in the air, then it is a full point. First blood is two full points. Broken bones to your opponent result in the loss of a full point for you. Being thrown from, or stepping out of the ring, results in the loss of a point. You go negative five points for any reason, and you lose the match."

Face fixed in the emotionless cop look of hers, Elexis nodded. "Understood, thank you."

Iona smiled and inclined her head in a slight nod. Expression turning serious, she looked at Gisella. "Let's have a good, clean fight to honor the gods," she said in a warning tone.

Smile a bit too large and power a bit too bubbly, Gisella nodded once. "Of course, Proxy Alpha Iona." Though the "Proxy" part, along with her title, was meant to be a dig, Iona didn't so much as flinch. But she didn't return the woman's smile either. She moved out from between them and held a hand up. "Warriors, ready yourselves."

Hands raised, fingers tight together, Elexis slid into a back stance that left her bladed toward Gisella. She was the very picture of calm and centered. Gisella shook her hands out and nodded.

"Begin!" Iona commanded. In a flash, the elder alpha was out of the way.

Gisella bounced on the balls of her feet like a boxer. She moved around Elexis in a dizzying, bobbing pattern. It was a distracting technique she liked to use. I knew it well from sparring with her myself. Elexis ignored the moving limbs, bouncing breasts, and swaying hair. Her eyes locked on Gisella's eyes. Such focus impressed me. A clear mark of a good fighter. Not that I thought Elexis would be distracted by bouncing breasts. Eyes flaring wide, Gisella's lips pursed in frustration.

She darted in. Her fist thrust at nothing but air as Elexis sidestepped the strike. Twice more Gisella attacked and Elexis stepped effortlessly out of the way. The woman was crazy fast for a new wolf. They danced like that for a while, exchanging strikes and blocks. The grace of Elexis's raw style moved me. I couldn't look away. Gisella landed a punch to Elexis's stomach. Anger flared in me. I stomped it down, convincing myself I didn't care.

The point was called and awarded. The fight continued.

Gisella threw a kick with snake-like speed. Suddenly Elexis stood behind Gisella. I hadn't even seen her dodge the woman's attack. Claws extended, Elexis slashed out. A surprised scream of pain came from Gisella as she arched her back away.

"First blood!" one of the corner referees shouted.

Iona stepped into the ring. Both fighters relaxed their guard and came to a ready position opposite each other. Four gashes on Gisella's back bled freely. Her wide eyes stared at the curved, inch-long claws extending from

Elexis's fingers. Iona moved around to Gisella's back to look at the wound.

"Confirmed. First blood and two points to Elexis! The score is two to half a point" she announced.

From where I sat, I heard Gisella's teeth grind. It made me smile. She wasn't quite powerful enough to partially shift in the middle of a fight—another thing I knew from sparring with her. But now she knew Elexis was. To be able to have control while one's adrenalin was pumping was rare among even *verndari*-level fighters.

"Warriors ready!" Iona commanded. When they nodded, she began to walk backwards out of the ring. "Begin!"

Before the words stopped ringing through the hollow, Gisella's body began to shimmer with the start of a shift. She crouched down onto all fours just before morphing into a brown and white wolf. Not a lot of fighters would have seen that for the telegraph it was, but Elexis did. Gisella launched into the air. Sliding on her back, Elexis flattened herself onto the sand. As Gisella soared over her, Elexis kicked her feet into the wolf's stomach. The kick sent Gisella soaring from the ring to crash into the spectators on that side. A roar of cheers rose from the crowd. Hand held out, Iona stepped into the ring. Gisella's wolf form skulked back in. Shaking sand from her hair, Elexis moved into a ready stance.

"Point to Elexis for the kick. Point removed from Gisella for leaving the ring. Three to negative point five. Warriors ready!" Iona announced.

The crowd erupted into more cheers, even those who had taken the brunt of Gisella's fall. The smile on Elexis's face made it clear she was enjoying the hell out of herself. And it made her radiant as a valkyrie.

The fight continued.

Leaning forward, elbows on my knees, I watched Elexis's every move. She was a force of nature. Every kick, block, strike, and spin was efficient and effective. No wasted movements on flowery presentation marred her style. The only fighter I'd ever seen who was better was the reaper. Elexis's fighting style was so wild and raw, it looked like Odin himself had blessed her with battle fury. In that moment, I wanted her more than I'd ever wanted anything.

It became glaringly obvious they were outmatched. She danced out of the way, dodging, dropping, and leaping over Gisella. Twice Gisella shifted between wolf and woman to try to get the advantage. She couldn't land another strike on Elexis no matter what she did. Elexis gained another point, looking bored and relaxed as she did it. Blood pouring from a split lip, Gisella doubled over, breathing hard. After the point was called, Elexis went on the defensive, relaxed as she blocked and dodged out of the way of the taller woman's strikes. She passed up several opportunities to end the match. Like a cat, she played with Gisella, tormenting her until the *verndari* was sweating and gasping for breath. If I hadn't known Gisella for the bitch she was, I would have felt bad for her.

Elexis's power shone like the moon. And like the moon, she drew me in until I wanted to dance naked in her light. Gisella's flared like the bonfire, a force that would soon burn itself out. There was no comparison. Somehow Elexis had been hiding her power up until now. But the fight revealed its true nature. I'd met alphas who didn't have the pull she did.

And I wasn't the only one who couldn't look away from her. Out of my peripheral, I caught Bain and Isak watching her with intense interest. I had to concentrate hard to keep my power from flaring up in response. The last thing I wanted was for them to think I was interested in her. All right, second to the last. I wanted them interested in her even less.

Finally, she took mercy on Gisella and ended the fight with a jumping roundhouse kick to her stomach. In human form, Gisella went down on all fours and stayed there, gasping for breath. The point was called and the match awarded to Elexis. Still, Gisella didn't rise. Once Iona let go of her wrist from raising it in victory, Elexis went to Gisella's side. She held her hand out to her. Gisella sat back on her knees, reached out, and slapped Elexis's hand away. Gasps erupted through the crowd. Beside me, my mother started to growl. Ignoring the warning, Gisella stumbled to her feet and moved away from Elexis. Elexis shrugged and walked back toward me.

My mother rose and went to Gisella so swiftly, the breeze of her leaving ruffled my shirt. As Gisella bent over to pick up her clothes, Gyda grabbed her by the hair and dragged her off into the crowd.

My father stood and took Elexis's hand, placing a kiss on the back of it. "You fought beautifully, Elexis Sandalius. I apologize for my *verndari's* rudeness. Please know, if you ever want it, you have a place among our *verndari*," he told her.

I stood as well, forcing myself to move slowly so I didn't seem eager.

Once I reached my father's side I froze, unable to speak, move, or breathe, not because of him but because of Elexis.

She smiled. Sweaty, blood-splattered, she looked like a Viking shieldmaiden of old. "Thank you, Alpha Ander." She left it at that, and I was glad. To say more could give the wrong impression.

My father didn't let go of her hand. "I do hope you'll share where you learned to fight like that. It was remarkable," he said.

She shrugged, starting to look a bit uncomfortable at the attention. "The street as a foster kid at first, then a mixed martial arts gym, then the police academy, then the Law Enforcement Martial Arts Association." Her words broke my paralysis.

"Wow. I didn't know you had so much training."

She turned her beautiful smile on me, and with it came her power. Heightened due to the fight, it washed over me in a wave strong enough to drag a lesser *varúlfur* under. And she wasn't even doing it on purpose. In that power I felt the potential I had suspected during her fight. I took her hand from my father, not caring how it looked. "I think Elexis might like to get cleaned up before the rest of the festivities," I said in as light a tone as I could manage.

The look on my father's face made it clear he was about to protest, but Elexis spoke before he could. "Yeah, thanks. I'd love that."

I inclined my head to my father in a show of respect. "Would you please excuse us, Alpha?"

Ander stepped aside. "Of course."

We started into the crowd. "There's a creek running through the hollow. I'll take you to it," I told Elexis.

People moved in to congratulate her, pat her on the back, or just reach out to touch her. She endured it all with heartfelt words of thanks and genuine smiles. But soon her crackling power told a different story, one of suspicion and discomfort at so many strangers at her back, touching her. I walked faster. Being used to the Friday-night lights and attention, I couldn't exactly understand her discomfort, but I sympathized. She stretched her legs out to keep alongside me. Soon we left the throng of people behind and entered a forest glowing with the light of the full moon. The sweet scents of pine and hemlock replaced those of wolves and fire. Water trickled over rocks not far away.

Elexis let out a big sigh. "Thanks, I needed out of that crowd."

"I thought you might. That isn't the only reason I brought you out here, though." My voice sounded deeper and a bit more suggestive than I wanted it to. But dammit, I couldn't help it. Now that I'd seen this wild, powerful side of her, I couldn't get it out of my head. The man in me tried to focus on how she had judged me and suspected I was involved in the bitings. The wolf in me couldn't focus on anything but how perfect a mate she would be, powerful, confident, self-reliant, equal in all ways.

"Then why did you bring me out here?" she asked.

I told myself I was imagining the sound of hope in her voice. I had to be. One kiss did not mean she wanted to jump my bones.

We stopped alongside the rocky edge of the creek. It meandered on through the forest ahead of us, its silver surface reflecting the moonlight. I sat on a fallen log and clasped my hands before me to keep them to myself. She sat so close, the heat of her body burned my skin, making it ache to touch hers.

"You just kicked a *verndari's* ass like it was nothing," I said.

She grunted. "She wasn't that good."

"Actually, she is. You are just that much better."

Moonlight played on the blue highlights of her hair as she shook her head. "Not this again."

I grabbed her hand. "Elexis, I'm serious. This is no time for modesty. You just proved to everyone watching not only could you be a top *verndari*, you are alpha material. I could practically hear Bain and Isak salivating while you fought."

"Ugh, gross. Well, at least on Bain's part. Isak is kind of hot, though..."

Laughing, I bumped her shoulder with mine. "Sure, if you like your men in their sixties," I teased.

She laughed with me. "That is just not right."

After a moment of listening to her beautifully honest laugh, I said, "Seriously, though, you just threw down the gauntlet to a lot of *verndari*, so you'll have to be careful."

"What's new?" she said through a sigh.

"That reminds me of the other reason I wanted to talk to you alone. Could you tell from Gisella's fighting style if she was one of the ones who attacked you?"

She shook her head. "If she was, she wouldn't have walked out of that ring." The bitterness in her voice warned me to tread carefully.

"Damn, sorry. I was hoping you might have caught a lead."

"Nope. Just a bitch with a grudge."

"With your potential, you're going to come across a lot of those."

Letting out a fierce growl, she flew to her feet. "I'm sick and tired of people expecting so much out of me. It only ends badly for them." Her reaction took me completely by surprise. Pain etched deep lines into her face.

"I didn't mean to—"

"No one ever does," she interrupted.

Another growl came from her. She strode to the creek, plunged her hands in, and began to scrub at the blood on them. Her claws had extended again. I gave her a moment to herself while she washed. By the time she splashed water on her face, she breathed a little easier.

"Who did you lose?" I asked gently.

Her shoulders slumped. "My mentor, Lieutenant Perez. They said it was a wolf attack while he was out hunting." She turned a sharp eye on me. "I hunted down the wolf who attacked him, but when I went to shoot him, he shifted into a man, then attacked me."

"James," I breathed.

"Yes, the bastard. But as much as I hate him and want to bring him to justice, I also know he isn't the only one to blame."

I rose and started toward her. "No, Elexis. None of that is your fault."

Popping out of her crouch, she spun toward me. "Don't try to placate me. We were investigating a death by wolf attack. The signs were there. I just couldn't wrap my head around it." She swallowed hard before going on. "Perez chose to go on a hunting trip near where the attack happened. I was too busy with another case to go along. I should have known..."

Her head dropped, and I wanted desperately to lift her chin, but the hostility radiating off her made me think twice. "What, that werewolves were real? That everything you thought you knew about the world was wrong? No. No one in your position could have known."

Her head jerked in my direction, fangs bared. "But part of me did know. I suspected, deep down. I felt it. And I'm of one of the *varúlfur* bloodlines. That's how that works, right? You only survive if you are of a bloodline. So

I should have trusted my instincts. If I had half the potential Perez thought I did, I would have."

Moonlight shone on a tear trailing down her left cheek. I brushed it away, my thumb lingering on her soft skin. For a second, she leaned into my hand. But then she pulled swiftly away.

"I don't need you to make me feel better. I don't want you to. What I want is to catch James and the people behind the bitings." She sniffed once, put her shoulders back, and started walking. "I need to get back."

It took all my willpower not to go after her and take her in my arms. All her bitterness made sense now. I had no idea she'd been grieving. No one shared that little tidbit of information with me. Then again, no one shared any information with me anymore.

When I didn't follow, Elexis looked back over her shoulder at me. "You coming?" Her tone was lighter, forced, but lighter.

Still, I couldn't help but try to lighten things a little more. "A guy doesn't like to be asked that. He prefers a woman knows when he's coming."

She took a big, dramatic step away from me.

"What are you doing?" I asked.

"Moving in case Thor decides to strike you down for that horrible line," she said with a laugh.

"Hey!"

The laughter that spilled from her sounded a bit tired, but I'd take it. Anything was better than the profound sadness that had gripped her a few seconds ago. She'd just bit my head off and here I was caring about her feelings. Maybe Thor had already struck me.

CHAPTER TWENTY

ELEXIS

The rest of the night was a blur of food, wine, ancient Norse music, and even a bit of howling at the moon, literally. It turned out werewolves really did that. Raul hadn't been kidding. The alphas all wanted me to join not only their packs, but the ranks of their *verndari*. No one else challenged me, but I could see the caution and veiled hostility in the eyes of several *verndari* in all the packs. Nearly every single male of *verndari* level or higher asked me to dance at some point in the night. But the two most persistent were Bain and Isak.

Thankfully, Raul kept them all mostly at bay, though I did get sucked into one dance with Bain and two with Isak. True to his promise, when people started taking their kids home, Raul whisked me away with excuses of police paperwork to file. I breathed a sigh of relief as the forest swallowed the noise of the festivities behind us.

I wasn't sure if I wanted to be alone with Raul after I'd spilled my darkest secret to him, but I knew I didn't want to be around all those people anymore. They didn't know me, they didn't want *me* in their pack. They wanted my power. That annoyed the hell out of me. Or maybe into me was more accurate, because that's how I felt, like the Norse demi-Goddess Hel, filled with spite, regret, and a need for vengeance I had no way to quench.

"That was uncomfortable," I mumbled as I negotiated my way through a patch of ferns.

"I don't know, you looked pretty comfortable dancing with Isak," Raul said, tone more than a touch bitter.

Feeling his eyes on me, I smiled and shrugged. "What can I say, the man can dance. Looks, personality, and talent on top of it. What's not to like?" I waved a hand. "Seriously, though, he isn't my type."

Out of the corner of my eye I thought I saw a muscle in his cheek twitch. I tried not to think about what that meant. And I tried not to be happy about it. Both attempts failed.

"Any luck with feeling the power of your attackers?" he asked.

"No. I tried, but like I said, I didn't get a good feel for them that night. I didn't know how to. Now that I do, it's too late."

He grabbed my hand. "It's not too late. We'll find them. At least after your fight with Gisella, people are less likely to mess with you."

"I don't know about that. I got a lot of dirty looks from *verndari*."

"Yeah, well—"

I stopped and held a finger up to his lips. A fire started to burn behind his amber eyes as he gazed down at me. Desire softened his features. The warmth of his breath did all kinds of naughty things to me. But I couldn't let that distract me. I'd heard something. I listened hard for it. There it was—two male voices arguing in urgent whispers. Giving Raul a look I hoped conveyed the need for quiet, I withdrew my finger from his lips. He raised a brow but didn't say anything.

Careful to place each step precisely on the rocky ground of the hollow, I started to creep forward. Bright moonlight made it easy to see the path before me. Even seeing the ground, I wasn't as quiet as Raul. The man moved like a ghost. But then, he'd had his abilities since puberty, so he had a bit of an advantage over me. We crested a small rise. Through the trees, a hundred feet or so away, stood Bain and Dustin. Arms flailing as he paced back and forth in front of Bain, Dustin ranted.

"Assassins, really? Ayra is my friend. This is going too far!" The urgent words were almost elevated above a whisper.

Eyes going wide, Raul looked at me. I grabbed his hand and pulled him into the shadows of a thick group of trees with me. Low-hanging, feathery pine boughs helped conceal us.

"The point isn't to kill her, so much as distract her," Bain said, voice surprisingly gentle.

Dustin stopped before him and leaned close. "So much? Really?" he hissed.

Bain grabbed the man's face in both hands. Afraid for Dustin, I took a step out of the trees. He might be a member of Bain's pack, one who stuck close to him, but he was still a gentle person with low power who couldn't defend himself against someone like Bain. Raul pulled me back, his grip on my hand tight. He shook his head at me.

Bain sighed. "We have to keep her away from the key long enough for the awakening. This is almost over. You only need to stay strong for a bit longer. She'll be fine, trust me," he said.

The key? An awakening? Could that be connected to the bitings? I moved a step closer. Something cracked beneath my foot. Bain let go of Dustin's face. Both men turned in our direction. Bain started to walk toward us.

I gave Raul a desperate look. He all but tore his shirt off, grabbed me, and pressed me against a tree, molding his entire body to mine. A moment of claustrophobic fear and distrust swept through me. The feel of his muscular chest and his hot groin against me raised a surprising desire that burned it all away. Our lips found each other in the dark with magnetic ease. His mouth opened over mine, tongue slipping tentatively inside. When he withdrew, my tongue followed his. Warm and wet, he tasted complicated, like a great Cabernet.

The logic of needing to make out with him to keep from getting caught took all the guilt out of it. I gave myself over to the moment. For believability, of course.

His hands cupped my butt, strong arms lifting me off my feet with an ease that made my breath catch. I wrapped my legs around him, locking my ankles together, pulling his groin against mine. The hard length of him against my opening made me groan into his mouth. I wanted the clothing between us gone. Our kiss became hungry, our fangs rubbing against one another's. It was a strange yet erotic sensation. My hands worked their way around his muscular back, claws tracing across his taut skin. He slid a hand up my shirt.

Footsteps approached, bringing the reality of why we were groping each other slamming back. The pressure of Bain's power came with them. I opened my eyes. Raul's cheek-length brown hair covered my face, obscuring anything beyond it, but effectively hiding me as well. The footsteps passed by less than ten feet from us, then faded away. Both Bain and Dustin's power soon disappeared into the forest.

Raul's hand stopped at my ribs. His tongue withdrew from my mouth. He set me down on my feet and took a step back. "Sorry about that," he whispered, not sounding in the least bit sorry.

Instantly, I missed the feeling of him against me, of our breaths mingling into one. "Don't be." His brows rose and he smiled. I pushed off the tree to follow him. "Raul, I—" My words cut short as my hand pressed into the groove created by the tree trunk and a branch. Something small, cool, and hard moved beneath my fingers. It rattled like a tiny chain. I dug it out and held it up. Moonlight glinted off a gold pendant in the form of three triangles woven together. Engraved on the triangles were the names Didrik, Lísandra, and Draupnir.

Chills exploded across my skin in the form of bumps. Holding the necklace before me, I stepped out of the trees.

Raul turned to me. "What's wrong? What is that?"

"Lísandra's necklace."

CHAPTER TWENTY-ONE

ELEXIS

lthough our wolf's eyes—and nose in Raul's case—were able to detect everything just as well on a moonlit night, we went back to that spot the next day. With him sleeping on the couch in what I had come to think of as the game room, we'd been able to get an early start. Thankfully, he rose at the crack of dawn just like I did. A big part of me had wanted him closer than the couch, much closer. But the mood had been ruined by the likelihood of Lísandra's death.

We found a few strands of her blond hair on the tree branch and a single drop of old blood in the grooves of the bark. While none of it was conclusive enough evidence, it painted a clear picture to me. A struggle had occurred that resulted in her necklace being torn off and lost in the tree. What happened after was hard to tell. But I got a very bad feeling. From all the pictures of her wearing the necklace, and knowing Didrik had given it to her, I knew she wouldn't have left it behind. If she were alive, she would have come back for it.

Despite being totally blind-sided and half out of his mind with anger, Raul had texted Ayra the night before and warned her about the assassins. His concern for her and Sonya made me realize the depth of my misjudgment of him. I felt like an idiot. Some detective skills. The trauma of having been attacked and bitten by James shouldn't have blinded me so thoroughly to the fact Raul was nothing like my attacker.

Later that afternoon, I broke the news to Iris. After a few tears and a glass of wine, we found an old jewelry box of Lísandra's and put the necklace in it. Holding the wooden box close to her chest with one hand, Iris raised her wine glass with the other. "To Lísandra and Didrik. May they be dining together at Odin's table in Valhalla," she said in a voice clear and strong despite the moisture in her eyes.

I clinked my glass against hers. "To Lísandra and Didrik charming the cloaks off the gods." She almost smiled.

We drank the last of our wine in their honor. Letting out a long, shuddering sigh, Iris put her glass on the speckled marble kitchen bar. She tucked a lock of teal hair behind her left ear—her new color being something she called a mermaid ombre. It started out blue a few inches below her blond root line, faded into green, then turned to teal. The way it set off her green eyes was stunning. I was more than half looking for a reason for us to shift so I could see how it looked on her wolf form.

"Are you coming to the meeting?" she asked.

"Meeting?"

"The AVW, American Viking Werewolves."

My brows rose. "Sounds downright criminal. What is it exactly?"

"Nothing criminal, I promise. We're a group of *varúlfur* from all different packs, and even a lot of lone wolves, kind of an umbrella pack that encompasses a bunch of different packs. We share information to make us all stronger, safer."

"There is another group, right? The AVV. What's the difference?"

"Yeah, the AVV is the American Viking *Varúlfur*. They hold more traditional beliefs and customs and are usually the older generations."

I let out a short, harsh laugh. "So their names virtually mean the same thing." Iris smiled and shrugged. Suspicion started to prickle at me. "Does the AVW believe werewolves should be out to the world?"

She gave me a look like she had known my mind would go there. "Some do. Bain is one of them, and he believes that. None of them claim to support the unsanctioned bitings, and I honestly believe most of them don't. But I don't believe Bain."

"Sure, I'd love to go." Any information I could glean at this point would be a good thing, and members of this group could be involved.

A motorcycle with a seriously powerful-sounding engine rumbled up my driveway. I knew the sound well—a Suzuki Hayabusa, one of the fastest bikes on the market. Jackson Hole was no Sturgis—thank the powers that be—but we'd had our fair share of motorcycle rallies. And a cop always knew the sound of something that could outrun them. Iris started toward the front door and I followed, more eager to see Raul than I cared to admit. I'd seen the bike in his garage. It had to be him. I smoothed out my blue peasant's blouse, wishing I'd worn something a bit less girlie. Such outfits made me uncomfortable around guys, particularly those I liked.

Soft footsteps barely disturbed the gravel of the driveway. Their cadence was another sound I knew well—Raul. A deck board creaked as he crossed it. Iris opened the door before he could knock. He wore beige jeans that fit just tight enough to hint at more than adequate attributes, a tucked in button-up silk shirt the color of the darker flecks of brown in his eyes, and a brown Cordura jacket. The jacket surprised me. He didn't normally wear unnatural fabrics. But I wasn't going to complain. It made him look even sexier than normal, very biker-like in a fast and furious way.

His amber eyes drank me in slowly, as if he'd been waiting all day to do so and was determined to take his time. My power flared like it wanted to reach for him. Hell, he looked so delicious, *I* wanted to reach for him. I pulled my power back in and swallowed my libido. Like everything where my wolf was concerned, it wasn't easy. That it could rule me so completely irked the hell out of me.

Despite the new clues, we were no closer to solving this case. Distraction of any kind was not a luxury I could afford.

"What's with the jacket?" I asked, doing my best not to sound breathy like a bitch in heat.

He made a motion with his head, indicating the motorcycle over his shoulder. "Our skin is tough, but not impenetrable." He drew a hand through his ruffled hair. "I belong to this group, sort of an umbrella pack, but with a committee instead of alphas. We're having a meeting tonight. I thought you might like to go."

The hesitant tone of his voice made him sound like a nervous teenager asking a girl out for the first time. It was kind of charming. "I would. Iris just told me all about it."

His mouth worked a few times before words came out. "Oh, uh." His gaze moved to her. "You beat me to it."

She shrugged. "I'm here a lot."

I looked down at my shorts and bare feet. "I'll ride with you. Just let me get some jeans and shoes on."

He smiled, amber eyes brightening. My insides tried to melt at that look, but I cooled them off with thoughts of the investigation. I stepped aside and beckoned for him to enter. His gaze fixated on my legs, and he made a sort of strangled grunting sound of approval. I left him in the foyer with Iris as I went and changed. The thought of being on a motorcycle behind him sent a thrill of heat through me that stirred my power. I did my best to drive the thoughts away as I pulled my jeans on. By the time I laced up my black boots, I had my sex drive mostly under control. I wanted to believe the attraction was based on the fact I hadn't gotten laid in close to a year, or on the instincts of my wolf side. But deep down where I didn't want to look, I knew it was more than that.

As I wove my hair into a quick braid, I brought my focus around to the whole point of going—which wasn't to have Raul's body between my legs. When I walked back into the foyer, Iris was putting on a leather jacket, a helmet sitting at her feet.

"Whoa there, girlfriend. We just drank an entire bottle of wine," I said.

She gave me a disarming grin. "Over the course of two hours. Couple that with *varúlfur* and Norwegian metabolism, and I'm good."

I thought about arguing for all of a second before I realized I didn't feel the slightest bit tipsy. "Well shit, that could get expensive," I murmured.

Both Raul and Iris laughed. Iris patted me on the shoulder as she stood from picking up the helmet. "For sure. I've already let Luke know we're going out and he'll need to keep an eye on the cameras, so we're good to go," she said. She handed me the helmet. "You can use my extra helmet. You might need it with this crazy driver." She motioned with her head toward Raul.

A short laugh came from him. "Look who's talking. You always leave me in the dust."

She shot him a broad smile. "German technology can't be beat."

I gave her a half-smile as I accepted the helmet. "Thanks, I think."

Watching the two of them engage in such friendly banter softened something in me. Raul was kind and friendly toward her, despite the fact she was an outcast. Many in his position would have jumped at the chance to treat someone as an inferior. It spoke volumes about him I hadn't been open to reading before. And since Iris accepted him so easily, it made me think maybe I had been too harsh on him.

We started for the front door. I looked up at the hidden camera in the massive antler chandelier overlooking the foyer and waved at Luke, who I knew was watching. From the little table on the wall leading to the kitchen, I grabbed my phone. The new app I had downloaded onto it would allow me to check the cameras and give me alerts if any of the alarms were tripped. So, in essence, I wasn't leaving the outcasts completely alone. Still, it didn't feel good. I closed the massive double doors behind us and armed the security system.

When I hesitated with my hand on the door, Raul touched my shoulder. "Don't worry. No one knows they're here. Besides, everything you've done for them has made them safer." His words were barely more than a whisper, as if he were worried someone might be listening. It made me even more reluctant to leave.

Iris strode off to where her bike was parked beneath an ancient pine tree to the left of the house. I did my best to adopt her carefree attitude. The smile I gave Raul almost felt genuine. At the bottom of the steps, his charcoal-gray motorcycle crouched like a predator waiting to attack. Okay, maybe it wasn't the bike that was intimidating so much as the idea of riding on it behind Raul. My resistance to the pull between us was already wearing thin. This was not a good idea.

He took his jacket off when we reached the bike and handed it to me. A huge, round patch covered most of the back—a wolf's head formed of knot work surrounded by a wheel of Norse runes, all stitched in silver. Above the wolf was a rocker that read: AVW. Below it was one that read: Montana. Leaning close enough I could smell the mild aloe shampoo he used on his dark brown hair, Raul pulled the keys from one of the coat pockets.

"I've been a *varúlfur* longer, so my skin is tougher. This will protect you if we go down," he said.

"Why would we go down?" I asked in a strangled voice.

"We wouldn't! That's not what I mean. I...um..."

Iris snickered in the distance. Her motorcycle started up.

"You know she was kidding, right? I'm a good driver. You don't have to worry," he said.

Cocking my head, I put his jacket on. "We'll see," I said, fighting to keep a straight face. I had nothing against motorcycles, and I actually believed him. He was just too easy to mess with.

Raul's scent of pine and aloe, along with light, pleasant undertones of a wolfy musk engulfed and distracted me. The desire to burrow deep into it and roll all over until the scents covered my skin gripped me, hard. To hide my reaction, I pulled the full face helmet on. I could still smell him, taste his scent on the air, and hear his heartbeat, but at least he couldn't see how it affected me.

"So, there are more divisions of the AVW and AVV in other states," I said. It was vital I get my mind on something else before I straddled a powerful, vibrating machine and pressed up against this man.

"Just over eighteen thousand," he said before putting his helmet on.

"Wow," I managed.

He shrugged. "It doesn't sound so impressive when you consider there are over three-hundred and fifty million people in America."

He had a point there. It reminded me that despite all the bitings, werewolves were an endangered species.

The bike rumbled to life at the turn of a key. Blood rushed to my nether regions as he swung a leg over. Silk sleeves hugging his bulging biceps, legs straddling that machine, he looked even sexier than I had imagined. Forcing my desire down deep, I got on behind him. He reached back, grabbed one of my hands, and pulled it up around his waist.

"Better hold on. This thing is fast enough to come out from under even a *varúlfur*."

I wrapped my other arm around him as well, just to be safe. The designer silk shirt he wore did nothing to hide the valleys and planes of his hard abdominal muscles. My fingers wanted to explore further, but I forced them to be still. It took a mile or so of open road and fresh air to clear my head.

Not sure he'd hear me, and only half wanting him to, I said, "You and

Iris are on pretty good terms." As soon as the words were out, I knew he'd hear me. Hell, I could hear his heartbeat.

"Are you jealous?" he asked in an amused tone. Though his voice was a bit muffled from the helmet, it was easy to hear, even over the wind noise.

"No. Surprised is all. With her being an outcast and you being fallen." I tried to make the words light so they didn't sound as condemning as they felt.

He stiffened against me a bit.

"I don't mean anything bad by that. I just didn't know how else to put it," I said.

Nearly a minute later, he responded. "After Didrik was killed, I spent a lot of time in the library. I went over all the books I could on pack law, trying to find a loophole to catch Bain in. We sort of bonded over our hatred for the man."

I didn't get the vibe they'd been lovers, and that made me happier than I cared to admit. "You didn't find anything," I said.

He accelerated a bit around a corner, making my heart thud with excitement. His answer came after his speed leveled out on a straight stretch. "Nothing. The bastard is meticulous at covering his bases."

Meticulous didn't seem to be Bain's thing. His clothes were always haphazardly thrown together, and his hair looked like he braided it and left it for a week at a time. Even his home was that of a casual bachelor, with beer bottles on the deck railing and clothes slung across the outdoor furniture. From my chat with him, I would say he was good at avoidance and misdirecting. Meticulous was not a word I would choose for him, though. But I didn't want to start an argument while riding bitch on a crotch rocket with a guy who could barely stand me half the time.

The winding road forced me to mold myself to Raul's back and move with him and the motorcycle. Conversation died off, which was a good thing, considering how tongue tied I got from being so close to him. The warmth of his body seeped into mine. His power wound around me, feeling as real and solid as he did. The strength and stability of it drew me in deeper. Resting my helmeted head on the back of his shoulder, I gave myself over to the sensation of him against me and all around me, of moving in time with him. There was something instinctual and right about it, as if this was where I belonged. That should have made me nervous, but it didn't. Not yet, at least.

The empty road wound like a curled ribbon through the forest of sweet-smelling evergreens and birch. Sunlight filtered down through the tall trees, leaving long, intermittent shadows across the blacktop. Raul kept his speed under seventy, even on the straight stretches, giving me the impression he was in no hurry. We didn't catch up to Iris. The contented feel of his power, coupled with the way he leaned back against me, made me hope our destination was far away.

I clung tighter to him, enjoying the muscular body beneath my hands. My little finger brushed the waistband of his jeans. The image of him naked, fighting like a Viking of old, flashed behind my eyelids again. I kept my eyes closed, enjoying the memory far more than I should have. The urge to let my hands trail lower surged. From the way his power felt, all charged and excited, I knew he would welcome it. His silk shirt allowed my other fingers to slip lower without any resistance. The edge of his jeans lay just beneath all my fingertips now. The desire to touch more left me breathless.

My resistance nearly caved, but then we rounded a corner and came upon a roadside bar tucked into the trees. A wooden sign with letters formed out of copper pipe spelled out "AVW Clubhouse." Smokey gray windows lined the front of the large, red-brick building. Not even my wolf's vision could see through them. Motorcycles and sports cars of every kind and color filled the parking lot.

Equal parts excitement and disappointment filled me as Raul parked next to Iris's motorcycle. I was eager to question people but reluctant to let go of him. He took his helmet off and hung it on the bike's mirror. Voices and bluesy music came from inside the building. Only two other people were working their way through the parking lot. I held onto Raul a moment longer. His hand covered mine where it rested on his abdomen. I mustered up my willpower, pulled my hand free, and jumped from the motorcycle. Hurt flashed in his eyes before they flicked toward the two guys walking through the parking lot.

Shit. I hadn't meant for it to look like that.

Determined not to take a leap backwards in my relationship with him —even if it was just a working one, I grabbed his hand. "No, Raul, I—"

"Hey Raul, who's this pretty little thing on your arm?" came a man's voice as they veered our direction.

Both tall men wore leather jackets sporting the same patches as the ones on the back of Raul's. The speaker had a shaved head, a blond goatee, and a broad smile. The second guy leered at me appreciatively from behind a shaggy mop of brown hair.

Now Raul pulled *his* hand free of mine. "Hey Chris, John." He nodded to each as he said their name. "This is Elexis Sandalius, my partner."

"Partner? Is that slang for something, Anderson?" Chris, the goatee guy teased.

Raul laughed, but it sounded a bit forced. "No. HHPD asked me to work with her on the bitings case."

"So you're single," John said in a suggestive tone.

Raul's brow furrowed, and a cord popped out along his jaw.

I decided to play John to my advantage. "Maybe. What's your take on werewolves coming out to the world?" As I talked, I took Raul's jacket off, handed it to him, and took a few steps toward John. His height gave him a good look down my low-cut blouse.

He smiled. "Depends how you feel about it."

I shrugged. "Haven't decided yet."

We all started to walk toward the building.

"In that case, there are pros and cons both ways, I guess, depending on how you look at it. I don't much like the idea. I live in Montana because I like the peace and quiet. Coming out to the world would end that," he said.

"Yeah, but we'd be able to shift anywhere we wanted, run anywhere we wanted. We wouldn't have to hide what we are," Chris said.

I slowed my pace until he walked alongside me as well. "So you're for it."

His face scrunched up, and he shook his head. "I didn't say that. The last thing I want is to see our kind become some government experiment, or be forced into encampments. But I would like to be able to shift without worrying about being shot," Chris said.

John made an unhappy grunting noise. "Yeah, thanks to all the bad media from those condemned killing people, it's a dangerous time to be a wolf."

"Condemned?" I asked.

"It's what we call the wolves who go mad when they go through the *verða* and start killing people. Or maybe they were mad to start with," Raul said from right behind me.

My cop instincts told me these guys were being honest. They weren't involved. When we reached the door, I dropped back by Raul's side. John and Chris each opened and held one of the double doors. Music and voices poured out in a wave that threatened to suck me under. I turned my werewolf hearing down until the sounds were tolerable. The wolfy musk wafting out of the room took my breath away. It wasn't a bad smell—just strong. No one was actually in wolf form. Werewolves just carried that scent as part of their natural smell.

People filled the stools along a bar running nearly the length of the room and sat at tables throughout it. There were easily several hundred. I recognized a lot of them from Hemlock Hollow, even a few from my basement. Members from all three packs were present. Dozens of strangers from out of town filled the tables as well. They were a rough-looking bunch in their patch- and rocker-adorned jackets or vests. Many were tall, broad, and blond, but not all. In fact, I picked out at least four different races.

Many eyes turned our way, and only a handful of those who did were unfriendly. Most people were engaged deep in conversation, some of it companionable but most of it political. I turned my hearing back up as we walked in. A lot of heated talk centered around the news stories about wolf attacks, poachers, and newly bitten. Even more discussed the seeker and the reaper.

Several people called out greetings to Raul as we wove our way through the tables. He answered each with a smile, calling them by name. Iris waved from a table against the far wall. Raul waved back and started her way. Getting there took a while because he had to stop often to chat with people. Their interactions with him were casual and respectful, making it clear most of them held respect for him, particularly the outcasts. He asked them about their packs, mates, or children, showing genuine interest in their answers. The respect they gave him surprised me after how I'd seen him treated in Hemlock Hollow, by his own pack even. It made me wonder how much of that was due to Bain's influence.

Once we reached Iris's table—at which sat two other outcasts from my basement—Raul pulled a chair out for me. First, I was pleasantly shocked he would openly associate with the outcasts. Second, it was becoming clear the whole gentlemanly thing wasn't an act. I smiled at Iris as she pretended to introduce me to the two others at our table: Jamie, a twenty-something red-headed woman with an A-line bob, and her tall, dark-haired, skinny boyfriend, Dennis.

I sat down just as a waitress showed up at our table—a pretty brunette woman who looked no more than twenty. But being a werewolf, it was difficult to tell her age. "Can I get you anything, darling?" she asked.

"Water, thanks."

She nodded and looked to Raul. "I'll take a glass of cabernet sauvignon. Make that two."

The waitress dipped her head, smiled at him from beneath her lashes, and strutted off. Her short, pleated skirt almost flashed her butt cheeks. Raul didn't even glance her way. I raised a brow at him. "Two glasses?" I asked.

"One for you, one for me."

I shook my head. "I'm working. *We're* working." I didn't even try to keep the critical tone from my voice.

The crooked grin he gave me made me tingle down to my toes. "Yes we are, and people talk more openly to a lady with a drink in her hand," he said.

Brows raised, I tilted my head to the side and inclined it. "True enough," I admitted.

While we waited for our drinks, we chatted about random things with Iris, Jamie, and Dennis. Nothing too revealing, considering the super hearing of everyone in the room. Iris carried the conversation easily in her overt and energetic way. One got a buzz just being around the woman, she let off so much energy. She had a sharp sense of humor that touched on the dark side cops were so familiar with. Maybe it was part of why I clicked with her so well.

The way she led the conversation gave me the perfect cover to nod and engage slightly while I listened to other conversations throughout the room. Unfortunately, everyone else was either being as careful as we were about their topics of choice, or they had nothing nefarious to talk about. Finally, our waitress returned. She set two glasses of red wine before Raul and a tumbler of what smelled like rum and lemon juice in front of Iris.

Grinning, Iris saluted her. "You read my mind, sweetheart."

The waitress laughed and inclined her head to Iris before asking for our food orders. The place served the regular variety of pub food, from which we each made our choices. Once she left, Raul took his glass of wine and stood. "Shall we mingle before the food gets here?" he asked me with a pointed look.

I picked up my wine glass and stood as well. "Sounds like a good plan." I looked to the others. "Sorry to duck out on you, work to do and all."

Iris waved a hand. "Go, detect things."

Dennis and Jamie smiled and nodded.

I followed Raul into the throng of people. Their chatter flowed around us in waves. I focused in on it, listening for key words. People stopped us here and there to chat with Raul and ask to be introduced to me. They treated him like an old friend, one they respected and valued the opinion of. Not one of them we spoke to seemed to believe he had bitten in Sonya of his own free will, even though they clearly didn't know the whole story. Many commented on how brave he was to remain in Hemlock Hollow and put up with the politics trying to devour him. The way these people saw him, it made me see him in a new light.

I stayed close to him, often touching his arm or his back. Partly, I wanted to deter the men who looked at me with interest or lust, but mostly I just wanted to touch Raul. I found myself looking forward to the ride home. People talked freely enough, eager to give their opinions on the bitings, those involved, and the damage it was doing to werewolves' anonymity. But none admitted to having any information on the whereabouts of Calder or James. It was one dead end after another.

After almost half an hour, Raul led us back to our table as our waitress brought our food. Iris raised her brows. I shook my head in answer. We talked with her, Jamie, and Dennis between bites, mostly about the news regarding the wolf attacks, a topic that wouldn't attract prying ears. Shortly after we finished, a dark-haired woman stood up on the bar and howled a long, eerie note. Bumps rose along my arms. I wasn't sure if I'd ever get used to hearing a human make that sound. The entire room fell silent.

"Welcome to the July meeting of the AVW. Tonight's first topic is the report of wolf attacks in our individual territories and the media coverage. In Flathead, we've had six reports in the last two weeks, two of them confirmed. From what our source in the coroner's department says, they were *varúlfur*. The media covers the topic at least once a week."

She jumped down and a blond man vaulted up to take her place. "In Lincoln, we have reports of two attacks. Both turned out to be false. News talks about wolf attacks once a week or so."

He jumped down and another took his place. The reports went on and on. Sometimes alphas spoke on behalf of their packs or territories, sometimes *verndari*, and even lone wolves in a few cases. Each county in Montana had reported attacks, and though not all of them were real, too many were. And too many were confirmed to be condemned werewolf attacks. The numbers rose on the interior counties, both on attacks and news coverage. From listening, it was easy to gather that the condemned doing the attacking were following a path through Montana and down into Idaho. Dozens of accounts were given until finally, the same dark-haired woman who had started the flow of information jumped back up onto the bar.

"Each attack pushes us closer to discovery, which endangers our freedom, our way of life, our children. This world is ripe for a fight, and they won't hesitate to turn it on us," she said.

Murmurs and a few shouts of agreement and alarm came from the crowd. She held up a placating hand. "Now the seeker and the reaper are doing their part to stop the condemned. But we have to do ours as well." Her gaze found Raul. "Raul Anderson, what news of the investigation?" She beckoned to him to come up as she got down.

Raul strode through the murmuring crowd and took his place up on the bar in one easy leap that sent a thrill through the predator in me. "Ayra Valdísdóttir is closing in on the worst known perpetrator involved in the bitings, Calder Valdísson. When she and I spoke last week, she had tracked him to Idaho, where she hopes to intercept him," Raul began in a voice that carried strong and confident throughout the room. He addressed them with an ease that reminded me how much of his adolescence had been spent in the spotlight. Yet he wasn't cocky or arrogant. I liked that.

"Thanks to Detective Sandalius, Hemlock Hollow's new lead investigator on the case," he paused and indicated me with a nod and a wave of his hand, "we have expanded our list of suspects and found new evidence we hope will lead to a swift resolution."

My heart fluttered. The man was modest and quick to give credit where it was due. I was in so much trouble.

All eyes turned to me. The murmuring increased tenfold. More than a few people gave me a nod of respect and offered up words of gratitude. Raul went on, taking the heat off me. "There haven't been any attacks near Hemlock Hollow, but due to the wolf preserve there, we're the focus of media attention at least once a week." He swallowed hard and his fangs flashed beneath the bar's canned lighting when he went on. "One of the wolf packs we protect was slaughtered by a human poacher."

Gasps and cries of anger washed through the crowd. When they died down, Raul continued.

"Only one pup survived. Detective Sandalius and I were able to get the other pack to take him in. It proves the point that many are looking for a place to lay blame, an imagined evil to fight. The public will turn on us if they find out we exist." Nodding at several agreeing comments, he paused to let the crowd settle. "It's happened before, and it will happen again, which is why we need your help. If any of you know any information about anyone biting in someone against their will, and who did it, please reach out to Detective Sandalius or myself."

Many called out thanks and encouragement to him. The dull roar of conversation started up the moment he jumped to the floor. People rose and started to mingle. A large group surrounded Raul and began talking to him.

Beneath it all, I caught the mumbled comment, "Stupid pawn doesn't know shit about who's really behind it. He's too naïve to look that close to home." The words ended in a slight growl. That growl had a familiar timber to it.

Chills tore through me. I had heard it before, on a rainy night while alone on the road. I rose so fast I bumped the table and Iris had to catch our drinks. The voice had come from the far right-hand side of the room. Too many people were already standing and mingling for me to see the source. I started in that direction.

"Elexis, what's wrong?" Iris asked.

"It's one of them," I whispered over my shoulder as I moved into the crowd.

Focusing on my hearing, I followed the sound of his voice. He complained softly about Raul's arrogance. I caught a glimpse through the throng of people. The voice belonged to a man of medium build—well, medium for a Viking—sitting at a table with one other man. I put his face to memory: a prominent brow over muddy eyes, a square jaw peppered with week-old stubble, a wide nose. The man with him had his back to me. All I could tell of him was that he had dishwater blond hair and broad shoulders.

People approached me, asking questions about the investigation. "Just a second, I have to find someone..." They blocked my way. I wove through them as best I could without drawing attention to myself.

"Raul, I heard one of them. They're here," I said in a low voice, hoping he'd hear. Sure, *they* might hear, but I was banking on them not understanding what I meant.

I shot a glance in his direction at the same time his head turned my way. My expression must have said what I didn't dare because he cut off his conversation and started to move my way.

Through the throng of people I met the gaze of my muddy-eyed attacker. Those eyes widened and his mouth dropped. He flew to his feet and started for the back door. Dishwater blond guy followed him. Muddy Eyes moved with a pronounced limp. Even with that limp, they were going to make it to the door before I could cut them off. A frustrated growl tore from me. People soon tried to move out of my way, but they moved in the wrong directions, making things worse. With a thrust of my head, I indicated the fleeing pair to Raul. He nodded. In an impressive jump, he shot over the heads of the crowd and onto the bar. The pair disappeared out the door. Raul ran down the bar like a highway, using it to make it across the room in seconds. He leaped for the door, catching it just before it swung shut.

I took Raul's lead and jumped onto a table. From there I launched myself to the bar and hit the wood top running. Chaos and questions erupted all around. Some seemed to figure out what we were doing but too slowly. They started to move away from the door a second later when I made it to the end of the bar and jumped down. I flung the door open. It slammed into the wall so hard, the windows shook. Motorcycle engines revved to life as I stepped out into the sun. Two motorcycles tore out of the parking lot seconds before Raul reached them on foot. They left him in the dust.

People flooded out behind me, catching the scent of a hunt.

"Raul, what's going on?" Morene's voice came from behind me. The worry in her tone struck me all wrong. What little hair I had on the back of my neck in this form tried to rise.

Fury rolled off Raul as his head shot in our direction. "Those are the guys who attacked Elexis," he said through a growl, the words just barely recognizable.

"That's not possible. They're Draupnir members. None of our pack would dare—"

"They would and they did," I cut her off.

The shocked look she gave me appeared genuine, but...

A third motorcycle engine roared to life. I turned back in time to see Raul's Hayabusa tearing out of the parking lot. Morene flew past me in barely more than a blur, her long brown hair streaking out behind her. I thought I heard her say, "Those sons of bitches. They won't get away." She got behind the wheel of a red sports car I didn't recognize on the far side of the parking lot, firing it up faster than most could move ten feet. I ran halfway across the parking lot before she laid rubber on asphalt and disappeared down the road.

"Dammit!"

Iris's vanilla and bark scent whipped around me as she ran past. It pulled at me. "Come on! You can ride with me," she called back.

I bolted after her. She handed me her helmet as she started her motorcycle. "What about you?" I asked even as I pulled it on.

Shooting me a crooked grin, she knocked a fist against her aqua hair. "My head's harder."

Arguing would only waste time, so I didn't bother. I climbed on behind her. As soon as my hands locked around her waist, she took off to the roar of a powerful engine revving for all it was worth. If I hadn't been gripping her so tight, she would have left my ass sitting back in the parking lot. I suddenly became infinitely grateful for the helmet. The attack had proven I was far from immortal. I didn't want to test just how far.

Wind tore at my clothing and threatened to whip my hair free of its braid. I looked over Iris's shoulder at the speedometer. Ninety and climbing. My stomach dropped. I moved my gaze to the road ahead of us. Trees flashed by on both sides so fast it looked like we were barreling down a green tunnel. The thrill of the hunt pumped through my blood like a drug, making my heart pound harder. Though the speedometer maintained a steady rise, and Iris worked the gears like a pro, I wanted to go faster. We whipped around corners, our knees almost touching the pavement due to our speed. Still, I needed more. As much as I wanted to catch these bastards, part of me didn't want the chase to end. Now I understood werewolves' obsession with fast vehicles.

The road straightened and I saw for what had to be close to a mile. Raul sped not more than a quarter mile ahead of us. There was no sign of Morene's car or the two Draupnir members' motorcycles. I listened hard, straining to hear through the full-face helmet. Wind and motorcycle engines were all I could hear. Clinging with my thighs to the bike, I let go of Iris and took the helmet off.

"What are you doing?" Iris asked.

"Listening."

She didn't chastise me or slow down—which earned her all the points. I poured my concentration and power into my hearing. Distant shouts came to my ears. I recognized Morene's voice among them.

"Take a left there!" I said, pointing to a dirt road just ahead.

Helmet still in hand, I thrust my arms around Iris and gripped tight. No time remained to do anything else. The motorcycle's tire squealed as she got on the brakes hard. The rear tire started to slide out. Every muscle in my body clenched. She gunned the gas at just the perfect time and righted the bike before the front wheel touched the dirt. We plummeted down the dirt road at eye-watering speed.

"Traitorous bitch!" came a man's voice from just ahead. Pain filled the words. It was hard to tell over the rev of the motorcycle, but it almost sounded like a wet gurgle followed.

"You were just as much a part of this. You'll never see the halls of Valhalla. You'll burn on Muspelheimr!" came another man's voice. A man's pained scream followed, pitching up high into a wail that abruptly cut off.

The motorcycle crested a hill. In the dip below, Morene's red sports car idled like an angry cat. Beneath its front wheels lay a crunched motorcycle. Another motorcycle lay in the middle of the dirt road. Three bleeding bodies lay scattered through the wreckage, two without heartbeats. The heart of the third thundered, strong and steady as if fresh from a run or a fight. Long, brown hair spilled around the prone form as she writhed on the ground, a hand held against her bleeding stomach.

Before Iris could fully stop the bike, I leaped from the back and ran to Morene's side. I dropped the helmet and tore my shirt off. Balling it up, I pressed it to the woman's bleeding stomach. She let out a little cry. Her eyes fluttered like she might pass out. The wound was bad, two claw marks cutting all the way down through the skin and muscle. One of the men had tried to eviscerate her and had nearly done it.

The engine of a second motorcycle roared down the road behind us. Head rolling toward one of the bodies, Morene tried to sit up. I held her down.

"Don't try to move. You're hurt pretty bad."

Iris walked over and checked the two bodies. She looked at me and shook her head. Suspicion burned in her eyes as they moved to Morene.

"I can't let them get away..." Morene said in a fading voice.

Iris glared at her as she returned to our sides. "No need to worry about that. They're dead," she said in a dark tone. It made me remember those men had once been her packmates.

Morene tried to sit up again. This time I wasn't so gentle about holding her down. She had a lot of strength for someone hurt so bad. Behind us, the approaching motorcycle came to a stop. Footsteps beat a fast rhythm in our direction. With them came the feel of Raul's power.

"No! Oh, Odin, I didn't mean to kill them. Gods, I killed them!" A sob tore from her. She swallowed hard. "What am I going to tell their families? Not just that they're traitors, but they're dead. And Bain, he'll be so pissed." Her head rolled in my direction. "They tried to kill me. You'll tell him, won't you? He likes you. He'll listen to you." The desperation in her voice and eyes felt over the top. But that could be because I feared she killed them on purpose. Dead men couldn't identify my third attacker, which seemed a little too convenient.

"Just lie still," I told her.

Raul dropped to his knees beside her. "What the hell happened?" he asked.

She reached for him, eyes rolling his direction. He cradled her hand in both of his. "They fought me—" A harsh cough cut off her words.

"Easy, don't try to talk," Raul soothed her.

Iris and I exchanged a look. I was glad I wasn't the only one who thought Morene was full of it.

"How bad is it?" Raul asked me. The worry in his voice ate away at my callousness—a little.

"All the way through the muscle. It is best if I leave the pressure on," I said.

He nodded and looked back to her. "Where's your phone, sis?"

"In my car."

He patted her hand before laying it on the dirt. "Hold tight. I'm going to get it."

Her eyes went wide. "Don't call him, please don't. He'll be so mad," she begged. Those wide eyes glistened with moisture.

Raul's brow pinched, and his lips drew in a tight line. "You need your pack to heal you. Let me worry about Bain."

After a second's hesitation, she nodded once, slowly. When he rose, she let out a long, shuddering breath, and her eyes closed. Face held in a rictus of pain, she kept them squeezed shut tight. A dark green T-shirt appeared before me. I looked up and found Iris standing there in a green bra. She nodded down at Morene. "Yours is bleeding through."

My blue silk shirt had turned purple. Blood oozed up around my fingers. "Shit, I liked that shirt." I accepted Iris's and placed it on top of mine.

It was a lot of blood. I had no doubt the guys had been trying to kill her. What I did doubt was that she hadn't meant to kill them. Which raised the questions: who was she trying to protect, and had it been an order from Bain, or was she hiding something from him?

CHAPTER TWENTY-TWO

RAUL

I'd always wanted to get behind the wheel of my sister's brand new Porsche, but not like this. Not after I'd just watched her most trusted *verndari* load her into the back of a van, bleeding and in pain.

"She'll be all right. She's strong, and she has a whole pack to dogpile with and heal her up," Elexis said, offering me a smile from the passenger seat.

Her power reached out to mine, soothing it. Breathing a little easier as I pulled out onto the road, I looked at her. My T-shirt hung on her, the neck low enough to remind me of the glimpse I'd gotten of her lacy black bra. If I had been in my right mind I would have taken a much longer look.

"I know, it's just, what if the third attacker is a Draupnir member too? Is she truly safe with them?" I asked.

She made a snorting sort of laughing noise. "I wouldn't worry. Your sister can hold her own."

"Yeah, but she's in a nest full of Loki-loving vipers."

Throaty laughter filled the car. The sound of it almost made me smile. "What?" I asked.

She shook her head. "It's just...you have a way with words sometimes," she said through bouts of more laughter.

I enjoyed her amusement and the sound of her—alive, breathing, and well. The night could have ended much differently. It was a bit of good luck, or divine intervention, that Morene was the only one hurt. The need to touch Elexis overwhelmed me. I put a hand on her arm.

"Thank you for helping her."

Her smile softened from humor to something else. "Of course." She stared at me for several seconds, looking like she wanted to say more, but she didn't.

"I'm sorry we didn't catch them alive. I know how frustrating it must be with a third one still out there," I said. It tore me up, and now we had no way to find out who her third attacker was. A big part of me was pissed at Morene for taking the opportunity at a lead from us, which made me feel like the worst big brother ever.

"I know, Raul. It isn't your fault," Elexis said.

I slapped a hand on the steering wheel. "But it is. I should have realized they'd turned down that road. If I had, my sister wouldn't have gotten hurt, and your attackers might be in custody instead of dead."

"Don't beat yourself up, seriously," she insisted. The gentleness in her dark blue eyes washed over me, not judging or blaming.

"How did you and Iris know to turn there?" I asked to derail the conversation.

Her face went blank and tension sang through her power. "I heard them."

"Wow, I didn't even hear them, and you were wearing a helmet."

She looked out the passenger window. "Well, not exactly."

"But I saw it on the ground beside you."

Gaze fixed on the forest racing by the window, she answered, "I hung onto it, but I took it off so I could hear better."

I grabbed her hand. "Elexis! That's crazy. Until you've been a *varúlfur* for at least ten years, your body is only twice as strong as a human's. Your head hitting the asphalt will still do a lot of damage."

She wouldn't look at me, but she didn't pull her hand away either. I couldn't let it drop. "Elexis, please. I don't want anything to happen to you." It spilled out on a wave of desperation before I could even think about it.

Free hand going to her chest, she turned to me with a shocked, over-the-top dramatic look. "Why Raul Anderson, you sound worried about me," she teased.

"I am," I admitted. Hiding it was getting tiresome. Besides, seeing someone I cared about bleeding out in the dirt put things into perspective. If she rejected me and judged me like everyone else, so be it. But not putting myself out there meant I'd never know.

The softness in her eyes made part of me jump to attention. She smiled, and the world ground to a halt. Her hand slid out from beneath mine, caressed my cheek, and turned my head gently forward.

"In that case, you should watch the road," she teased.

Her hand trailed slowly down my neck, over my bare chest, and to my leg. Fire erupted everywhere she touched. It warmed instead of burned, yet it felt like it could roar through me and consume all in its path. She took her hand away, and the temperature in the car dropped ten degrees.

"Raul, there's something I don't get," she said.

"What's that?"

"People in this town talk like you're a womanizer, and it feels like the rep goes back before what happened with Sonya. Yet your fiancée was the one who cheated on you. And in the weeks I've known you, you've been nothing but respectful to every woman I've seen you interact with. What am I missing?"

I wanted nothing more than to pull the car over and kiss her until the rest of the world—and our clothes—fell away. If we weren't on the way to drop off Morene's car, I would have. The urge passed as I realized I had to tell her what I'd done. I focused on the twilight shadows creeping over the road.

"When I was sixteen, I wanted nothing more than to be my father's First *Verndari*, his right hand man. But he's a hard man to impress." I swallowed my shame and pride and continued. "My sister said she would back me and tell him I was the man for the job if I did something for her. You've got to understand, my dad treated her like she was Asgardian born, not just a princess, but a goddess. So her word would have been all I needed."

Elexis turned sideways in her seat and watched me with interest. I had to fight the urge to fidget. Finally, she didn't think I was an ass and I was about to blow it. But it was better if she heard this from me.

"She had a crush on this guy, Tyler Viðarsson, a member of the Draupnir pack before Bain killed Didrik." The deep oceans of Elexis's eyes started to look stormy. Looking back at the road, I pushed on. "But Tyler had been dating the same girl for the past three years. Morene had seen his girl eyeing me after a football game, and she got an idea. She convinced me to seduce her so she and Tyler would break up. I wanted to make Morene happy, get in my father's good graces, and I was a horny teenager. So I agreed."

I glanced back at Elexis to see her reaction. That damn blank cop look hid her as well as a mask. When she didn't respond, I kept going to fill the silence. "It worked in one way. Tyler broke up with his girlfriend and started dating Morene a month later. But rumors spread from school to the town. My father found out what I did."

"What about Morene's part in it?" The protective tone of her voice made me feel a little better.

"He never knew. I wasn't going to rat my sister out."

Those stormy eyes narrowed. "So, you got the reputation of being a player, got on your dad's bad side, and she got the guy. Not cool." Anger darkened both her tone and her power.

I shrugged. "Yeah, but I wasn't exactly innocent."

"No, but she's older. She manipulated you. And she didn't support you with your dad like she said she would."

On one hand, my hackles rose over the comment about Morene, on the other, it felt good to have someone voice my innermost thoughts.

"Is that the only time she did anything like that to you?" I didn't like the cop tone in her voice.

It took all my concentration to keep my eyes on the darkening road. "Yes. What do you mean?"

Elexis raised a placating hand. "I'm just a neutral mind here, working things out."

"What things?" The words came out harsh and clipped.

"Things like two of my attackers being from Draupnir, the third being female, and the other two now conveniently dead so they can't identify her. Dead by Morene's hand, a woman who has worked her way into a proxy alpha position of the Draupnir pack."

The words dumped over me like a bucket of ice water. "Are you accusing my sister of attacking you?"

"No. I'm just looking at the facts and not ruling out the possibility," she said quickly.

"Well you should because she would never do that."

Her power developed a guarded feel to it. She turned forward in her seat. "I get it. She's your sister. You're being a good brother defending her, but—"

"No. I'm the screwup, not Morene. Everything she has ever done has been for the pack. She's gentle, sweet—"

"And manipulative, and hasn't hesitated to sacrifice you in the past for her own needs. Like I said, I get it," she snapped.

Power flared between us, hot enough to spark.

"No you don't. You have no family. How could you possibly understand?"

Silence fell fast and hard. Her energy crackled and popped, each pop stinging me like embers from a fire. We rode in painful silence for nearly a mile. I wanted to take the words back but couldn't open my fool mouth to do it. At a stop sign, I finally worked my jaw loose, but she spoke first.

"Who found Sonya and told you where she was?"

All the words I'd been about to say evaporated. Of course, it had been Morene, but only because she was the best tracker around and Bain had made her. Doubt tickled at the back of my mind. I refused to let it in. She was my sister.

Elexis sighed. "I can see you making excuses for her in your head. Until you can stop doing that, don't come after me." She jumped out of the car, slammed the door, and disappeared into the darkness.

CHAPTER TWENTY-THREE

ELEXIS

By the time I stormed through the ferns clogging the ditch, the bastard drove off. Once I ran out of curse words in the English language for him, I started going over the ones I knew in Icelandic. Unfortunately, I ran out of those even quicker and had to start cycling back through. Anger rode through me like a drug, raising my power and making it feel hot as the Sahara in July. I was about to lose it utterly and completely. If I didn't shift on my own, the choice would soon be made for me. When I reached the trees, I stripped down, body vibrating with the change before I even dropped the last bit of clothing.

From head to tail, I shook my black fur coat out. It always felt like it had been pressed flat beneath my skin after I first shifted. It was in my head, I knew, but that didn't banish the feeling. Besides, it felt good to shake, like I was shrugging off all the bad energy of the day. And today there had been plenty. Just when I thought Raul and I were making progress, that I was starting to understand him, he turned around and became a huge pain in my ass. A gorgeous, loyal one with golden eyes that dug into my soul like the probes of a Taser.

Shaking my head, I started to run. With each step, another thought of him faded away until nothing but the forest and I remained. For once, it felt good to give over to my instincts and just run. Trees whipped by, ferns, boulders, hills. The moon pulled at me, drawing me deeper into the forest, inviting me to run with it. So I did. Sometime later I stopped next to a moonlit stream for a drink and realized I had no idea where I was. Could this be the stream that ran through the hollow? I wasn't sure. Worse, I had no idea how to get back to my clothes.

Tail sagging, I did a little circle, tripping over one of my feet in the process. The place didn't look, sound, or smell familiar. My ears flicked back and forth. A sound carried to me, a human sound. Light on my feet so I wouldn't be heard, I followed it. As I walked, I focused on trying to recognize my surroundings. The bridge couldn't be too far from here. When I'd gotten out of the car we'd been about halfway between the bar and Hemlock Hollow, and I'd run a few miles. Hopefully, it had been in the right direction. I was nearly on them when I realized what I was hearing—a male voice in the throes of passion. I froze. Ears pricked forward, I listened and waited, hoping they hadn't heard me. I caught glimpses of them through feathery boughs of fir. They weren't more than fifty feet away.

Moonlight shone off beads of sweat working down a tall, slender man's bare back. He knelt behind his partner, buttocks flexing as he pumped. I knew that build, that dishwater blond hair—Bain. It took a moment for my wolf eyes to realize the figure he knelt behind was another man. The brown hair and boy-band pretty face were also unmistakable—Dustin. From the euphoric look on Dustin's face, the situation was clearly consensual.

Fear of discovery paralyzed me for several seconds. Did it threaten an alpha's position to be gay? I didn't know. What I did know was Bain wanted me to think he was interested in me, and he wanted everyone else to think he was looking for a mate—a female one. That had to mean he didn't want people to know he was gay, which meant I was in danger.

Both men were so caught up in each other, they hadn't noticed me. Yet. I started to back away, tail fanning behind me to check for obstacles. My heart felt like it pounded higher and higher into my throat with each step. I wasn't exactly great at moving as a wolf yet. A branch tripped me and I ended up on my tail. The ferns squishing beneath my butt sounded like a four-alarm fire. The couple didn't look my way. I scrambled up and continued my painfully slow retreat. Once the fir tree fully blocked me from view, I turned and ran.

The second I could no longer hear them, my sprint became an all-out run. Horror and fear drove my legs faster and faster. How could Dustin want that man? He had seemed so gentle, so kind. And Bain was cruel, manipulative, and a killer on top of it. It made no sense. After about a mile, the crawling sensation of being followed raised my hackles all along my back. Ears flicking about, I listened. Every now and then I heard the faint sound of a paw touching the ground. Whoever they were, they were stealthy as hell, and definitely a werewolf.

I changed direction and headed for higher ground. I had to find somewhere to make a stand. Running away so I wouldn't be noticed was one thing, running from a fight was another altogether. I'd never done that and I never would, even if it meant I had to fight an alpha.

I stopped on top of a grassy hill with one lone hemlock tree twisting out of a rock on top. The thick forest all around the hill obscured both view and sound, but it would have to do. Besides, I could hear them coming. No, not them, one wolf. He was so light on his paws I had to concentrate hard to hear him. I wanted to shift back. My fighting skills as a human were far superior to my fighting skills as a wolf. But I couldn't. Fear and instinct wouldn't let me. Teeth bared, I braced myself as he crested the hill. The skin along my back tickled and twitched as every hair on it stood on end.

The brown wolf's head, with its white-tipped ears, wasn't who I expected to poke up over the hill. Relief powerful enough to leave me shaking flooded through me. I shifted to human form and stood.

"Raul?" I asked, though I knew it was him.

By the time his gaze dragged its way up my body to my face, he had shifted into a man: a hot, sweaty, naked man. I suddenly had no idea where he was looking because I couldn't keep my gaze on his face. I became acutely aware of my own nakedness but made no move to cover myself. This time it wasn't out of a desire not to seem prude.

"Thank Odin I found you. You're not easy to track, woman," he said through a long, relieved sigh.

He strode over to me, and I had to force myself to look up at his face because watching him walk naked, parts swinging, was too much. Then I remembered I was pissed at him.

"Yeah, well, I didn't want you to find me," I said with a lot less bite than I intended. I dug deep for my anger, wanting its fire back.

Shaking his head, he walked closer. My gaze made its way up to his arms, catching on the Norse knot work tattoos there. He looked entirely too delicious naked. It wasn't fair to my stressed mind.

"I know, and I deserve that. I shouldn't have said the things I said, and I definitely shouldn't have drove off. I'm so sorry. I'm the biggest idiot in the nine worlds."

The words got me to look at his face. Sincerity and worry made deep pools of his amber eyes. Moonlight softened the lines between his brows and made his five o'clock shadow shine with highlights. His power pulled at me, reaching down into my very center. I stepped toward him without meaning to.

I shrugged. "Maybe not the biggest. I've heard this Loki guy has done some pretty idiotic things. I mean, having sex with a horse, really?"

A nervous laugh came from Raul. "Well, he is a shapeshifter, so I'm sure he was in horse form when he did it. So it's not like it sounds." He took my hands. "You're shaking."

His touch charged and emboldened me. "I saw something. There's someone else out here. We need to go, now," I insisted.

The worry in his eyes deepened. I shook my head as I saw a question forming on his face. "Later."

"Okay. My house isn't far from here."

I stepped away from him and shifted back to wolf form. As much as it bugged me, I was a far better runner as a wolf. His paws hit the ground beside me a second later. We jogged back into the cover of the trees. I did my best to keep my pace relaxed and not pull ahead of him. It had been him all this time following me, not Bain. There was no need to rush.

Eventually the rhythm of running combined with the scents of the dark forest to soothe the tension out of me. The terrain started to look familiar once I relaxed. Hemlocks filled with hundreds of tiny brown cones started to outnumber the taller pine trees. The ground became rockier. The scent of wild roses and grapes filled the air. Both grew near Raul's back patio. Raul's own scent was all over these woods in old trails. The smell of humans and civilization—pavement, a cold barbecue, metal, wood, and a cooling vehicle—filled the air. The trees thinned to reveal Raul's modern home of glass and angles clinging to the side of the hollow.

My hackles finally lay down. The crawling sensation of my hair standing up eased more with each step. Right now, Raul's house looked like the best place on earth. We shifted back to human form as we reached the front door. For good measure, I listened for the sounds of anyone else before walking across the threshold. I even said to hell with my dignity and gave the air a good sniff. Nothing. I stepped inside, closed the door behind us, and locked it. One of Raul's brows rose before his gaze drifted down to my naked body. I enjoyed the feel of him looking at me for all of a second before I remembered I was pissed at him. Crossing my arms over my breasts, I shot him a harsh look.

"You left me," I snapped, all the fear of the possibility of being seen by Bain pouring out in my acidic tone.

"You got out of the car and ran off before I could stop you." He sounded sorry, but...

"You drove off."

He took a step closer. Gods, he smelled good, like aloe soap, pine forest, and wolf. I tried not to notice how amazing he looked naked, but I failed.

"I did, and I am so, so sorry for that. I was mad and stupid. I only drove a half mile before I turned around. But when I got back, you were gone."

"So you agree you were stupid for not listening to me?"

A muscle in his stubble-covered cheek twitched. "Yes."

"About my objective deductions regarding Morene."

The same muscle twitched again. He looked away. "Yes."

My jaw dropped. "What? Really?"

His fingers touched my arm, which was close enough to my breasts to make them react in a way I didn't want them to at the moment. My anger started to slip away, and I tried to cling to it. Eyes boring into me, he caught my gaze and held it.

"Really. I'm not saying I believe she's involved in the bitings. But I can't deny she's manipulative, driven, and overprotective. If she thought you were a threat to me in some way, I have to admit she might attack you. I wanted to think she wouldn't, but I may have been deluding myself."

My arms dropped away from my breasts. "What brought on this revelation?"

He turned to put his hands on the kitchen bar as if he needed its support. All that naked, muscular flesh of his threatened to distract me. The one eye of the large knot work wolf's head tattoo on his back felt like it was staring at me. The urge to touch him, to run my hands along the circle of runes surrounding the wolf, almost made me reach for him.

"What you said. You're a neutral party who is looking at facts. I was being emotional and letting it cloud my judgment." A big sigh came from him as he turned back to me and grabbed my hand. "I trust your judgment better than my own. I trust you." The words struck me with the force of a bullet.

His gaze moved down to our clutched hands. Mine followed until I realized how good the view was of his naked lower body. I wanted to throw him down right there on the kitchen floor and ride him, but he had to know what I'd seen tonight. I had to focus. I pulled my hands free and took a step away.

He went on, misunderstanding my distance. "She killed those two men, and she didn't have to. She's made it clear she doesn't like or trust you. I don't know what she's capable of anymore."

A shiver traveled through me. Raul walked to the couch, grabbed the red chenille throw from the back of it and returned. He wrapped it around me without a word, hands lingering on my arms as if he couldn't stop touching me.

His eyes were a bit distant. "I didn't think she had it in her to kill a person, let alone two. I was wrong. Maybe this alpha thing is getting to her."

I covered one of his hands with mine. "Don't blame yourself for being a supportive brother." Looking away, I mustered up my willpower. "Raul, I saw something in the forest."

His gaze focused on me in an instant. "What?"

Another shiver traveled through me. "It's going to require a drink."

The heat of his hand left my arm, and I almost regretted asking for the drink. But then he went to the wine fridge beneath the bar, opened a bottle of red wine, and the heady scent filled the air. He handed me a glass and sat down at the bar. I turned away because I couldn't tell him while he was sitting there naked, tattoos and half-hard hot bits displayed. Knocking back a long drink of liquid courage, I steeled myself, and then told him.

His face scrunched up into a look of utter disgust, baring all eight of his fangs. "Oh Dustin, by Thor, how could you?"

"I know. He seemed like such a nice guy. Who'd have known he had such bad taste in men?"

Raul shook his head. "I never would have guessed."

"But did you know Bain was gay?"

"Definitely not. He hid that very well."

"Why would he do that? Does it threaten his position as alpha?"

Cocking his head to the side, Raul looked up as if thinking. "Not in this century. There still has to be a male and female alpha, to balance the power. But they don't have to be a mated pair."

"Then why would he hide it?"

He shrugged. "Old fashioned fear, maybe. He was born in 1952, grew up in the sixties when a gay man was still dragged through the streets and beaten to death in some states."

I shook my head. "Something about that doesn't feel right. I think there's more to it, I just can't put my finger on what."

"There is one thing. If whoever he chose as a female alpha mated and that mate decided to challenge Bain for leadership, he would be within his rights to do so."

Chills worked over me, making me clutch the throw tighter. "You don't think he would choose a female and try to convince her he was straight, do you?"

"I don't know. If I could figure out how the guy's mind worked, he'd be behind bars."

I took another long drink of wine. It went down smooth, leaving behind an aftertaste of dark cherries. Knowing Raul didn't buy the cheap stuff, I felt bad for drinking it so fast. "I was afraid they had seen me, smelled me, or heard me, something. I thought for sure he was chasing me and would try and kill me if he caught me."

Raul stood and took me by the shoulders. "You don't have to worry. He wasn't. There was no one in the area but the two of us." He smiled. "Wait, you said 'try.' You think you could have beat him?"

Heat radiated from him, but most intensely from his eyes. His hands were brands on my arms. Those eyes bore into me, and I wanted them to go deeper.

"I damn sure would have tried," I breathed.

A low growl came from him. "That is so hot." The raw need in his voice made muscles low in my body clench.

His hands slid slowly up my arms to cradle my face. I let the throw drop to the ground and set my wineglass on the bar. He looked down at me as if seeing me naked for the first time, eyes wide and dark with passion. The look alone did things to me only a man's touch had ever been able to do. My arms slid around him, hands exploring the muscles of his lower back. Every part of him was fine, and I wanted to touch all of him. We both stepped toward one another at the same time. We melded together in a way that felt natural and oh so right. The length of him—all hard and eager—pressed against my stomach. Oh what I wouldn't have done to be six inches taller in that moment so I could have shifted just right and moved his erection between my legs.

Our bodies separated when he bent down to kiss me. I missed the heat and pressure of him for all of a second before his lips urged mine apart. One of his hands worked its way down around my waist while the other massaged my right breast reverently, expertly. Sensations shot from it straight down between my legs. Heat and wetness followed. That one touch drove me out of my mind with need. As we kissed, I explored his body with my hands, touching all the curves and muscles I'd been admiring every day since we met. When I reached between his legs and grabbed the length of him, he gasped and broke our kiss.

Such an overwhelming desire filled his amber eyes that they reminded me of molten lava. Power reared up within me in a hot wave that flowed out to reach for him. The pressure of his own power rising in response filled the room with a crackling presence. The two fronts collided and swirled together just as we did. So many sensations hit me all at once: his hands exploring my body, the feel of his taut skin beneath my fingers, our power flowing together to combine into a force greater than anything I had ever imagined. I became drunk on all of it.

His hands cupped my butt and lifted me. I wrapped my legs around his waist. The pressure of his length trapped between my leg and groin drove me wild. I'd never wanted a man so badly. The power of the need scared me a bit, but the fear only heightened it instead of making me want to pull away, which came as a bit of a surprise. Maybe it was his power mingling with mine in a way that felt perfectly natural. A shock of cold shot through me as he sat me down on the marble bar. But then he pressed between my legs and branded my most intimate parts with his own. My thighs clenched automatically, wanting him closer, but the angle was all wrong due to my grip.

I forced my legs to unlock as he reached down between us. The bar height combined with his own was perfect. His hard length slowly slid into my wet heat, and my world exploded. As he entered me, so did his power. It flowed into every part of me until it filled me to bursting. White spots appeared before my eyes, so many they blocked my view of him for a second. The pressure of him inside me built as he pushed in deeper, groaning with the effort and pleasure of it. I leaned back onto the bar to give him a better angle. In no hurry, he leaned with me, his lips seeking mine again. His soft lips urged mine apart with a nudge, and our tongues danced. That sensation combined with him moving inside me had me breathing as if I'd just run a marathon.

After a long, mind-blowing kiss, he straightened, leaving me leaning back on the bar on my elbows. His hands massaged my breasts, tweaking in just the right spot at just the right time. The crest of an orgasm started to build in me already. One of his hands moved down to play with the pleasure point between my legs right above where he and I joined. I was ready to roll over the edge of oblivion at the first hint of his touch. Somehow, he kept me on that precipice for what felt like an eternity as he sped the rhythm of his thrusts. I watched him pleasure me, awed at the joy he took in it, and the look of adoration he bathed me in. It brought me to release even faster.

The intensity of my orgasm left me spent, sprawled back onto the bar, muscles twitching, gripping him inside me. Power washed out of me in a wave that knocked our wine glasses over. They rolled across the marble and clinked to the floor, one of them shattering.

Raul threw his head back and laughed. "Wow!"

He stopped moving inside me, and it felt like the world ceased to spin. Keeping us joined, he scooped me up and moved us to the couch. Thanks to his strength and agility, I ended up on top without us parting. Talents upon talents, this man.

"Sure we won't destroy the couch?" I asked.

A crooked grin pulled up one corner of his mouth and dimpled his stubble-covered cheek. "Don't care."

Hands on his chest, I started to move. Grin growing larger, he looked up at me as if I'd hung the moon. I'd been ready for lust, need, or even passion, but not this reverence. It thrilled me in all new ways. We found a rhythm together, his hips rising to meet me as I descended. Our movements became perfectly in sync, like instinct. With his hands on my hips, guiding my movements, he brought me again before taking over. The release of my power blew a magazine and hardbound book off the glass coffee table. This time, we both laughed.

In a new position, that perfect rhythm came right back with surprising ease. By the time his breathing became short and his thrusts grew frantic, he had expertly brought me back to the edge again as well. As he spent himself inside me, another orgasm shook my body. Our combined explosion of power left us in a tsunami-like wave. The huge picture windows overlooking the hollow shook as if from an earthquake. Above us, in the point of the vaulted ceiling, the modern metal fan rocked back and forth. Exhausted laughter came from both of us.

For several minutes we lay together on the couch, my body resting half on his, my head on his chest. I listened to the amazing sound of his rapid heartbeat beneath my ear. His arms wrapped tight around me; his head leaned against the top of mine. I'd never felt so close to someone as I did in that moment. The fear I expected that thought to provoke never came. My instincts told me this was right, that flawed and imperfect as he was, *he* was right. I didn't ever want to move.

CHAPTER TWENTY-FOUR

ELEXIS

The warmth and pressure of Raul's lips on mine lingered even after his Cherokee had pulled out of the driveway. A long, content sigh slid from me as I closed and locked the double doors of my house. Iris was working at the library, and the outcasts were either in the cabins or basement, leaving me virtually alone for the time. The quiet house felt expectant. It had to be the storm building in the gray skies outside. I watched out the stained glass window to one side of the doors, but the streaking rain obscured all but Raul's tail lights as he went around a bend in the driveway. If I listened hard enough, I could hear the constant patter of rain even through the insulated roof. Today would be a day for staying inside with a good book. Or maybe one of Didrik's journals. Intent on finding one, I turned to head for the library.

I'd wanted to spend the Saturday in bed with Raul, but he needed to have a candid talk with his sister, and I wasn't about to screw up that progress. He seemed genuinely suspicious of her now. He'd even brought up how she hadn't returned his calls for days after I'd been attacked. It tore him up to admit she might be under Bain's thrall, but he was finally admitting it to himself. I wanted to go with him. She was dangerous. But I knew this was something he had to do on his own. And despite how I felt about the woman, it was clear she loved and adored him.

More out of habit for comfort than because of the chill, I wrapped my sweater tighter around me as I started into the quiet house. The hardwood floors felt cool beneath my bare feet. The storm had replaced the July heat with a building cold that felt more like October. Now that I paid attention, it was actually a bit chilly in the house. The basement got far colder than the upper house. I started that way to check. Couldn't have the little ones in the basement getting cold. Did young werewolves get cold before they'd gone through the *verða*? I needed to chat with them more to find out these kinds of things.

Halfway down the steps, I heard a noise that stopped me in my tracks. A scratching or brushing sound carried through the wall to my right. The weird thing was, as far as I knew, there was nothing behind the wall except for insulation and support structure. It didn't sound like a mouse or anything of the sort. I did hear a little heartbeat, but it wasn't *that* little or fast. This was a werewolf heartbeat.

At the bottom of the stairs, I turned toward the sound and found myself at a cinderblock wall. I ran my hands along the gray, painted surface. No imperfections or seams marred it. At the shadowy corner where the two walls joined, air moved through a paper-thin gap. Feeling along the short, triangular-shaped wall beneath the stairs, I found it. One of the cinderblocks in the darkness near the bottom of the wall depressed at my touch. Hydraulics hissed; the wall drew back and slid aside. Soft light illuminated a twenty-by-twenty or so room. Bookshelves lined three walls. The fourth was covered, floor to the angled ten-foot ceiling, in a beautiful mural. In the middle of the room stood a desk, a stool, and an easel. The scents of old paint, chalk, and graphite lingered.

A small boy sat on a plush, blue rug near the mural. His blue eyes widened beneath blond bangs as he looked up at me from the book he had open in his lap.

The hardwood floor of the room felt warm in comparison to the concrete of the cellar, but not by much. The moment I passed beyond the wall, it slid closed behind me.

"Sigur, what are you doing in here?" I asked.

Eyes going impossibly wider, Sigur popped up, clutching the book to his tiny chest. "I'm sorry. I know I'm not supposed to be in here. I know," he said, glancing longingly at the bookshelves. "It's just..."

"You like stories," I finished for him with a smile.

Gaze cast down at the book he held, he nodded. The bottom edge of the cover revealed the author—Dr. Seuss. Another glance at the shelves revealed at least a third of them were filled with children's books. I realized beneath Sigur's scent lingered a very faint woman's scent. It clung in every corner and on every surface.

I ruffled Sigur's hair as I walked past. "It's okay, I like them too."

He trailed after me. "You do? What kind of stories do you like? There are all kinds in here."

"I like people's stories," I said absently as I perused the canvases stacked near the easel.

The artwork was exquisite. The subject matter was wolves, wilderness, and Hemlock Hollow. Many of the paintings were signed by the artist Eren Donovan. At the bottom corner of the painting on the easel—a half-changed werewolf howling at a full moon in a rainstorm—the scrawled name caught my eye. I couldn't make out all of it, but I could read the first name.

"Lísandra," I murmured.

"Momma said this was her office, and it's a sacred place 'cause of it," Sigur piped in. "I always treat it with respect."

"I am sure you do, Sigur. You're a good boy," I said over my shoulder as I walked toward the mural wall.

The painting depicted the Hemlock Hollow *Bífrost* replica in exquisite detail, from the rainbow-hued steel, to the hollow beneath, and sky beyond it. Then it got weird. A figure was shackled spread eagle beneath the archway in the center of the bridge. Two others stood before him, one with a hand to the sky catching a bolt of descending lightning, the other clutching the free hand of the first, their other hand extending to the shackled figure under the archway. Lightning flew from the extended hand of the third figure and exploded across the chest of the shackled figure. In the archway behind the shackled figure spread an otherworldly, futuristic city with a ringed moon in its periwinkle sky.

"What the..." I caught myself just in time, remembering there were little ears in the room.

"That's the bridge to Valhalla," Sigur piped up.

Intrigued, I walked closer, fingers tracing the lines of the bridge.

"There's a book on it over here," Sigur said.

That drew my attention from the wall. Sigur pointed to a bookshelf. Seeing my interest, he grinned up at me before dashing over to the shelf. On his tiptoes, he reached as high as his little hands could and just barely grabbed the spine of a book. He cradled it like a prize, all gentle and reverent, as he carried it over to me. The sight of the leather cover gave me chills. It was another journal, but a big one, like the one I'd found Didrik's renderings of the bridge in. Leather worn to a smooth finish and dry around the edges told me this one was much older. That, and the old book smell it had to it. It also held traces of what I'd come to know as Lísandra's scent, a lot of traces.

I accepted it from Sigur.

"Careful, it smells old. Mamma says we have to be careful with old stuff," he warned.

I nodded. "I will be, don't worry."

As I walked to the stool, I eased the cover open. The first page nearly made me miss the stool when I sat down.

Building a Bridge to the Nine Worlds
Ingmar Heimdallrson

"Heimdallrson," I murmured.

"That means he's a son of Heimdallr, guardian of the *Bifrost*," Sigur said.

"Have you read this?" I asked.

Sigur shook his head. "Words are too big. But I like the pictures."

There was no way I held a book written by the son of a god. Was there? The subject matter certainly made me wonder. I wiped my hand on my pants to remove any oils before I turned the page. Hands on the stool, Sigur stood at my side on his tiptoes to peer under my arm at the book. I scooped him up and sat him on my lap. He looked on in a sort of awed silence as I flipped through the pages.

My heart sank as I realized it was written in Icelandic.

"Can you read this, Sigur?" I asked.

"A little."

"If I point out a paragraph, will you read to me what you can?"

He sat up as tall. "Yeah, I can do that."

Engineer drawings filled the first few pages. From what Sigur could make out of the writing on the pages opposite them, I gathered it was descriptions on the proper direction the bridge should run, how long it had to be, how reinforced, what material, even how much exposure to the moon was recommended. Then it got weird—well, weirder.

Next to a picture of a figure with its arms extended to the sky and lightning exploding all around it, was a page all about the seeker—or *leitar* as the book called them. Sigur was eager to show me the right word for them. It talked briefly about their Frigg-granted power to seek out those *varúlfur* on the edge of madness, but then it went into their ability to attract lightning. I would have assumed Sigur's translation was off, but the picture supported what he said. In all the things I'd read and heard, there hadn't been anything about the seeker being able to attract lightning. The next page had another picture of a figure and lightning, but this time instead of going into the figure, the lightning was shooting out of their hands. The page opposite it talked about the reaper, or *uppskera*. Sigur had a little trouble with this one, but I finally figured out he was saying it talked about her ability to channel lightning.

Chills traveled up my arms from where my hands held the book. This meant something. It connected with what was going on here in Hemlock Hollow. I could feel it deep in my gut where my cop's intuition lay.

The next page showed a figure with a literal third eye in their forehead. They stood on a bridge with an alien landscape behind them. Strange plants, two moons in the sky—one with rings—made the otherworldliness obvious. According to the book, this person was the key that opened the gate and navigated the path to one of the nine worlds. It called them the *lykill*. The chills in my arms exploded throughout my entire body. I looked up at the mural on the wall. It all clicked into place.

"That's what the bridge does," I murmured. Closing the book, I shifted Sigur on my lap. "Sigur, do *varúlfur* ever go to the other eight worlds?"

He giggled. "'Course not, silly. It's not allowed."

"Not allowed? Why?"

"'Cause we're the children of Fenrir and one of us might kill Thor during Ragnarök. So we were banned here. Everyone knows that story." He began to swing his legs, distraction clear on his face.

"You mean banished here?"

"That's what I said."

I set him on his feet and stood.

He looked up at me with wide eyes filled with excitement. "You don't know the story?"

I shook my head. With many hand gestures and more than a bit of acting, he proceeded to tell me the story.

Loki, brother of Odin, was jealous of Odin's rule of Asgard. He and the giantess Angrboða shifted to wolf form and mated, and the wolf Fenrir was born. (Much blushing and giggling followed this part.) The gods favored the wolf pup, but they knew he would grow big and strong like his giantess mom, so they raised him. When he got too big, they tricked him into being chained up. Fenrir's sons Hati and Skoll tried to convince Odin to free him, but Odin wouldn't. Tyr, son of Thor and God of law and justice—who lost his hand to Fenrir—convinced Odin to banish the children of Fenrir to Midgard so they couldn't kill Thor during Ragnarök.

Taking Sigur by the hand, I started for the door. The seeker, the reaper, the key, it was all starting to make a frightening kind of sense. I had to get to Raul, to tell him. Things with Morene were far worse than I had originally thought. The otherworldly paintings she was constantly bringing him, the way she always talked about the nine worlds and wanted to hear about his dreams, pushing him even though it cost him sleep, it wasn't sisterly interest. She thought he was the key.

CHAPTER TWENTY-FIVE

ELEXIS

By the time I returned Sigur to his mom, found a jacket and my keys, the deluge outside had reduced to a drizzle. I plunged into the misty gray with only one thought in mind: I had to get to Raul. The sinking sensation in my stomach told me the faster I did so, the better. He had gone to check on Morene, to see how she was feeling. I racked my brain trying to remember if it had been his idea or hers. My gut told me the answer mattered, a lot.

As I jumped into my truck and started it up, I checked my phone one more time. No response to my texts or the two voicemails I'd left Raul.

"Dammit," I muttered.

Gravel flew as I shifted the truck into first and put the gas pedal down. A figure appeared out of the mist in the middle of the driveway, not twenty feet ahead. I slammed on the brakes. The bumper of my truck stopped inches from a soaking wet Dustin. He was at the driver's side window in a heartbeat. I rolled it down.

"Dustin, what the hell?" I snapped.

"You're looking for Lísandra. I can take you to where they dumped her body," he said, so quietly I barely heard him.

His wide eyes darted constantly to the surrounding woods. Even the misty rain couldn't dampen the scent of fear wafting off him.

"Now? You tell me this now?" I snapped.

"It can only be now," he insisted.

He fidgeted and kept looking over his shoulder. The nervous energy around him made it clear he might bolt at any moment. I slapped a hand against the steering wheel, and he flinched and drew back.

"Dammit! Get in," I commanded.

He shot around the front of my truck and jumped in the passenger side so fast I didn't have time to check my phone again. I started a text to let Raul know what was going on.

Dustin looked at the phone like it might explode and kill us both. "Please drive, we don't have time."

I dropped it with the text only half finished and shifted the truck back into first. "Which way?" I asked.

"Left."

I turned left onto the paved road.

"If you are leading me into a trap, you'll be the first person I kill," I warned him. From what I'd read, *varúlfur* law permitted it.

He swallowed hard. "I'm not. Things aren't as they seem, not with the Draupnir pack, and not with Bain."

I flashed back to him and Bain in the woods, and wished I could scrub my mind of the memory. "Why don't you tell me how they really are then?"

"I'll tell you everything, but you have to drive faster."

"Where are we going?"

"Forest road 318, just beyond Draupnir land into neutral territory."

It was several miles away. I pushed the gas pedal down as much as I dared in the old truck.

"Start talking," I commanded.

The truck filled with the pressure of my power. Dustin flinched. "Bain was trying to run her out of town. He didn't want to hurt her. He loved her like a sister."

"That's one screwed-up family."

One corner of Dustin's mouth quirked up into a sad smile. "Yes it was." He tipped his chin up. "Take a right up there."

I did as he instructed. Gravel crunched under the tires. Trees towered over the half-dirt, half-gravel road, their evergreen boughs creating a canopy the rain had to work to get through. I didn't like how dark and deserted the road looked.

"We have to hurry," Dustin prompted me again.

I sped up as much as I dared on the wet gravel. "Why?" I asked.

"Because I don't want my absence noticed."

"Then why not just tell me where, go on your way, and let me call a team in," I pressed.

"This is how it has to be. I'm sorry." I didn't like the defeated sound of his voice. But I liked what he said next even less. "Bain's a good man."

My upper lip drew back from my teeth in disgust, exposing the fangs I couldn't stop from extending. "He killed his own brother."

"It didn't happen like everyone thinks."

The gentle tone of his voice, the soft, sad look on his face, revealed more than he was saying.

"Oh shit, you love him," I said.

He turned to look out the rain-streaked window. "Of course I do, he's my alpha."

"No. It's more than that. You're *in* love with him. The question is, has it blinded you?"

His head whipped in my direction so fast, droplets of water flew from his hair and landed on my arm. "No. It's made me see."

"You sound like you've drank the Kool-Aid."

A long sigh hiccupped from him. "You don't know, no one does, and I'm so tired of it." He almost sounded like he was going to cry. Oh hell, I couldn't handle that.

I held my hands up in surrender. "Okay, okay. So tell me."

"I will. After I show you. Turn left up there."

The trees parted just enough to expose a side road of dirt choked with grass and underbrush. It looked like it hadn't seen any foot traffic—let alone vehicles—in a very long time.

"I meant what I said, Dustin. If this is a trap—"

"It isn't. I swear to all the gods, it isn't." The earnest tone along with the feel of his power convinced me enough to keep driving.

Branches scraped along the sides of my truck now and then, making me cringe.

"I hope you're a true believer so Odin fries your ass if you're lying.

What does Bain want with the seeker and the reaper?" I asked, working up to digging information out of him.

Dustin cast a confused look my way. "Nothing."

"He blackmailed Raul into biting Sonya for a reason. What was it?"

"Like I said, I'll tell you after I show you."

We traveled the next few miles in tense silence. Twice I asked him how much farther, and twice he insisted not much more. Just when I was ready to throw his ass out of my truck and turn around, the road ended in a tangle of ferns and tall grass. I eased to a stop and turned a hard glare on him.

"What now?"

"Now we hike."

Before I could properly growl at him, he opened the door and stepped out into the drizzly morning. Despite his urgency—and in part because of it—I texted Raul one last time.

Be careful. Something big is up with Morene. Don't trust her. Dustin says he knows where Lisandra's body is. We're hiking out from the end of Forest Road 318.

The first part might not get him away from her, but the last part would. For good measure, I copied the text and sent it to Iris as well. Dustin tapped on my window, making me jump.

"Hurry," he said.

I nodded and started to zip up my jacket. The second he turned and started to walk off, I reached into the glove compartment and got my backup gun. Putting my foot up on the seat, I strapped the weapon to my ankle with practiced ease and speed, then pulled my jeans over it. Dustin would be able to smell it if he were paying attention, that and the one holstered at the small of my back. But I didn't care. In fact, I hoped he did. It might deter him from doing anything stupid. Regular bullets might not kill our kind, but when put in the right places—like a lung, a knee, or an eye—I was counting on it slowing even the most powerful down. And I was sure it still hurt like hell.

Mist cooled every inch of exposed skin the moment I stepped out of the truck. I zipped my jacket closed and put my hood on, regretting taking the time to do my hair. Dustin eyed me from beneath brown bangs dripping with rain.

"We should shift. We can get there faster that way," he said. The way his eyes flicked to the left when he said it made me think he was scared. Good.

"Not happening. I'd be stuck smelling wet dog all day," I said. While that did bug me, it was more about not wanting to give over to instinct in front of a near stranger. That, and I didn't want to leave my guns and cell phone behind. Those were weapons I was far more comfortable with than claws and fangs.

"It's better than the alternative, trust me. We need to hurry," he argued.

I motioned to where the trail ended in the thick underbrush. "Then get your ass moving."

Brow furrowed so deep it looked painful, he dropped his head and marched into the ferns. Taking considerable more care with my footing, I followed. I knew I could be walking into a trap—maybe even literally—so I wasn't about to take any unnecessary risks. The patter of rain on leaves made it hard to hear much beyond a few dozen feet, and impossible to distinguish smells. Dustin's slightly elevated heart rate told me he was nervous but not terrified. For the moment, it seemed, I was safe. Or as safe as I could be on a hike in the middle of nowhere with the lover of a psychotic alpha.

"What's the alternative?" I pressed him.

Before he answered, his gaze darted left and right. It didn't feel like he was afraid someone might be out here in the middle of nowhere. It seemed more like a nervous habit from a bottom-level pack member. Either way, it made me itch to have my gun in my hand.

"They'll realize I'm gone. They might figure out what I'm doing. If that happens, they'll hurt someone I care about," Dustin said.

"Who are they?"

We left the underbrush behind for tall fir trees. The almost sweet scent of wet fir and rich smell of soaked earth enveloped us. The fir boughs stretched so thick overhead the mist didn't permeate them.

"Lisandra first, then I will tell you."

His stubbornness was pissing me off. I could make him tell me, beat it out of him. But that would mean going all crooked cop, and I couldn't bring myself to go there. I racked my memory for anything about pack law which might allow me to do it and found nothing. Dustin belonged to another pack. Beating him, or even scaring him into thinking I would,

would put me at the mercy of his alphas, and that wasn't a place I wanted to be either. Frustration escaped me in the form of a vicious growl. Dustin flinched.

"Fine. Why are you showing me where Lísandra's body is?" I asked.

"Because she was my alpha once. I cared about her." The tenderness in his tone and the pain etching deep lines in his face revealed the truth of his words.

"What happened to her?"

His eyes squeezed shut tight for a moment, but he didn't stop walking. "She found out the truth and tried to avenge Didrik."

"Bain killed her."

He shot a glare at me. "No."

"Then who did?"

His lips pressed tight together, and he sped up his pace. Opening my mouth to accommodate the fangs that wouldn't retract, I matched his pace, letting him see them. Fear flashed in his eyes, but he didn't flinch this time.

"Why didn't you tell the chief where her body is?"

"Then I would have been involved. But this way, they'll think you figured it out."

"How long have you known where she is?"

"I just found out this week. Now was only safe time I had to tell you."

I concentrated on my breathing, trying to cool the anger boiling in me. He was telling the truth—or a version of it. I could both sense and smell it now that we were sheltered from the rain.

"You had nothing to do with her death?"

Watery eyes wide, he looked at me. "Gods no. I loved her like a mother. I can't stand the thought of her body lying up there. She deserves a proper Viking's funeral so her soul can find its way to Valhalla."

The terrain grew steep, making it harder to talk, so I backed off the interrogation. He wasn't giving me much I could use anyway. Ten minutes or so into the hike I started to recognize the area. Every now and then I caught glimpses of the hollow through the trees. We couldn't be far from the bridge. But then we veered off to the left, going deeper into the forest. Eventually, we worked our way back to the right. The rain had stopped, but everything was so wet and fragrant that if I had to find my way back, I'd have a hard time following our trail. At last we broke out of the trees atop a ridgeline overlooking the hollow. The bridge was so far back it was no more than a line on the horizon.

Dark clouds that looked like they were broiling up something nasty choked the sky and made it feel like dusk instead of late morning. The break from the rain didn't look like it would last long. Heedless of the slick rocks, Dustin started to climb down the face of the ridgeline. It wasn't exactly a sheer wall, but it was close enough. The bottom of the hollow lay a hundred or so feet below. At least he had picked a low part of the ridge.

"If you're trying to get me to fall and break my neck, it won't work," I warned him.

He kept climbing without offering a response. Cursing under my breath, I followed him. Sharp rocks dug at my hands and eluded my feet, making for very slow going. Thirty feet down I was over it. The next tiny outcropping I came to where I could stand with both feet, I scoped out the ground below. It looked like about seventy feet. The most I had jumped from since being bitten in was fifty, but I figured what the hell? The faster I got this over with, the faster I got to Raul and made sure he was okay. Wind whipped at my hair as I sailed down. It felt like I fell forever. I bent my knees and absorbed the impact as my feet touched down on the spot of dirt I'd aimed for. The shin splints, or at least minor pain I expected never came.

I grinned until I remembered why we were here. Impatience set in.

"Just jump, Dustin," I called up.

He shook his head and kept climbing. I took the opportunity to check my phone. Nothing. Worse than nothing, I had no signal. The last text I'd sent Raul showed it had sent. That was something at least.

Finally, Dustin's feet touched down at the bottom of the hollow. He turned a wide-eyed look of disbelief on me. "You don't look hurt."

"Why would I be?" I gestured to myself and bared my fangs at him. "Werewolf, remember?"

His eyes widened more at seeing my fangs, and he took a step back. "That explains it," he said in a soft voice.

Sighing and rolling my eyes, I asked, "Explains what, exactly?"

"I couldn't have made that jump without breaking a leg. You have the power of a *verndari*." He looked me over before adding in a worried tone, "Or higher."

I decided to use this. "Then you know what I can do to you if you don't tell me the truth."

Both of his hands rose in a placating gesture. "I will, I swear. We're almost there."

He strode off at such a quick pace, I had to jog to catch up to him.

The unique, musky scent of a cougar stung my nose. Traces of it covered this area. Probably more than one of them, but it overwhelmed my nose to where I couldn't tell. From going through the *verða* back in Wyoming, I had learned the big cats avoided my kind like the plague. Still, years of experience made me leery of them. We hadn't gone more than ten feet before the horrible stench of rotting corpses hit me like the gigantic hammer of a thunder god. Fighting back nausea, I covered my nose and mouth with my arm. There was no way this was just one body. It had to be a dozen, at least. My gun was in my hand and pointed at Dustin before I knew I was going to draw it.

"What the hell?" I demanded.

Power flared out of me and washed over him. He flinched as if it hurt. Cringing, he held his hands up. "Easy, easy. It isn't what you think."

"That's not just one body!" I snapped.

"No, it isn't. But if you take another whiff, you'll realize it isn't human either," he said in a voice tight with pain.

I took a very small breath in through my nose. After fighting a gag instinct, I realized he was right. It wasn't wolves like I feared it would be, though. "Is that...livestock?" I asked as I lowered my gun a bit.

He nodded. "Cattle, mostly."

"What the hell?" I repeated, unable to come up with anything more articulate while trying not to vomit.

"You'll understand in a second. Come on, it's just over the hill." He started to walk, but I didn't follow. With an exasperated sigh, he stopped and turned back. "You're not in any danger, I swear." The truth in his tone made me holster my gun and follow.

Everything about this felt like a bad idea, but my cop instinct wasn't screaming at me, so I kept going. My nose was another matter. As a detective, I'd smelled my fair share of dead bodies—and then some. But this was different. For one, my sense of smell was like a million times better now, literally. Then there was the fact that the stench of putrefying organs and flesh combined with the smell of a slaughterhouse in an absolutely nauseating combination. Before we even crested the hill, bones littered the rocky ground. Bits of flesh still clung to some. A hoofed leg covered half in hair lay to my right, a bleached femur ahead of me, part of a hip bone to my left. Several sets of horns were scattered here and there. None of it prepared me for what was on top of the hill.

Dozens of carcasses of cattle in varying states of decay lay in a small hollow just down the hillside. Having grown up in cattle country, I knew what it was without having to ask.

"A carcass dump," I murmured and immediately wished I hadn't for the rank air the words drew into my lungs.

Some ranchers hauled their dead cattle into the middle of nowhere to dump them, despite it being highly illegal. I looked from the pile to Dustin. "Oh hell no."

Holding his nose, he nodded. "Afraid so," came his muffled reply.

I pulled my phone from my pocket. No signal. "Is there anywhere in this damn hollow I can get a signal?"

He shook his head.

"And you're sure her body is in there?" I gestured to the pile.

"That's what I overheard."

Gaze glued to the grisly pile, I shook my head. "I'm hiking back to where I can get a signal, and I'm getting a team up here."

He took a step toward me. "We don't have time for that. They'll notice I'm gone. If we leave now, they might move her body, then we'll never find her," he said in a voice choked with emotion.

The pile of carcasses held my gaze like the aftermath of a train wreck. Through her pack members and her husband's writing, I had come to know Lísandra as a benevolent, loving woman who put others first.

"I can't leave her in there," I said through a deep sigh.

Swallowing my gorge with the skill born of years of seeing terrible crime scenes, I strode over to the pile. I grabbed a set of horns and hauled the first steer's body off the pile. My werewolf strength made it easy, my werewolf nose did not. Moving the carcass stirred up all kinds of nasty scents. Of course, it chose now to stop raining.

"Odin has a dark sense of humor I see," I mumbled.

Dustin gave me an odd look as he pulled a carcass from the pile. "I never thought of the Allfather as having a sense of humor."

"He has to."

He cocked his head at me. "You believe in our gods?"

I lifted a shoulder. "Let's just say I'm open-minded."

Talking made the smell worse, so we worked in silence for a while. I wanted to drill him for information, but the stench tried to cling to the roof of my mouth when I opened it too far. We got into a good rhythm of Dustin grabbing one side of the carcass and me the other. Only once did we make the mistake of flinging one and dropping it. The stomach ruptured and the stench magnified so much that Dustin stepped away and vomited. I came close to doing the same. The carcasses on top of the pile were fresher and easier to move. Deeper down, not so much. Decay had set in. Some sloughed apart in pieces. Dustin vomited twice more.

Sometime during our gruesome work, the sky darkened and the rain resumed falling. It made the already nasty work slippery and horrible. At least it kept the smell down. Through a cow's skeleton covered in bits of parchment-like skin, I finally saw a human foot emerging from a pair of blue jeans. Thunder boomed overhead, close enough to shake the ground.

"Oh Odin, there she is," Dustin gasped.

The rate of decomposition on the foot was all wrong. I shook my head. "No." I grabbed the cow skeleton and tossed it aside.

Each raindrop that hit my skin felt like it landed on a raw nerve. Even after decomposing in the summer heat for two months, I recognized the asshole who had bit me in.

"James?" Dustin exclaimed.

"Yeah, that's him," I said through a growl.

Someone had stolen justice from me.

"I suspected, but I never quite believed she had killed him too," Dustin said.

My attention snapped to him. "She? Who is *she*?" I demanded.

Dustin flinched as my power lashed out at him. "Morene. She killed Lísandra, and apparently James too."

"Why do you think Morene did it?"

"I know she did it. She bragged about taking a group of *verndari* out and killing Lísandra. She used it to keep Bain in line, let him know what would happen if he didn't do as she wanted," he said.

It was hard to tell with rain streaking down his face, but I thought he was crying.

Everything clicked together with a terrible finality. "She's the one behind all this, not Bain. She wants to open a gate to the other worlds, doesn't she?" I asked.

Looking down, Dustin nodded.

"The whole exposing us to the world thing was just a distraction," I said.

He nodded again. "For her, yes. For Calder it isn't, though. He believes *varúlfur* should rule this world, that we alone can save it from pollution and ruin. I think the two of them are using each other to get what they both want."

Oh no. "Raul. I have to get to him."

Neither my urgency nor my stinging power phased Dustin. He was too busy staring at the pile in horror. "There she is," he murmured.

He moved a cow carcass to the left of James's body. Another corpse lay there, this one far more decomposed, to the point of just leathery skin sunken against bones. Scraps of clothing hung here and there. Long, blond hair clung to the scalp in clumps.

Something stung the back of my neck half a heartbeat before I heard a gunshot. Another shot rang out. A blue and green feather appeared on Dustin's neck. He reached for it, swayed, and fell backwards onto the pile of dead cows. I turned in the direction the gunfire had come from. Rain bounced off two men holding rifles at the top of the hollow. Roaring, I started in their direction. Before I could reach the closest rock to take cover, one of them fired at me again. A stinging pain in my chest made me look down. Blue and green feathers attached to the end of a tranquillizer dart jutted out of my chest.

"Son of a—"

It was no small consolation that when the world swayed and went black, I fell into the dirt instead of on a pile of carcasses.

CHAPTER TWENTY-SIX

RAUL

Trees whipped by at a dangerous pace. With each deep breath, the scents of wet pine and hemlock filled me. Thunder rolled above an ominous cloud cover that made it nearly dark as night. Rocks slippery from the constant rain made for terrible footing. But I couldn't slow down, not with the words of Morene's text burning through my brain.

I found Elexis's last attacker. Meet me at the Bífrost.

I didn't know if her pack had healed her before she ran off to confront this person or not. If they hadn't, she was in danger. Even if they had, she could still be in danger if it was Bain. I pushed myself faster. Once I crested the next rise and broke out of the trees, the bridge came into view. Lightning crackled nearby, turning the wet, silvery surface of the bridge half a dozen colors. It made it look more like the real thing than a replica, like I could walk across it into Asgard. It also illuminated two figures standing near the archway at the center of the bridge. The darkness of the storm, combined with the distance, made it impossible to tell who they were.

Drawing on the energy of this place of power, I used it to push myself even faster. At this speed the pelting rain was almost painful. It made anything beyond twenty feet look like a misty blur and made the scents of damp forest overpower everything. I reached the beginning of the bridge. The two figures on it had a distinctively feminine shape. That was about all I could tell of them, except one was smaller than the other. I slowed to a jog as I started onto the bridge. Thirty feet away I knew from the feel of their power neither of them was my sister. But I recognized them both.

I slowed to a walk. A prickling sensation along my spine warned me the sharp teeth of a vicious trap were coming. But I couldn't turn back now. I resisted the urge to extend my claws and fangs. Fighting these two was not an option.

A plait of white-blond hair draped over the shoulder of the petite, yet athletic figure of the smaller woman. Her eyes shone electric blue in the near dark. The golden brown gaze of the second woman pierced through a wet curtain of her long, black hair to stab me with a fierce dislike. Despite the glare, she was gorgeous, with the almost exotic-looking angles to her face Native American women possessed, mingled with the height and build of a Norse woman. The combination struck me as powerfully as it had the first time I'd met her.

"Sonya, Ayra, what are you doing here? Where's Morene?" I asked.

It made no sense that the *leitar* and *uppskera* would be here.

The petite blonde, Ayra—reaper of the shifters—vibrated with a dangerous energy the likes of which I had never seen in any but her. She had grown stronger since she'd been away, a lot stronger. There was no way Morene could think Elexis's attacker was one of these two. If one of them wanted Elexis dead, for whatever reason, she would be. The thought made my claws itch to be extended.

"Why would your sister be here?" Ayra demanded in a suspicious tone.

Sonya took a step toward me, but Ayra stopped her with a hand on her shoulder. "If that bitch is the one who took Ty and Vidar, I will rip her apart myself," Sonya snarled.

Lightning crackled overhead, almost seeming to reach for her. Not good. This bridge was all metal.

I shook my head in confusion. "Took Ty and Vidar, what are you talking about?"

"They're missing. We both got a text from an unknown sender saying to meet here if we wanted to see them alive again," Ayra said, voice deadly calm.

"No. That doesn't make sense. She wouldn't…"

The press of another power came from the other end of the bridge a moment before a familiar voice. "Little brother, you made it. And Sonya and Ayra, how good of you to come."

"No," I whispered as I recognized Morene's energy a moment before she stepped onto the bridge. She was still too far away to see, but I knew the feel of my sister's power and the sound of her voice.

Ayra and Sonya turned toward her with murderous rage all but dripping from their energy. I dashed forward, putting myself between them and my sister. When they stepped after me, I held a hand out.

"Now just wait. There has to be a reasonable explanation for this. There's no way my sister would kidnap your mates," I said.

Sonya bared fangs at me, and Ayra shook her head. "Raul, you've always been blind where she's concerned," Ayra said.

I turned to my sister, who grew closer by the second. "Mor what's going on?" She couldn't possibly think these two had anything to do with attacking Elexis. Strong as Elexis was, she wouldn't have made it through a fight with Ayra and two other people. Sonya, possibly… And Sonya did still hate me a bit. I glanced back at the two of them. The look on Sonya's face was angry, but bewildered, and scared.

Morene stopped about halfway to me. Mist encased the end of the bridge behind her, making it impossible to see or smell if anyone else was with her. Though the rain fell steadily around her, she was close enough I could now make out her features. Excitement crackled around her. The hint of a smile tugged at the corners of her lips. As I passed under the ten-foot-high arch in the center of the bridge she held a hand up. I stopped and glanced around.

"That will do perfect right there, little brother," she said. The command in her imperious tone grated me all kinds of wrong ways.

Extending claws forced me to open my hands. "Tell me what's going on, now. Why aren't you surprised to see them?" I gestured over my shoulder. Power rolled off me, reaching for her. She flinched, eyes widening, filled with a mixture of surprise and respect.

"Because I invited them to come here," Morene said.

The press of Ayra and Sonya's power told me they approached behind me. "Her invite consisted of a hunting party of Draupnir *verndari* who drugged and abducted Vidar and Ty," Ayra said.

I turned toward her. "What? No. That's ridiculous. What would Morene want with your mates?"

Sonya's golden-brown eyes narrowed in my direction. "There's no denying it. We smelled traces of wolf's bane and chloroform at the scene, as well as her scent, and that of several of her *verndari*. The question is, are you involved?"

Both the seeker and reaper looked long and hard at me. Their power crawled over my skin. I ignored the urge to push it back, to resist. "Of course not," I said.

Ayra's power tugged at mine like a Band-Aid that wouldn't come off. I stopped resisting and let her pull a little of it to her. She drank it down like water, leaving me a little light-headed. I'd experienced the strange energy stealing once before from her, and it had scared the crap out of me. This time, I had expected it, wanted it. She looked at Sonya.

"He's telling the truth," she said.

Sonya growled. "Damn. I wouldn't have minded kicking his ass."

I shot a glare at my sister. "You *invited* them? These two have been through enough thanks to me. Explain, because my patience is gone."

Morene threw her head back and laughed. One hand resting on a hip, she stopped about twenty feet away. "Look at you, making demands of an alpha, and you being mid-level in the pack and all."

"A stand-in alpha. And I just reached *verndari* level again yesterday, and I shouldn't need to remind you that my ranking doesn't mean I'm any less powerful. In fact, I'm stronger now since I've been fighting daily for months. Now speak. Who attacked Elexis?" I commanded, throwing power behind it.

She staggered from the force of my power. Straightening back up, she whistled. "Impressive. Guess I can't argue with that." She smiled. "The woman who attacked Elexis is standing on this bridge." Her smugness destroyed my last nerve.

I opened my mouth to give another command when I felt the approach of other *varúlfur* from behind her on the bridge, a lot of them. Nine figures emerged from the misty rain. Three had their hands bound behind them.

Each bound figure was flanked by two others—*verndari* from the feel of their power. But the three they led were even more powerful, alpha level, easily. My power spiked when I recognized them—Vidar Balderson, Tyler Viðarrson, and—

"Elexis!"

"Ty!" Sonya called out.

"Vidar! You bitch, I'll kill you!" Ayra screamed.

The *leitar* and *uppskera* came up to flank me. Claws brandished and fangs bared, I lunged forward. Three of the *verndari* escorts produced knives and held them to their captives' throats. I hesitated, steps slowing.

Morene stopped me cold when she drew a gun and pointed it at Elexis's head. "Step back to the arch, little brother," she said, eyes on me but the gun glued on Elexis. The cold, calm tone of her voice made me unwilling to risk testing her.

I took three big steps backwards. Elexis's gaze slowly met mine, as if it took a lot of effort for her to move her eyes. Rain plastered her shorts, tank, and dark hair to her. Even over the rain I caught the scent of death, and it came from her. Aside from a few bruises, she didn't look hurt. And her eyes, anger filled them, not pain or fear. Seeing that gave me a surge of strength. To each side of her Tyler and Vidar moved with a telltale sluggishness. They'd been sedated.

"Morene, stop. If Bain's manipulating you, we'll handle him together. Just please, put the gun down," I said.

My gaze locked with Elexis's. Her captors had stopped her and the others a good thirty feet away. I'd never make it to them in time.

"He isn't, Raul. She is the one who has been manipulating *him*," Elexis said.

Morene glared at her. "Shut up, pig, the wolves are talking." Her attention turned swiftly back to me. "At first I thought she'd be too much of a distraction from your preparation, you being such a hopeless romantic and all. So I tried to take her out." She shot a quick glare at Elexis. "But she is one strong bitch. I hadn't expected that."

"*You* attacked Elexis?" I asked through a vicious growl.

She shrugged and smiled. Thunder boomed overhead as if Thor were watching and beating out a battle rhythm for us, drowning out her answer.

Lightning lit up the night. When Thor's drums faded, Ayra's laughter filled the night.

"Bitch, you are going to burn," Ayra said.

"Yes," Sonya agreed in a resigned tone. I recalled Sonya being all about healing and harming no one, not so...so hostile—except toward me. But then, she was dating my sister's ex, and my sister had just taken him hostage.

The men with the knives to Tyler, Vidar, and Elexis's throats looked to Morene. She held up a placating hand to them. "From the videos, I know Ayra needs Vidar to help her focus on more than one target at a time. You killed some of my best wolves in that park in Portland. But without Vidar at your side, you aren't likely to hit all three of my men with knives to your boyfriends' throats, as well as me. And that means at least one of them is going to die," Morene said. Her smile grew as she looked past me to Sonya. "And I know you aren't willing to make that sacrifice."

A low, steady growl sounded behind me, pulling at my power. "Don't underestimate me," Ayra warned.

Fists clenched at her sides, Morene took two steps closer to us. The gun she held trained on Elexis drooped. "No, Ayra Valdísdóttir, don't you underestimate me. I've been studying you. I know all about you. And until an hour ago, you had no idea I was involved in this." Her eyes flicked from one point behind me to another. "Neither of you did."

"You were in this with Calder?" Ayra asked.

Morene snorted. The gun drooped a little lower. "Calder was in this with me."

"Why, Morene?" I asked, needing to keep her distracted and get that gun further from Elexis. Now that she was closer, I could smell the silver bullets in the magazine. She had come prepared to kill people.

The look she turned on me was one of complete adoration. It threw me off guard. I almost didn't notice her move the gun completely away from Elexis. "This is all for you. The digital art I made for you, our long talks about the nine worlds over Saturday breakfasts, moving all the pawns into place, it was so you could awaken and fulfill your great destiny."

"What the hells are you talking about?"

Another bolt of lightning shot across the sky, brightening the landscape and making the bridge seem to glow half a dozen colors.

"The *leitar* and *uppskera* are pawns, but you, brother, you are the *lykill*," Morene said, eyes aglow with a crazed look.

"*Lykill?*" I asked.

"Yes, the key."

"I know what *lykill* means, but what you're saying doesn't make any sense."

"Look bitch—" Ayra began, but thunder swallowed her words.

When my gaze moved back to Morene, she was pointing the gun at Elexis again. "It's time. Move back under the arch."

"Why?"

Her fangs flashed. "Don't make me shoot your girlfriend. I don't want to do anything that would hurt you that bad, but I will if I have to."

Keeping my gaze on her, I started walking backwards toward the arch. More fangs flashed as Morene's smile grew. "Very good. This doesn't have to be hard. No one has to get hurt."

"Why don't I believe her?" Sonya mumbled behind me.

Morene thrust her head in Sonya and Ayra's direction. "Put his hands in the shackles on the arch."

I felt them moving in on both sides of me. "Why? What the hell are you doing, Morene?" I demanded.

The smile Morene gave me had a maniacal look to it I'd never seen on her. "I'm helping you fulfill your destiny. You are the key, the one who will open the gateway to the other nine worlds. Our kind can finally retake our place on Asgard."

I shook my head. "We can't go to Asgard. The presence of our kind there endangers Thor and could bring about Ragnarök. To try and return means you will never step foot in the halls of Valhalla, never dine at Odin's table, even after death."

Morene's eyes shone with a fervent look that gave me chills. "I don't want to dine at Odin's table. I want to sit at the head of it."

I moved out of Sonya's reach—and right into Ayra's. The reaper grabbed my left arm. I kept my attention on Morene, afraid to look away from the gun she had on Elexis. "You sound insane," I said through a growl.

"No more insane than a *leitar* and *uppskera* awakening for the first time in three hundred years. Why do you think I told you all those stories about the nine worlds? Encouraged the dreams that plagued you? You're special, Raul, so special," Morene said in a reverent tone. Fury and more than a bit of insanity filled her eyes as her gaze shifted to Ayra. "Do it, or I'll have my man start by reopening that wound in your *verndari's* back," she snapped, attitude going all fury and alpha, like Hyde surfacing within her.

"Sorry," Ayra mumbled in my ear as she began to lift my arm.

Every instinct screamed at me to resist, but I couldn't. The proof that Morene would follow through with her threat was written all over her zealous face. And I knew my sister all too well. Once she got an idea in her head, she wouldn't let anything stand in her way, not even family. I could not allow anyone else to get hurt because of me. It was best to play along with her delusion for now.

"All right, I'll do whatever you want. Just please, let the three of them go," I said.

Making a ticking noise, Morene shook her head. "Can't do that. I can see in Ayra's eyes that she knows I'm telling the truth. She won't do it if I let Vidar go."

I turned to look at Ayra just as Sonya grabbed my other arm. Energy shot from both of their hands deep into me. It struck something, awakened it with a breathtaking jolt. Power surged from my core all throughout my body. And I felt them, the nine worlds, as if they were physical things in the air around me and I could reach out and touch them. Other bridges and gateways lay on them, waiting to be tapped into. I saw them, like a map in my mind, with tunnels leading to each. The wonder of it was overshadowed with the implications.

"Yes! Now you see, don't you?" Morene said in a crazed tone.

"Yes," I moaned, caught up in the near-euphoric wonder of it all.

"What are you doing to him? Stop it!" Elexis yelled.

She made a sound of pain, and my eyes focused on the here and now. Blood trickled from a thin cut on her neck.

"No!" Vidar snapped, gaze on me.

Ty lunged toward the man holding Elexis. The scent of more blood filled the air despite the pouring rain trying to dampen it. The man holding Tyler had driven the knife blade a good inch into his neck, just in front of the carotid. Everyone went still.

"No one moves!" Morene roared. She pointed with her free hand toward the three of us. "Except you two. Chain his hands now or my men will cut the teacher's throat and re-open that wound in the *verndari's* back."

Ayra and Sonya lifted my arms and clamped on the shackles, stretching me out in the middle of the arch. Energy pulsed through it—which I now realized was more of a circle with me at its center.

"Good girls. Now Sonya, call down the lightning, and Ayra, channel it into my brother and direct it down the path he opens. Raul, focus on Asgard, open the gate," Morene commanded.

Tyler—the man whose girlfriend I'd stolen in high school because Morene convinced me to—jerked in his chains. "Morene, don't do this. If I ever meant anything to you—" His words turned into an angry groan of pain. Power had weighed heavy in those words. He had been trying to compel her with it.

"You didn't. You were no more than a means to an end, a way for me to get accepted into the Draupnir pack where I could start my work there."

Vidar made a snorting sound. "Your work?" He and Tyler exchanged a look when Morene's attention was diverted. They were going to try something stupid. I had to stop them.

"Yeah, what do you mean, your work?" I prompted Morene.

The answer came from behind us, in a deep, gravelly voice that took me utterly by surprise. "She means manipulating me to kill my own brother so she could take over the pack through me."

I turned as far as my bonds would allow and could just barely see Bain's tall, lithe form striding down the bridge toward us.

Power rolled off him, past us, and into Morene. She staggered back a step.

"Where is Dustin?" he commanded. "If you have hurt even a single lock of hair on him..." His words trailed off into a growl.

Morene raised her hand high and made a beckoning gesture. Another of her *verndari* approached from the mist-shrouded end of the bridge, leading a bound and gagged Dustin. "No need for such dramatics. Your boyfriend is fine," Morene snapped. "For now. Stop right there, or he won't be."

The gun in her hand moved from Elexis to Dustin.

"Why does he smell like death?" Bain demanded.

Morene grinned. "He's fine. He just discovered where I buried James and Lísandra's bodies, and showed the detective where they were. I allowed it because it kept them both out of my hair until I needed them." The delight in her voice made me sick.

She was proud of herself. My stomach began to cramp at the realization my sister was a crazed murderer. She really would hurt these people. She really would hurt Elexis. The instinct to shift and fight her rippled through me. I pulled at the shackles, but they didn't give in the slightest. The silver chafed my skin.

"I need to see for myself," Bain insisted.

Morene made a beckoning gesture. Claws clicked on the bridge behind us. I was able to turn just enough to see a big, lanky blond wolf running at me. Fangs bared, I braced for impact, but Bain soared over me and the arch and landed on the other side not ten feet from Morene. Teeth snapping, he let out a long growl before turning toward Dustin and emitting a small whine.

"I'm all right," Dustin said.

The hackles along Bain's back relaxed a bit. He actually cared about him.

"You killed Lísandra?" I snarled at my sister.

Morene held her free hand up in a placating gesture that had the opposite effect. "I know you cared for her, but it had to be done. She'd discovered the truth and was going to stop me. I couldn't let that happen." Her gaze shifted behind me. "Now do it, *leitar* and *uppskera*. My patience has run out."

Vidar cursed in Icelandic as the scent of more blood tinged the air.

"Fine! Just don't hurt them. Sonya, we have to do this." Ayra's defeated voice came from behind me. "I'm sorry, Raul. This is probably going to hurt, a lot."

"Good," Sonya mumbled, so quiet under her breath I barely heard it over the patter of rain on the bridge. I deserved that.

My gaze caught Elexis's again. Her eyes widened and she shook her head. "It's okay. Do what it takes to save them."

Thunder boomed. I turned enough to see Sonya and Ayra. Directly overhead, lightning crackled through the dark sky like a silver dagger cutting a jagged trail through the clouds and rain. Sonya stood with her legs apart, one hand up in the air, reaching for it as if calling to Odin himself. Her other hand clung to one of Ayra's. But she didn't need to reach, it came straight for her. The light extended to encase Ayra as well. Ayra's free hand extended toward me. I didn't even have time to think about bracing myself before lightning shot out of her hand and into me.

The world exploded in a wash of bright light and pain.

CHAPTER TWENTY-SEVEN

ELEXIS

A primal scream tore from me as I watched a ball of lightning engulf Raul. They were killing him, and I had to stop them. I grabbed the arm of the man holding a knife to my throat and yanked down on it. It hurt like hell, considering my wrists were bound together with rope soaked in something that burned my skin as well as my nose. Thankfully, my captor was distracted by the spectacle. When I felt air between the blade and my neck, I thrust my ass as hard and fast as I could back into the man's groin. He grunted in pain. Using his arm as leverage and my hips to thrust with, I twisted and sent him flying over my shoulder in a judo throw. Water splashed up around us as he hit the bridge hard.

I wrenched his arm back at an unnatural angle until it popped, then stripped the knife from his hand and cut my bonds. Groaning in pain, he flinched and held his good arm before him as if expecting me to stab him. Instead, I slammed the pommel of the knife into his head. He went limp instantly. I didn't think it would kill him, but at the moment, I didn't care. He had been ready to kill me, after all.

Chaos erupted around us. Bain had Morene's hand in his jaws. The gun lay in a puddle of rainwater on the bridge beside them. The tall, broad blond who'd been bound to my right fought with his captor. The ripped

African American guy in a superhero T-shirt had broken free and was fighting Dustin's captor. The guy who'd had a knife to his throat was nowhere to be seen. Dozens of people fought at the far end of the bridge behind us. Some were Arnoddr members, but the others...

"Iris?"

Turquoise braids whipping about her, Iris spun, kicked, and blocked like someone out of an old kung fu movie. After taking down two big men, she nodded my direction and smiled. She'd gotten my text and had come for Raul and I with a bunch of the outcasts. I smiled back at her before spinning away. I lunged toward Raul, whose silhouette was outlined by crackling lightning. Out of the corner of my eye, I saw Bain release Morene and bound toward Dustin. Arm dripping blood, Morene staggered in between Raul and me.

The bright white of lightning faded behind her, replaced by a steady glow of yellow. Looking past her, I saw an impossible sight. Lightning no longer engulfed Raul, thankfully. But that was the only good thing. Instead of the seeker, reaper, and the bridge behind him, I saw an alien landscape similar to one of the paintings in his house. A world of charred black mountains and molten lava rivers burning bright red swaths across the landscape unfolded. Two moons hung in a pale pink sky. Shapes moved in that sky. I was pretty sure that wasn't Asgard.

Morene lunged at me while I was distracted. As she bore me to the ground, she shifted into a wolf. Jaws snapped for my neck. Hands buried deep in her dark brown fur, I held her away from me. Writhing like a crazed thing, she broke free of my grasp and bit down on my arm. Sharp canines buried deep in my flesh. I cried out, the scream quickly followed by a curse. Rather than pull away, I shoved my hand deeper into her mouth. She gagged and let go. I shoved her off me and launched myself up.

"Stop this, Morene. He's your brother. You don't know what this will do to him," I said.

Snarling and snapping, she rolled to her feet, shifting back to human form as she did so. When she stood, she had the gun in her hand. A wicked smile cut across her face as she leveled it on me.

"I know exactly what it will do to him. I've been preparing him for this moment for the last ten years. Now get out of my way or I will kill you," Morene said.

"No. You aren't getting to Raul, or that gate. You've broken all kinds of human and *varúlfur* laws. You will stand trial for them," I said.

Something flew through the air between us. I couldn't be sure, but I'd almost swear it was a war hammer, Iris's hammer. It connected with the gun in Morene's hand and sent it flying over the edge of the bridge into the dark sky. I shot a quick glance in the direction it came from. Iris saluted me and winked before returning to her own battle. In my moment of distraction, Morene launched herself at me. I sidestepped, but couldn't completely avoid the reach of her claws. Pain burned in three lines down my forearm. Warm blood welled up to mix with the pouring rain covering me.

We danced about one another in an exchange of blocks and strikes, all in the eerie otherworldly glow coming from Raul and that damn arch. I needed to get to him. The spike of his power worried me. Morene landed another blow, a punch to my solar plexus that left me gasping for air. Dammit! I couldn't allow myself to get distracted. Still sucking air, and not caring, I threw a front kick into her back as she tried to spin away. I needed to give over to my instincts or else I'd never make it through her to Raul. Before she could recover or I could second guess myself, I shifted into a wolf. My clothing exploded, little bits of it splatting everywhere onto the wet bridge. The scent of her blood drove me half out of my mind. Well, out of the human half, at least. My wolf half loved it. The smell drew me in like a beacon. Blood ran down her right front leg in a steady stream. Iris's hammer must have done some damage when it tore the gun from her hand.

I had to do the one thing that scared me more than any other, give over to my wolf instincts completely. If I didn't, I wouldn't beat Morene. I could feel that in the pressure of her power. While becoming the type of monster that had killed my mentor and bitten me in against my will terrified me, losing Raul terrified me more. On top of that, the outcasts deserved someone to fight with them, to fight for them.

I loosened the tight reins of control I constantly kept on my wolf half, then I dropped them completely. Only a moment of fear rose up before my power flared and replaced it.

Morene and I went for each other's throats at the same time. I ducked at the last moment, making her miss by a mile. I, on the other hand, got a mouth full of fur before she was able to spin away. As she did, I kicked out with my left back leg. My elongated claws—far longer than a normal wolf's —raked down her side, tearing flesh. Not a very wolf-like move, but effective. A surprised whimper escaped her. She was an idiot if she thought I was going to limit my fighting style to that of a wolf when my human side had such great fighting instincts as well.

She came at me again, lips pulled up, a growl rumbling from her open jaws. Behind her the glow of that other planet—or plane, or whatever it was—outlining Raul flared brighter. Something came from it, passing right through Raul as if he were incorporeal. It flew up into the dark, dripping sky. I caught a flash of red scales and leathery wings. Another shape followed it, this one covered in golden scales. An elongated neck, four legs with talon-adorned feet tucked up high, and a tail that ended in a fork made me think maybe the drugs that had knocked me out were having side effects. The gold one took off after the red creature. *Dragon*, my mind wanted to say, but there was no way. No fucking way.

The air was shoved from my lungs as Morene's wolf form struck me in the side. We toppled to the ground together. My claws scraped against the metal of the bridge, desperate for purchase, trying to stop me from going over the edge. I stopped sliding just as I felt open air beneath one hind foot and my tail. Heart trying to pound out of my chest, I scrambled back to put several feet between me and the edge. It was a few hundred feet fall from the middle of this bridge. Even if werewolves could survive that, I was sure it would hurt like the unholiest of hells.

Morene came at me again. I called up my wolf instincts and used the adrenalin pumping through my body. Free of fear and concerned only with protecting my pack—Raul—I slashed, bit, and grappled until I had her pinned on her back. The scent of her blood surrounded us. She cowered and whined as I snapped my jaws before her face. Her body warmed and vibrated beneath me. A moment later her wolf blurred, then she became a woman. Rather than continue to fight like I expected her to, she turned beseeching, tear-filled eyes to me. Wounds on both of her sides, down her right arm, and across her abdomen, bled freely. None of it smelled like arterial blood. Regardless, I smelled enough of it to know she had to be getting weak and was in a lot of pain.

"Just let me go, please. I'll step through that gate and you'll never see me again," she pleaded.

My wolf wanted nothing more than to clamp jaws on her throat and finish her. The instinct was so strong I could barely fight it. I shifted to my human form. The need to eliminate a threat cleared away, leaving me with rage instead. But I could control that, mostly. Keeping my claws long, I gripped her throat tight. Bright little spots of blood welled from where the tips dug into her flesh.

"No. You will answer for everything you've done. Lísandra and all the others will have justice," I snarled.

"What do you care? You didn't even know her," Morene snapped. Her head turned ever so slightly, gaze going to the gate where Raul stood.

He wasn't alone anymore. Ayra and Sonya stood to his left, working on his shackles. To his right stood a figure that took my brain a moment to process. It was a lithe woman with massive brown and gold wings sprouting out of her back. The wings rose high above her shoulders and swept down to touch the bridge. Long blond hair hung down between them. An angel? No, a...

"Valkyrie," I whispered.

My world just rocked clean off its axis. First dragons, now valkyries. The dragons I could have written off as drugged, or not seeing clearly through the rain. But the valkyrie stood not thirty feet from me. There was no denying her. After being bitten and turned into a werewolf, it shouldn't have surprised me, but it did. A few small crackles of lightning traveled across the dark clouds overhead. My hands convulsed tighter around Morene's throat. Her gagging brought me back to myself and made me ease my grip a bit.

"No! They'll close the gate." Her wild eyes returned to me. "Let me go. I'll give you money, property, whatever you want. It's yours."

I grabbed one of her hands, tweaked it until she was forced to roll away from the pressure, then used her movement to flip her onto her stomach. Taking that same hand, I turned it around at a precarious angle and held her still with the pressure. I glared down at her. "Don't make me cut you again. It would be hard to explain in the report." I would have given a lot for a pair of handcuffs. Looking down at my naked body, I realized I would have given a lot for a shirt too.

The valkyrie helped Sonya and Ayra open Raul's shackles. His hands didn't fall from them. Ayra tried to pull his hand down and went through him as if he were no more than a hologram. More flying figures approached through the sky of the other world glowing behind him. The need to go to him almost made me abandon Morene.

"What's wrong? Help him," I called out.

The valkyrie turned to look at me. "Is she his lover?" she asked of Ayra. She sounded human enough. But the wings were definitely real, and not at all human, no matter how my brain tried to rationalize it. Her gaze locked on mine.

Ayra shrugged. Soft footsteps sounded across the wet bridge to my right. Out of the corner of my eye, I saw Iris approaching. "Yes," she said.

The valkyrie's eyes locked on mine. "He needs you."

Iris knelt next to me. "I've got this. Go to him." As soon as she had a grip on Morene's arm, I shot up and bolted to Raul.

I stopped a few feet short, due to both not knowing what to do and the immense pressure of power rolling off him. Fear stilled my hands. Not a fear of pain, I didn't care about that, but a fear of finding him incorporeal to the touch. The winged woman standing at my side didn't help matters. Though she stood only a few inches taller than me, her wings rose up another two feet above her head and spread out behind her, making her look massive. They had to span fifteen feet when opened.

"Do you care for each other? Are you a mated pair?" she asked.

I looked at Raul. His gaze was fixed on something elsewhere. Though he looked in my direction, he wasn't seeing anything in this world. The wonder on his face gave me some comfort. At least he wasn't in pain. But seeing him like this made me ache terribly. What if he couldn't pull out of it?

"Very much," I whispered. As to the second question... "I don't know. I'm not sure what that means."

"Then talk to him, try to bring him back. Touch him if you can," the valkyrie said.

I moved closer, stepping into the massive waves of power rolling off him. It stung, a lot. Not caring about the pain, I forced myself another few steps until I was no more than two feet from him. My hair whipped out behind me, carried by the wave of power stirring up a wind all its own.

This close, his body didn't quite look solid. "Raul Anderson, you come back to me. Do you hear me?" My voice choked in my throat, becoming too solid to get out.

Movement in the alien world behind him tried to draw my attention, but I wouldn't let it. He was all that mattered.

One of my hands rose toward his face, longing to touch that week-old scruff he never quite shaved all the way. What I wouldn't give to feel it brush my skin one more time... I leaned close to his ear. "I will not lose you, not after I just found you. You belong to me, to this world. Do you hear me?"

His eyes moved as if searching for the sound of my voice. Swallowing hard, I closed the distance between my hand and his face. The pressure of power burned with an intensity that screamed at me to move away. I refused to. Through all that power and heat, I couldn't feel his beard, his skin, only pain.

"You have to close the gate, Raul," I said. My attention flicked to the shapes flying toward us in the distant pink sky. "Things are getting through to this world. You have to close it."

He became more and more transparent with each passing moment, as if he was fading from this world.

The next words caught in my throat, and I had to swallow hard before I could get them out. "Come back to me. I can't lose you."

Painfully slow, his gaze focused on me. The heat scorching my body subsided to a bearable blaze. Behind him, the alien world started to fade away. He became more and more solid, as if he was stepping back into his body. Stubble scraped my palm.

"Elexis," he breathed, like my name gave him life.

I threw my arms around him and clutched him tight. His heart beat strong and steady beneath my ear. Tears slipped from the tight creases of my eyes. "You came back to me," I gasped against his chest.

His arms wrapped around me, solid and strong. "I'll always come back to you."

Our lips collided with a desperation born of what might have happened. People rushed past us—Ayra and Sonya from the unmistakable feel of their immense power. I didn't care. In that moment, all that mattered was Raul, his arms around me, his breath mingling with my own.

He was here with me, truly here. The tremendous anxiety over possibly losing him started to slowly release its death grip on my throat. Our kiss turned languorous instead of desperate. Eventually, our lips parted. He leaned his forehead against mine and let out a long breath.

I pulled back to look into his amber eyes and punched him softly in one arm.

"You had better, Raul Anderson," I warned him.

He chuckled as he took his shirt off and handed it to me. I didn't care that it was wet and three sizes too big. It smelled like him, and that brought me an immeasurable amount of comfort. He started to growl as he looked behind me. The menace in the sound made the hairs on the back of my neck stir. I knew the cause of his reaction before I turned. Bain.

Behind us, the valkyrie stood not far away, one combat boot on Morene's back, golden-brown wings draped around her like a living cloak. It reminded me of how a bird of prey protected its kill. Rain streaked down her blond hair, making her look like a wet dream instead of the drowned rat I felt like. Not far from her, Iris stood watching Morene's prone form, fists clenched. To their left Bain embraced Dustin with a tenderness I wouldn't have thought the man had in him. Beyond them, Ayra and Sonya were embracing the tall, broad blond man and the African American man who had been held captive with me. Several bodies lay around them. A scattering of the outcasts stretched back the remaining length of the bridge.

Raul stormed past me—giving the term an all new meaning for me with the intense roil of his power. "Bain!" The name was barely audible through the growl that came with it.

Bain released Dustin, pushed the smaller man behind his back, and turned to face Raul. Hands spreading wide, Raul extended his claws as he marched on him. Bain took a step away from Dustin and went down on one knee as Raul reached him. Confusion dug deep furrows between Raul's brows. He pulled up short, stopping just before reaching the man. Upper lip curled back from his fangs, he snarled down at him. "What is this?"

Bain lifted his head just enough to meet Raul's gaze. He looked back down almost immediately. "Submission," came Bain's gravelly voice, sounding tired and defeated.

Raul shook his head. "What? Why?"

I approached slowly, stopping right behind Raul. If I touched him, I feared I might ignite his fury, but I wanted to be close enough to stop him from doing something he'd regret. "I think I know," I started.

Bain gave me a sad half-smile. Raul's head turned my direction, but he didn't take his eyes off Bain.

"You wanted me to find out about Morene's plan. That's why you signed the rental paperwork so fast. You knew about the artwork in Didrik and Lísandra's house that I'd find. You needed our help to get out from under her," I said. Nodding, he swallowed hard and dropped his head. I went on. "I think you suspected the outcasts were living there, and you wanted me to help them. I also think you hoped if I became your co-alpha, I could defeat Morene."

Tears welled in his eyes. "I knew how smart you were the moment I met you. I knew you'd figure it out." His gaze shifted to Raul. "I never wanted any of this, not the alpha position, not to open the gates to the nine worlds, and certainly not to kill my own brother." Deep pain laced his tone, the kind I had heard when drunk drivers involved in a fatal accident realized what they'd done.

"Then why did you do it?" Raul snapped.

Bain's sharp gaze stabbed to where Morene was pinned to the ground by the valkyrie's boot. "Because she has wolves in place waiting for the word to kill Dustin's entire family line, and finally him." That sharp gaze shot to Raul, then me, and became beseeching, desperate even. "Please, only you can stop them. Elexis, you defeated Morene. They are pack-bound to listen to your command."

I looked from Bain to Dustin, whose brown eyes were bloodshot from tears that mingled with the decreasing rain. "I'll do everything I can to stop them, you have my word," I promised.

Dustin swallowed hard, bottom lip trembling. "Thank you," he whispered.

Wicked, feminine laughter tittered over the distant rumble of retreating thunder. "She'll never save them all, Dustin. Which do you think will fall to my assassins before she roots out everyone loyal to me? Your baby sister? Mother? Father? Or one of your dozens of beloved cousins? Maybe all of them," came Morene's strained voice.

I started to march in her direction, but the valkyrie stole my thunder.

She hauled Morene up, lifted her off her feet, and held her suspended in air. "Someone about to face the wrath of Odin the Allfather would be foolish to make threats that could get them drawn and quartered. And on Asgard, we still serve out that term of justice literally."

The blood drained from Morene's face, leaving her looking stark and ghostly, but a spark lit her eyes. "You're taking me to Asgard?"

The valkyrie made a high-pitched snorting sort of noise. "No, *varúlfur*. That is a place you'll never see. You will stand trial on Muspelheimr."

I felt Raul's power flare. He gritted his teeth and dropped his eyes from his sister. I went to him and took his hand. His fingers wove through mine and gripped tight. As she began to choke and sputter, the valkyrie lowered her to the ground.

"Raul, little brother, do something. You can't just let them kill me," Morene pleaded.

Raul let go of my hand and walked over to his sister, each slow step full of more menace and rage than any charge or lunge could have been. The valkyrie tensed, her hand tightening around Morene's arm.

"You have offended the gods, the *gods* Morene. You endangered Lord Thor with a stupid stunt that could have started Ragnarök. And the worst part is, you meant to. You deserve to stand trial, and you deserve whatever punishment the Æsir decide to carry out." Raul's words were so cold they sent chills through me. But he was right.

Morene thrust her chin out. "Even if they torture me, or kill me in some horrible way? If they blood eagle me?"

Raul twitched at the last part, but he turned it into a sneer. "No chance of that. You're not royalty."

"But I'm an alpha, and daughter of an alpha. They could, Raul, please!" she begged, but he had already turned and started to walk away from both her and Bain.

I stood as straight as my tired body would allow. "You aren't an alpha anymore, Morene," I proclaimed in a voice that carried through the dark and stormy night. The weight of the eyes of the outcasts on the bridge tickled along my skin, calling to my wolf. But there were more.

I followed the feel of werewolf energy and looked into the gap the bridge spanned over. Hundreds of eyes stared up at me, some human, some wolf. Something instinctual in me knew they were made up of a majority of the remaining outcasts and the Draupnir pack. It felt as though a little thread connected each of them to my power. The sensation felt strongest from the outcasts, as if their threads were thicker. The strangeness of it overwhelmed me. I swayed on my feet. Raul appeared at my side, a hand on my arm to steady me.

"What is this?" I whispered to him.

Iris answered as she approached. "The pack bond. You defeated Morene and Bain submitted to you. You're our alphas now."

My wide eyes skittered across all those looking up at us before finding Raul's gaze. Part of me wanted to panic at the idea, but another much bigger part wanted to protect these people, not just because I cared about them, but because they were *my* people, my wolves. The foreign feeling left me speechless. Suddenly, I understood what being a werewolf meant. My instincts didn't seem so scary anymore.

Wings beat at the air, turning all eyes, including mine, skyward. It wasn't dragons like I feared it would be, but four more valkyrie descending from the misty, pre-dawn sky. Ayra—the pale-haired, ghostly looking werewolf reaper—approached the valkyrie standing with Morene. Small though that woman was, she radiated more power than I'd ever felt from anyone. Though I knew she wasn't a threat to us, part of me wanted her away from the outcasts.

She extended her hand to the valkyrie. "Thank you, Holly. This will never happen again. You have my word."

Of course she knew her name. A freaking valkyrie!

Holly shook her hand. "I know. I trust your word. Thank you for helping close the gate. This could have been a lot worse than it was."

Ayra nodded to her, turned, and walked back to the towering dark-skinned mountain of muscle waiting for her. They clasped hands and disappeared into the mist swallowing the end of the bridge. After a long look at Holly, the dark-haired seeker and her blond Viking followed. Huge wings beat at the moist air. From behind the archway—which now looked like nothing more than decorative architecture—came three more valkyrie. They moved through the air with all the grace and danger of giant raptors. I wouldn't have thought humanoids could fly gracefully, what with their legs and all, but these three managed. They landed on the bridge and swept their wings down around them with an almost regal air.

They wore modern enough looking clothes—slacks, shirts that clasped at the neck and opened along the back, and roman-style sandals. It was a far cry from the golden armor I was used to seeing them wearing in artwork. Two were blond and fair-skinned like Norsemen, but the third was a woman with skin as dark as that of Ayra's boyfriend.

Holly looked to the dark-skinned woman. "You saw what happened, Imani?" she asked.

Imani nodded. "We did. Lord Odinsson has declared the woman and the man must stand trial." As she spoke she nodded toward Morene and Bain.

"No!" Dustin cried. He lunged forward and grabbed Bain's hand. Tears streamed from his red-rimmed eyes. "Please don't take him to Muspelheimr. He did it only to protect my family and me from *her*," he spat the last out as he shot Morene a piercing glare.

The look Imani gave him was almost sympathetic for a heartbeat before it turned hard. "That is for the Æsir tribunal to decide. The Lord has decreed they must stand trial, therefore they must."

Bain leaned his head against Dustin's. "It is as it must be. I knew the consequences, and I would make the same choice again to protect you. I have to answer for that," Bain said.

A sob slid from Dustin. "But you regret it. You didn't want to do any of it," he cried.

"That will be taken into consideration during the trial. All things will be," Holly said.

Keeping a tight grip on Bain's hand, Dustin straightened and turned to her. "Is there any scenario in which he'll live?"

"Yes," Imani answered.

Dustin swallowed hard. "Is there any scenario in which he'll be allowed to return here?"

"No."

Rather than bow or break like I thought he might, Dustin straightened even more. "Then I want to go with him. His fate will be my fate. What he did, he only did because of me."

Imani nodded. "You may accompany him as his witness. But you will never be able to return either."

"I accept that," Dustin said without hesitation.

A new respect for the man grew in me, along with a deep sadness. Morene had ruined so many lives. I shot her a vicious glare as Holly clamped some wicked-looking shackles around her ankles and wrists that Imani gave her. Not wicked because they looked medieval, but the opposite. Outfitted with a digital display, they smelled of silver. All right, maybe a little medieval with the spikes around them that dug a bit into the skin, and looked like they might go farther in if she struggled. The look Morene gave me in return was beseeching, begging even.

"Don't let them do this to me," she whispered.

My brows pulled down tight over my eyes. "Let them? I would do it myself if they weren't here. Okay, maybe not the Muspelheimr part, but definitely the cuffs and prison part. You blackmailed a man to murder his own brother, threatened his lover's entire family, murdered a wonderful woman, and cast out everyone loyal to her. Not to mention the whole threatening-the-gods part. If this Muspelheimr really is a place of lava and fire, it's exactly where you belong."

She shook her head more at each sentence. "My brother will come to blame you. He'll hate you."

Raul turned his back on her. He took my hand in his and started to walk away from his sister. "No, I won't." His cold tone made the rainy night feel chilly.

She called after us. "You're the law in this town. Don't let them just take away a murderer who should stand trial. Please! Raul!"

His hand tightened on mine, but he kept his pace slow and steady. Wings beat at the night behind us, retreating to a place I had thought was only myth. From the flare in Raul's power, I knew it hurt him to keep walking, but he did it. No sooner had I thought about soothing him than my power poured out of me and flowed over him in a warm wave. He breathed a sigh of relief, and his hand relaxed around mine. I hadn't even known I could do that. When we reached the people on the bridge, they parted like a curtain. Iris and two others I knew as outcasts who had been Didrik's *verndari* came first. They bowed deep, exposing their necks to us, with Iris going so far as to move her hair out of the way.

The weirdness continued. Out in the hollow, the mist had lifted enough for me to see those of the Draupnir pack who had gathered were all on their knees. And as we reached each person on the bridge, they went down onto a knee, some struggling to do so despite injuries they had sustained during the fight with those loyal to Morene. I reached for one of them, but Raul stilled my hand.

"But they're hurt. Why are they doing that?" I whispered.

He brought my hand to his lips and kissed the back of it lightly. "Don't freak out." I gave him a look until he went on. "They're submitting to their new alphas."

Though I kept my shit together and continued walking from the bridge with my head high, inside I freaked out like no one's business, but in a good way. I had a pack, a family. No matter what happened after tonight, that was pretty amazing.

CHAPTER TWENTY-EIGHT

RAUL

I watched Elexis button the top button of her royal blue blouse and unbutton it for the sixth time. I wanted to remove it from her completely, but if I did that again, we'd be late. Instead, I flipped the kronur through my fingers, needing to keep them busy. The coin was a poor substitute for what I wanted to do with my hands. When finished, she moved to the standing mirror and fussed with her hair again, arranging the black and blue locks she'd been working on for the last hour. I walked closer, the desire to touch her overwhelming me. Her nervous energy filled what had once been Didrik and Lísandra's room with enough pressure to make a tea kettle whistle. It was our room now, scattered with a mixture of my modern bachelor furniture and what Elexis had kept of Lísandra's.

"We don't have to do this, you know. If you aren't sure—"

She spun on the ball of her bare left foot and pressed a finger to my lips. "I've never been surer of anything. I just..." She looked down as her voice trailed off. "I don't want to screw it up. I want it to be perfect."

I slid my arms around her waist and pulled her close, breathing deep of her gun oil and vanilla scent. "It doesn't have to be perfect. You're perfect, and that's what matters."

She made a cute snorting sort of sound. "Hardly."

I kissed her nose. "You're perfect for me, and for them. That's all that matters." To emphasize my point, I pressed my hips to hers, letting her feel how perfect my body thought she was.

She groaned and put her arms around my neck. "If you keep that up, we're going to end up in bed again and we'll be late."

A little growling noise rumbled from me. "My love, you're the one keeping it up."

The sound vibrating through her drove me wild. "You're trying to distract me," she said.

"And it was working." Knowing she liked it, I let just a bit of my fangs extend as I gave her a crooked grin.

"Stop it, Raul! I really don't want to screw this up." The anxiety in her voice stabbed me.

I shoved the coin into my pocket, took her hands in mine, and bent at the knees until I could look her in the eyes. Their beautiful dark blue depths tried to suck me in, but I couldn't let them, not with the entire pack waiting on us. But more importantly, not when that wasn't what she needed. "Elexis, you don't have to do this. You can still back out," I said.

She rolled her eyes, pulled one hand free, and smacked me in the arm. "Of course not, you big jock. I just don't want to screw it up."

"What's that about my big cock and screwing?"

Laughter bubbled from her as she smacked me again. "Raul! I'm serious."

My shoulders rose in a half-shrug. "All right, if you must have me again. But I'm just warning you, everyone will hear."

She laughed harder. Chuckling with her, I pulled her close. "Seriously, though, the ceremony doesn't have to be perfect, because you're perfect, to me and those *varúlfur* out there."

"To the outcasts maybe, but not to those of the Draupnir pack, those who remained."

I snorted, replicating the sound she made when she was annoyed. "Anyone who doesn't think so can hit the road with their tail between their legs."

A long, slow sigh slid from her, heating my blood. "I know. I'm still a bit uncomfortable with the whole assaulting people being legal thing, but in their case, I'm good with it. It's just...those who stay are going to be my...

family." She gripped my one hand tight and looked me straight in the eyes. "*Our* family."

Too choked up for words, I pulled her close and kissed her. After a long, breathless few seconds, I pulled away.

"Just when I had convinced myself I didn't care if everyone heard..." she murmured through a lopsided grin. The words almost stopped me from retrieving the manila folder from my nightstand.

She accepted it with a smirk. "A folder, how thoughtful of you." Despite her sarcasm, she opened it with a look of anticipation. Curiosity radiated off her. Eyes widening, she flipped a page over. Her eyes widened even more, and she gasped. "You discovered who my birth parents were," the words were the barest of whispers.

"I used a strand of your hair. I hope that's not too creepy. The chief helped." I hadn't meant to add that last part. It made it sounds creepier, if anything.

Instead of answering, she took two steps back and sank down into a wingback chair beside the mirror.

"The Haitian mafia. Holy shit, does that mean what I think it means?" she asked, wide eyes lifting.

"They belonged to a crime syndicate controlled by the Columbian *varúlfur* mafia, but your father was Mexican American and your mother was Costa Rican. She was from an old *varúlfur* line, but he was human."

Her jaw worked, but no words came out. After a moment, she started to laugh. The humor in her eyes convinced me it wasn't hysterics. At least, not completely. She wiped away tears. "And I'm a cop."

I moved close enough to stroke her arm. "They came to America, had you, and didn't go back. The evidence is spotty, but it looks like the mafia killed them for leaving but not before they were able to hide you in the foster care system."

She took a long, shuddering breath, and flew from the chair into my arms. Joy and sadness in equal measures radiated from her energy. She gripped me so tight I could barely draw in a breath. The way she nuzzled against my neck drove me crazy, but I kept my desire reined in. Now was not the time. Finally, she let go and drew back just enough to look me in the eyes.

"Thank you. This information is the greatest gift anyone has ever given me."

I smiled a bit sheepishly. "You're welcome."

"I love you, Raul Anderson."

The words filled a void in me I hadn't even known existed. But even more so, they were the most honest, free of any ulterior motive thing anyone had ever said to me.

"I love you too, Elexis Sandalius."

Rising up on her toes, she pulled me down into a sweet, gentle kiss completely uncharacteristic for her. I found I liked it just as much as her take charge, hungry kisses. Maybe more for the vulnerability it showed. Just as I had forgotten about the ceremony, a knock sounded on the door. My distraction had been so complete, I hadn't even heard footsteps approach.

"Hey, lovebirds, they've started to gather." Iris's amused voice carried through the heavy wooden door to our bedroom. She could hear everything down to our accelerated heart rate, so I had no doubt she had heard what we'd been doing for the last two hours.

"Actually, they've been gathered for the last half hour," came Leif's amused voice.

When I drew away from the kiss, I found Elexis blushing a deep red. It looked sexy as Helheimr on her. Grinning, I rubbed a thumb along her cheek. She started for the door, smacking my butt on the way.

"We're coming, Iris," Elexis said.

Through the door, I heard Iris mumble in a good-natured tone, "You have been for the last two hours."

Pausing at the door, Elexis fussed with her blouse again. I smoothed the back of it over the waistband of her linen shorts and rested my hands on her shoulders. Leaning close, I whispered. "You look perfect. Don't worry."

She turned to me and whispered, "What if I say it wrong?"

The door opened. Leif sat in an antique-looking wingback chair with his long legs kicked up on an end table, a copy of *Sports Illustrated* open in his hands. He dropped the magazine onto the table and stood with blurring speed. The big grin on his face as he looked at the two of us made me grin back. Iris stood leaning against the wall with a hand on one hip, her multi-hued hair unbound and hanging about her shoulders in soft, frothy waves of aqua, green, and blue. She grabbed hold of Elexis's right hand and pulled her over the threshold.

"*Stelpa*, they think the nine worlds of you. It won't matter what you say," Iris said.

"The outcasts, sure, but maybe not those who stayed in the pack," Elexis said quietly.

Inclining her head, Iris gave her a hard look from beneath long eyelashes. Power crackled from her. "Those who don't are a threat to you both, and therefore to the pack. We have driven out any threats to the pack so Draupnir can be strong and whole again."

"We got them all, trust me," Leif assured her.

The tension went right out of Elexis. Her shoulders relaxed and she smiled. "That is only part of why we chose you two to be the pack's First *Verndari*. Thank you, Iris and Leif. I needed that."

Though Iris shrugged like it was no big deal, I saw how much it meant to her written on her face. "Any time, *stelpan mín*." The Hemlock Hollow equivalent of "my girl" was no small endearment, particularly to call someone who had been an outsider less than a month ago. I loved that the two of them had grown so close.

"And hey, I stayed, and I am loyal as an *einherjar* to you both," Leif said, his blue eyes filled with conviction.

Elexis reached up and patted his cheek. "I know, Jörgensson. But that's because you're a good cop who takes the 'protect and serve' thing very seriously. And because you're a good friend to Raul."

Pink tinged his cheeks. "And to you, Elexis."

Squaring her shoulders and lifting her chin, she nodded. "Let's do this. If I keep you from Karman and the baby through one more feeding, she may want to skin me alive."

Blushing hotter, Leif gave her that big, goofy smile of his that had made all the girls in high school swoon. "Naw, she's waiting outside with the others. The baby is with our sitter."

Elexis nodded, stiffened, and took a few deep breaths.

Flicking a hand in the air, Iris shook her head. "Don't sweat it, Alpha Detective, or would that be Detective Alpha? Anyway, we're not going off to war, we're going to your coronation." That hand flicked back my direction as she turned to lead the way. "And yours, of course."

I caught her smirk before her head turned in the direction of the huge hall yawning before us. Nervous tension flowed off Elexis in waves hot enough to burn. I took hold of her hand as we followed after Iris and Leif, weaving my fingers through hers.

"We could be," she grumbled.

Leif shook his head. "No one will challenge you, not after so many saw you defeat and humble the last alphas."

I appreciated him not mentioning Morene's name. Being spared the sting of hearing it was a kindness. The deer in the headlights look didn't leave Elexis.

"Relax before your energy burns the house down," I whispered.

Wide eyes turned my direction. "Is that a thing? Can we do that?" The panic in her voice made me feel bad for teasing.

A laugh slipped from me. "No, no, don't worry."

She struck me in the arm again. "You're possibly the worse *kennari* ever," she teased in a light tone.

"Possibly," I agreed.

When we walked out the massive double front doors of the Draupnir alpha's home—our new home—she was smiling. Mission accomplished. She paused and took a few deep breaths before following Iris around to the back of the wraparound porch. Her hand gripped mine so tight, the bones in it moved, but she kept her smile and her confident stride. It made her even sexier, which made me want to take her back upstairs as soon as possible. Or maybe just out into the woods...

What was left of the Draupnir pack, along with all of the *útrýmt*, covered the acres of green grass stretching out behind the house. Though twilight had settled over the land, softening everything with shadows, my wolf eyes saw each person, even two acres back into the trees. My best guess put them at just over three hundred in number. From the feel of their power, two-thirds of them were *útrýmt*—most of which I recognized from those who had lived in secret around this very property—and the remaining were what was left of those who had stayed under Morene and Bain's rein. Each held a small, unlit wooden torch that had been soaked in pungent lamp oil. The scent tickled my nose, but not in an unpleasant way because of what it represented. With a nod to us, Iris and Leif stepped down off the deck and joined the front row of the crowd. A man handed Iris a torch.

Their energy crackled with excitement and anticipation. Respect filled their eyes, something I hadn't seen directed my way since I'd bitten Sonya. The effect it had on me must have shown because Elexis's hand tightened around mine and she gave me a breathtaking smile. A united front, we stepped to the edge of the deck overlooking the gathering. Our gazes met again, and I nodded to her.

Swallowing and lifting her chin, she looked back out at the crowd. "Every decision Raul and I have made, good and bad, has led us to this place," she said in a confident tone that carried over the hushed crowd.

I took my cue. "Every struggle and triumph has led us to each of you, to this pack."

Together we said, "We have defeated the Draupnir alphas, and we seek to take their place to protect and lead you."

Elexis drew in a deep, shuddering breath. I took a step closer to her until our shoulders touched, giving her the added strength of as much of my touch as I could. We had practiced this part over and over, but she kept forgetting the words.

We continued speaking together. "I knew Bain and Morene, who came before me." The power of each word reverberated out from us over the land, like a wave spreading.

The crowd echoed us in a soft murmur. "We knew Bain and Morene, who came before you."

We spoke the next line, power building more with each word. "I knew Didrik and Lísandra, who came before them."

Again the crowd echoed us, even the very young who hadn't been alive in their time. The words were more about knowing their legend, their ways, acknowledging they had been alphas, than having known them personally.

Together Elexis and I finished, "I knew the succession of alphas before me, on back to the loins of Geri, first of Odin's wolves."

She didn't miss a single word. As much as she joked about the old gods, I worried she might not get the next part quite right. Our eyes met as we spoke it. "We seek to lead with the wisdom of Odin, the mercy of Frigg, the bounty of Sif, and the strength of Thor." The conviction with which she said it moved me.

The tangy scent of a steel wheel rolling across flint drifted to my nose. The lighter in Iris's hand sparked to life. She touched it to the torch she held, which erupted into a small flame. Next, she touched it to the torch in Leif's hand. Power rolled off her as she turned to the crowd.

"Those who would honor our new alphas, bring forth your flames to create a fire as a beacon to the gods so they may bless this coronation," Iris said in a booming voice.

She and Leif started to walk back through them. They parted like a withdrawing sea, making a path to the huge pyramid of stacked branches in the center of the backyard. Eerily silent for such a large crowd, they waited and watched us. I smiled at Elexis. She smiled back, face filled with a light that had nothing to do with the rising moon overhead. Hand in hand, we stepped down off the deck onto the grass. The members of the Draupnir pack watched us with a sense of reverence as we passed through them. More than a few tears glistened on cheeks here and there.

Before us, Iris and Leif reached the towering pile of branches. Iris held her torch against them until a few caught fire, then dropped it in to add to the pile. Leif followed suit. To the right of the bonfire, twenty feet or so away, stood a round dais of expertly stamped and stained concrete atop three stairs. Iris and Leif stepped up two steps, to the level just below the platform, and beckoned to us to take our place on top of it. We did so, turning to watch as more and more members of the pack approached with lit torches. Iris and Leif began a chant that the pack echoed.

"Hail Odin, he who brings the pack wisdom." When they repeated it in Icelandic, I joined in.

Hundreds of torches lit the night, all approaching as they murmured the words back at them, at us.

"Hail Frigg, she who brings the pack fertility and mercy." Elexis's grin grew as they repeated it in Icelandic, her lips moving along with the words, trying them out.

Each pack member in turn laid their torches to the bonfire before taking their place around the bottom of the dais. With everyone who did, I felt a string of power weave and connect Elexis and me to them. It became intoxicating and sobering at the same time. Each thread was a responsibility, a life that was now part of our family.

"Hail Thor, he who brings the pack strength."

Their voices were now so numerous, they filled the night. This time Elexis said the majority of it in Icelandic along with us. It was almost as if she remembered the foreign words better.

"Hail Sif, she who brings the pack the bounty of the land." Again we repeated it in Icelandic.

Hundreds of torches soon turned the pile of branches into a bonfire that could no doubt be seen for miles. I hadn't noticed a single person without one. But then, with Leif's help, Elexis and I had done our best to root out anyone loyal to Morene and send them packing. It hadn't been hard. Most had fled the night we defeated her and Bain.

The pack spoke the final intonation along with Iris, their combined voices filling the night. "We ask that you bear witness and bless the coronation of the Draupnir pack's new alphas." This part, Elexis and I didn't repeat. It was for the pack, and the pack alone, to beseech the gods.

It felt as though Elexis and I stood on an island surrounded by a sea of power, a sea we controlled the ebb and flow of. The rush was unlike anything I'd ever experienced, the humbling sense of responsibility making the Bowl game my senior year in college feel like nothing in comparison. Not even opening the gates to the nine worlds had felt quite like this.

I did my best to memorize each face staring up at us, filled with such hope and trust. Inspired by their devotion, I finally forgave myself for allowing my sister to blackmail me, for going against everything I believed in and biting in Sonya. Forgive, but never forget. I would spend every day of the rest of my life making up for it. The last of the walls I kept around myself disintegrated, and the energy of those gathered flowed into me. They were our family now, our pack. If it ever came to it, I would fight and die for each and every one of these *varúlfur*.

Leif's chest puffed out. "Are there any who would challenge the alphas of the Draupnir pack?" he asked in a voice that boomed above the roar of the growing bonfire. The question was so full of menace, it came as no surprise when no one stepped up or spoke out. Several people took a knee, then several more, until finally every person gathered, including the children, had done so. They all tilted their heads to the side, exposing their necks in a show of submission and trust. I inclined my head to Leif, and he grinned his big, goofy grin in return and bowed.

I looked to Elexis. Firelight danced across her as if competing with the shadows for a chance to touch any part of her they could. Moisture shone in her beautiful sapphire blue eyes, but a smile turned up her lips. She gave me a slight nod.

Together we said, "May the Draupnir pack thrive and prosper!"

The crowd erupted into whoops, hollers, and howls. I threw my head back and howled with them, and was pleasantly surprised when Elexis did the same. I waited for her cue, to see if she felt up to the next part. As I had told her before, it was voluntary and not all alphas did it. She started to unbutton her shirt and pride for her exploded through me. She dropped it on the dais and started unbuttoning her shorts. Before the sight of her naked could make more than pride explode through me, I started to strip too. Heat emanated from her a moment before her naked form shimmered. Seconds later she stood on all fours in her wolf form. Her black fur with its subtle blue streaks here and there made my breath catch —right before I shifted as well.

Elexis nuzzled against my shoulder, joy shining in her blue eyes, which were now startling amidst all her black fur. While casual, the touch meant so much more to my wolf side. With it, she marked me as her mate, her pack, for all to see. It was a very wolfish thing to do. She had come a long way with accepting her instincts. Basking in her vanilla and gun oil scent, I rubbed my snout along hers, marking her as mine as well, but also as an equal. She regarded me with something no one had ever looked at me with —unconditional love.

She let out a long, beautiful howl. Compelled by something deep inside, I took up the chorus with her. The pack joined us, three hundred plus wolves strong, singing of our unity to the moon and to the gods themselves.

***

Thank you for reading! Did you enjoy? Please add your review because nothing helps an author more and encourages readers to take a chance on a book than a review.

And don't miss more from Heather McCorkle at www.
heathermccorkle.com

Until then read more paranormal romance like <u>EDGE OF THE WOODS</u>
by City Owl Author, Jules Kelley. Turn the page for a sneak peek!

You can also sign up for the City Owl Press newsletter to receive notice of
all book releases!

SNEAK PEEK OF EDGE OF THE WOODS

BY JULES KELLEY

Before Eve knew of her clairsentience, mortuary science seemed like the perfect career choice. She'd gravitated to the profession for the quiet and lack of drama, only to find out that dead people never shut up. Irony was one evil clown.

She locked the front door of the funeral home and extended her umbrella, stepping into the night after a draining day of consoling the panicky deceased. Fat raindrops drummed a litany of heartbeats. Reflections of red and green streetlights turned puddles into glimmering pools.

A breeze batted a few loose curls into her face and made her shiver, but the air's aroma of autumn leaves lifted her mood.

One backwards glance at the bronze plaque above the doorbell sneaked a smile onto her lips. *Evelyn Conley-Adyemi, Funeral Home Director*. She was a damn good mortician and adept shepherd to those who departed with unresolved issues and needed her help to pass on to the afterlife. Reminding herself of the contributions she made helped to ease the stress of difficult days.

Tucked in the back pocket of her pants, Travis Williams's spirit warmed her butt cheek. He'd stay put for a little while, attracted to her life force. Time to hurry home and process him before he faded away. Or worse.

Eve hustled through her Old Louisville neighborhood, rubber boots splashing against the sidewalk. Rain struck its rhythm against her umbrella. Vintage gas-lamp porch lights lit her path. From someone's stoop, the yellow glow of jack-o'-lantern mouths and eyes warded off sinister spirits.

She tipped a nod at a grinning pumpkin. Malevolent forces were not to be trifled with. A chill shot up her back, but she pushed aside memories of her past blunder and focused on the voice of Travis inside her head.

"And that's when I decided to take a more aggressive approach to my stock market portfolio. Stupid me, never listening to that financial adviser." Travis droned on about his life story for several blocks. The tale of Travis was remarkably average and semi-charming at best, but she didn't mind being a sounding board for the dead. They provided decent company in her three-thousand-square-foot house, lounging in the containers she'd blessed for them until she got the signal that they were ready to pass, like Travis was. Every spirit followed a distinct process as unique as their individual personalities.

The Victorian mansion she'd inherited from Grandpa Barney would soon welcome the elements of Travis's spirit still clinging to the earthly plane. After she did her ritual, the noblest parts of him would cross over with grace. His body, well, that was worm food.

Death was a complex process with a lot of moving parts, but most people didn't want the details. Eve told the dead man's young widow and their daughter that God had transported Daddy to heaven. A simple, safe, half truth.

The intersection stoplight turned red. Eve paused at the end of the sidewalk and peeked inside the popular neighborhood Italian restaurant to her right. Happy couples enjoying each other's company over wine and pasta packed the quaint place at the end of the block. The sight pricked her heart.

Her unsmiling reflection, a faint apparition in water-splattered glass, stared back at her. Eve looked younger than her thirty-five years—the tawny skin on her freckled face lacked one single crack—but nonetheless it was time to give up on dating. Men couldn't get past the mortician thing. Besides, if her shit-ass ex taught her anything, it was that love stinks worse than a lifelong alcoholic dead on the slab.

An emotion born of equal parts envy and self-righteousness curdled near her navel as she people-watched from the outside. She didn't need romance. She had a calling in life. A spiritual purpose, one she could not afford to stray from again. Not since she'd made an unforgivable mistake last year.

"Walk," the crossing sign instructed in its electronic voice, interrupting her thoughts before they took a dark turn. A white stick figure, pixelated legs swinging, flashed on the signal box. While Travis reminisced about his favorite beach vacation, Eve resumed movement.

Soon she came to her wrought iron front gate and fumbled with the slick latch until it opened. Keys jingled as she fished them from her purse while taking careful steps down the slippery cobblestone pathway to her door. Her own Halloween pumpkin, carved in the pattern of an arched cat, bathed the front steps in festive tones. The flame of the candle inside of it flickered as if amused. The neighborhood decorations committee did an amazing job keeping up with the details, lighting her jack-o'-lantern while she was at work.

Under the brick canopy shielding her concrete stoop from the downpour, she closed her umbrella.

"Excuse me. I need your help." A man spoke in a posh English voice quickened with distress. The worry in his tone prevented an onset of terror, but she clutched the pepper spray canister on her keychain all the same.

She reluctantly turned to face him. A sense of uncanniness froze her mind at the first sight of the angular, familiar face looking down at her. Though he stood in the shadows, she recognized the distinctive cut of his aquiline nose.

Could he have some connection to her past? Might he be a cousin or friend of the dead woman she'd wronged? "Help with what? Who are you?"

Eve scanned him, searching her memory. He was white, or perhaps multiracial like her, with ear-length dark hair secured in a blue bandana and a few days of stubble crawling over a jawline as defined as the rest of his elven facial features. Large hands disappeared into the pockets of black jeans painted onto stilt-like legs. Lean arms went on for days. Palpable sadness offset his striking looks, all of it adding up to a compelling impression prompting her to forgo telling him to get lost.

"I need to talk to you. Please. I mean you no harm whatsoever. I realize I should have rung first, but I wanted to explain my outlandish predicament in person. I was afraid if I phoned you and launched into the entire story, you'd figure me for a prankster and hang up straight away."

He pressed his lips into a line. The pleading manner of his speech left her no lingering doubt of his honesty, and the way his head hung and his broad shoulders drooped triggered an ache beneath her breastbone. What remained of her initial spark of fear died. Nothing about this man was threatening or sketchy. Rivulets of rain sluiced down his sleek leather jacket, enhancing the tragic energy around him. Poor guy walked over without an umbrella. Eve relaxed her grip on the pepper spray.

"Okay, I'm listening. But I'm sorry, you look so familiar and I can't help but be distracted by this sense that we've met before. Have we?" Who *was* this person? Someone from mortuary school, a long-forgotten high school acquaintance? No, she'd never known any Brits.

A half-smile curved his mouth as he stepped out of the shadows. Though darkness obscured the color of his irises, night couldn't hide the playful glimmer in his gaze. "Bet you've seen me on the telly."

"You're on television?" A screeching gust of wet wind blew his scent in her direction, and she caught whiffs of wet leather, cigarette smoke, and spicy aftershave mixed with male pheromones. A tingle chased through her, an effect of the intrigue. And *maybe* Mr. Mystery's sexy aroma. Eve's ex smelled like beer and lazy hygiene, a contrast heightening her sensory enjoyment of the man in front of her.

Mr. Mystery withdrew his hands from his pockets and rotated a ring around the longest, shapeliest finger she had ever seen. He wore a couple of additional rings, none of them wedding bands. Ridiculous that she noticed that in the first place, worse that she got a minor head rush when she did.

Still playing with his hands, Mr. Mystery looked Eve in the eye. Maybe what interested her most about this man was how large he loomed despite his nameless, anonymous status. Like some old-world deity walking amongst mere mortals. "All over it. Music videos, interviews, documentaries and whatnot."

"Are you famous?" If so, what the hell was a famous person doing at her place, soaked to the bone and in trouble?

"Yeah." The smug yet shy way he spoke the word, and the hint of a cocky smirk that accompanied it, sent warmth spreading through her core. Dude had a presence. One of those people whose personality expanded to fit the room, who strutted through life like sidewalks were catwalks. Even drenched and under duress, he projected panache down to his toes. Wild ankle boots, fuzzy and printed to look like a spotted cow's foot, adorned the toes in question.

But she would not become a star-struck mess. Protecting Travis came first, and the window of time to do so closed by the minute.

"I need that explanation now, the whole part where you tell me who you are and why you walked through the rain after dark to come to my house. Because I'm in a hurry." She propped the umbrella against a wall and folded her arms over her chest, forcing herself to stop thinking about his gorgeous face and trim body, his killer style. It didn't matter.

Besides, she looked like crap. Damp conditions made a frizzy disaster of her ponytail of black curls. The acrid odor of embalming fluid hung around her like always, and Travis's bereaved widow had snuffled tears and snot all over the shoulder of Eve's cute new blazer.

"You know the name Jonnie Tollens?" He spoke his name with crisp pride as he squared his shoulders and straightened his spine, gestures indicating she should know of him. With his posture corrected, Jonnie towered above her five-six frame.

"I don't." She'd have to stand on her tiptoes to kiss his lush mouth, not that she was entertaining such a notion. Nope. She was not.

He waved a hand in the air. "Look, it doesn't matter who I am. I need your help. I've heard what you can do with spirits."

Her stomach dropped, taking the stirrings of attraction with it. Word about her ability had gotten around. Since last year's *incident* involving a dead cult member, she had no desire to be famous or infamous. She should tell him to take a hike. But the broody Brit appealed to her empathy, so she afforded him another opportunity to explain himself. "Heard how? From whom?"

"Overheard someone backstage talking about your work. They had a business card."

Travis talked about the final chapters of his story, his chemo treatments, meaning she needed to get inside and deal with him. "If you know who I am, you know I have a very specific ability. Ensuring the souls of the troubled dead pass safely into the afterlife." *Except the one you failed.*

Eve swallowed. She stuck the front door key in the lock. One time, one person, one failure. One person whose tortured screams still haunted her nightmares on those nights she managed to steal sleep from the sadistic claws of insomnia. One person whose family's letters threatening to kidnap her and burn her at the stake made checking the mail a dreadful task.

"I know." His tone came out curt and more than a little droll.

At this point, Jonnie was wasting her time and thereby putting Travis at risk. Hadn't he registered the whole part about who she could and could not help? What did he want from her?

Eve turned around to face him, pulling out her key ring as she did. "Do you see the problem here? I help dead people."

And speaking of dead people, she had about five minutes to send Travis on his way. Another fuckup would not happen on her watch, and Mr. Mystery amounted to a big roadblock standing in the way of her goal.

"I realize that."

She indulged an exasperated sigh. "You keep repeating that concept, but allow me to restate the chief issue. I help dead people. You, by contrast, are alive."

"I'm just going to blurt it all out."

A confused chortle popped from her throat. "Fine. Make it quick."

"I underwent a medical procedure that caused some alarming side effects. My blood is toxic, and I need these under-the-table transfusions to prevent lapsing into a coma. I don't want to use the V word quite yet, but there are other symptoms that make me think it applies in this case. Changes to my body, new things happening every day. Fangs. Cravings. You see, I think I am dead. Or undead, rather. So perhaps you can help me pass over."

Undead? Fangs? The V word, as in vampire? This guy was delusional. Vampires came up now and again in the pages of the trusty encyclopedia of magic she'd scored while thrifting with her mom, sure, but Eve figured the mentions were allegorical. Monsters didn't roam the streets of downtown Louisville or fly into bedroom windows at night. Heck, she'd never even met another person with gifts like hers.

"Sounds like you need a malpractice lawyer, not a spiritual guide to the afterlife."

"Fine. I'll show you proof, if that's what it'll take to convince you." Jonnie took a step closer and pinned Eve with his stare. The whites of his eyes darkened. His pupils stretched to vertical slits. Her pulse accelerated, then dropped low, lower.

Her mind grew foggy and fuzzy. Then it blanked. The air left. Her jaw fell as she stared into his eyes. She could only gawk. Nothing more than his eyes existed in the word. His eyes were all that had ever been or would be.

Keys fell from her hand and clattered on the ground.

"Do you believe me now?" His voice spoke inside her mind.

She felt her head bob up and down like a manipulated marionette.

"I swear to you I'm not alive anymore, not in the normal sense," he whispered out loud, enunciating his syllables like each one dropped a bombshell revelation.

The spell broke. Eve sucked down air, desperate for breath. Her heart did fluttery things, like its beats were catching up after hanging in stasis.

Spacey and shaking like her blood sugar had plummeted, she pulled it together enough to gather up her keys. Too amazed to be terrified, she scrambled to make sense of what happened. Was he a super powerful psychic? Had he hypnotized her? "What the fuck was that all about?"

"I'm sorry. I don't know." His voice trembled, and he backed away with a palm over his mouth. Raindrops glistened on his lashes like dew on blades of grass. "But I don't like it. It's a new development, and it's driving me barking mad. There's more. It's a lot. Help me, Evelyn, you're my last hope."

He knew her given name, meaning he'd done his research.

"I don't think I can. And you need to let me help those I'm able to assist. Speaking of which, I have a soul in my pocket who needs to pass over." Whatever troubled Jonnie, she couldn't even begin to think about how to alleviate it.

"Please give it a try, Eve."

"I apologize, but the answer is a firm no. Goodnight." She turned to her front door and resumed unlocking it. Seconds passed without a reply from Jonnie.

She'd rejected him in his time of desperation. But what could she have done? Without more information, nothing. But damn, failing people in need tore her apart.

"Jonnie?" Eve turned, but where he'd stood, an empty spot remained. He was nowhere to be seen amidst the darkness shrouding her tree-lined historic neighborhood.

Well, she tried. Eve let herself inside, kicked off her wellies, and dropped the umbrella in its stand.

No time to waste, no time to wallow or brood. Clearing her head of the encounter with Jonnie, Eve bolted up the creaky spiral staircase leading to her second floor, then coiled her way around the tighter one that twisted upward to the third level. She dashed down the carpeted hallway and turned the crystal doorknob leading to her sanctuary.

"Okay, T-Bone, let's get you home." In her pocket, his soul pulsed happily at her utterance of his frat-house nickname.

Jars holding ghosts crowded the surface of her oak vanity. Celtic knots and crosses patterned pewter and ceramic containers in various shapes and sizes. Mom theorized that Eve's powers came from her Irish heritage, and thus kept her stocked up with sacred Irish artifacts, in other words stuff she found at yard sales.

A quick check confirmed that the golden lights of other ghosts filled her Irish jars with warm and cozy reminders of life.

Smiling despite the urgency of her situation, Eve hustled to her other antique dresser, the one covered in allegedly sacred Nigerian artifacts (stuff Dad scored off online shopping websites). Her supernatural abilities bred loving competition between her weird, wonderful, accepting parents. She bet the ghosts would hang out in old sour cream containers without complaint, but this way her family had a quirky tradition.

Finding one of the woven jewelry baskets empty, she scooped Travis's spirit from her pocket, a wad of pale golden light about the size of a glass eye swarming around her fingers. Quickly, she shucked his clingy essence into the box and closed the lid.

Now came part two.

Eve sat in the middle of the floor and closed her eyes. A few deep breaths lowered her brain waves to the proper state to access the spirit world. Soon, voices filled her head. So many voices, all speaking at once, blurred together into gibberish. She needed to keep breathing, or according to her big reference book of magical and esoteric things, she could have a brain aneurism.

A low hum, similar to the "om" chant her yoga teacher used, sounded in her ears.

"Your name is Travis Williams, and I give you permission to let go."

"Are there people where I'm going?" Travis whispered with the typical blend of amazement and fear.

It touched her how vulnerable folks were as they prepared to pass over. At the end of the day, humans wanted to be with others. Wanted to be loved. And she was grateful, because among her family and friends, she had plenty of love in her life. Plenty.

"Yes." She meditated, focusing her attention on making a blue light spark in the void. The light would lead Travis into the afterlife, a place rich with the companionship and affection the dead sought. Eve knew this in her heart.

A plume of blue fire, the hue so saturated it surpassed the flame on her gas stove, burst into being. "Do you see it?" she asked.

"I see it."

"Follow my voice, Travis. Into the deep."

He did, and his essence drifted away from her mind until the fire flared and blinked into nothing.

She concentrated on her breath until the trance lifted. Her lids wanted to stay down, but she urged them open. A little groggy but otherwise fine, Eve rose, yawned, and strolled out of the sanctuary. Blowing out a breath, she wiped away the cool sweat beading on her brow.

The threat of the flame changing to red haunted her during ceremonies. It was anyone's guess what type of mishandling allowed the red flame to ruin a transitioning ceremony. Her reference book called it The Thief, and according to her reading she'd sent poor Lacey to a place of grief and suffering. Extensive research into demonology and door opening hadn't yielded any answers on how to save the girl. Eve frowned, a sour slosh roiling her insides.

Entering her living room, she forced the sight of mahogany bookcases, overstuffed furniture, and low lighting to relax her. She hadn't banished the young woman on purpose. Likely, the girl carried some residual negative energy from the creepy Hollywood cult her parents saved her from before she'd killed herself. These facts, though horrible, tempered Eve's guilt.

Nope. Still your fault. Before she could fall down the rabbit hole of obsessing, she curled up on her paisley couch, picked up her vintage rotary phone's receiver, and dialed her best friend Meg's number. Her emotional state improved as the dial spun through digits. The heaviness and smooth feel of the inherited retro artifact made for a comforting reminder of her favorite grandfather.

After one ring, a click came through the line. "Are you calling because you're finally ready to try speed dating with me?" Meg teased in a Kentucky twang muted by living in metropolitan Louisville.

Rolling her eyes, Eve twirled the chunky curlicue cord around her fingers. "I think I have plans that night. Like staying in and pulling out my own fingernails with rusty pliers."

Meg huffed. The self-styled matchmaker extraordinaire had been trying to find the perfect guy for Eve since their days at Manual High School. An exercise in futility, but Meg's stubbornness didn't let her see that. "I didn't even tell you which day."

"My point exactly." Eve tapped her temple like Meg could see the gesture. Sparring was part of her and Meg's love language, and neither would have it any other way.

"So, what's up?" In the background, one of Meg's cats meowed.

"I had kind of a weird night." Would Jonnie come back? How would she feel if he did?

"With a ghost?"

Eve laughed. What a blessing to have friends and family who supported her gift and didn't judge.

Jonnie's scent lingered in her nostrils, and the way his dark eyes blazed nagged at her. There was something big about their encounter, something important. Though on most days her mind worked like a bear trap, irksome memory loss bothered her. She'd forgotten a significant detail about their meeting. "No. Before that. I met a famous person."

On Meg's end, a metallic object clattered to the ground. "What? Who?" Surprise raised her voice.

"You know who Jonnie Tollens is?" Flush crept over Eve's cheeks. *Jeez,* listen to her acting like a teenager, gossiping on the phone about hot celebrities.

A big gasp. "Shut up."

"I take it that's a yes."

"You really need to start listening to more than Bach and Beethoven. He's in that Chariotz of Fyre band, the one with all the pyrotechnics and stuff. They're playing downtown tonight."

Eve sat bolt upright on her comfy sofa. Maybe she could reconnect with Jonnie and apologize for driving him away. "What time?"

Meg barked out a laugh. "Like, right now. You're acting weird. What's going on? Wait. Shut the front door. Is there something you aren't telling me? Did you hook up with him?"

The suggestion planted a half-formed fantasy in Eve's mind. What would his slim figure look like naked? Did he have tattoos, piercings? She squeezed her legs together, attempting to halt a tingling pressure between them. "Of course not. He came by unannounced, asking me about my work with the ghosts."

"Whoa. That's random. What was he like?"

Eve flinched. What a jerk move she'd made, dismissing him. "He was acting off. Desperate. He'd walked over without an umbrella. It seemed like an urgent situation."

Dull pain gathered below her ribs. She had let Jonnie down royally.

"Weird. Was he strung out on drugs, you think?"

Snaking the black plastic coil up her forearm, she considered Meg's question. "I don't think that was it."

"Well, I'm so curious it isn't even funny. You wanna go loiter by the arena and see if we can catch him after the show gets out?"

A long shot, but she'd take it if it meant giving Jonnie another chance. Her calling obliged her to use her unique power in service of others. Perhaps he had a dying loved one who needed her assistance. Déjà vu rippled through her mind. He'd said something about someone being not alive. "You're sure you don't mind?"

"You kidding? This is the most interesting thing that's happened to me all week."

Eve would get to the bottom of her beguiling celebrity encounter. "Let's do it."

"Be right there."

She set her receiver in its cradle and reclined on her couch. What had he said, done, that was so odd? Drawing a blank, she stood. With any luck, she'd link up with him later. Belly buzzing in anticipation, Eve ran to her bedroom and hurried into a dress.

Don't stop now. Keep reading and grab your copy of EDGE OF THE WOODS by City Owl Author, Jules Kelley, and find more from Heather McCorkle at www.heathermccorkle.com

NOTES & GLOSSARY

GLOSSARY:

Æsir: The Norse gods and goddesses, often just referred to as gods.

Berserkr: A bear shifter, or werebear.

Draugr: (draugar, plural): Norse for "again-walker," the Hemlock Hollow packs' term for a vampire.

Einherjar: Warriors chosen by Odin.

Fallið: A werewolf who has disgraced themselves in the eyes of their alphas and their pack, and has fallen in ranks to the bottom of the pack for it.

Gungnir: The spear of Odin.

Kennari: The Hemlock Hollow packs' term for a teacher.

Konunglegur: The Hemlock Hollow packs' term for royalty or wolves considered to be of high birth.

Leitar: The Hemlock Hollow packs' term for the seeker of shifters on the edge of sanity.

Lögreglu: The Hemlock Hollow packs' term for police or law enforcement.

Lykill: The Hemlock Hollow term used for the "key," the *varúlfur* who can open the bridges to the other nine worlds.

Ósigur: Hemlock Hollow's term for a *varúlfur* defeated in battle.

Ráðið: The Hemlock Hollow packs' term for council.

Stelpa: Hemlock Hollow dialect of Icelandic for girl, or maid.

Uppskera: The Hemlock Hollow packs' term for the reaper of shifters.

Útrýmt: A werewolf who has been outcast from their pack, either due to a falling out with the alpha, or an alpha takeover.

Varúlfur: The Hemlock Hollow packs' term for werewolf.

Verða: The Hemlock Hollow packs' term for the process of becoming a werewolf.

Verndari: The Hemlock Hollow packs' term for a protector.

WHO'S WHO OF THE PACKS:

REINHARD PACK:

Alphas: Ander Árgeirson and Gyda Björnsdóttir.

Mentioned Members: Raul Anderson, Oliver Gilmerson, Jagger, Tamara, Leo Ragnarson, Leif Jörgensson, Gisella, Eva, Hati, Nathan.

DRAUPNIR PACK:

Alphas: Bain Robertson, and Morene Andersdóttir as his first *verndari,* standing in as the ruling female until he finds a mate.

Mentioned Members: *Útrýmt:* Vidar Balderson, Tyler Viðarrson, Iris, Luke, Jamie, Dennis.

ARNODDR PACK:

Alphas: Isak Gunnarsson and Iona Hákonssdóttir as ruling female until he finds a mate.

Mentioned Members: Ayra Valdísdóttir, Calder Valdísson, James Jóndórson, Dustin, Abela Aronsdóttir, Óli Larson, Brigid Thomasdóttir, Elí Gabrielson.

For more on the packs of Hemlock Hollow, visit Heather at
www.heathermccorkle.com

THE NORSE NINE WORLDS (ACCORDING TO THE CHILDREN OF FENRIR SERIES)

<u>Asgard</u>: Home of the immortals, the Æsir (male gods) and Asynjur (female gods), often simply referred to as the Æsir.

<u>Niflheimr</u>: A world of fog and mist that is more often than not cold and dark. Home of the *niðhöggr*, dragons, children of Jormungandr.

<u>Muspelheimr</u>: A world of heat and fire, covered with lava flows, burning gas pockets, and hot pools. It is home to the fire giants and fire demons.

<u>Midgard</u>: Home of the humans.

<u>Vanaheimr</u>: Home of the Vanir, a wild, nature-loving people said to be able to see into the future. Also where valkyrie are originally from and where many of their race still thrive.

<u>Alfheimr</u>: Home of the light elves, lovers of art and music. It is a lush, wild world overflowing with game and abundance. As a planet with two suns, a lesser and a greater, most places on the planet get only six hours or less of darkness. This causes rapid growth in plants, which helps support massive, dinosaur-like creatures.

<u>Svartálfheimr</u>: Home of the dark elves. This planet is far from its solar system's only sun, making it a harsh and inhospitable world to most vegetation and creatures. The surface is riddled with extreme lightning storms. Most people and animals live in the vast underground caverns that cover the world.

<u>Jötunheimr</u>: Home of the giants. A rocky world covered in massive forests and wild lands riddled with rivers. The mountains are so high, they are constantly covered in snow.

<u>Helheimr</u>: Home of dire wolves and smilodon cats along with many other creatures seen only in the darkest myths and legends. It is a world of snow and ice, cold and dark due to its distance from the sun in its solar system.

For more on the nine worlds according to the Children of Fenrir series, visit Heather at www.heathermccorkle.com

Want even more paranormal romance? Try EDGE OF THE WOODS by City Owl Author, Jules Kelley, and find more from Heather McCorkle at www.heathermccorkle.com

There's something lurking in Pine Grove, Montana, and its bite is vicious.

Haley Fern has been the alpha of her local werewolf pack for less than a year, when their law enforcement liaison retires, and Leland Sommers, a man who knows nothing about werewolves or their world, is hired in his place.

What could be an awkward situation turns complicated when the man shows up his first day on the job with an injured teenage boy he found on the road—a boy Haley knows has just been bitten.

But discovering who bit the kid isn't as easy as it seems, especially with Leland asking questions and looking at Haley the way he does.

Can the alpha figure out who is attacking innocent people on her wildlife preserve and protect her pack? Or will the new sheriff and her growing attraction to him put her entire world in danger?

Please sign up for the City Owl Press newsletter for chances to win special subscriber-only contests and giveaways as well as receiving information on upcoming releases and special excerpts.

All reviews are **welcome** and **appreciated**. Please consider leaving one on your favorite social media and book buying sites.

For books in the world of romance and speculative fiction that embody Innovation, Creativity, and Affordability, check out City Owl Press at www. cityowlpress.com.

ACKNOWLEDGMENTS

To my fans and readers, old and new, thank you for choosing this book from all the options out there. I appreciate you more than I can ever express. It is thanks to you that I keep getting to do what I love most. And a special thanks to those who leave reviews on retail sites because those reviews help boost the book on the site and make it more "visible" to new readers so it doesn't get lost in the sea of many, many books published each year.

Thank you to the amazing City Owl family. That includes my wonderful editor, Yelena Casale, the rest of the City Owl team, as well as every one of the authors in the flock who are so selfless and supportive of each other and me. I love you all!

ABOUT THE AUTHOR

HEATHER McCORKLE is an Amazon bestselling author of paranormal romance, historical romances, urban fantasy, and steampunk. She lives in the Great Northwest with her amazing husband and horizontally challenged cat. As a Native Oregonian, she enjoys the outdoors as much as the worlds she creates on the pages. When she isn't writing, reading, or editing, you can find her on the ski slopes, or prepping for ski  season by hiking, mountain biking, and paddleboarding. She has been known to play an excessive amount of disc golf, but still claims to be mediocre at it.

www.heathermccorkle.com

 twitter.com/HeatherMcCorkle

 instagram.com/heathermccorkle

facebook.com/authorHeatherMcCorkle

pinterest.com/heathermccorkle

ABOUT THE PUBLISHER

City Owl Press is a cutting edge indie publishing company, bringing the world of romance and speculative fiction to discerning readers.

Escape Your World. Get Lost in Ours!

www.cityowlpress.com